Books by Marina Fitch

THE SEVENTH HEART
THE BORDER

THE
BORDER

MARINA FITCH

ACE BOOKS, NEW YORK

This book is an Ace original edition,
and has never been previously published.

THE BORDER

An Ace Book / published by arrangement with
the author

PRINTING HISTORY
Ace mass-market edition / January 1999

All rights reserved.
Copyright © 1999 by Marina Fitch.
Cover art by Diane Fenster
This book may not be reproduced in whole or in part,
by mimeograph or any other means, without permission.
For information address: The Berkley Publishing Group,
a member of Penguin Putnam Inc.,
375 Hudson Street, New York, New York 10014.

The Penguin Putnam Inc. World Wide Web site address is
http://www.penguinputnam.com

ISBN: 0-441-00594-2

ACE®
Ace Books are published by The Berkley Publishing Group,
a member of Penguin Putnam Inc.,
375 Hudson Street, New York, New York 10014.
ACE and the "A" design are trademarks
belonging to Charter Communications, Inc.

PRINTED IN THE UNITED STATES OF AMERICA

10 9 8 7 6 5 4 3 2 1

For Mark, for everything

ACKNOWLEDGMENTS

Many thanks to my cousin Fernando for sharing his memories and stories, and to Teresa Heinz Bruns, the Silver Sage, for helping me with my herbal research, which I then tailored to suit my purposes. I would also like to thank Marty Schafer for correcting my Spanish (among other things) and for being such a good friend. And a special thanks to Mr. Schafer's 1997 sixth-grade class at Calabasas School for teaching me all about *chupabracas* (misspelling intentional).

AUTHOR'S NOTE

Several characters in this novel are bilingual. Although written in English, dialogue that is spoken or heard in Spanish has been set between » « instead of standard quotation marks.

THE
BORDER

PART ONE

ONE

LUZ HOVERED AT THE EDGE OF ROSA'S VISION LIKE someone glimpsed through rain-blurred glass. "Get out of here," Luz said.

Rosa touched the charm, a silver girl, that hung from her neck. Morning sun baked the narrow Tijuana street, coaxing the stench of aged urine from the pavement. The odor blended with car exhaust and the aroma of fresh tortillas from the *tortilleria* down the street.

Rosa's stomach lurched. *Not morning sickness. Not now, not here . . .*

She started at a sharp toot and stepped back between two parked cars. A red taxi stopped beside her, blocking the street. The driver, a hard-eyed man, studied her, then dismissed her. *Am I too respectable to hustle*, Rosa wondered, *or too poor?*

The driver smiled. Rosa followed his leer.

Two buildings down, four prostitutes in thick, shiny stockings leaned against a peeling hotel. One swayed forward on black heels, arching her back. She resettled against the wall. Her sheer dress, the buttons straining across her breasts, looked more like a sexy nightie, the kind Rosa had seen in Señora Mendoza's catalogues. The prostitute gazed at Rosa, her expression closed and proud. *They buy my body*, the look said, *but not my soul.*

Rosa lowered her hand from the charm. "They're younger than I am."

"Sixteen, seventeen," Luz said. "At least nine years. Rosa, get out of here before someone decides to hurt you."

Rosa nodded. Stepping onto the sidewalk, she hurried past three men gathered in front of a red-curtained doorway—a bar, one of many on Calle Jon Coahuila. The curtain pulsed to the beat of loud salsa music. The tallest man stepped in front of her, devouring her with a hungry gaze. Rosa swerved around him and into the street.

A skinny man with a drink-pocked, eager face appeared beside her. »Señorita,« he said, touching her only with his words. His voice had the feel of sweaty, anxious hands.

Luz flared brighter. "You don't want to know these people," she said. "Look at him. His clothes look like they're made from soiled sheets."

"Luz," Rosa warned. Not that it mattered. The man couldn't hear or see Luz. Only Rosa could.

Encouraged, the man shuffled closer. »Señorita, this is not a good street,« he said in Spanish. »You must go. Are you looking for a nice place to eat? I will show you. But please, come.«

They walked to the end of Calle Jon Coahuila, then out onto the Avenida de Constitución. "Get rid of him," Luz said. "I can't believe that creep asked you to meet him in the red-light district—"

»Now you are safe,« the skinny man said. »Señorita, that is a very bad area. Just last week, I saw a gringo, fifty, sixty years old. He walked down Coahuila and two men, they grabbed him. One held him like this.« He wrapped an arm around his neck and wrenched his head back. »The other, he kicked him in the—he kicked him, then he took his wallet. No one did anything. Who knows? They might have knives. Or guns. They dropped the gringo. He lay on the ground for three, four minutes, twitching like this.« The skinny man flailed, as if he'd stepped on a live wire. »Then he got up and walked away.«

"And that's what *you* need to do," Luz said. "Walk away. Now."

Rosa smiled. »Thank you,« she said in Spanish. »I'll be fine now.«

The man nodded. »Yes, you will be fine. Do you need a place to eat? I know some good places. Not very expensive.«

»Ah, I understand,« Rosa said. She pulled a two-peso coin from her pocket and handed it to him.

His eyes sparkled. »Thank you, señorita. Thank you.« He pressed the coin to his palm. »Señorita, how did you come to this area? You are a nice lady . . .«

"You've paid him for his gallantry," Luz said. "Now get out of here before he figures out another way to be useful."

Rosa crossed Constitución. »Someone arranged to meet me at Miami Bar,« she said over her shoulder.

»Meet you?« The skinny man caught up to her. »Who? Perhaps I can find him for you.«

Luz bristled. "Rosa . . ."

"Pedro Gallo," Rosa said.

The skinny man bobbed his head. »I know where to find him. Go in here and wait. I'll bring him to you.«

He pointed to a restaurant. The greasy, salted aroma of roast chicken spilled from the frontless, three-walled room. A large woman with bleached hair gestured to Rosa and pulled out a white plastic chair. Rosa hesitated, then entered the restaurant. She sank onto the chair. The skinny man was gone.

The blond woman smiled and set a napkin on the table. »What would you like?«

The scent of chicken fat filled the restaurant. Bile peppered Rosa's throat. »Seven-Up?« she said.

The woman's smile never wavered. »Sprite. One moment, señora.«

"Rosa, what are you doing?" Luz said. "This idiot arranged to meet you in the red-light district. Are you really willing to trust him with your life?"

"You've turned down every coyote I've talked to," Rosa whispered. She picked up the napkin and folded it into a square. "I'm desperate, Luz. I need to cross."

Luz hissed. "I told you, *I'll* lead you across—"

"Like you led Papá?" Rosa said. "Like you led me and Mamá?"

The blond woman returned with the Sprite. A straw bent over the bottle's lip. »How far along are you?« she asked in a low voice.

Rosa took a sip of soda. »Three and a half months. How did you . . . ?«

The woman winked. »I have four of my own.«

Someone scraped a chair across the floor. Rosa looked up, hands folding and unfolding the napkin. A soft, paunchy man with a crooked mustache plowed toward her table, the skinny man trailing behind.

»There she is!« the skinny man said. »You see? Just as I told you.«

The paunchy man turned. »What, are you still here?«

The skinny man backed away. »I . . . well, I thought . . . I found her . . .«

The paunchy man raised his hand as if to strike. »You crazy little bastard—«

The skinny man backpedaled out of the restaurant. The paunchy man swaggered toward Rosa. He grinned, the poorly trimmed mustache sliding to one side. »Señorita Rosa?« he said. A gust of sour beer buoyed her name. »I am Pedro Gallo.«

"Ah, yes," Luz said. "Well worth waiting for. Can we go now?"

Rosa stood. She set the napkin on the table. It now

resembled a rat. »Pardon,« she said. »There's been a mistake.«

The coyote's smile sagged. He raked the fringe of his mustache with his teeth. »Señorita, a mistake? But you said you needed someone to help you cross. I can do that. I can take you all the way to San Diego.«

Luz sniffed. "He'll take you all the way to Hell."

Rosa brushed past the coyote.

He snatched at her arm. »Señorita—«

The blonde stepped in front of him. »You need to pay for the señorita's drink,« she said.

The coyote muttered a curse. Rosa slipped from his fingers and out of the restaurant. She hurried to the corner, away from the smell of chicken fat, before stopping to suck in a lungful of air. It tasted of diesel and rotting vegetables. Her stomach settled a bit. She turned the corner and headed toward the Avenida de la Revolución. "Oh, Luz," she said. "He's the worst yet—"

A hand caught at her arm. "Damn him," Luz muttered.

Rosa turned. The coyote, Pedro Gallo, tightened his grip. »Señorita, I can help you,« he said. »Why won'r you trust me?«

"Why is he so desperate?" Luz said. "With so many people who want to cross the border, why chase you?"

Rosa eased away from him. »So many people want to cross. Why chase me?«

A hurt look masked the coolness in his eyes. »I want to help you. A woman alone . . .«

"Ah, a woman alone," Luz said. "Ask him about Dolores, the woman who hired him to take her across last week."

»Like Dolores?« Rosa asked. »The woman who hired you last week?«

He dropped her arm. »I don't know anyone named Dolores.«

Luz leaned closer to Rosa. "Sure he does. He took

her to a shack, on this side of the border. Till it was safe to cross, he told her. Some of his friends—a couple of coyotes, a couple of smugglers—they were waiting. After they'd each taken a turn with her, he beat her so she couldn't talk or run. Then he took her to the border and left her there. The border patrol picked her up an hour later.''

A chill bled Rosa's warmth. »Dolores,« she said. »You and your friends had your way with her, then you beat her. But you took her across, didn't you? To a place where the Migra were sure to find her.«

The coyote crossed himself, backing away from Rosa. »Keep your money. I don't want it. I try to help, and I am insulted.« He spat at her feet and stalked away.

Rosa stood very still, waiting for the sun to warm her. She fingered the silver girl dangling from the chain around her neck. "Is she—is Dolores dead?" she asked.

"No," Luz said. "But she lost an eye. And her life's savings."

Rosa shivered. "May God have mercy."

"As He sees fit," Luz said.

Rosa released the charm. She plunged into the flow of tourists and vendors, letting the current carry her to Avenida de la Revolución. A young girl thrust a bag of *churros* at her, a man held up arms draped with silver chains. Tables lined the sidewalks, heaped with plaster dogs with flock coats, beaded necklaces, earrings, blankets, a king's ransom in cheap treasures. Men in dinner jackets called out to the passing gringos, trying to lure them into bars and clubs blaring bass-heavy music. One man inserted himself between a gringo couple. "Two-for-one margaritas," he said in English, gesturing to a stairway. "You can eat here. Our water is clean."

Rosa swept past, avoiding them as if they were rocks in a stream. The men ignored her. So did most of the vendors. They saved their breath for the tourists.

But not the children. The children thrust packets of gum at everyone.

Rosa suppressed a shudder. There weren't as many children here. Perhaps the crowds were too thick or too tall; the children could be easily overlooked. They had been impossible to overlook her second morning in Tijuana when she went to Plaza Viva Tijuana to see the border. . . .

»YOU DON'T WANT TO GO TO VIVA TIJUANA,« TÍO HECTOR had told her as she left his apartment. »It will break your heart.«

Rosa looked into her uncle's kind, sad eyes, the lids fleshy and weighted. Gray streaked his mustache and temples, soft folds cupped his eyes. How old he'd grown since he'd moved to Tijuana two years ago. How old and how sad.

Rosa smiled. »Ah, Tío. I just want to see the new fence—«

»It's solid, a sheet of metal,« Hector said. »Not like the wire fence they had when your papá crossed. People say it's electrified—«

»Let her go,« Hector's girlfriend, Gloria, called from the bedroom. »If it will get her out of Tijuana sooner.«

Hector's mouth thinned to a harsh line. He started to speak, then closed his eyes. The muscles throbbed along his jaw. His face softened when he opened his eyes. »Rosa, there are better places to see the new fence—«

»But the plaza is near the pedestrian crossing,« Rosa said. She leaned forward and kissed his cheek. »I'll be fine, Tío. I just need to see.«

Hector sighed. »God be with you, Rosa. And may He protect your heart.«

It proved to be no idle blessing.

Children met Rosa at the green bridge that spanned the culvert and dropped down into the plaza. A small girl, no more than six or seven, a box of pastel chewing gum clutched to her chest, stopped Rosa with an out-stretched hand clutching a wand of pink-violet-green-yellow Canel's. »*Chugala*,« the girl said. Then in English, "A quarter. I give you this for a quarter."

Rosa stared down into the thin, fierce face. The girl's black eyes searched Rosa's for any sign of weakness. "I give you five for a dollar," the girl said.

Please, God, Rosa prayed, *that my child never has to walk these streets.*

»Two pesos for one,« Rosa said.

The child's pupils widened a second. She nodded and handed Rosa the wand of gum. Rosa pressed a coin into her palm.

Children flocked to Rosa's side, pecking at her with gum and paper cups. »Señora, señora, señora,« they cooed, pigeons desperate for any crumbs.

Please, God, please, Luz—not my child.

Rosa slipped the gum into her skirt pocket, then felt to see how many coins she had. She needed a few pesos for something to eat. If she didn't eat, she'd be sick. If she didn't eat, her own baby would weaken. She withdrew her hand with what little she dared give away. Five pesos, divided among cups and palms, divided among small, hungry faces with eyes already well-versed in contempt. Too many small, hungry faces, not one of them more than nine years old.

Rosa held up her empty hands. »That's it,« she said. »That's all.«

The children darted away, scattering among the tourists that strolled across the bridge. One boy rushed to a gringo couple, his gum wand held high. A beard of dirt blackened his chin.

The gringa blinked. Her shoulders bowed under the weight of the child's poverty. She fumbled open her purse.

The man touched her wrist. "Don't, Paula," he said. "Remember what Reverend Thompson said. Giving them money won't help them. Give a man a fish—''

Paula glared at him. "I don't have a fishing pole, Eric," she said, digging through her purse. "This child is starving *now*. He's suffering *now*. I can't wait for him to grow up to fulfill your stupid cliché."

Stung, Eric withdrew his hand. "I know how you feel. But it won't make any difference. He'll be out here again tomorrow—''

"But at least he'll have had something to eat," Paula said, handing the boy a dollar. He offered her six wands of gum, but she closed his fingers over the bill. She smiled. When he failed to smile in return, her own smile widened with weary resignation. »Go with God,« she told him.

"You're teaching him to rely on handouts, not himself," Eric said.

Paula turned away. Her eyes settled on Rosa without seeing her. "I can't look into that face and hope he understands how noble I am and how I only have his best interests at heart while he starves."

Rosa's heart caught. The gringa's eyes were a clear, rain-washed blue. Just like Papá's.

The gringa's gaze flitted to a five-year-old boy singing to the squeaks and grunts of a toy accordion. Rosa retraced her steps, wading through the clamoring children. For her baby's sake, she needed to cross—soon. For her baby's sake, she needed to find Papá and her sister, Mary. She needed more than Luz to achieve that miracle.

She needed a good coyote. . . .

A COLLEGE STUDENT SLAMMED INTO HER, JARRING HER from past to present. He staggered, almost stepping off the curb into the Avenida de la Revolución. He grasped the bill of his cap. "Hey, lady," he said, "I'm real sorry. Uh, *con perdón*—''

A second college student grabbed his arm. "Jason,

check this out. This lady's got one of those sweater things. Only this one's got an alien on it. Real *X-Files* stuff.''

The two students gathered around a street vendor's rack of colorful hooded sweaters. The top one had a *chupacabra* printed on it. Rosa smiled. With its skull-eyed head, talon hands, and gremlin body, the creature did look a bit like an alien.

The vendor patted the sweater. "*Chupacabra*," she said. "Is not alien. Is vampire. Sucks blood from goats."

"Cool," Jason said.

Luz sniffed. "Cool. Until he meets one scurrying around the farm."

"I wouldn't mind meeting one in the desert if it meant I was crossing the border," Rosa muttered.

She turned down Quinta, leaving the crowd behind and heading deeper into Tijuana. Fewer vendors blocked the sidewalk; those who did sold tacos and fruit. Rosa slowed as she passed one of the fruit vendors. Clear plastic cups overflowed with knobby guanabanas and cut watermelon, papaya, and pineapple. No strawberries. Hector said they grew strawberries in el Norte, in Watsonville, California. Someday he hoped to go there, to eat the luscious red fruit.

Someday she hoped to raise her child there, with Papá and Mary.

Rosa turned down Madero, then glanced at Luz. Luz stayed just at the edge of sight. "So far you've turned down five coyotes—" Rosa began.

"*You* turned down the last one," Luz said.

"Me?"

"Did you see the origami you made out of that napkin? A rat. A diseased, vicious beast. Just like that jerk."

Rosa frowned. "I wasn't paying attention to what I was making—"

"Trust your hands," Luz said. "They know."

"My hands." Rosa rolled her shoulders. "You turned

him down before I picked up the napkin. Luz, if we meet one that's only a little bad, will you give me your blessing?"

"One who curses and drinks too much tequila? Gladly."

"We'll never get to Watsonville if you don't stop being so careful."

"I'm here to protect you," Luz said.

"Like you protected Papá."

Luz smiled. "From Ireland to here. Until he sent me to you."

Rosa nodded, her chest clenched around the memory of Papá's face. She held his summer-blue eyes and his tumbled, honey-brown curls for the space of a breath—then let him go. *Soon, Papá,* she promised. *In Watsonville. In California . . .*

»*Hola, mamacita,*« one of the men from the auto repair called. He made a smacking sound and blew her a kiss.

»Leave her alone,« a second mechanic said. »Are you trying to embarrass her?«

But he used the word *embarazar,* not *avergonzar.* To embarrass . . . or to make pregnant. The other men howled with laughter.

Rosa gritted her teeth, wishing for the hundredth time that Hector's apartment had even one building between it and the auto repair.

The wrought-iron door to the apartment complex stood open. Rosa stepped into the shaded passage that led to the first floor of the white and turquoise box. Drab with neglect, the stucco walls looked truly white only from a distance. Up close, every stain, every wash of dirt and grit, added to the building's yellow-gray pallor.

Rosa's nostrils flared involuntarily. Urine. Urine and dried feces. So different from Hector's neat, tidy house back home.

She tried to peek through the lace curtains shielding

the front window, but could see nothing. Or no one. Both Hector and Gloria should be at work. Rosa stopped in front of the door and arched her back. "We'll hunt for coyotes later," she said, reaching for the knob. "I need to rest—"

Gloria's voice sheared through the apartment's thin walls. »You said she would be here a night, two at the most. She has been here five. If you have to find her a coyote yourself, then do it, but get that *bruja* out of my home.«

Rosa let her hand drop.

»Gloria, be reasonable,« Hector said. »A woman alone, in her condition . . . she can't trust just anyone.«

»Well, she obviously trusted *someone*,« Gloria said, »or she wouldn't be in 'her condition.'«

»Gloria, *cariño*. Why are you so angry with her?"

»I'm not angry. I'm afraid. She's crazy, Hector. She talks to herself, even stops to listen like there's someone there. She hears voices, I know she does. God help us, Hector. Suppose the voices tell her to kill us?«

"Just her," Luz said. "You can spare him."

Rosa shot her a dirty look.

»Gloria, she's harmless,« Hector said. »She's frightened and alone. So she talks to herself. What harm in that? Her papá talked to himself.«

»Ay, wonderful! She comes from a family of lunatics!« Gloria's voice became muffled. »Hector, either she leaves tonight or I leave.«

Hector chuckled softly. Rosa imagined him stroking Gloria's hair. »*Cariño, cariño*,« he crooned. »She's my niece.«

»She's crazy. And not only that, the *bruja* has put a spell on you—«

Rosa backed away, then hurried down the corridor to the street. She followed Madero away from the apartment building and the auto repair. Family or not, she refused to come between Hector and his girlfriend.

Luz leaned into Rosa. A gentle warmth glowed along Rosa's skin. "I'll find a place where you can rest," Luz said. "And a coyote. I'll protect you, Rosa. If you let me."

If you let me. Rosa shook her head. Not that the choice had been hers in the beginning.

It had been Papá's.

Here on the border, so many things dissolved into Papá. Like a ghost or a lost dream, he waited for her on the other side. That last night, before he vanished into California forever, he had prayed to the darkness, his voice the tail of a shooting star.

"Go to my Rose, Eileen," he had whispered. "Be with her."

TWO

"ROSIE," PAPÁ WHISPERED, HIS FINGERS BRUSHING HER cheek. "Rosie, wake up."

Rosie peeked from under her blanket. A trickle of moonlight seeped into the room. The moon's breath, Papá called it, exhaling color back into the world. Rosie rubbed her eyes. "What time is it?" she mumbled.

"Time to get up," Papá said. He smoothed the hair from her face. "Mary is up and dressed hours ago."

Rosie sat up. The covers on the other side of the bed had been thrown back, the pillow knocked to the floor. "Where is Maria?"

"Mary," Papá said. "From now on, she is Mary and you are Rose."

"I'm always Rose," she said.

Papá laughed, his voice full and round in the dark. "Always. My Rosie, my Star of the County Down."

Rosie giggled. *That's my Rosie*, he always told people. *Conchita had two girls, the first for her and the second for me. A beautiful little girl who looks just like her mamá.*

She did, too. She had Mamá's broad cheekbones and dark eyes, her brown skin. Eleven-year-old Maria—*Mary*—looked more like Papá, with her peach skin and blue eyes. But Mary's hair was pure night, just like Rosie's and Mamá's.

"Where is Mary?" Rosie asked.

"She's helping Mamá," Papá said, handing her a green dress. "It's time you were helping her, too."

Rosie yawned, then climbed out of bed and pulled on the dress. "But why are we getting up so early? Can't I help her in the morning?"

Papá shifted. Moonlight spilled across his face. "Rosie," he said, "we're going away. Far away."

"To Ireland?" Rosie said, suddenly awake. "Are we going to Belfast? Do I get to see castles?"

Sadness made Papá look old. "Oh, darlin'," he said. His voice got that funny lilt. It happened every time he talked about "home." "We'll not be going to Ireland. We've to go to California—"

»Miguel,« Mamá said, stepping into the room. »Don't confuse her with whys. She won't understand. She's too young.«

"She's seven," Papá said. "She'll understand—"

He stopped suddenly, tilting his head to one side. "Yes, of course," he said to no one, then turned to Mamá. "We've got to go. Rosie, help your mother. Speak to her in English whenever we're alone. She needs to practice."

"I have enough practice, Michael," Mamá said. Her English was heavily accented.

Papá stood. "You need to be able to pass, Conchita. When we get to the border. Let Rose and Mary talk to you—"

He stopped again and listened to the night. "Yes, yes," he said. "We're away."

He took Rosie's hand and led her from the room. He paused in the doorway and gazed into Mamá's eyes, then kissed the corner of her eye, her cheek, her chin. "We've got to go," he said.

• • •

TÍO HECTOR'S GREEN PICKUP TRUCK RATTLED TO A
stop. Huddled against the back of the cab, Rosie pressed
closer to Papá. She wound her arms around him until
her arms crossed Mary's. Mary gripped her hands.

Rosie looked up into Papá's windburned face. "We're
not going to get out here, are we, Papá?" she asked.

Papá's frown cleared. He kissed the top of her head.

Rosie peered over the side of the truck at the village
of cardboard shacks and crumbling houses built of garbage. A wiry boy chased a smaller one around a mound
of broken crates and rotting vegetables. The older boy
had no shirt, the younger boy no pants. Neither had
shoes. Dirt covered their skin like a rash.

Papá banged on the cab's back window. »Hector! Not
here!«

»What kind of lunatic do you think I am?« Tío Hector
shouted through the glass. »You, I might leave here. But
Conchita and the girls?«

Papá slapped the window. The truck's engine
drowned out Tío Hector's laughter.

Rosie peeked through the window. Beside Tío Hector,
Mamá prayed over her folded hands. *For the dirty children*, Rosie thought. *And for us*.

The truck lurched forward, then swung wide. Rosie
stretched to see over the side of the truck. A shack made
of corrugated tin and boards had fallen into the street.
A woman in a torn, storm-gray dress smothered a small
fire with a seat cushion, then smacked a dog licking at
a can of beans.

Papá pulled Rosie down. "There but for the grace of
God," he said. He held her and Mary tight, until Tío
Hector's truck shuddered to a stop again.

Tío Hector jumped out and came around to talk to
Papá. »The bus station,« he said. »Conchita thought it
would look like you took the bus from San Diego for
the day.«

Papá nodded. "Are you ready, girls?" he said. "We're here."

"We crossed the border?" Rosie asked.

Papá smiled. "Not yet. We're in Tijuana."

Tío Hector helped Rosie and Mary climb down from the truck while Papá rechecked the contents of the battered suitcase. Mamá fussed over Mary, then Rosie, smoothing their wind-swirled hair with her fingers. »You look like you've been caught in a hurricane,« Mamá said. »For days. Weeks.«

»*For days*,« Mary said.

"English, Mary," Papá said.

Setting the suitcase down, Papá turned to Tío Hector. They hugged clumsily, patting each other's backs. Tío Hector released Papá, grasping him by the arms. »Go with God,« he said.

Papá pulled Tío Hector into another hug, then pushed him away. »You are a better friend than I deserve,« he said.

Tío Hector kissed Mamá and Mary goodbye. He crouched to kiss Rosie. Rosie's eyes filled with tears.

Tío Hector pinched her chin. »Ay, niña. Don't cry. You are going to a better place.«

»But will you come see us?« Rosie said.

»I will. In California. You won't lose your Tío Hector.« Then Tío Hector climbed into his truck and drove away.

Papá took Rosie's hand, tucking the battered suitcase under his other arm. He looked at the people around them, his gaze flitting from face to face until it fell on a gringo with sun-bleached hair. Papá turned his back on the man. "Over here," he said, herding his family away from the gringo.

"Hey!" the gringo shouted. "Hey, buddy!"

"What should we do, Eileen?" Papá whispered without slowing. He listened, as if this Eileen, this personal patron saint, was answering him. After a few seconds, he pursed his lips. "You're sure?" he said.

Mamá glanced at him, her mouth drawn tight.

The gringo caught up to them and grabbed Papá's arm. "Hey!" the man said. "Is it good to see another American! Listen, you got to help me, man. These fucking beaners—sorry ma'am—they totally ripped me off. I mean, they took everything. I don't even have two centavos to rub together. If you could loan me, you know, just a couple of pesos . . ."

Papá removed the man's hand. "I'm sorry. We're down to our last pesos ourselves. We've just enough for a meal, then we're heading back home."

The gringo ran a hand through his tangled hair. He thought for a minute, then his eyes brightened. "Maybe you could give me a ride to San Diego—?" His face crimsoned. "Right. You just got off a bus. Like, you really got a car."

Papá smiled, a bare curl of the lip, and turned to go. "Sorry. Good luck to you."

Mamá urged him forward. "Come, Charley, the children are hungry," she said, her English clipped and careful.

Papá nodded. Mary's face squinched. "Charley?" she whispered.

Rosie peeked at the gringo. He stared at the ground, shaking his head. "It's cool, it's cool," he said, then looked up. "So, like, you aren't American, are you? Where you from?"

Papá froze. He touched his upper lip with the tip of his tongue and turned to the gringo. "Of course I'm American. Why do you say that?"

The gringo shrugged. "I don't know. Just the way you say stuff. You're Canadian, right?"

Papá relaxed. He chuckled, an almost giddy sound. "Canada's still part of the Americas last time I checked."

The man frowned, puzzled. He blushed and nodded. "Oh, right, right."

Papá smiled again, a real smile this time. "The children are tired. I've got to go. I hope everything works out for you."

The gringo shrugged, an apologetic smile on his face. "Sure, I understand. It's just been so long since I spoke English, you know? Hey, good luck to you, too, man! Have a nice day!"

Papá nodded and led them out onto the street. He stepped around the corner of a building, dropped Rosie's hand, and crossed himself. "Jesus, Mary and Joseph," he prayed.

Mamá touched his shoulder. He hugged her, hard. Releasing her, he took Rosie's hand again. They hurried away from the bus station.

Rosie plodded beside Papá, thinking about the gringo. "Papá," she said after a couple of blocks, "is Ireland in Canada? I thought you said Ireland was far, far away?"

Papá squeezed her hand. "Ireland *is* far, far away. So far away, that today we're going to pretend we're from Canada, just so we don't confuse people."

"Oh."

"So now we're Canadian Mexicans?" Mary asked.

"Yes," Mamá said, meeting Papá's eyes. Her cheeks hollowed. They did that when Mamá was scared. "Now your father is Canadian. He has never been to Ireland."

Papá took a deep breath and held it. He looked at Mamá, his gaze caressing her face. Rosie's chest tightened. She wanted Papá to look at her like that, as if she, too, held him together.

ROSIE HELD MARY'S HAND AND FOLLOWED HER through the crowded streets. Some of the boys looked at them—well, they looked at Mary.

At almost twelve, Mary's body had begun to make

promises. She looked long and skinny, except her *chichis* stuck out a little. The boys studied her as she walked by, appraising her the way Mamá appraised a mango. *Is she ripe?* their eyes seemed to say. *Will she ripen soon?*

The boys seemed to want something. So did some of the men—the ones with hungry eyes. The ones who looked like crazed roosters. Rosie drew closer to Mary.

Mary looked down at her. "Are you afraid?"

Rosie shook her head. "No. We're just going to the market."

Mary eyed her coolly. "I'm afraid."

Rosie blinked. Was her sister teasing her? Or trying to get her to admit she was frightened? "Because we're going away?"

"Because of the men who are after Papá," Mary said.

Rosie stopped. "What men are after Papá? Why?"

Mary frowned. "I'm not sure. I heard Mamá and Papá talking about it the night we left. I couldn't sleep."

Rosie drew even closer to Mary. Mary had these . . . premonitions sometimes. She knew when something was going to happen. She could feel it, she said. Maybe not *what* was going to happen, but she knew *something* was about to. A lot of times she woke, sat up, then slipped from the bed she and Rosie shared and went to the bedroom door to listen. Many times she'd overheard Mamá and Papá talking about things like Papá's boss not being able to pay this month or a new priest coming from Mexico City. When she was four, Mary woke up and heard Mamá tell Papá she was pregnant. "And I knew," Mary had told Rosie more than once, "that I was going to have a sister. A sister who looked just like Mamá."

None of these premonitions would have seemed so strange if Mary had been a light sleeper, but Mary slept like the dead. One *Día de los Muertos*, Rosie had decorated Mary with marigold pollen and marigolds. She had even set a sugar skull on Mary's chest. Mary slept through everything until Mamá came in and screamed. . . .

Rosie slipped her hand in her sister's. The crowds grew thicker as they walked on. Within a block, vendors lined the street, their stalls made of tattered plastic and old pipes. "What did Mamá and Papá say?" Rosie asked. "About the men?"

"The men are from Belfast," Mary said. "They're after Papá for something he did there. They want to kill him."

Rosie swallowed. "What did he do?"

"I don't know," Mary said, "but he had to do it. That's why he left Ireland. That's why he stayed here."

"No, it's not," Rosie said, pulling away from her sister. Anger replaced fear. "Papá came to Mexico for a vacation and then he met Mamá. She was the most beautiful woman he had ever seen. He couldn't leave her, it would be like tearing his heart from his chest. He didn't leave Ireland because he had to. He wanted to."

Mary gave her that older-sister look and shrugged. "If you say so."

"That's what Papá said." Rosie glared at Mary. "It is."

Mary bent close to Rosie. "What else was Papá going to tell us?" she whispered. "When we were too little to know to shut our mouths?"

Tears sprang to Rosie's eyes. "But he *does* love Mamá. He *does*."

"Oh, Rosa." Mary smoothed a tear from Rosie's cheek. "Of course he does. And he loves us. But Papá got into some kind of trouble in Ireland. That's why he came here. That's why we're going north. Come on. Smile for me. Let's get that bread and cheese. And if we have a little extra money, we'll get a tomato. What do you say?"

It was a bribe and Rosie knew it. She loved tomatoes. Rosie nodded. Mary took her hand again.

They stopped at the first stall, Mary politely inquiring the price of a loaf of bread. »That is too much,« Mary told the woman behind the table. The bartering began.

Rosie turned away to see what treasures were for sale. The man at the next stall had mounds of jalapeños, serranos, and Anaheim chiles. Next to him stood a table draped in black cloth. Bits of silver and shiny tin—*milagros*—peeped from the dark folds. Rosie glanced at Mary. She and the vendor still haggled over the bread. Rosie walked over to look at the *milagros*.

Donkeys, people, and houses shimmered against the black cloth. Rosie reached to touch a silver girl in a flared skirt—

A coarse, dry hand covered the *milagro*. A woman in a black dress leaned over the table, her forehead nearly touching Rosie's. »You need a miracle?« the woman said.

Rosie drew back her hand. »No, señora. I was—I—«

»Everybody needs a miracle.« The woman removed her hand. The silver girl gleamed. »These have been blessed by Father Rudolfo. They will protect you and help you win your heart's desire. If you're pure. Are you pure, niña?«

Rosie's throat tightened. She hadn't been to Mass in over a week. Not since they left home. Did that mean she was no longer pure? »I don't—I don't know,« she stammered.

»Ah,« said the woman. »Well . . .«

"Your man said he's got children," someone nearby said in an odd, thick English. "Two wee girls. Can you believe it? The fucking cunt."

"We'll find him, Hewitt. Haven't we tracked him this far?"

Rosie's shoulder blades squeezed together. She turned slowly.

Two gringos strode past the stalls. The taller, a blond

man with a square jaw, swept the market with a chilly glare. His blue eyes gleamed like painted tin. "He won't be here. He's probably miles away by now. What a waste of time. He'll be hiding till he feels it's safe to cross."

"The bastard needs to eat," the other gringo said. A stocky man with sandy curls, his calm felt more dangerous to Rosie. "So do we. Have you got any pesos left or did you spend them all on tequila?"

The blond man swore. "Of course I have pesos. Do you take me for an eejit?"

The other chuckled. "Calm yourself, Hewitt—" he began, then stopped. "Look at your one, over there. She's got a bit of Irish in her or I'm an ass. Look at those eyes."

Rosie tensed. The man was staring at Mary.

Mary paid for the bread and stepped away from the stall. She counted her money, then looked up with a frown. "Rosie—?"

The sandy-haired man joined her. He smiled. "Hello, miss," he said. "I was wondering, could you help us? My friend and I are lost."

Rosie held her breath. *Don't speak English, Mary*, she wanted to shout. *Pretend you don't understand.* If she yelled it in Spanish—but what if these men knew Spanish?

Mary backed away.

"Please, miss," the man persisted. "We've only come down for the day and we haven't a clue where we are. If you could help us, we'd be grateful."

Mary shook her head and shrugged, still backing away.

The blond man, Hewitt, blocked her escape. "Come on, darlin'. We won't hurt you."

Mary curled around the bread. »*Leave me alone.*«

"You make the girl escared," the woman from the bread stall said in slow English. "You leave her *solo.*"

"We mean no harm," the sandy-haired man said. He smiled again at Mary. "You understand me, don't you, darlin'?"

Mary hugged the bread tighter, her gaze fixed on the man as if terrified and uncomprehending.

»*Solo*,« the woman said, stepping from behind her table. »Ay, Nando! Quickly!«

A thin, mustachioed man with sad, angry eyes shoved his way through the gathering crowd. The sandy-haired man held up his hands. "A little misunderstanding. Come on, Hewitt. We'd best be going."

But Hewitt grabbed Mary by the arm and jerked her to him. The bread fell from her arms. "You understand every word, don't you, darlin'?" he said. "Where is he? Where is Sean Devlin?"

Rosie pressed her lips together. So they weren't after Papá—

The sandy-haired man grasped the blond by the shoulder. "Hewitt!"

Hewitt shrugged him off, then released Mary. "Tell Devlin we're onto him."

The two gringos walked away. Mary picked up the dust-coated bread. The woman hissed, nudging Nando. Nando stormed after the gringos, clamping a thick hand around Hewitt's forearm. Hewitt turned, ready to swing, but Nando beat him to it. He punched the gringo in the face. "The señorita," Nando said. "You buy her *un otro pan*. Bread. You buy."

"You fucking cunt!" Hewitt growled.

Nando hit him again.

The sandy-haired man inserted himself between Hewitt and Nando. "You've made your point," he said. "How much will the young lady be needing for the bread?"

"Twenty pesos," Nando said.

Hewitt sputtered. "You fucking thief—"

"I am wrong," Nando said humbly. "Twenty-five."

"For the love of—"

"Shut your gob, you bastard," the sandy-haired man said. He dug into Hewitt's pocket and fished out a wallet. He handed Nando the money. "If you could tell the wee girl how sorry I am . . ."

Nando took the money and stalked off. The two gringos departed under a haze of glares.

Nando handed Mary a fifty-peso note. She thanked him, then paid the woman for a new loaf of bread. She cradled it in her arms along with the fallen one.

Rosie came unrooted and ran to her sister. She threw her arms around Mary's waist. »Those two men,« she whispered. »I thought they were looking for Papá.«

Mary rubbed Rosie's shoulders. »They might be,« Mary said. »Come. Let's go.«

»But Papá's name is Michael.«

»His name is Papá,« Mary said. »Nothing else. Remember that.«

Rosie frowned, puzzled. She nodded, then followed Mary through the stalls.

Mary stopped at the table draped in black cloth. She picked up two of the silver girls and asked the woman how much. They haggled for a minute, then Mary bought both *milagros*. She handed one to Rosie. "Here," she said. "It's always good to have a miracle waiting."

»IT IS NEARLY SIX,« MAMÁ SAID, RISING FROM THE BENCH to look down the street. Worry tinged her voice. »Your papá was supposed to meet us here half an hour ago.«

»He'll come, Mamá,« Mary said.

Rosie bit her lower lip. What if he'd met the two gringos from the market? They didn't seem like nice people. And if Mary was right and Papá wasn't just Michael Connelly but was also Sean Devlin . . . like an actor. Actors used many names. . . .

Rosie searched the street. Shadows reached to catch strolling couples, swaggering boys, a worried gringo with a map . . . but not Papá. Mamá sat down again. The old man on the bench next to theirs belched. With his head thrust forward and his shoulders hunched, he looked like a turtle. Or Tío Gerardo. The man lifted a bottle to his lips, rocking backward to get the last drop.

Mamá sighed. »He'll come when he comes. Maria, help me with the food.«

Mamá tore the bread into jagged chunks while Mary sliced the cheese with a plastic knife. When Mary finished, Rosie handed her the tomato. Mary cut that, too, using a piece of bread as a cutting board. She gave Rosie a thick slice of tomato and the soggy bread, draping a slice of cheese over the open-faced sandwich.

Papá strode toward them, dust puffing under each step. He carried a huge bag in his arms. "I got them," he said. "Pray to God they fit."

Mary's voice was low. »Speak Spanish, Papá.«

Something in her tone stopped Papá. He looked at her.

Mamá took Mary by the wrist. »Maria, don't be disrespectful to your papá.«

Mary lowered her head without shifting her gaze from Papá's. »Forgive me, Papá.«

Papá finally nodded, as if waking from a trance. »Certainly, Mary. Now, why do you want me to speak Spanish?«

»We met two gringos at the market,« Mary said. »They were looking for Sean Devlin.«

Papá paled. He set the bag at Mamá's feet.

»One was blond, the other was sandy-haired,« Mary said.

»They didn't sound like *yanquis*,« Rosie said, anxious to be helpful.

Papá crossed himself.

Mary held Papá's gaze. »They talked like you did before Señora Mendoza moved to Nuñez. Before you asked her to teach you to talk like a *yanqui*.«

Mamá wrapped the bread in paper. She stood. »This is too open. Maria, Rosita, cover the food and gather your things.« She turned to Papá. »During your search, Miguel, you must have seen an abandoned house or a doorway . . .«

Papá scooped up the bag and the small suitcase at Mamá's feet. »I know a place. Ay, Conchita, that you and the girls should get mixed up in this.«

»We are part of you,« Mamá said. »Of course we are mixed up in this. Hurry, *mijas*. Lead us, Miguel.«

Papá nodded. »This way.« He turned suddenly to Mary and Rosie. »Look, if anyone asks you your last name, tell them it's Solano. Use your mother's family name, don't use Connelly. Until we cross the border.«

Mary and Rosie nodded.

Papá took a deep breath, exhaled. »This way,« he said.

They walked through the maze of streets, passing closed shops and fenced houses. One house, fortified behind a brick-and-iron fence, had wrought-iron bars on each window. *We'd be safe there*, Rosie thought. *The gringos would never find us.*

She caught up to Papá. »Papá, why do those men want you?«

»This is no time for stories, Rosita,« Mamá said. She smoothed a stray hair from Rosie's face, then patted her cheek.

They walked the narrow streets in silence.

ROSIE AND MARY STOOD SIDE BY SIDE IN THE CENTER of the abandoned warehouse. Mamá and Papá studied them, their faces striped by the sunlight slicing through the wooden slats. Wadded paper, splintered crates, and mounds of rotted fruit littered the floor. Buzzing flies crackled like static. And the smell! Rosie tried breathing through her mouth. A big mistake—the air tasted like rotted fruit, metallic and over-sweet like medicine. She wrinkled her nose.

Lifting her foot, she scratched the back of her calf with her new sneaker. She teetered and reached for a stack of crates. Mary caught her by the upper arm. »Don't lean on that,« she said in Spanish. »It isn't safe.«

"English, Mary," Papá said. "What do you think, Conchita?"

"Mary might pass for a *yanqui* girl," Mamá said. "Rosita will not."

Papá opened his mouth as if to argue with Mamá, but only shook his head and scratched the back of his neck. "Mary could pass. Mary looks like a North American. Rosie looks like she's wearing someone's discards."

Rosie looked down at the new clothes. A pair of jeans, her first ever, and a cotton blouse. The cuffs of the jeans had been rolled up, the waistband cinched tight with a plastic belt. The blouse, covered with purple and blue flowers, hung like a dress.

The sneakers fit.

"Tuck the blouse into the pants, Rosita," Mamá said.

Rosie did. Papá winced. "Worse," he said. "She looks like a charity case. I tried, Conchita. These were all I could find."

"She can cross in her own clothes," Mamá said. "In her little blue dress."

"But she looks like a Mexican!" Papá said.

Rosie pressed her lips together to keep her lower lip from trembling. Mary took her hand. "She is a Mexican," Mamá said quietly.

Papá turned scarlet. "I didn't mean—Conchita, we stand a better chance if we all look like *yanqui*s. It's not features and coloring, it's dress and expression and the way we carry ourselves."

Mamá sighed. "I know."

"Try on the dress I got for you," Papá said, suddenly

eager. "Let's see if it fits."

Mamá ducked her head. A shyness weakened her smile. "Right here?"

Papá grinned. "Don't look, girls. Your mamá is modest."

Rosie lowered her eyes and stared at a crumpled paper at her feet. If she unfolded it, what lines would it bear? How deep would the creases be? She imagined it spread out in front of her, a map of tiny roads and rivers, some intersecting, some veering away, some knifing across others in deep slashes. In her mind, she smoothed the paper a bit more, felt the wrinkles with her palm—

"Conchita," Papá breathed.

"Oh, Mamá!" Mary said. "You look beautiful!"

Rosie looked up. Mamá stood in the center of the abandoned warehouse, her full figure ripe in soft, burgundy cloth. The dress fitted her bust snugly, then flowed into a swingy skirt that fell to her knee. Pearl-white buttons shone from the top of the scooped neck to Mamá's waist. Mamá *did* look beautiful. She looked as if she'd stepped out of a magazine, one of those fancy women's magazines Señora Mendoza got from California. Rosie held her breath—

Then exhaled, her heart growing heavy. Mamá looked beautiful—but she still looked Mexican.

ROSIE MURMURED AND SCRATCHED THE SIDE OF HER face. She snuggled deeper into Papá's lap, clinging to sleep. He stroked her hair, singing softly. The words chased her fleeing dream:

> "I said, says I, to a passerby, 'Who's the maid
>   with the nut-brown hair?'
> He smiled at me, and he said, says he, 'That's
>   the gem of Ireland's crown,
> Young Rosie McCann from the banks of the

Bann,
She's the Star of the County Down.' ''

"What do you say, Eileen?" Papá said in a low voice.
"Can you guide us across?"

Rosie strained to hear a response, any response: Mamá
saying, "Miguel! Not in front of the children," or
Mary's mumbled, "God be with us," nearly drowned
out by her footsteps hurrying away. Or maybe Eileen
herself, this guardian angel Papá turned to for advice and
comfort. . . .

Sometimes Eileen was no comfort to Rosie. Like now.

"I can't leave them behind," Papá said. "Yes, yes, I
know. It might mean the difference between life and
death. But Eileen, they *are* my life. Without Conchita
and Mary and my wee Rosie, I have breath, not life."

Papá's fingers lifted the hair from Rosie's cheek,
tucked it behind her ear. "How could I ever leave my
little star?"

Silence replied. Rosie's ear ached with listening. The
silence said, *Mamá and Mary are gone. It is just you
and Papá in the old warehouse. Would he speak so
freely to Eileen if they were here?*

"Yes," Papá said. "I can feel them, too. How the
devil did they track us here? We took such a scrambled
route . . ."

Papá sighed. "I know, I know. Twelve years it's taken
them to find me. You'd think they'd have forgotten by
now. One pub, one wee, lousy pub—right. Speak *yanqui*, please. One *bar*. Satisfied, Eileen?"

Rosie's nose tickled.

Papá chuckled. "I know. I can feel her wakefulness.
But she's not afraid of you. Not like Conchita and
Mary." The humor left his voice. "Please, Eileen. Help
me find a safe crossing. If anything happened to this
little one—"

Rosie sneezed.

Papá lifted her into a sitting position. "Good morning,

my little star," he said. "You slept a long time."

Rosie rubbed her eyes, squinting into the gloomy shadows. "Is it really morning?"

Papá laughed. He tickled her. "Do you think I'd let you sleep *that* long?"

Rosie giggled and tried to tickle him. Papá jerked away and rolled into a ball. He was pretending, Rosie knew. He wasn't ticklish at all. She continued to tickle him, climbing across his back and draping herself around his neck. He swung her into his lap, biting her with kisses. "Mamá and Mary will be back soon with a light supper," he said. "And then we'll cross the border."

Rosie struggled to sit upright. "Papá? Who is Eileen?"

Papá raised his eyebrows. "Eileen is my guiding light. She led me safely to Mexico and now, God willing, she will lead us all to California."

"Is she an angel?"

"No—" Papá jerked upright. "*Here*? How—?"

He jumped to his feet, tucking Rosie under his arm. They crept to a stack of broken crates near the door. Papá held a finger to his lips. Rosie clenched her teeth until her jaw ached.

Footsteps approached. "Tijuana's too fucking big," a voice said. Hewitt. "We'll not find him here."

"It's not too big," the sandy-haired gringo said. "All of Mexico is too big, but Tijuana? If we can't find our man here, then what are we about?"

The footsteps stopped beside the door. Rosie and Papá pressed closer to the stack of crates. Papá's lips moved in silent prayer. Afraid she might make a sound, Rosie followed along in her head: "Hail Mary, full of grace . . ."

The hot, stinging smell of cigarette smoke drifted through the window. "It's too bad we didn't meet the Yank before we went to the market," the sandy-haired man said. "That girl—I'd bet my life she's his daughter. No doubt the other was around and about as well. No matter. The Yank will be with us tonight. And if he finds Devlin or the girls before then, he'll stick to them like glue."

Papá's prayers stopped. His eyes narrowed.

"What makes you so sure he'll help us?" Hewitt said.

"Didn't we promise to feed him? Didn't we offer him a night's lodging? There's no way a wanker like that is going to pass up that opportunity." The cigarette butt he wedged between two slats fell to the floor. Its ash glowed red in the dusk, then faded. "He'll be there. And after we find Devlin, we'll dispose of him."

Hewitt's laugh had a nasty, dirty edge. Rosie shrank closer to Papá. "We could do it here," Hewitt said.

"We could," the sandy-haired man said. "Come on, then. We'd best talk to that coyote again. See what he's heard about an Irishman and his family."

Footsteps tramped away. Rosie started to rise, but Papá held her down. He hugged her close to his chest and whispered in her ear, "Not yet." They waited a long time, until evening shadows hid the far wall. Papá said, "Go to the door, Rosie. Peek through the slats. Do you see them?"

She leaned into the rough boards, twisting her head one way, then the other. "No one, Papá."

Papá stood. "Ah, Rosie. If I could spare you this—"

Footsteps clattered toward them. Papá grasped Rosie's hand and pulled her back to the stacked crates. He relaxed as "*Gracias a la vida*" drifted to them, made hesitant by Mamá's nervous humming. "At last," he said, releasing Rosie.

Mamá forced open the door and entered the warehouse. She was alone.

●   ●   ●

»HE WOULDN'T LEAVE HER ALONE,« MAMÁ SAID, LEADING Papá and Rosie toward the city center. »I went back to the *taqueria* to get straws. When I came out, he was talking to her, asking her where her papá was. She dropped something and bent to pick it up. When he stooped beside her, she signaled me over his head to go.«

Papá's hand crushed Rosie's. »You left her there?« he said.

»What was I to do?« Mamá said. »It scares me to death, Miguel. She is eleven years old. In a city like this, anything could happen to her. But the *yanqui* wouldn't leave her alone.«

Papá mumbled something and tightened his grip. Rosie winced. »Papá,« she said. »You're hurting me.«

Papá's shoulders slumped. "Oh, Rosie. I'm sorry."

Mamá turned down a narrow alley. »Before we went into the *taqueria*, she told me, 'Mamá, if we get separated, I'll meet you at the bus station.' 'If we get separated?' I said. 'Niña, we had better not get separated.' 'A feeling, Mamá,' she said.« Mamá crossed herself. »One of her premonitions. Why, Miguel, what does the *yanqui* want with us?«

Papá's grip started to tighten again. »He's working for them.«

Rosie slipped her hand free and clutched his wrist.

Mamá faltered a step. "The Udea?"

"UDF," Papá corrected. "I should have gone on ahead alone, then sent for you and the girls. How could I have been so selfish?"

"Not selfish," Mamá said, placing a gentle hand on Papá's arm. "How could you send for us without giving yourself away?"

Papá shook his head. "I don't know, Conchita, but I would."

They gazed at each other for a long time before looking away.

»I DON'T SEE HER,« MAMÁ SAID, SCANNING THE BUS station. She pulled at Rosie's new blouse and jeans. Had they been lettuce, Rosie thought, they'd be shredded by now. »Do you see her, Miguel?«

»Maybe she's in the toilet,« Rosie said.

Papá squinted into the twilight. »Good thinking, Rosie. Conchita, why don't you go check—?«

Mary hurtled out of the shadows and threw herself at Mamá. She wrapped her arms around Mamá's waist as if she would never let go. »Oh, Mamá,« she said. »He wouldn't leave me alone. He followed me all over town. And then those two men from the market passed us and nodded at him like they knew him.«

»How did you get away?« Papá asked.

Mary turned to him without releasing Mamá. »I walked into an apartment. I sat in the living room for ten minutes. He left.«

»Probably to tell the others he knew where we were staying,« Papá mused. He looked at Mamá. »It's too dangerous here. We have to cross tonight. The man I bought the clothes from said there's a hole in the fence a safe distance from customs. He said the Migra don't patrol that stretch very often. Mary, go to the toilet with your mamá and change into the jeans.«

Mamá took Mary's hand. She walked toward the restroom, stopped. She dragged Mary back. »Miguel, I've been thinking,« she said. »It could happen again. We could get separated. We need to arrange a place to meet or—or where we can get word to each other.«

»Ay, Conchita,« Papá said, touching Mamá's cheek. »That's not going to happen. We won't be separated—«

»But at some point, maybe we should be,« she said. »If being with me and the girls means that you can't make the crossing, you have to promise me you'll go on alone—«

»Conchita—«

»Promise me,« she said. »I will not go another step, I will not follow you, unless you promise. If these men find you, they'll—« She bit her lip, glancing at Mary and Rosie. »I would . . . rather think of you far away and alive, in California, then to have you—to have you . . .«

Papá wet his lips. He traced Mamá's cheek with his fingers. »But how would I find you?«

»We'll return to Nuñez,« she said. »Promise me, Miguel.«

Papá withdrew his hand. His eyes deepened with a terrible hurt. »Take Mary to the toilet—«

»Promise me,« Mamá said.

Papá swallowed. The words came out hoarse and strained. »I promise.«

Mamá nodded. She hurriedly kissed his cheek, then led Mary away.

Papá crouched beside Rosie. He looked up at her, his face pale and shaken. "Rosie," he said. "Rose, once we cross the border, you must only speak English. If someone speaks to you in Spanish, pretend you don't understand. And if anyone asks where you live, you're on vacation from Fresno. Will you do that, my little star?"

Rosie nodded.

He pulled her into his arms. "Ah, Rosie, Rosie. Your old man loves you, you know that. Whatever happens."

THEY WEREN'T THE ONLY ONES WHO KNEW ABOUT THE hole in the wire fence.

Groups of people waited, whispering to each other and pointing. No one wanted to go first. »It's unlucky,« a man in a black T-shirt told Papá. »The first group across usually gets caught.«

»You've crossed here before?« Papá said.

»Many times,« the man said. »I work in Los Angeles. Once a month I come home for a weekend. Then I go back to work.«

Papá nodded. He drew Mamá, Mary, and Rosie aside. "Remember," he said. "English only once we cross. We're the Sayles family. We just wanted to see the border for ourselves."

A hush fell over the crowd. Rosie craned to see. A group of five men darted through the hole, then turned like a flock of ducks and ran back, chased by jeep headlights. The headlights strafed the fence, then jounced into the dark.

»Sacrifice yourself, Antonio,« someone joked, »so the rest of us can get across.«

A young man with a thick mustache and a baseball cap turned and made a rude gesture at the speaker. The speaker laughed. »Careful, Antonio,« he said. »There are children here tonight.«

Antonio straightened. »Children?« he said. He frowned, looking over the crowd until he spotted Mary and Rosie. He pushed his way to Papá. »You are trying to get your family across?« he asked.

»Yes,« Papá said.

Antonio's eyes narrowed. »You look like a gringo. Why do you need to sneak across?«

»I'm French,« Papá lied. »I've been promised work if I can get into the United States—without going through customs.«

Antonio shrugged. »We all have work if we can cross.« As he started to turn away, he saw Mamá. He stared at her. She stared back without flinching.

»Your wife,« Antonio said. »She is Mexican.«

Papá nodded.

»If the Migra stops you, they won't believe she's a gringa.« Antonio stroked the ends of his mustache. »It will be harder for you, especially with the two little girls.«

»If the Migra stops me,« Papá said, »they will send me back to France.«

A grin spread across Antonio's face. »You are illegal? In México?«

Papá nodded again.

Antonio chuckled to himself. »Ramiro, what time is it?«

»Nine-thirty,« someone said.

Antonio patted Papá's shoulder. »We will create a distraction for you. Be ready.«

»I need ten people,« Antonio said, pacing between the little knots of people. »Enough to fill the Migra jeep.«

Someone groaned. »Forget it, Antonio, you ask too much.«

»Hey, it's early,« Antonio said. »Besides, they are too busy here to beat you. They'll put us in the jeep, bring us back, and we can cross again later.«

»Go fuck yourself, Antonio,« someone else said.

»Careful,« Antonio said with a wink at Papá. »There are children here tonight.«

MAMÁ AND MARY STOOD NEAREST THE HOLE IN THE fence. Rosie hung back with Papá. "Is this safe, Eileen?" Papá whispered.

A short, thick man with curly hair punched Papá's arm. »Be ready,« he said.

Papá nodded.

Thirteen men eased through the hole in the fence, then broke into a run.

It seemed at first the men might make it. The fastest of them, Antonio, spurted into the dark, outdistancing the others by several meters. He dropped behind a bush before headlights pierced the night.

Within minutes, the Migra collected eleven men and piled them onto the jeep. Some clung to the roll bar, others to the sides. The Migra drove them away. As soon as the red taillights faded, Antonio popped up from behind his bush and waved.

"Now," Papá said, pushing Mamá through the hole in the fence.

Mamá dashed toward Antonio, followed by Mary. Rosie balked.

Papá shoved her forward. "Run, Rosie. I'm right behind you."

Rosie slipped through the fence and ran as fast and as hard as she could.

"Damn it to hell!" someone shouted behind her.

Rosie glanced over her shoulder and stumbled.

Hewitt and his sandy-haired friend watched through the hole in the fence. Hewitt pointed. "It's him, sure as I'm standing here! Come on!"

Papá scooped Rosie into his arms and crashed through the bush where Mamá, Mary, and Antonio were hiding. »We can't stop,« Papá said, grasping Mamá's hand and jerking her to her feet. »They're here. They saw us.«

With a curse, Antonio bolted.

"Hey, Devlin!" Hewitt shouted. "It's only a matter of time."

"And place," the sandy-haired man added. "If the Yanks catch you, you'll be sent back. There'll be a grand welcoming party for you, Sean."

"Eileen, help us," Papá whispered.

They ran toward the sleepless city lights, Papá still doubled over to carry Rosie, Mary dragging Mamá by the wrist. The pumping of Papá's legs joggled and bounced Rosie. She squirmed. "Set me down, Papá," she said. "I can run."

"But can," Papá panted, "you run . . . fast enough?"

"I can run, Papá," Rosie said.

He swung her to her feet. Rosie raced ahead, her fear contained only by the exaggerated breathing of her family. Her heart tried to match the broken rhythms of their feet hammering the dry earth. Houses loomed ahead on the edge of the desert. Houses with yards and parked cars and fences—places to hide. Rosie forced her aching legs to run faster.

The metallic whine of a Migra jeep growled behind her. Rosie lunged for the safety of the houses. Her feet finally slapped against asphalt.

Mary darted past her, veering around the corner of the first house. Papá followed, his big hand catching Rosie's shoulder and urging her along. A few steps behind, Mamá huffed and wheezed. Then Mamá fell.

Papá's momentum carried him forward, his fingers sliding along Rosie's arm. Rosie ducked and circled back to Mamá.

Mamá dragged herself to her knees, gasping for breath. She retched, but did not vomit. Rosie bent to gather her mother's hair. Mamá wiped her mouth with the back of her hand. »It's all right, niña,« she said, rising unsteadily to her feet.

The Migra jeep washed them with its headlights as it ground to a stop.

Two men in uniforms climbed out of the jeep. "Just some woman and her kid," the youngest said. He walked up to Mamá and grabbed her arm. "Come on, sweetheart. It's been fun, but it's time to go home now, *comprendes*?"

The older gringo pushed his cap up. "That Mick said he saw another Paddy go through the wall. Maybe we should look around."

"Man, you know 'em all, don't you?" the young one said. "Every racial slur in the book. Come on, *niña*. You, too."

He nudged Rosie, then pulled Mamá toward the jeep. Mamá cried out, dropping to her knees.

The younger gringo frowned. "She's hurt, Parton," he said, kneeling next to Mamá. "Shit, she's bleeding. Uh, *señora, hablas inglés? Un poco?*"

"She doesn't speak English, you moron," Parton

said. "She's a wetback. Whoa, buddy! Hold it right there!"

Rosie glanced over her shoulder. Parton had drawn his gun. Papá stood beside the nearest house, his hands raised above his head. He stared at the gun barrel, at the man, then at the young gringo feeling Mamá's leg. Mamá cried out again. "I think she broke it, Parton," the young gringo said. "Must've hit that curb pretty hard."

Papá's face registered nothing but bewilderment. "What happened? What's going on here?"

The young man looked up. "Nothing, sir. Sorry to disturb you. Just caught some illegals trying to cross."

Papá stepped forward. "Is she all right? What did you do to her?"

The older man edged closer to Papá, his head cocked as if listening for something. A cold knot formed in Rosie's stomach. He was listening for an accent, an Irish accent.

"We didn't do anything," the young man said. "She fell. I think she busted her leg."

"Well, for God's sake, help her," Papá said. Then he turned to the older gringo. "And you, get that thing out of my face. My taxes pay your goddamned salary. I don't need this kind of crap."

Rosie almost smiled. Papá sounded just like Señora Mendoza.

Parton lowered the gun. "Sorry, sir. Let's go, Vedder."

Vedder slipped his arm around Mamá's waist and lifted her onto his hip. "Lean on me, that's it. *Niña*, get on your mom's other side and help her out, okay?"

Papá's prayer was so faint, Rosie wondered if she'd really heard it. "Go to my Rose, Eileen," he said. "Be with her."

Someone appeared at the edge of Rosie's vision. A voice, a woman's voice, whispered, "I know your papá told you to speak English, but all that's changed. If you speak English, if you let on you know it, your papá will be at the mercy of the two Irishmen or others like him. If you let on, your papá will die.''

Rosie looked away from Papá. She stared at the dirty toes of her new sneakers.

"Niña?" Vedder said. "Honey, *comprendes*? *Ayuda* your mom, *niña*. Okay?"

Rosie rubbed her nose with the back of her hand, then slipped her arm around Mamá's waist.

Mary stepped around the side of the house. "Dad?"

"I told you to stay inside," Papá said.

"I was scared," Mary said. "What's happening? Who are these people?"

Papá put his arm around Mary's shoulders and marched her toward the house. "This doesn't concern you," he said. Together they turned the corner and were gone.

"Let's get these two to a hospital," Vedder said. "Come on, *niña*. *Ayuda* your mom. Put the gun away, Parton. The poor kid's already scared to death."

"It's all right, Rosa," the woman's voice said. "You just saved your papá's life. It's all right. I'm with you. I'll help guide you."

Rosa turned her head a little to look at the woman. The woman stayed just beyond her vision.

"I'm Eileen," the voice said. "Eileen is an Irish name for light. You can call me by my Spanish name: Luz. I'll be the light that leads you."

THREE

ROSA TRUDGED DOWN AVENIDA DE LA REVOLUCIÓN, eyeing the occupied benches in front of the Jai Alai Fronton Palacio. Music spilled through the open windows of the sports bar/arcade on the corner. As Rosa walked past, an old man swayed to his feet and shuffled away. Rosa hurried to claim the shaded bench. She sank onto the cool metal slats.

Between the heat and the baby, the worrying and the waiting, her energy was all but depleted. What was it Mamá used to say? *Waiting will wear you to the bone faster than scrubbing floors.*

Mamá should know. Mamá had done both for seven years.

»You don't need to work in the hotel, Conchita,« Hector told her again and again. »Let them find someone else to scrub their floors. With the money Miguel sends you—«

»I can't count on that money,« Mamá said. »I don't know when it's coming or how much it will be. Better to work and know how much money I have.«

Then, after seven years, Mamá sent Papá's letters back unopened. »Gone,« she wrote in her crabbed handwriting. »Nobody with that name here.«

There was no money or word after that. Hard lines formed around Mamá's mouth; her lips became brittle and stiff. She clenched her teeth as if holding in her bitterness and frustration. She refused to speak English. She never mentioned Papá.

But she still wore the wedding band of entwined roses.

Rosa coiled her hair and lifted it from her shoulders. The breeze dried the sweat on her neck. Poor Mamá. Seven years she'd waited for a man who never sent for her. Seven years, each strung like a bead on a thread of promises and renewed hopes. No wonder Mamá cut the thread.

Rosa removed Mamá's wedding band from her pocket and weighed it in her palm. She'd waited almost four months for Jorge, her baby's father, before her own thread of hope snapped. Four months was enough. Enough for her to understand the crushing weight Mamá had borne. Enough to realize the waiting would leach the life from her, drying her out and making her as brittle as Mamá, even though she had never loved Jorge the way Mamá loved Papá. Oh, she'd loved him—he was the father of her child. Or maybe she'd loved his promises. . . .

»I'll take you with me,« he'd told her, that night he coaxed her out to the arroyo. He tucked a strand of hair behind her ear. »To Bakersfield, to California. We'll have an apartment of our own, you and I. You won't have to share your bed with your cousin's wife and her children—you won't have to share it with anyone. Only me. And you won't have to listen to your aunt blame you for your uncle leaving Nuñez or your mother's death.« He kissed her cleanser-reddened hands. »You won't have to clean hotel rooms anymore. You know how to type. You can get a job anywhere in California. Maybe even for some lawyer—or a rich doctor.«

"Don't sleep with him, Rosa," Luz warned. Rosa made a slight, go-away gesture with her hand.

Jorge tucked another strand of hair behind Rosa's ear.

Her ear ached with the pressure. He added another strand. »You'll make more money than me,« he said, head cocked to one side. »Ay, Rosa. We'll be rich in California.«

Rosa twisted her neck. The hair tumbled free. »And our children?«

»Will go to school. They will have everything.«

"Rosa . . ." Luz said.

»And we'll look for Papá?« Rosa asked. »And Señora Mendoza?«

Jorge tucked another strand of hair behind Rosa's throbbing ear. »Of course.« He kissed her. »I'll go first, to find a job and an apartment in Bakersfield. I'll write to you as soon as I get there. And in a month, I'll come for you.«

No letter arrived for Rosa; Jorge's mamá received one each week. Whenever one arrived, Señora Partida and her friend would walk over from the post office and sit outside the hotel until Rosa got off work. Then Señora Partida would brandish the letter and tell her friend, »Look, Guillerma. I have a letter from my Jorge. He says he's sharing a trailer with six other men. He has a good job, in construction. He's making lots of money. Ay, look at this! He sends me twenty dollars!«

One day, after three and a half months and a morning of roiling queasiness, Rosa set aside her cleaning basket and approached the señora. "Don't tell her about the baby," Luz warned.

"Why not?" Rosa whispered as she crossed the hotel lobby. "Perhaps she'll be more willing to give me the address if she knows I'm carrying her grandchild."

"Don't tell her," Luz repeated.

Señora Partida elbowed her friend when Rosa appeared. »Look, Guillerma,« she said, waving a new letter at her friend. »My Jorge has a girlfriend. She's a North American. He's going to marry her soon and get his green card.«

Rosa faltered a step, then passed the two cackling women.

»But he could have found a North American girl here,« Guillerma said.

»Ah, no, Guillerma. Only a *bruja* taught to act like a North American.«

Rosa's cheeks burned. She quickened her pace.

"Where are you going?" Luz said.

"Home," Rosa said. "It's time I told Tía Inez about the baby."

"Bad idea. I think we should talk this over first—"

"Before too long, I'll start showing," Rosa said, scowling at Luz. "Maybe I should wait and see if she notices."

As soon as Rosa told her aunt, she wished she'd waited. Tía Inez slapped her, then dragged her by the hair to the bedroom. She flung Rosa to the bed. »I took you and your sainted mother in when she fell ill, I feed you and house you and this is the thanks I get!« she shouted. »Not only do I have to house you, now I have to house your bastard. And look after it, too, I suppose, or are you planning to quit your job? You drove your uncle out of my house—«

"Ask her who cuckolded him," Luz muttered.

»—killed your mother—«

»Mamá had a tumor,« Rosa said.

»—and now you plan to ruin me!« Inez concluded. »God had no mercy the day your father arrived in Nu-ñez. . . .«

Rosa swallowed to rid herself of the memory's bitter taste. She glanced at the Jai Alai Fronton Palacio. A colorful statue teetered in the courtyard out front, its arms spread wide, poised to fall or take flight. *Just like me*, Rosa thought. At least poor Mamá, with all her loneliness and pain, had not had to face the shame of abandonment. Everyone, especially Inez, treated her with tenderness and respect, trying to ease her sorrow. Rosa winced. Everyone but her daughter.

What an insensitive brat she'd been. Especially at twelve, when it seemed all she wanted to talk about was Papá. »Tell me about him, Mamá,« she'd said over and over. »Tell me the things that I was too young to see or understand.«

The lines around Mamá's mouth became harsh. »No.«

»Please, Mamá. Why hasn't he sent for us?«

But Mamá's jaw clamped tight. Rosita searched Mamá's face. Fear coiled there, and anger . . . and boundless sadness.

Now Rosa understood that sadness, but it had perplexed her at twelve. She, too, missed Papá and Mary. A day didn't pass that she didn't beg God for their return. But if someone mentioned them to Mamá, she shrank like a poppy at sundown. Her eyes seemed to see only things very far away—and never revealed.

Rosita's childish mind tried to get a glimpse of the sights that haunted Mamá. She saw the two Irishmen coming up behind Papá on a dark, lonely street—

She buried the thought. No. No, Mamá worried that Papá had found another woman. That he had married some blond *yanqui* woman. Loni, that was her name. Or Darryl. Thin and blond, with a tiny, perfect nose and flawless teeth. Darryl wore pale blue silk to set off her sapphire eyes. She fussed over Mary, pretending Mary was her own daughter. She even gave Mary a gold locket with a diamond heart, but Mary refused to wear it. Instead she wore a simple chain with a silver girl. Darryl said, "But Mary, it's so crude. Let me get you something nicer."

Mary looked past her—at Papá. "This is a *milagro*, a miracle," she said. "It will help me find my sister. *I* haven't forgotten her."

And Papá, the grief showing only in his eyes, would turn away, as he had that night on the border. . . .

Rosa pressed against the back of the bench and closed her eyes. The tortures she had dreamed for herself at twelve! But they had been better than worrying that the Irishmen had found Papá. They had been better than imagining him dead.

She turned the ring in her hand, pressed it to her palm, then pocketed it. This ring, this little bit of worn gold, was all Mamá had been able to leave her—the only thing Rosa could touch as she might Mamá's cheek or hand. Mamá's hands. Rosa winced. At the last, as the tumor devoured Mamá to the bone, the ring seemed to grow larger and larger, absorbing Mamá's life, preserving it in the bright metal. . . .

Rosa opened her eyes. The statue trembled in the shimmering heat. Wiping her sweaty forehead with the back of her hand, she looked around. A newspaper lay on the bench beside her. She picked it up. A tourist paper, *The Tijuana Reader*. She began tearing it into squares.

"You will get across," Luz said. "I promise you."

Rosa folded a page, then tore it. "Before the baby's born?"

"At least a day."

Rosa stopped tearing the newspaper and jerked to look at Luz. Luz stayed just at the edge of sight.

"It was a joke," Luz said.

Rosa shook her head. She ripped another square. "I need to cross, Luz. And I need a coyote. There are no holes in this new wall. You've seen it—it's slick, solid metal."

"I'll find you a way—"

"Luz, I can't wait any longer," Rosa said. "I have no home, and, except for Tío Hector, Papá, and Mary, no family." She forced her hands to still. "I don't want my child to grow up like those children in the dump. Do you remember them, Luz? The children playing in the garbage when we tried to cross with Papá?"

"Rosa, that won't happen to you or your daughter—"

Rosa began folding the last square, her hands creasing the paper with vicious strokes. "And I don't want her to grow up like those children selling gum at Viva Tijuana, full of contempt—Daughter? It's a girl?"

Luz smiled and nodded.

A thrill surged through Rosa. A girl. She had hoped the baby was a girl—

A shiver followed the thrill. How did Luz know the baby's sex? Sometimes Rosa wondered if the border between them had blurred. What would happen if it dissolved?

She abandoned the thought. "I need to get to Watsonville, Luz," she said. "I hope Papá's still at that address Tío Hector saved from the last letter."

She imagined Papá and Mary welcoming her into their home, their hands straying across her belly to touch this new life, this daughter. Her own hands continued to fold the paper as if they had minds of their own. After a few careful creases, a flapping bird nested in her palms.

"Your papá," Luz said.

Rosa turned the newsprint bird over in her hands. With its wings lifted high, the little bird looked as if it was ready to fly away and leave her behind—like Papá.

She touched the silver girl. At least Mary had left her this. What miracles had Papá left her?

Many. He'd left her Luz. And his love for Mamá.

Rosa stroked the paper bird, then pinched its tail and pulled. Its wings fanned the hot air. Papá had loved Mamá—with every look, with every touch. And, despite her adolescent fantasies, Rosa knew why he had never sent for them. Mamá's note was only part of it. He had never sent for them because of the Irishmen who came to Nuñez and found their way to Hector's, looking for her and Mamá.

»Did you make that?« a childish voice said.

Rosa looked up. A boy no more than seven stood in

front of her, his face smeared with rubbery, dried ice cream. He pointed to the flapping bird. »Did you make that?« he said again.

»Yes, niño,« she said, handing it to him. »Would you like it?«

The boy nodded. He pulled at the bird's wings, then held it up. »Lupita! Edgardo! Look!«

Several paces away, leaning against the wall of the sports bar, stood another seven-year-old boy. Beside him, head bowed, stood a girl of nine or ten. The girl's gaze met Rosa's and held it for a few seconds. Then the girl bit down on a smile.

»Would you like me to make something for you, too?« Rosa said to the boy leaning against the wall.

Edgardo's face lit up with a grin. He hurried to Rosa's side. »One of those,« he said, pointing to the flapping bird. »Just like Josué's.«

Rosa selected another piece of newspaper. After a few quick folds, she handed Edgardo a flapping bird. She looked up at the girl. Lupita still stood beyond reach, her gaze fixed on Rosa's hands. »Would you like something, too?« Rosa asked.

Lupita blinked and stepped back. She nodded.

Rosa beckoned with her hand. »Come here. I won't hurt you.« A blur raced between them. »No, Josué. Don't pull the wings. Hold the chest and pull the tail. There, Edgardo's got it. That's how you make the wings flap.«

Amid shouts and squeals, the boys guided the paper birds high above their heads. Longing dimmed Lupita's eyes. She watched the birds dive and swoop.

»What shall I make you?« Rosa said.

Lupita shrugged.

"Trust your hands," Luz said.

Trust my hands, Rosa mused. She shook the tension from her fingers, then cleared her mind. She picked up the next piece of paper, ready to fold it, but the paper didn't feel right. Without looking, she let her fingers sort the torn squares. Something about the texture of the last sheet felt right, a certain tooth and weight. She began to fold, a sudden drive and urgency flowing through her hands. She hurried through a series of valley and mountains folds, creased, unfolded, refolded. She let her mind drift, allowing her hands to create without hindrance. Lupita crept toward her. Rosa peeked at the girl. Lupita's shyness dissolved into fascination. Rosa glanced at the animal forming in her hands, stifling her surprise. A black panther—for this shy, gentle child?

I'm trusting you, Rosa told her hands. She crimped the front legs, then handed the paper animal to Lupita. »A panther,« she said.

A smile seeped across the girl's face, a predatory, cat-like smile. A wakening power gleamed in her eyes. She stroked the sleek paper flanks, then darted after the boys with a snarl.

"Luz," Rosa said, "if I unfolded that piece of paper and studied its creases, would I understand why a panther was the right choice?"

"Panthers are graceful and strong," Luz said. "That's how Lupita imagines herself in her daydreams. And someday, she'll make that grace and power hers. In *this* world."

Rosa sighed. "I wish I could see the way you do."

"You do. But you see with your hands. Trust them. They'll guide you."

Rosa folded a crane. "That's what Señora Mendoza said."

"And did you listen to Señora Mendoza?" Luz asked.

FOUR

"KATHY," SEÑORA MENDOZA SAID, OPENING A PACKage of origami paper. The top sheet, a rich royal blue, seemed to glow in the late afternoon sunlight. "You're old enough to call me Kathy. It won't kill you."

Rosita scooted her chair deeper into the shade until she butted up against the glass-topped wrought-iron table. This late in the afternoon, the Mendoza's adobe walls trapped the courtyard's heat and held it. The captive heat wavered, enraged and spiteful. Rosita sponged the sweat from the back of her neck with a worn handkerchief. "Kathy," she said. She wrinkled her nose.

Señora Mendoza removed two sheets of paper from the package, one blue, the other a vivid hibiscus red. She raised her eyebrows, amusement widening her delicate almond eyes. "Doesn't feel right, huh? No, I bet it doesn't. Not after seven years." She set the blue sheet in front of Rosita. "Try Kathleen. It's a little stiffer. Maybe that'll feel more respectful."

"Kathleen," Rosita said. Her fingers skimmed the slick, smooth surface of the origami paper. "It still doesn't feel right. What's wrong with calling you Señora Mendoza?"

Señora Mendoza reached for the cigarette smoldering in the abalone shell at her elbow. "If you're going to talk like a real American—well, a real Californian, anyway—you've got to start calling everyone by their first names, regardless of how old they are. You're fourteen. No self-respecting teenager calls anyone Mr. and Mrs. anymore. Not in California.''

"Kathleen," Rosita said again. She grimaced. "Maybe they'll just think I'm old-fashioned."

Señora Mendoza took a drag on her cigarette. "No one's old-fashioned in California."

Rosita smoothed the paper again. Señora Mendoza should know. She visited her family in Atherton twice a year—for a month at Christmas and another two months in the summer for the Kimura family reunion. She'd be leaving for the reunion in a month. . . .

Señora Mendoza returned the cigarette to the abalone shell. She rubbed her thumbs across her fingertips, then picked up the red paper. She began to fold, quickly and precisely. "You people are too class conscious down here," she said. "In the States, they're just racist."

"That's the same as class conscious," Rosita said, leaning forward. She watched as the paper transformed under Señora Mendoza's persuasive fingers. She couldn't tell yet what Señora Mendoza was making—

The señora's hands stopped, the origami only half formed.

Startled, Rosita looked up. Señora Mendoza gazed at her, her eyes hard and dark as avocado seeds. The lines tracing their bay-leaf perfection had been etched as deep as the lines around Mamá's mouth. And as harsh. Señora Mendoza lifted her chin. Her short, blue-black hair brushed the collar of her white blouse. "Don't make that mistake," she said. "Race and class are never the same."

She reached for the cigarette. It collapsed into a pool of ash. She pushed the abalone shell away, then pressed its lip with her finger. The shell rocked, its reflection on the glass pulsing like heat. "Your English is good," she said, her gaze meeting Rosita's again. "It's really good.

But that wouldn't matter there. Not to lot of people. They'll always suspect you, because you don't look white enough. And there's nothing you can do about that. No matter how you dress or act, no matter how little you practice or even know about what they consider your culture—they'll suspect you. When it comes time to round up all the illegal aliens, they'll take you. When it comes time to blame someone for the way things are, they'll blame you. You're not them and they can see it. They *do* see it, every time they look at you."

She leaned toward Rosita. "Class can be learned," she said. "It can be faked, maybe even acquired. People make money or marry it all the time. Not race."

Rosita shrank back. Sunlight sliced her shoulders and neck.

With the barest of nods, Señora Mendoza turned back to the origami. She completed it with several quick folds, then set a winged horse on the table. "Look at it closely," she said.

After a minute, she unfolded the winged horse and smoothed the paper with her palm. "There," she said. "Now, find Pegasus."

Rosita took a deep breath and stared at the red paper. Lines crossed and recrossed the square. She frowned at the paper, turning it over to look at the same triangles and squares overlapping each other on the white side of the paper. A leg emerged from the lines—or, rather, what would become a leg. Three more legs, two wings, a neck and head—

"Trust your eyes, but more than anything, trust your hands," Señora Mendoza said. "Even if you don't think your eyes are taking in the whole pattern, they are. But it's your hands that will translate those patterns." She tapped the paper. "It's the patterns that will help you. You can use them to copy what I've done, or you can use them to create something of your own. But remember—study the patterns. And trust your hands."

"She's right," Luz said.

Rosita traced the winged horse's neck with her finger. "I can do this," she said.

"I know you can," Señora Mendoza said. "Remake my Pegasus, then make one of your own. Then I want to teach you another skill, one almost as useful as origami."

ROSITA TRUDGED ALONG THE ROAD TOWARD TOWN, THE dust following her in puffs like small dogs. She readjusted her grip on the small, portable typewriter, the beige case resting on her thigh. It rose and fell with each step she took, her dress crumpled and damp, caught between the typewriter and her leg. Rosita shifted the typewriter into her arms, hooking the paperback book between her elbow and her thigh. "Portable," she grumbled. "About as portable as Mamá's bed."

"Have you ever seen a regular typewriter?" Luz said.

"You know I haven't," Rosita said. "What good is this thing, anyway? There are no tildes, no accents. There's only one question mark—there's only one exclamation point. It's stupid."

"It's an English typewriter," Luz said. "That's why Kathy—"

"Señora Mendoza."

"—wants you to use it. So that when you get to California, you won't have to pick fruit or clean houses. You'll stand a better chance of being mistaken for a native."

The book worked its way from under her arm and fell to the dirt. Rosita pressed her lips together and glared at the battered lump of paper. Wait till Mamá saw the cover on this one! She'd crossed herself three times when Rosita brought home the one about the girl who went to the prom and had blood poured over her. She'd say a rosary over this one, the way the woman's breasts looked ready to burst from her dress. A smile twisted the corner of

Rosita's mouth. She banished the grin, determined to be "put out," as Señora Mendoza said.

With a sigh, she squatted, set the typewriter on the ground, and placed the book on top of it. A plastic and metal box, a fat book—*and* Señora Mendoza had wanted to send a box of paper home with her, too. The woman was crazy—

"Rosita," Luz said.

Rosita swayed to her feet. "Hmm?"

"No English," Luz said. "Not to these men."

Rosita jerked to look. Two gringos walked toward her, one blond, the other red-haired. Rosita hugged the typewriter to her chest. "What do they want, Luz?" she whispered. "Can you feel it yet?"

"Not yet," Luz said. "They're thinking too hard about something else. One of the men is sick . . . the food doesn't agree with him. Wait. The redhead spotted you."

The red-haired gringo grasped the other man's sleeve. The two of them stopped, then approached Rosita slowly. Rosita forced herself to keep walking. "*Yanquis?*" Rosita whispered.

"Irish," Luz said.

Rosita's heart faltered for a second. Irish. Looking for Papá. Trying to find him through her and Mamá.

She knew now why Papá left Ireland—and why he left Mexico. Mamá and Luz had been forced to tell her after her cousin Leandro, Tío Hector's son, had stopped her on her way home from Señora Mendoza's one evening. She had just turned ten. . . .

»Your papá is a murderer,« Leandro said. »He killed people in Ireland. Lots of them.« He pretended to wield a machine gun. »Gunned them down. *Ch-ch-ch-ch-ch!*«

Rosita held herself to keep from trembling. A terrible certainty fisted her stomach. Papá had done something, she knew. Something dangerous. Was it possible? Had he really shot people?

»He—he did not,« she stammered.

Leandro aimed at her with his imaginary gun. »Gunned them down.«

"Luz?" Rosita pleaded.

Luz's silence chilled her. Rosita ran all the way home.

Mamá met her at the door. Looking down into her tear-streaked face, Mamá pulled her inside. »Who did this to you?« she said. »Who made you cry?«

Rosita backed away from Mamá, as if distance would make it harder for her mother to lie. »Papá,« Rosita said. »Did Papá shoot people in Ireland?«

Mamá's eyes grew hard as onyx. »Who told you that?«

»Leandro. He said Papá gunned people down.«

»Hector.« Mamá spat the name. Then grief softened her anger. She gestured for Rosita to come to her.

Rosita refused, backing farther away. »Did he?«

Mamá looked up, as if beseeching God. Taking a deep breath, she bowed her head. »Your papá was a freedom fighter,« she said, her voice low and flat. »He joined the *guerrilleros*, hoping to take his country back from the English. One night he bombed a cantina, one that belonged to an Englishman.«

"I warned him not to," Luz said.

Rosita swallowed.

Mamá pressed her lips together, made a kissing sound. »It was late at night. No one was supposed to be in the cantina.«

"But there was," Luz said.

»A rich man was visiting the cantina owner,« Mamá said. »A very powerful rich man. He hated the *guerrilleros* and was using his influence to get the English to send more soldiers to the village.«

"That night the rich man convinced the others to round up all the *guerrilleros* and anyone thought to be friendly with them, anyone Catholic, and have them arrested," Luz said. "Those who were suspected of being part of the *guerrilla* were to be shot—accidentally."

Rosita pressed against the wall.

»Miguel, not knowing the men were meeting in the cantina, threw a bomb through the window,« Mamá said.

"When I understood what the men were planning," Luz said, "I told him, 'Go on, Sean. Do it.' It was eight guilty lives in exchange for dozens of innocents."

"They were—they were not all innocents," Rosita murmured.

Mamá leaned closer. »Say it again, Rosita?«

"Many of the people the men wanted to kill were," Luz said. "Including boys your age."

»What did you say, Rosita?« Mamá coaxed.

Rosita wet her lips. »It must have been horrible.«

Mamá nodded, her shoulders sagging. »It was. Seven men died. The rich man survived, but he was in the hospital for many months. Your papá knew that the rich man's friends would kill him, so he fled.«

"I told him, 'Warn the others, then go,'" Luz said. "People died that night and people were saved. I led your papá here. And, when the rich man's friends tracked him here, I led him away. . . ."

Rosita looked down as the gringos drew near. The blond one tried to catch her eye. Gringos thought Mexican girls shy and modest. She hurried past them with one last furtive look. Tiny veins reddened the blond man's face, like the scarlet veins in a blood orange. The red-haired man, with his walnut-brown eyes, smiled at her. She looked away. Handsome . . . how could Papá's enemy be so handsome?

"Hello, miss?" the blond gringo said. "Could we have a word with you?"

Rosita squeezed the typewriter to her chest and kept walking.

"Señorita," the red-haired man said. "*Momentito, por favor.*"

Shocked, Rosita swung to face the gringos.

Spanish. None of the Irish had ever spoken Spanish before.

The red-haired gringo's smile widened. »I'm looking for an old friend of mine, Michael Connelly. This town is the last address I have for him.«

Rosita hesitated. Usually the Irish asked for Sean Devlin. Maybe this one *was* a friend of Papá's. Rosita studied the red-haired gringo. A friend of Papá's . . . impossible. The man looked twenty-four or twenty-five— five, maybe six years older than Mary. He would have been a baby when Papá left. . . .

»Your Spanish is good,« she said, to distract them from her long silence. Then the very devil entered her. She cocked her head. »Most *yanquis* don't bother to learn Spanish.«

This time the two men started.

Clearly puzzled, the blond gringo frowned. "Ian, did she call us Yanks?"

Ian shook himself. "Never been called *that* before. Although it might well work to our advantage . . ."

He cocked his head, just as she had, only to flirtatious effect. »Most *yanquis* have no one as beautiful as you to inspire them.«

"Flattery," Luz said.

"I know, I know," Rosita muttered.

Ian leaned closer. »Excuse me? I couldn't hear what you said.«

Rosita blushed, cursing herself silently for responding to Luz. »Nothing. I must go. I'm late—«

»Can I walk with you?« Ian said, falling in step beside her. He reached for the typewriter. »Let me carry this—«

Rosita jerked to the side. The book and the typewriter would give her away. »Please, leave me alone. I'm late—«

»I won't slow you down,« Ian said. »I just—you're

so beautiful. You're like a rose in the desert, so fresh and tender and perfect.«

Rosita bit her lower lip, fighting the thrill rising inside her. A rose in the desert . . .

"Romantic crap—*bad* romantic crap," Luz said. "What kind of filth seduces a fourteen-year-old girl? This is the sleaziest one they've sent."

Rosita glared at the man. »What kind of filth seduces a fourteen-year-old girl?« she said.

Ian's jaw dropped. »Fourteen? But I thought you were at least seventeen—« He called over his shoulder to the blond, "It's the younger one," then tried to look embarrassed. »I'm sorry if I was disrespectful. Your beauty . . .«

Rosita locked her jaw, then glanced back. The blond man followed several meters behind, giving his friend every opportunity to enchant her. He waved to her. Rosita scowled and swung to face the road ahead. Within fifteen meters, they would reach the edge of town and her house. Should she go in or pass by?

»What's your name?« Ian said.

Rosita ignored him. If Mamá was outside, she would go in. If Mamá was not, she would go to the cantina and look for Tío Hector. And if the men would not leave her alone?

»Niña,« Ian said, »I'm sorry. Forgive me. I'm just trying to find my friend—«

Rosita nodded toward the blond gringo. »He's back there.«

Ian inhaled with a slight whistle. »*He* is. I'm trying to find another friend, Michael Connelly. Miguel Connelly. I was told he lives here.«

Rosita glanced sideways at the house. Mamá was not there. Rosita kept walking. Her feet molded to the round cobblestones.

"Go to the church," Luz said. "Go to Father Ruiz."

The cantina, Rosita thought.

"I can feel your resistance," Luz said. "Go to Father Ruiz. Anyone else might lead them to your papá."

Rosita took a deep breath. She headed toward the church.

»I haven't seen him since I was a child,« Ian said. »My father talks about him often. They were inseparable. They played football together, went to dances together.« He chuckled. »For a while they even dated the same girl.«

"My God," Luz said in a strangled voice. "It can't be. Ask him his name."

Rosita hugged the typewriter. »What's your—?«

»Rosita!« Leandro called, hurrying toward them. A twitch of smile bristled the fuzz on his upper lip. »So the gringos found you. They asked Papá about you—«

»Rosita,« Ian said. He touched her chin. »So you are a rose in the desert.«

Rosita pulled away. »Please, señor—«

"*Ask him his name*," Luz repeated.

Leandro shifted from foot to foot, his chest puffed like a tomatillo bursting its husk. »*Mira*, señores. I told you. Every day she walks this road from Señora Mendoza's—«

»I don't know your name,« Rosita said to silence Leandro. If he told them about her English lessons, they'd know. They'd know she was Michael Connelly's daughter. »You know my name. It's only fair.«

Ian shrugged his eyebrows and nodded. »True,« he said. He watched her closely. »My friend here is Jackie Lyttle.«

The blond man offered a slight bow.

Still studying her, Ian said, »And I'm Ian Elliott.«

Rosita held his gaze. Luz said nothing.

Rosita shifted the typewriter a little on her hip, then brushed past the Irishmen. »A pleasure to meet you,« she said.

Leandro's pride dissolved into confusion. »Rosita,

where are you going? They've been waiting to speak to you all day. They're old friends of your father's.«

Rosita forced herself to walk slowly. »To church. To talk to Father Ruiz.«

"Where is she going?" Jackie Lyttle asked.

"To church," Ian said. "To talk to the priest."

"Fucking papist cunt," Jackie said. He started after her.

Ian caught him by the arm. "And where are you going? We'll talk to her later. Let's go find the mother." He switched to Spanish. »Leandro, where is Señora Connelly?«

Rosita glanced over her shoulder. Leandro's face had become as hard and opaque as painted glass. He turned from the men and walked away.

Ian jogged to catch up to him. »Leandro—«

Leandro glared at him, nostrils flared. »I know enough English to know what a 'fucking cunt' is,« he said. He spat at Jackie's feet. »Stay away from my cousin.«

Rosita sped up. "Luz, that man. Who is he?"

Luz hissed. "He's the cantina owner's son. Stay at the church tonight. And tell Father Ruiz to send for your mamá."

PINK DUSK BLUSHED ACROSS THE WHITE WALLS OF THE sacristy. The brass handles on the wardrobe dulled in the dim light; shadows swallowed the wooden crucifix. Rosita set Señora Mendoza's book on the bench between herself and Mamá and stood. She winced as the nerves in her legs released streamers of lightning pain. Stumbling a step, she reached for the light switch.

»No,« Mamá said.

Rosita withdrew her hand. She returned to the bench and sat.

Mamá picked up the book. Her upper lip curled in

distaste. »Look at this. You shouldn't be reading this anyway. Such trash.«

Rosita slid the book from Mamá's hands, imagining the cover through Mamá's eyes. The woman bursting out of her dress was not the worst of it—a man held the woman, dangled her backward, ready to ravage her with a kiss. Behind them flames danced. Rosita smiled. The very gates of Hell.

»It's a classic, Mamá,« she said. »They even made a movie out of it. You saw it. *Gone with the Wind.*«

Mamá waved the book away. »Trash. Don't let Father Ruiz see it.«

Silence filtered into the sacristy with the dark. Rosita stared at the crucifix, trying to hold it with her eyes to keep it from disappearing. *We need you*, she told Christ.

»Mamá,« she whispered. »Do you really think those men would hurt us?«

Mamá twisted her wedding band. »The others left us alone. I pretended not to understand them and told them nothing. They talked to others and learned only that your papá crossed the border. These two . . . they're different.«

Rosita waited. She blinked and the crucifix disappeared, swallowed by darkness. »How, Mamá? How are they different?«

Mamá took a deep breath. »They know more. They know your papá's name, the name he used here. And the redheaded one knows Spanish. He also has photographs and claims to be an old friend.« Mamá turned in the darkness. »He showed the photographs to Hector. Did Leandro tell you?«

Rosita shook her head. »No.«

»He also said he had greetings from his papá that he wanted to share with Michael Connelly's family,« Mamá said.

Rosita touched the silver girl at her throat. »From his papá?«

"Welcome to Hell," Luz said.

Mamá touched Rosita's knee. Rosita nearly leaped off the bench. »They have guns,« Mamá said. »Guillerma saw them. At the hotel when she brought them fresh towels.«

Rosita closed her eyes and said a quick prayer. When she opened her eyes, she searched the darkness for Christ. Silence deepened with the night.

"Rosita," Luz said. "Rosita, get out of here. Now."

Rosita reached for the typewriter. "Where?"

Mamá tensed. »Rosita?«

"Leave everything," Luz said. "I'll guide you. But get out of here now."

Rosita stood. "This is a church—"

"Do you think that matters to them?" Luz said. "*Go.*"

Rosita held her breath, exhaled. »Mamá, we have to go.«

Mamá's fingers whispered in the dark as she crossed herself. She swayed to her feet. Rosita took her hand.

"This way," Luz said.

A flickering blur passed by the side of Rosita's face. It drifted in front of her, a dim star hovering near the door. The star's glow illuminated Christ's face. Rosita tugged at Mamá's hand, leading her out of the sacristy and into the cool night air.

Luz floated in front of them, then darted around the church. Rosita followed as Luz passed the low adobe wall surrounding the cemetery and climbed the hills.

Mamá stopped. Rosita tugged at her hand. »Mamá, please. It's not safe here.«

»And it is safer in the hills?« Mamá tried to slip her hand away. »There are ghosts and bandits in these hills. Leandro saw a *chupacabra*—«

Rosita tightened her grip. »Mamá, please.«

Luz flared. "Hurry."

Rosita yanked Mamá's arm and dragged her from the shelter of the cemetery.

Luz led them along a dry arroyo, past scrubby brush and weathered trees. As they dropped beneath the crest of the first hill, a truck rattled to a stop behind them. The engine ticked. Tío Hector's truck. Rosita held her finger to her lips, shushing Mamá. They peeked over the hill.

"Rosita," Luz said. "There's no time for this."

The truck waited outside the church. The rectory door opened, spilling light onto the foot-polished ground. Rosita ducked lower. Father Ruiz called out. From the truck, Tío Hector answered.

»You see?« Mamá whispered, pushing past Rosita. »It's only Hector.«

The truck's passenger door squealed open. The blond gringo stepped out.

Mamá froze.

"Hurry," Luz said.

Rosita grasped Mamá's hand and pulled her away.

They ran, stumbling over rocks and tangled roots. Luz fled deeper into the hills, then veered suddenly, leading them back to the rocky bed of the arroyo. Rocks and pebbles scrabbled and shot from under their feet. Mamá hurtled forward, catching herself with her outstretched hand. Rosita reeled her to her feet.

»There's nothing out here,« Mamá panted between breaths. »Nowhere to hide.«

"Luz?" Rosita said.

"Hurry," Luz said.

Rosita took a deep breath and plunged on. Mamá had no choice but to follow. They tripped and staggered along the dried stream until they came to three huge boulders leaning into the rocky hillside. The arroyo skirted them. The light slipped between a niche in the boulders.

Rosita stopped. Beside her, Mamá trembled with fatigue, choking for breath. »What . . . now?« she gasped.

The light reappeared in the niche.

"No, Luz," Rosita whispered. "We can't fit there."

"You can," Luz said. "Trust me."

Rosita headed for the boulders. Mamá stumbled after. »Rosita, are you crazy?« she whispered.

Rosita drew even with the first boulder. She lay a hand on the cooling rock and pulled herself around. A crack opened up between the first boulder and the second. A crack wide enough to slip through.

Rosita gestured with her hand. »Mamá, in here.«

Mamá studied her. »Just like your papá.«

»Yes, Mamá,« Rosita said. »The same.«

Mamá shivered. She joined Rosita beside the narrow opening, hesitated, then slipped through. Rosita followed.

The crack led to a chamber just big enough for the two of them to sit side by side. They huddled together, hugging their knees to keep from touching heat-leeching rock.

Luz faded. Darkness filled the chamber. "You must be absolutely quiet," Luz said.

»Not a word, Mamá,« Rosita whispered.

Mamá's hair brushed Rosita's knee as she nodded.

Again, the darkness held them in a prison of silence, but this time so complete, Rosita could not even imagine Christ's face. She prayed to God and to the Virgin and to Luz. Her ears ached with the strain of listening.

After what seemed hours, exhaustion overwhelmed her. She slept.

ROSITA WOKE TO A SHARP PAIN IN HER ANKLE. A GROAN escaped her before the blackness reminded her where she was. Something struck her ankle again, waking the nerves—Mamá, jerking in her sleep. Rosita scooted as far from her as the chamber permitted.

"They're coming," Luz said.

Rosita stiffened. She placed a hand over Mamá's mouth, startling her awake. She placed her mouth beside Mamá's ear. »The gringos are here,« she whispered.

Mamá pushed Rosita's hand away. The air in the little chamber soured with fear.

Voices seeped in like dawn—slowly at first, then expanding to fill the silence. *All gray tones*, Rosita thought. *No real color yet, no real words.* She shifted, facing the crack in the rock.

Jackie's words began to take shape. "What . . . think they . . . way?"

"Their footsteps . . . hills," Ian said. "They just disappeared. Must have . . . riverbed. Bloody rocks . . . hidden their footsteps."

The shuffle and crunch of rock on rock grew louder with the men's approach. They stopped next to the boulder. Rosita grasped Mamá's hand. "It's all right," Luz whispered. "They're just stopping to rest."

Rosita clenched her jaw.

Rocks grated. Someone sitting? "We don't have much to go on," Jackie said. "Your one couldn't be sure where the letters were coming from."

"We'll find him," Ian said. More scattering of rocks.

"It's brilliant, really," Jackie said. "Send the money from different places so no one will be able to trace it."

Ian snorted. "Brilliant would be cutting the cunt off forever. No trail, no ties. Didn't your one say he's got the other daughter with him?"

"Aye."

Gravel shifted again. Someone paced near the crack.

"A real bastard, that one," Ian said. "Robs a woman and child of a husband and father, then sets about having his own family. Shatters the very core of a community, then goes away to start another. When I find him, I'll wring his fucking neck."

"A bullet's too good for him," Jackie agreed.

"Good enough for the mother and the girl, though.

Think how grand it will be to tell him about it as he's pissing and begging for mercy, how the small daughter took a bullet to the head. Might even shoot the older one in front of him.''

Rosita curled around her writhing stomach. Mamá's hand tightened around hers, not in fear but in strength. *We're going to die, Mamá,* Rosita wanted to say. *Why are you urging me to hold on?* Bile coated her mouth.

The gravel continued to clink and crunch. ''The whole bleeding family,'' Jackie said. ''Now, didn't he leave you a wee bit more than that? You'd your mother—''

''A bit more!'' Ian's voice thickened with a snarl. ''My mother lost her father, her brother and her husband in that fire. She'd little heart left for anything after that. And didn't I see it myself, my father running from the burning pub, jacket aflame, and the bastard Sean Devlin rising up from behind the wall and shooting him dead? Five years old, I was. Could you take more from a child?''

Jackie hissed and uttered an oath. ''You're sure it was Devlin?''

Mamá's grip nearly severed Rosita's wrist.

''Who else?'' Ian said. ''And he's going to pay for it, with his blood and the blood of those he loves.''

A scream built in Rosita's chest. *How could Papá do such a thing? How could—*

''It wasn't your papá,'' Luz said. ''Your papá never shot anyone—''

''Ian, come and take a look at this,'' Jackie said, his voice suddenly loud.

Gravel scattered. As Ian stood? ''What is it?'' Ian said.

Rosita held her breath—

''What do you think?'' Jackie said.

''About what? This frigging crack? You couldn't fit a dog through that.''

"You could, though. Maybe even a woman. Or a girl."

Scorn colored Ian's voice. "Could you, now? Well, then, wriggle your way in, Lyttle, and drag them out."

Gorge burned Rosita's throat. She stuffed her fist in her mouth.

Jackie laughed, a surprised, ugly sound. "Sure, I'd never fit. But you—"

"I will on your arse. Who knows what kind of creatures are in there? Snakes—"

"Snakes! How'd you come to be afraid of snakes, man? You've never seen one!"

"Haven't I? I've seen them at the bloody zoo." Ian's voice moved away. "I'm not going in there. You want to let some snake tear the flesh from your face, you go on. I'm following the river."

"Ian, we've been after them all night—"

"How far could a woman and girl go?" Ian said. "A little farther, then we'll go back to your one."

Jackie moved away from the crack. "I hate informers, whichever side they're on. I say we shoot the monster first chance we get—"

Their voices trailed away. Rosita's stomach spasmed, splashing her throat with bile. Mamá stroked her wrist. »We'll stay here at least another day,« Mamá whispered.

Rosita swallowed hard. She did not want to spend a day with the contents of her stomach. Touching the *milagro* at her throat, she begged God to help. Luz remained silent.

DIM LIGHT TRACED THE GAP BETWEEN THE BOULDERS. Late morning, early afternoon? Rosita shifted, trying to relieve the pressure on her bladder. »Mamá,« she whispered, »I don't think I can hold it any longer.«

»You'll have to,« Mamá said.

"I told you, it's safe to leave," Luz said. "Go to Señora Mendoza's—"

»Mamá, they're gone,« Rosita said, pressing at her crotch with her fingers. That helped a little. »We'll be safe—if we don't go home. We'll go to Señora Mendoza's.«

Mamá sniffed. »How do you know? Is it the voices? You're crazy, just like your papá.«

Rosita pressed harder. »One voice, Mamá. And it led us safely here.«

»And it led your papá away.« Mamá sighed. »Before the others could find him. All right. We'll trust your voice.«

Luz warmed to a glow, then left Rosita's side. A wandering star flickered in front of Rosita. Luz illuminated the crack.

Rosita crawled to the opening. Her legs, stiff and cramped, responded sluggishly, refusing to straighten. She dragged herself through the crack. Rock scraped her thighs and shins, grating her skin. At last she stumbled, blinking, into the sunlight. She staggered a few steps. Squatting over a bed of rocks, she lowered her panties and peed.

Nothing had ever felt so wonderful. She doubted anything would ever feel this wonderful again.

Mamá pulled herself from the slit between the boulders. Shading her eyes with her hand, she squinted at the sun. »Late morning,« she said. »Thanks be to God and insanity. Now where does insanity want us to go?«

ROSITA PECKED AT THE TYPEWRITER WITH TWO FINgers, glancing over her shoulder at the click of Señora Mendoza's pumps on the kitchen's painted tiles. Her shoulders hunched in anticipation of the heavy laundry room door wheezing open. She propped the typing book against the box of detergent on the pine folding table, then placed her fingers on the keys, as Señora Mendoza had taught her.

The door opened. Señora Mendoza grabbed the back of a chair and set it between Rosita and the washing machine. She watched Rosita type a sentence. "It's coming," she said. "Don't cheat. Use both hands. This is your ticket out of the fields and canneries."

Rosita's cheeks warmed. She typed another sentence.

"The Irishmen are gone," Señora Mendoza said. "They took the bus to Mexico City an hour ago."

Rosita withdrew her hands from the keyboard. She knotted them in her lap. "They were here a long time."

"A month. We can send for your mom. She's probably going out of her mind at my mother-in-law's." Señora Mendoza chuckled. "Good old Irma. She'd do anything for anybody—including kill them with kindness. What do you want to bet your mother's gained ten pounds and has a suitcase full of Irma's old hand-me-downs—every one of them black?"

Rosita tried to smile. She gave up and bit her lip. "Señora Mendoza . . ."

Señora Mendoza sighed. "I'll never be Kathy, will I? Hey, it's all right. What's up?"

"Is . . ." Rosita hesitated. "Is anyone dead?" she asked.

And braced herself. Tío Hector. Tío Hector had to be the informer. Leandro had said, *They asked Papá about you.* He told Mamá that the men had shown Tío Hector photographs of Papá. Perhaps Tío Hector had been taken in by Ian's story about being an old friend of Papá's. Perhaps. But he was still the informer. And Ian intended to kill the informer.

"Did . . . the Irishmen shoot anybody?" Rosita said.

Señora Mendoza reached over and squeezed Rosita's knee. "No."

Rosita glanced at the ceiling, offering thanks to God.

She turned to Señora Mendoza. "They said they were going to kill us," she said.

"I know."

Tears stung Rosita's eyes. "They said that Papá shot someone. As the man was trying to escape from a fire that Papá—Papá set."

Luz crackled to light. "Your papá didn't shoot that man—"

"But he could have," Rosita said, rubbing her eyes. "He threw the bomb."

"Could have . . . ?" Señora Mendoza frowned, confused. "Rosa," she said, placing her elbows on her knees and leaning closer. "Do you understand what's going on in Northern Ireland? Do you know what it is your father was fighting for?"

Rosita licked a tear from the corner of her lip. She shook her head.

"There's a war going on up there, Rosa," Señora Mendoza said. "Whatever your father did, he did because he felt he had to. To protect his own, to gain his freedom. Just like the civil war here, in the early part of this century."

Fettered sobs trembled along Rosita's shoulders. "Not Papá. Papá wouldn't kill anyone."

"In a war, people kill." Señora Mendoza looked down into her cupped hands. "It isn't right, but they do it." She looked up again. "It was war, Rosa. And it may not be an excuse and it may be terrible, but people do terrible things in a war because they think that's the only way the people they love will survive."

Rosita choked on her tears.

"Rosa." Señora Mendoza took Rosita's hands. She massaged them gently. "You love your father and he deserves your love. And, until you've worn his soul, until you understand why he did what he did, don't condemn him. Pity him. Feel for him, that he thought he had no other choice, that he was so desperate, so frightened, that he had no other choice. Feel sad, angry—feel hurt that he had to go to war.''

"Those men," Rosita said, "they're at war, too."

Señora Mendoza leaned even closer. Her eyes burned. "Yes, they are. But you can hate them. They're the enemy."

FIVE

HECTOR SANK ONTO THE BENCH BESIDE ROSA IN THE cool twilight. The colorful statue in front of the Jai Alai Fronton Palacio balanced beneath the first star. Hector handed Rosa a plastic cup of cut pineapple. »You can cross without a coyote,« he said.

"He's right," Luz said. "It would be more risky—"

Rosa picked up a wedge of fruit with her fingers. Juice trickled down her palm, slow and sticky. She bit the pineapple, the strings of sweet pulp lodging between her teeth. Flapping birds, *pajaritas*, cranes, and sea gulls flocked at her feet, an aviary of newsprint. She'd been sitting on the bench all afternoon, listening to the sports bar's music and staring at the jai alai statue. She'd even made an origami jai alai player. »I've crossed without a coyote,« she said, »and been brought back. I can't run—«

"You're pregnant, not disabled," Luz said.

»Not fast enough.« Rosa sucked her fingers. »Do you have a napkin?«

Hector pulled a handkerchief from his pocket. He handed it to her. »There are better places to cross. Your papá chose a bad one. A lot of people follow the highway.«

»And get run over or stranded on the median. No,

thanks.« Rosa wiped her hands. »I'll find a coyote. Soon. Tell Gloria not to worry.«

Hector opened his mouth, then pressed his lips together. He chewed his mustache. »There's the river. I can get you plastic bags for your feet.«

Rosa shook her head. »I'd be too worried that some of the water would contaminate me and hurt my baby. Besides, I can't run—«

»Fast enough. I know.« Hector stood. »Come back to the apartment. Gloria is out with her sister tonight. She'll be home late. Besides, it is my apartment, not hers.«

»Tío, I don't want to come between you—«

»My worry, not yours,« Hector said, offering his hand. He helped her to her feet. »You need rest. The baby needs rest. And tonight, I'll look for the coyote.«

Rosa shuffled through the birds. »Tío . . .«

"Let him," Luz said. "This feels right."

Rosa balked, then nodded. »All right. But be sure he's honest.«

Hector grinned. »As honest as a coyote can be.«

They headed down a side street, turned at the next corner. Rosa popped a piece of pineapple in her mouth. The street looked familiar. Either she had walked down this one earlier today or eighteen years ago. She imagined Papá at her side, holding her hand. Or Mamá scolding her for whimpering about her swollen feet.

»Some people cross in daylight,« Hector said.

"Oh, *that's* good," Luz said.

»Just walk across as if they do it every day,« he said. »Wait until the North American customs people are busy, then sneak through—«

Rosa shook her head. »I tried to sneak through in a crowd. And I'm still in México. I want a coyote—to be sure I make it this time.«

•   •   •

ROSA STRETCHED AND ROLLED OVER ON HECTOR'S sofa. The lumps in the stuffing refused to give. She wriggled, curling around one knot and grinding at another with her hip. The thin blanket worked its way loose. It slipped to the floor.

Rosa groaned and lay still. "Who needs a blanket?" she muttered.

"You do, to protect you from these damned fleas," Luz said.

"There are no fleas," Rosa said.

"Then what bit you behind the ear?"

Rosa ran a finger behind her right ear. She traced a bump, only a little smaller than the knots in the sofa. "All right," she said. "There are fleas. It's a place to sleep."

"The sooner you get out of here, the better," Luz said.

Rosa grunted assent, then closed her eyes.

"Let me guide you," Luz said.

Rosa opened one eye. "Like you did the night Mamá and I hid in the arroyo? I can't hide in any more boulders, Luz."

"Let me guide you, Rosa. I'll get you there."

Rosa sat up, propping herself with her elbow. "I told you—I want someone who's crossed before. A person with experience."

"I hadn't been inside that boulder before." Luz's voice softened. "Rosa, don't you trust me?"

Rosa's gaze wandered the stained walls. "I do. But something like this—" She frowned. "Luz, why don't you try to guide me in everything? Why don't you stop me when I make a wrong choice?"

"What good is free will if you don't use it?" Luz said. "What will you learn if I tell you what to do?"

Rosa nodded. The watermark on the far wall reminded her of a man's profile. Jorge's profile. "Luz, *are* you an angel?"

Luz sighed. "How many times must I tell you? No. I am not an angel."

Rosa tried to peek at her out of the corner of her eye. "A demon?"

Luz scowled. "No, not a demon. Or a fairy. Or a banshee. I could kill your papá for filling your head with such nonsense." Her scowl deepened. "And I'm not the blessed Virgin. I could kill your mamá for *that* one."

Rosa grinned. "I'd never mistake you for the Virgin." She sobered. "Luz, can you really kill people?"

"With what?" Luz said. "No. I keep people alive. If you have to label me, call me a life force. A spirit."

Outside, someone stumbled past the apartment, pausing to shout curses at the night. Rosa listened. Not Gloria. "Luz, why do you only know what people are thinking sometimes? Why not all the time?"

"What do you mean?" Luz said.

Rosa pulled at a tuft of stuffing seeping from the sofa's frayed cushion. "Well, like Hector. For years, we all believed—even you—that he was the one who told Ian Elliott and Jackie Lyttle our name was Connelly. And all the time it was Inez."

"Inez. If I could get my hands on *her* . . ." Luz shifted, a faint blur of light. "A person's mind has to be open. Your papá kept secrets from me—yes, I know. Hard to believe. And as for Hector, he didn't know how they found out and figured he must be to blame. Even now that he knows the truth, he accepts her guilt as his own. If only he had stressed to her how dangerous it was to tell strangers about your papá, if only he hadn't let her know where most of the postmarks came from. If only."

Rosa pulled at the thin blanket. *If only*, she thought, and realized she still blamed Hector. But how was he to know he couldn't trust his wife?

"Does he still hate her?" she said. "After what she did to him—"

"I'm surprised he hasn't killed her," Luz said. "I think he's baffled by her. She cheated on him and bore a stranger's child—what more shameful, hateful thing could she do to him? But to keep it a secret for ten years, to delay her revenge? The woman has the patience of Satan—"

"Do you think it was revenge?" Rosa asked.

"In his younger days, Hector sowed his wild oats. He even had a brief fling with her friend Guillerma. Inez knew how to hurt him. And then she rubbed salt in the wound by confessing that she was the one who told the Irishmen about you and your mamá. For years he lived with the fear and shame that *he* had somehow led them to you. And that somehow *he* may have inadvertently led the Irishmen to your papá. He worried—he still worries—that your papá is dead. But now he knows he's not the traitor. And he has a chance to help his niece and his good friend."

Rosa held her breath, locking it inside with her teeth. "The Irishmen—did they kill papá?"

Luz's voice dimmed like a star at sunrise. "I don't know," she said.

A HAND CUPPED ROSA'S SHOULDER. SHE MURMURED and turned to face Jorge. Without opening her sleep-encrusted eyes, she reached to stroke his face. Her fingers met a wiry mustache and a coarse, stubbled cheek.

Rosa grasped the blanket and sat up. The crown of her head smacked someone's chin. She blinked, trying to loosen the crust welding her eyes shut. A relieved laugh escaped her. »Tío,« she said.

Hector rubbed his chin. »I knew better than to wake you. But I was afraid you'd leave in the morning before I had a chance to talk to you.«

"Before Gloria chased you out," Luz said.

»It's all right, Tío.« Rosa relaxed. »Did you have any luck?«

Hector smiled. »Excellent luck. I'll take you to meet your coyote in the morning. You cross tomorrow night.«

"I can still feel the glow of the coyote on him," Luz said. "He's found a good one."

Rosa took Hector's hand in both of hers. »You trust him?«

"Yes," Luz said.

»With your life and the baby's,« Hector said.

Giddiness bubbled up in Rosa. »Would you trust him with yours?«

Hector's smile widened. »Yes. Even with mine.«

THE COYOTE LEANED BACK IN HIS CHAIR, BALANCING IT on two legs. His thick, strong hands held a cup of coffee tucked between his thighs. *A trusting man*, Rosa thought. One swift kick at a chair leg and the coffee would scald his crotch.

Rosa played with the ring in her pocket. »He looks too young,« she whispered to Hector.

»Looks,« said Hector. »He's twenty-nine. Are you going to stand in the doorway all morning or are you going in?«

»In a minute,« Rosa said. She withdrew her hand from her pocket and fingered the rough stucco that framed the restaurant door. The man looked safe enough, but so had some of the others. So far Luz had been maddeningly quiet. If she could just ask Luz, without attracting attention . . .

The coyote sipped his coffee, gazing over the rim of the cup into some unseen distance. A dreaminess dwelt there, in his dark brown eyes—dwelt in his entire smooth-skinned face. He raised one hand from the cup, tugged at the bill of his Padres cap, then lowered the hand. He rested the cup between his legs again.

"Get closer to him," Luz said. "I can't feel him from here."

Rosa stepped into the restaurant. Hector followed.

The coyote turned toward them the second they moved. A broad grin split his face, the lines at the corners of his mouth and eyes conjuring his age. He eased the chair to the floor, then stood. »Hector,« he called.

Hector shook his hand. The coyote turned. »You must be Rosa,« he said. »I'm Ernesto.«

To her surprise, he shook her hand as well, his palm warm from the coffee. Such a gringo thing to do, shake a woman's hand on first meeting.

"This one feels good—so far," Luz said. "Get him talking."

Rosa nodded. »With pleasure.«

»Please, come sit with me.« Ernesto pulled out his chair and offered it to Rosa. »Would either of you like anything? Coffee? Chocolate?«

Soon mugs of chocolate steamed between Hector and Rosa's hands. Hector prompted Ernesto to explain his price and the crossing. »I know a very safe place,« Ernesto said. »The Migra rarely go there. Beyond New Tijuana, beyond Otay Mesa. The wall ends there and there are places to hide if we need to. The Americans haven't leveled all the hills yet.«

»And the price?« Rosa said.

He ducked his head to the side and tugged at the bill of his cap. »Well . . .«

The price was impossibly low.

Rosa stared at him. »How can you—?«

Hector kicked her under the table. His face betrayed nothing.

"Quiet," Luz said. "Do you want him to raise it?"

Ernesto traced the rim of his coffee cup. »I'm not doing it for the money. That will cover my expenses.«

"He's serious!" Luz said.

»Once a month I help people cross into the U.S.«

Ernesto sipped his coffee. He made a face. »I'm going to get a refill—«

»You're not Mexican,« Rosa said, then bit her lip. »I mean . . .«

An amused smile curled Ernesto's mouth. »Why do you say that?«

»You—well, your Spanish is very good, but your accent . . .« Rosa's cheeks warmed. *Deeper and deeper.* »It's a little . . . different. And . . .« She fluttered her hands.

Hector glanced at her, his eyebrows rising just a fraction. Rosa swallowed a sigh.

"It's all right," Luz said. "He likes your honesty."

Ernesto laughed. »No, I'm not Mexican. I'm Mexican-American. I'm from California, third generation. I had to learn Spanish in school.«

Rosa frowned. »In school?«

»My parents refused to talk Spanish around me and my sisters while we were growing up.« Ernesto shook his head. »They were afraid we wouldn't get ahead if our English wasn't flawless. It's an assimilation thing. Try to make your children part of the dominant culture so they won't have to deal with all the prejudice and so that your culture won't hold them back. It doesn't work that way. The children just lose their heritage.«

»You talk like a college professor,« Rosa said.

Hector grunted and got to his feet.

Rosa turned to him. »Where are you going?«

»You don't need me here,« he said. »Come say good-bye before you go.«

He navigated between the tables and chairs, seeking the open seas of the street.

»Your uncle?« Ernesto asked.

Rosa glanced at the sludge in the bottom of her cup. »My mother's brother.« She set the cup on the table and pushed it away. »If your parents protected you from your

Mexican heritage, why are you here? Why are you doing . . . what you do?«

Ernesto took his cap off and ran a hand through his thick black hair. »Ah. They made a big mistake. They sent me to college. Once I got there, I got involved with MECHA, a Chicano-activist group. I decided I wanted to help my people. So—« He leaned toward her. »I became a paralegal. And I decided to help those who, like my parents' parents, needed to leave Mexico to survive. People like you.«

"This one," Luz said. "Go with this one."

Rosa smiled.

SIX

ROSA LIFTED HER KNAPSACK FROM HECTOR'S CRATERED sofa and swung it over her shoulder. If Ernesto told her she'd have to leave it behind, so be it. She could do without the toothbrush, comb and two dresses. When she got to Watsonville, she could buy new panties. What she couldn't replace were Señora Mendoza's diamond earrings or Mamá's wedding ring. She touched the collar of her dress; the earrings still clung to the interfacing. She dipped her hand into her pocket, slid the ring onto her finger, then released it. The band slipped free.

Hector cleared his throat. »You have your mamá's ring?«

Rosa nodded and withdrew her empty hand. »So, Tío. Will I see you in Watsonville?«

Hector kissed her cheek. »*Niña, niña*. How can I resist when I know there is such beauty waiting for me there?«

Rosa feigned indignation. »Tío! Do you forget who I am?«

Hector smiled. He bowed with exaggerated gallantry. »The daughter of my sister and my reason for crossing. Should I decide to cross.«

"We need to go," Luz said.

"I'm going," Rosa muttered. She walked to the door. »God be with you, Tío. Thank you for your kindnesses.«

Hector waved away her gratitude. »It's nothing,« he said. He folded his arms over his chest, unlocking them at the creak of the opening door. »I'll go with you to meet the coyote,« he said, hurrying after her.

Rosa turned, surprised.

"Rosa," Luz prompted. "We need to go."

»Just to see you there safely,« Hector said, taking hold of the door. »At night, it's not always safe for a woman alone.«

Gloria goes out alone, Rosa almost said, but something in Hector's face stopped her. It wasn't only her safety that deepened the knot between his brows. Longing lingered in his eyes, a quiet sadness as if he couldn't bear to see her go. *We are family,* he'd told her when she first arrived in Tijuana. *You are my sister's child.* And now that bit of home, that tie to another world, stood at the door—stood at the border—about to leave him behind.

As he left me behind, Rosa reminded herself, *with that monster Inez.*

Still . . .

»I'll be safe,« Rosa said. She leaned over and kissed his cheek. »Wait here for Gloria. Tell her the *bruja* is gone.«

Hector winced, looking away. »Ay, *niña*—«

Rosa winked. »It doesn't matter what she believes. It matters what we believe.«

Hector pulled her into an embrace. »Be careful in California.«

Rosa slipped away. »Be careful in Tijuana.«

"*Rosa,*" Luz said.

Rosa stepped out into the dark corridor and pulled the door shut behind her.

Luz nudged her with a smear of light. "Come on. We don't want to be late."

Rosa nodded and walked toward the center of town. Melancholy descended on her like a saint's blessing. She glanced over her shoulder at Hector's scarred and weathered door. His eyes haunted her to the very depths of her heart. She was leaving home, leaving everything behind.

She cupped her stomach, felt the gentle swell of the baby. No, not everything. This little bit of home dwelt in her.

And she was on her way to Papá and Mary, to her past and future home.

SEVEN

HECTOR WAITED, HAND ON THE DOORKNOB. HE glanced at the living room—all traces of Rosa were gone: her little bag, her shoes, even the impress of her head on the threadbare pillow. Everything gone . . . except a little donkey of folded paper, peeking from beneath the sofa.

Hector squatted and retrieved the paper animal. A donkey or a horse? He squinted at the finely shaped head, the arch of the neck. A horse, a running horse. Hector tucked the animal in his pocket.

Enough waiting. He yanked open the door and stepped out into the corridor. The smell of shit and rotted fruit wafted toward him. His nose wrinkled. He had left Nuñez for this—this infested shit heap. He must have been crazy. Perhaps in following Rosa, he was being crazy again.

Rosa stood at the corner, waiting to cross Madero. A car spewing salsa music drifted past her. The driver hooted and leaned out the window. »*Dios mío!* So many curves and me without any brakes!«

Rosa ignored him, hurrying across the street in the wake of his thumping bass. The smallness of her in the darkness—her blue and white flowered dress rippling with each step, the sway of her long, black hair—reminded Hector of his sister at that age. Ay, Conchita . . .

what a beauty. No wonder she turned the gringo's head. And their daughter, their Rosa, with her sweet caramel skin and dark eyes, her cheekbones rising like wings above that rose-petal mouth.

The other one, Mary—she'd looked like Miguel. What did she look like now? She must be thirty, past the first bloom of womanhood. A handsome woman, perhaps, but not Rosa.

Hector turned the corner. Rosa strolled down the street, her step light, even weighted by the unborn child. She nodded and said something—to no one. Hector closed his hand, gently, as if to cradle her in his palm. Since her papá had disappeared into the North, she'd done this, talked to the air beside her.

To her papá, Hector thought.

To God, said those who felt kindly towards her. *To demons*, said those who did not. *Bruja*, they called her. *Witch*.

Up ahead, Rosa turned onto Revolución. Hector hurried to close a little of the distance between them. Only a little. If she saw him, she would stop, give him that amused, reproachful look. The one that said, *I'm not fragile, Tío. You don't need to look after me. I will be fine.*

He agreed. Throughout her short life, hadn't she proved her resourcefulness and her strength? The day the last two Irishmen came to the village—

Shame seared Hector's cheeks. The day Inez betrayed Conchita and Rosa. The day she cuckolded him, sleeping with the blond gringo.

The bitch. Why had that life-sucking spider waited ten years before publicizing his shame? »Yes, the blond one,« she told her friends while sitting in the plaza. »Look at my Juanito. Look how pale he is, like coffee with cream. How could he be Hector's?«

And the women would all turn and stare at Hector as he walked past. One evening he overheard Lucia Partida say, »You know, Inez, the horns suit your Hector.«

If this is what the women said, what were the men saying? He imagined his friend Carlos sitting at the cantina, shaking his shaggy head. »The poor *cabrón*!« he would say. »And to have to raise the spawn of his shame as his own!«

Humiliation consumed Hector, turned his heart to ash. After ten years and with the Irishman long gone, he could not extract revenge. Unless he took it against Inez. Or the child. But little Juanito, with his angel's face and pretty smile—better to make Inez suffer. And he knew a way that would hurt her worse, and longer, than any constraint or beating.

He would leave, vanish. Force her to live the last of her days as a deserted woman, as a failed wife . . .

But why had the scheming bitch waited ten years to tell? And only weeks after Conchita died.

Hector slowed. After Conchita died . . . Inez loved Conchita. She hated Rosa, called her the little *bruja*. She and Hector had argued long and hard about whether Rosa should get her mamá's wedding ring. Inez wanted Conchita buried with it. He wanted Rosita to have it. »It will mean a lot to her, to have something of her mamá,« he'd said. And watching Rosa touch and weigh the ring whenever she grew thoughtful or sad, he knew he'd been right.

Inez had smouldered about that ring for days after Conchita was buried. Her eyes narrowed and her nostrils flared whenever her gaze settled on Rosa. Perhaps getting rid of him was Inez's first step in getting rid of Rosa—

Rosa waded into the tourist section. Crowds eddied and flowed around her, submerging her. A few steps later, she popped back into sight like a cork. It was the dress—modest, almost chaste—against the backdrop of slinky, shimmery gowns. She looked plucked out of time. Again, Hector's hand closed.

She could take care of herself. She'd only give him the look.

Like that time she was eight . . .

He had come across her about a kilometer outside Nuñez. Facing away from him, she perched on a rock overlooking the dry arroyo. She stirred the dirt with a stick. »That's not true,« Rosita said to no one. »I don't talk to you when other people are around and the other children still won't play with me. They don't like me because I know English.«

Hector slowed. His son, Leandro, had come home from school the day before with tales about Rosita. »You can't sneak up on her,« he'd said. »She always knows you're coming. Like she has eyes in the back of her head. And you can't play tricks on her. She knows what you're going to do.«

»Then don't play tricks on her,« Hector had said.

Rosita stirred the dirt, then jabbed hard with her stick. It broke. »They don't want to learn English. They want to play. Just not with *me*.«

Hector started to walk on. Then Rosita flung the stick away and brought her forehead to her knees. »They used to play with me,« she said, her voice laced with tears. »Before Papá and Maria left. Before you came.«

Hector stopped. An ache filled his chest. He slid his hands in his pockets and sifted for coins, old keys, anything. His right hand unearthed a package of Canel's. Concealing the gum in his cupped fingers, he approached Rosita.

Without turning, she straightened and said, »Hello, Tío.«

A shiver crept across Hector's shoulders. He stood beside her and offered her his fisted hand. »Rosita,« he said, »perhaps you can help me. I found dust in my pocket just now. Maybe you can help me turn it into a little gum.«

She lifted her face to his. Despite the muddy streaks

stippling her cheeks, she gave him the look: *I'm all right, Tío. You don't need to worry about me.*

Hector hesitated, then started to withdraw his hand. Rosita's eyes shifted to the side for a second; then she smiled with a child's awkward charm. She giggled. »Do we have to turn it into gum?« she said. »Couldn't we turn it into a little ice cream?«

He turned his hand over and opened it. »Too late. We've already made gum. But maybe, if we reach town before supper, we can stop at Guapo's. . . .«

Hector turned sideways to avoid a gringo and his woman. The woman glared at the gringo, spitting out something in English. The gringo's lower jaw jutted forward, his eyes narrowing. Hector hurried out of striking distance and nearly collided with Rosa.

He ducked into a doorway. She stood in the middle of the sidewalk, gazing up the stairs leading to the Cactus Club. Her mouth twisted to one side with distaste. "This is it," she said to no one. She stepped between two men shouting about margaritas and climbed the stairs to the disco.

Hector sighed and crossed the street to the Villa Colonial souvenir shop. From the bench out front, he would be able to see her leave.

He pulled a packet of Canel's from his pocket. He thanked God the disco did not have a back door.

HE HAD NO GOOD REASON TO FOLLOW ROSA. ONLY THAT he wanted to see her safely out of Tijuana, that he loved her like a cherished daughter, had loved her since that day on the bank of the arroyo. Something in the child— her brightness, or the contradiction of her loneliness and self-sufficiency—appealed to him. Or perhaps, if he was being honest with himself, it was her need for him and his attention that made him feel important, almost godlike. Whatever the initial attraction, it had forged a bond between them—firm, affectionate, and unbreakable.

He had strengthened the bond with ice cream—strawberry, without fail—and sweets, taking her to Guapo's once or twice a week. Sometimes she chattered, sometimes she sat quietly, one little knee touching his. The first few times, she questioned him, »You were a good friend to Papá?« she would ask, eyes begging for confirmation. A warmth would then take root in him, deep as the roots of mountains, and Hector would tell her: »Yes. Your papá and I were great friends. We had many adventures together.«

Rosita would tilt her head, listening to other voices, then nod. »Yes,« she'd say. »You were good friends.«

On her silent days, they simply sat side by side, at Guapo's, outside the cantina, on a bench in the plaza. But whether talking or quiet, her little hands were never still. She folded and refolded any scrap of paper that came within her reach, sometimes folding some magnificent animal or flower, only to unfold and smooth it to study the creases. He began carrying a small notebook of graph paper wherever he went. He and Rosa would sit and he would fish the notebook from his pocket. Tearing out a sheet, he would hand it to her. She then folded the paper into a square, tore off the extra, and began to transform the square into an eagle or a giraffe, an iris or a lily.

Sometimes she made a rose. These she gave to him, every single one. That look returned to her eye, the one that gently reminded him she could take care of herself. »Now you can relax,« she'd say. »Now you can protect this rose.«

EIGHT

THE WALLS OF THE CACTUS CLUB THROBBED. ROSA LAID a hand on the yellow stucco. Salsa music pulsed under her fingers, the song's beat insistent and excited. She pulled herself into the writhing mass of bodies, wedging her way into the disco. Musical instruments and papier mâché masks hung from the walls and stucco arches above her. On the floor, bodies concealed the tables and chairs; it looked as if the owner had decorated with bodies, dozens of them, hundreds, sweating and writhing, clutching beer bottles, clutching each other. Rosa's cheeks warmed. Everything seemed so . . . sexual. So lurid. Women stuffed into short skirts and child-sized blouses, their breasts threatening to overflow. Men sleek and hungry, their jeans hugging their crotches and bottoms. And most of them, all but one or two, were gringos.

Rosa took a deep breath, coughed up clouds of cigarette smoke. Why had Ernesto arranged to meet in the tourist section? She must stick out like a topaz among diamonds.

She squeezed past two gringo couples downing shots of tequila. One of the men grinned at her. "This is the *real* Mexico," he told his friends. "Didn't I tell you I'd find the real Mexico?"

Right, Rosa thought. Disgusted, she wriggled past.

"Over by the window," Luz said. "At a table, talking to a short man with a black and gray mustache."

Rosa raised herself on her toes to see over the crowd. Ernesto sat by the huge, paneless window, Padres cap pulled over his eyes, a big grin on his face. He raised a bottle of Coke to his lips, laughed suddenly, then set the drink down untasted. The other man's cheeks swelled into two tomatillos. The mustache hid any smile.

Rosa lowered herself. The crowd churned around her. She plunged between the swaying bodies, swimming toward Ernesto.

Someone caught her wrist. "Hey, señorita," a tall, hatchet-faced man said. "Come dance with me."

Rosa wrenched her arm away. "I didn't come to dance."

His eyes glittered. "No? Then this must be my lucky night. You came to fuck?"

Rosa gritted her teeth and shoved her way toward Ernesto. What did she expect? A woman alone in a place like this—in a town like this.

"He's following you," Luz said. "Ask him if he's gotten rid of that little present the last woman gave him."

Rosa's jaw dropped. "Luz!"

"It'll get rid of him," Luz said.

Rosa turned to the man and asked. He shriveled, fading back into the crowd. Rosa pressed on till she reached Ernesto.

He saluted her with the bottle of Coke. »Ah! There you are! As soon as the others arrive, we'll go. Would you like a Coke? A Corona?«

The short man appraised her with a glance. He dismissed her.

"Get out of here," Luz said. "Something's wrong. Get out of here."

»I, uh, no, thank you,« Rosa said. »If we have time, perhaps I could use the toilet?«

Ernesto raised his bottle and pointed to the nearest corner. »Over there. I won't leave without you.«

Rosa thanked him and hurried to the bathroom. It was empty. Rosa lowered the knapsack to the black-and-white tile floor, settling it next to one of the stalls. "What now? You liked him this morning—"

"Something's clinging to him," Luz said. "I don't know what it is. Something bad. You can't cross with him."

"Luz—"

"I'll find you a way across. Anything. Just don't go with him."

"Luz, I've already paid him," Rosa said.

"You can get more money. Can you get another life?"

Rosa held onto the sink and bowed her head. Luz bowed with her. "This morning, he was fine, wonderful," Rosa said. "You trusted him. Perhaps he had a bad afternoon. Perhaps he got some bad news from home that has nothing to do with the crossing. Is that possible?"

Luz straightened, disappearing from view. "It's possible. He may have found out that his girlfriend is leaving him or that his car needs a complete overhaul."

Rosa rolled her shoulders and pushed herself upright. "So it may have nothing to do with the crossing. I trust him. I'll take my chances."

"Rosa—"

"Rosa, nothing." Rosa picked up the knapsack and went into a stall. Might as well pee now. Who knew when she'd get another chance. "Free will, remember?"

Heels clattered across the tile floor. "And I told him, you put my hand down there, you better be willing to put a diamond on my third finger," a woman said.

Rosa finished her business and left the bathroom.

"Rosa, listen to me," Luz said. "Something bad is clinging to him. Be careful. Keep your eyes open."

"Luz," Rosa muttered, threading her way through the dancers.

"It might not be him," Luz said. "It might be one of the other *pollos*—"

Rosa rolled her eyes. She wound her way to Ernesto. Two other people had joined him and the short man. Rosa pressed her lips together. Like her, none of them looked as if they belonged in this or any other disco. The short man looked too old and sad to do more than drink beer and ogle women. The woman, in her late twenties, wore faded green slacks and an embroidered blouse, while the other man, a robust thirty, thirty-five, wore crumpled jeans with work-bleached knees. Rosa smoothed the skirt of her flowered dress. Had Ernesto wanted to draw attention to them, he couldn't have done a better job.

Rosa sat next to the woman. They exchanged nervous smiles.

No one said anything. Rosa looked around. One of the masks hanging on the arch above Ernesto caught her attention. The severity of its melon-slice nose and pointed chin crumbled under the sadness of its pink eyes. It seemed to implore her—

"Leave," Luz said. "Don't cross tonight."

Ernesto raised the Coke bottle to his lips. He lowered it untasted, again, this time smiling at the street below. »There he is! Let's go.«

Rosa peeked out the window. A brown van, a pitted Econoline, waited at the curb. A tattered Mexican flag quivered in time with the idling engine. Rosa frowned. The van looked like it might rattle apart any minute.

Ernesto touched her shoulder. »Ready?«

Rosa nodded and pushed herself to her feet.

She and the others followed Ernesto downstairs. *Like ducks*, she thought, and imagined someone wringing their necks as they stepped out onto the sidewalk. She hesitated at the door, then stepped between the two men in dinner jackets shouting and gesturing at the tourists. "Two-for-one margaritas!" they said. "We have nice dance floor! Come see!"

Cool air washed over Rosa, chilling the sweat on her skin. She hadn't realized how hot she was. Or how densely packed the disco was.

She straightened. *Maybe Luz sensed the danger in a stranger standing near Ernesto—*

"Luz—" she whispered.

»Ladies and gentlemen,« Ernesto said, opening the van door, »your limo is waiting.«

Luz flared. "Rosa, don't get in—"

Rosa followed the woman into the dimly lit van. There were no windows; the only interior light came from the broad windshield. The driver glanced at Rosa in the rearview mirror, then stared straight ahead. The woman settled onto the only clean pillow. Rosa sat on a dust-streaked yellow sofa cushion. The man in the faded jeans climbed into the van next.

Luz sighed. "Fine. If you're going to do this, get close to each of the others, one at a time. If you can. I want to feel them."

Rosa murmured low in her throat. She scooted her cushion closer to the woman.

"Great sorrow in this one," Luz said. "She is tired of watching her husband leave every spring. Tired of waiting for him to return, hoping he will make it in time for Christmas. This last year, he didn't come home at all. During the Posada, she locked herself in her house and refused to answer. Each night when the neighbors came, pretending to be Mary and Joseph, she crouched beside the door, waiting for their knocks and their calls to end. Then she crept back to her worn, wooden chair and sat in the dark. The sounds of the Christmas fiesta reached through her walls, but could not touch her heart. Her heart had disintegrated to dust, scattered by the winds of her husband's absence."

Rosa hugged herself. This woman's life, with her husband's long absences, the uncertainty of when she would see him again—if ever—had been Mamá's. And had already become Rosa's, waiting for news from Jorge, wondering what he would say when he learned she was pregnant. . . .

"The money he sends is good, but she doesn't want money," Luz said. "She's lonely. She wants him. So she's going to find him. She has an address in Hanford. She'll go there, even though she's heard rumors that he has another wife in California."

Rosa hugged her knapsack. Pain boiled in this woman, but not threat. Ernesto hopped into the back of the van and shut the side door. Rosa shifted until her knee brushed the leg of the man in the faded jeans. He kept his gaze trained on the driver's back, only a twitch at the corner of his mouth betraying his awareness of Rosa.

Luz sighed. "Well, *this* one isn't tragic, at least. This one had a good job in Fresno until a month ago. Tending grapes. Then he got into a fight with another worker over a truck. As they drove through a gate, he opened the passenger door to kick out a soda can. The door got dented. The driver yelled at him and told him to get out of the truck. He told the man, 'What are you worried about? It's not your truck, it's the *jefe*'s.' The man told him again to get out. So he hit the man. That night, the Migra came to his house. Two weeks later, he was back in Mexico. He's tried to cross the border on his own eight times since he got back and has been caught every time."

Rosa sniffed. Eight times. Perhaps Luz had sensed his bad luck clinging to Ernesto.

"He's not the problem," Luz said. "See if you can get close to the driver."

The older man climbed into the passenger seat and slammed the door.

"Or the lecher," Luz added.

Ernesto leaned close to Rosa. »Are you all right, Rosa? Are you comfortable?«

"The bad feeling is dissipating," Luz said. "Still . . ."

Rosa smiled. »A little nervous.«

He patted her knee, then sat back with his shoulders against the van door. »All set, Luis,« he said. »You know where to go.«

The driver turned. A young man with a round, smooth face and bristly, cropped hair, he grinned at his passengers. A silver tooth gleamed in the dim light. »Welcome to the Border Express,« he said.

THE VAN GROWLED ITS WAY THROUGH THE NIGHT, A windowless cage on wheels. Rosa thanked God and the Virgin that she'd had the foresight to pee at the disco.

No one spoke during the trip—except Luz. "Get close to the driver when we get to wherever we're going," Luz said. "The old man—I would have felt something at the disco. Of course, if the driver has to get the van back tonight, he won't be coming with us. And if the whole thing is a setup, he's probably in on it . . . forget what I said. Stay away from him. Far away. And from the coyote."

Rosa brushed at the cheek nearest Luz as if flicking at a fly.

"It may be nothing," Luz said. "Humor me, okay?"

The van lurched to a sudden stop. The engine snarled like a puma guarding a dead lamb, then fell silent. The sad woman crossed herself.

»Here we are,« Ernesto said.

He yanked open the van's side door, then jumped out. The desperate man scrambled after him. The older man pushed open his door and stepped down. He stood for a minute just outside the van, his fingers hooked in his belt loops, before ambling away. Ernesto held out his hand to the sad woman. She accepted it, stepping cautiously from the van. "Don't let him hold your hand too long," Luz said. "You may need to run."

Bent over in a crouch, Rosa balanced in the open doorway, the knapsack dangling from her shoulder. A broad, flat plain stretched before her, dotted with low, scrubby bushes. A weathered, dying tree wilted a few meters away. She looked for the solid metal fence. Nothing. Standing, she peeked over the roof of the van. The end of the fence split the landscape in the distance.

Ernesto took her hand. »Soon you will be in America,« he said.

"Soon you'll be in *California*," Luz muttered. "What is it with these North Americans? They think they're the only ones on the continent."

Rosa thanked Ernesto. She moved away. A spurt of urine hissed in the still night, followed by the smell of soured piss. Rosa suppressed a sympathetic smile. Someone was afraid.

The man with the graying mustache stepped from behind the side of the van, zipping up his pants. Rosa turned her back on him and gazed across the desert. She imagined the fence creasing the dusty plain like a fold in paper. Imagined she could see the border.

»Rosa,« Ernesto said, touching her shoulder. »Will the pack slow you down if you need to run?«

»If it does, I'll toss it,« she said.

Ernesto smiled. »Good. I'd rather you arrived safe.«

He walked over to the driver.

"He's fine," Luz said, surprised. "Whatever was clinging to him is gone. I don't understand—"

The van roared back to life, circled the small band of people and drove away. »Come here, everyone,« Ernesto said, waving them toward him. »The border is only a few meters from here. We'll cross as soon as the Migra does their nightly sweep—«

»They've done it,« a low voice said.

Rosa turned toward the voice. A tiny orange glow—no larger than a papaya seed—floated from behind the tree. A man followed the light from the shadows, a tall, gaunt man with curly black hair. He walked toward them, his gait unhurried. The squareness of his jaw and forehead made his head look like a section of the fence.

»Ah, you decided to join us,« Ernesto said, stepping forward to meet the man.

Rosa moved aside.

»I'm tired of being sent back,« the newcomer said. After a last drag on his cigarette, he tossed it.

The desperate man grunted. »You're not the only one.«

Ernesto returned to his *pollos*, the newcomer beside him. Rosa readjusted the knapsack and waited for Ernesto to continue his instructions. The newcomer slouched beside Rosa. Expensive cologne tickled her nostrils.

Luz choked. "God save us. It's *him*."

NINE

HECTOR SAT UP, LEANING FORWARD ON THE BENCH. ER-
nesto, the coyote, stepped out onto the street, followed
by Rosa and the other *pollos*. He led them to a brown
Econoline idling at the curb in front of the disco. Exhaust shrouded the van, congealing in Hector's lungs.

The Econoline blocked Hector's view of Rosa and the
others. He raked the ends of his mustache with his teeth.
What were they doing? Were they getting into the van?
If he stood, took a few steps, he could see. But then
Rosa would see him—

The van grumbled and shuddered. It leaped forward,
then sped down Revolución.

Hector pushed himself to his feet. Crossing the road,
he stood at the curb, watching the Econoline disappear.
That was the end of it, then. Rosa was gone, out of his
life. California was no place for an old man like him.
Certainly not Watsonville. He'd heard about the strawberry and lettuce fields there. In the fields, a man was
old, useless, at forty. At fifty-seven, he was well past his
prime. »Goodbye, Rosita,« he whispered, then turned
back toward the center of town.

A glint of metal winked at him from the gutter.

Probably a peso. Hector squatted and felt along the
darkened street. A ring caught at his fingers. Holding it

to the light, he sagged. It was Conchita's ring, the one with the little roses.

He stood, pressing the ring to his palm. Rosa would be heartbroken. It was all she had of her mamá, the one last object she could look at and touch to help her recall Conchita's comfort and strength; the last symbol of her parents' love. »People swear he never loved her,« Rosa had told him once, holding up the ring. »That's not true. This proves it.«

Hector squinted down the street. The van had long since disappeared. If there were only some way he could get the ring to Rosa . . .

A mosquito-pitched whine stuttered from the alley. The whine grew louder until a young man on a motorbike squealed out onto the street. »Hey!« he called. »You miss the bus? You the one Ernesto was waiting for?«

Hector smoothed his mustache. »I—«

The young man scolded him with a shake of the head. »You're very late. Ernesto doesn't wait for anyone. Come. I know where to go. I'll take you there.«

Hector eyed the motorbike. So small. The seat barely held one.

»Come on,« the young man said. »If you want to catch up to them.«

THE MOTORBIKE WOBBLED OUT OF A SWEEPING TURN. »Please, God, have mercy,« Hector prayed. He didn't dare let go of the young man's waist to cross himself.

»Don't try to help me,« the young man said over his shoulder. »If you lean into the curves, we'll dump the bike. Just sit back and relax.«

»Relax?« Hector said. »The way this thing shimmies and whines?«

»Great, isn't it?« the young man said, a proud grin in his voice.

Hector forced himself to think about something else.

They would catch up to the others and he would give Rosa the ring—Why not go with her? The coyote was missing a *pollo*. Perhaps he would let Hector take the *pollo's* place. He should have left a note for Gloria. *Cariño, I am following the bruja. Forgot to ask her to cast a spell on you. With love, Hector.*

Hector smiled. A note like that, she'd never let him into the apartment again. Was that so bad? Perhaps it was time to leave Gloria. Perhaps he should go to Watsonville. There was nothing here for him anymore. There must be something an old man could do—

Headlights sped toward them, winked off and on. The young man stopped the bike.

Hector frowned. »I thought you said we needed to hurry.«

»We do,« the young man said. »But that's the van. The driver can tell us if they've made the crossing yet.«

The van stopped beside them. »Hey, Alfredo,« the driver said. »What are you doing out here?«

Alfredo nodded toward Hector. »A late one. Doesn't Ernesto count his chicks?«

The driver laughed. A tooth flashed silver. »You better hurry. Ernesto was giving them the talk when I left.«

»Don't run unless you have to, listen for snakes, follow me,« Alfredo said.

The driver shrugged. »Close enough. I've got to get this thing back. Hey, old man, good luck in California. Stay away from the Migra.«

The driver gunned the engine and sped away.

Alfredo aimed the motorbike into the darkness. »Don't worry, old man,« he said. »If they've already left, I'll tell you how to find the safe house. You can do it yourself. You can cross without Ernesto.«

Cross the border . . . did he want to? It seemed he was destined to, as if God and the spirits were beckoning him to join Rosa in California. Ah, well, *ni modo.* It couldn't be helped.

TEN

ERNESTO GESTURED TOWARD THE NORTH. THE DESERT extended beyond the sweep of his hand. »No lagging or stopping once we cross,« he said, turning to the half circle of faces. »Not until we reach the hills. The hills offer a little protection, so we'll be safest if we move quickly. Does everyone understand?«

»Of course,« the newcomer said. He paced the outside of the half circle, stopping beside Rosa.

Luz hissed. "Get away from him. Fake a coughing fit, anything. But get away from him."

Ernesto considered each of their faces before continuing. »We need to watch for snakes—«

Rosa crouched to check her shoe. When she stood, she took a step to the left, placing the desperate man between herself and the newcomer. She jostled the lonely woman. The woman glared at her, then leaned forward to hear Ernesto's instructions.

Ernesto's voice skimmed Rosa's attention. »We shouldn't have to worry about the patrols. Not if we move quickly—«

Rosa crossed herself, then let her voice escape in a prayer. "Why is he so dangerous?"

"I don't know," Luz said. "There's just something about him. Remember the coyote who raped the woman and left her where the Migra would find her?"

Rosa nodded.

"This one feels worse."

Rosa crossed herself again. "What is he planning to do?" she mumbled into her folded hands.

"I'm not sure," Luz said. "He seems to be assessing everyone—"

»Does everyone understand?« Ernesto said again.

The others nodded and murmured yes. Rosa did the same.

»All right,« Ernesto said. »Let's go.«

Rosa hung back, letting the others get ahead of her. The newcomer followed close at Ernesto's heels. If she could pull Ernesto aside, warn him about the newcomer . . .

"Stay here," Luz said.

Rosa pressed her lips together. Here, kilometers from old Tijuana. Except for the road and the end of the wall, there was nothing. New Tijuana glittered a few kilometers away, but all she knew about the town was that there was a border crossing and a *maquila*—a factory— there. It might be as rough—rougher—than old Tijuana. And at night, alone, the odds of being beaten and raped . . .

She could wait till morning and walk to the *maquila*. Then she could take a bus to old Tijuana and return to Hector's apartment. And Gloria.

And wait for another coyote . . .

"I'm going with the others," she said. "If he wants money, he can have it. Papá and Mary will have money."

"Rosa—" Luz flared, then dimmed. "I hope that's all he wants."

ROSA PLODDED ALONG AT THE REAR, GAZE FLICKERING across the barren mounds rolling across the plains. Her gaze lingered for a minute on the desperate man's back. His shoulders had lifted and his tread had lightened since they crossed the border. Ahead of him, the lonely woman's head swung from side to side as if the scrubby bushes and the rocky soil were somehow special— holy—because they belonged to California. The older man held his head a little higher. Ernesto and the new-comer trudged on.

Rosa took a deep breath. Nothing. The air tasted no sweeter. She scuffed at the dirt with the toe of her shoe. The ground felt no richer. It promised no more than the dust of Tijuana.

She shook her head and smiled. Only the people had changed. Why had she expected more? Only people be-lieved in borders.

Ernesto stopped at the base of a low cliff, ushering the group into a dark gully. »There's a road up there,« he said. »We don't want to be seen.«

"Tension is building in the creep," Luz said. "Get close to him, just for a few seconds."

"You told me to stay away from him," Rosa said.

"We need to know what he's planning. Be nonchalant about it."

Rosa sniffed. *Be nonchalant.* The creep ambled just behind Ernesto, several meters ahead of her. Rosa hur-ried to catch up, then paused. Best to have some sort of escape route planned in case the creep tried something. She turned in a slow circle.

The land lay creased and worn like an unfolded ori-gami. She tried to understand the pattern of the land and what it could be made into, how it could be used. If it were refolded, would it be a dog, friendly and eager to please? Or would it be a scorpion, ready to sting this small band of pilgrims, anxious to poison them?

She peered into the night. Ahead rose more of the barren swells. Behind, across the desert, the lights of New Tijuana and the Otay Mesa border crossing glit-tered. Above, to the left, the cliff. To the right a dirt road running parallel to the border. Rosa's eyes widened.

Beside the dirt road stood two portable toilets. Toilets, here, in this barren landscape?

Ernesto touched her arm. »We'll rest here a few minutes,« he said. »Are you tired?«

Rosa shook her head.

He guided her toward the gully. »We need to hide. Sometimes the Migra come to use the toilets, so they don't have to go back to their headquarters. There are some rocks here to shelter us—«

»Ernesto,« Rosa said. She stopped, resisting the push of his fingers. »Ernesto, the man who joined us before we crossed. I have a bad feeling about him.«

Ernesto studied her. »A bad feeling?«

Rosa folded her arms across her chest. The knapsack slid from her shoulder.

"Set it down," Luz said. "Leave it. We can come back for it after the thief leaves."

Rosa set the knapsack down. »I don't know how to explain. It's just a feeling—«

"A strong one," Luz said.

»—but I wanted to warn you. So you can watch him.«

Ernesto clasped the back of his neck. »And this feeling. You've had it before.«

»It helped Mamá and me escape once,« Rosa said. »From some men who wanted to harm us.«

Ernesto released his neck and straightened. »Thank you, Rosa,« he said.

»It's nothing,« Rosa said.

"He's not sure whether to believe you," Luz said. "But he'll be alert. You can still turn back. Just walk away. Tell him you need to pee. The baby is pushing down on your bladder. I can lead you from here."

Rosa shuffled to the lip of the gully. No more than an indent in the cliff face, it provided a little shelter. *But shelter from what?* she wondered. Moonlight, the Migra, sun . . . robbers? She glanced at the creep. He crouched in the darkest shadows, smoking a cigarette. The older man huddled beside him, forehead touching his knees. The desperate man and the lonely woman sat with their backs nestled against the slope. Ernesto joined them. The creep stood, his back to Rosa. He tossed his cigarette away.

"I don't like this," Luz said. "I don't like this at all. Forget what I said about getting close to him. Just get out of here. *Now.*"

Rosa glanced over her shoulder at the dirt road and the portable toilets, then backed toward them slowly. If she could slip inside one—

»No one causes problems,« the creep said, drawing a gun from his waistband. He aimed it at Ernesto. »And no one gets hurt.«

Ernesto rose slowly to his knees. The desperate man did the same. The older man just sat there, his eyes heavy-lidded and calm. His fingers kneaded his thighs. Had they been plows, deep furrows would have rent his pants.

The lonely woman fingered her rosary. Prayer bubbled from her lips.

The creep aimed the gun at her. »No problems,« he said. »That includes problems with God.«

"Fear of God," Luz whispered. "He may be afraid to kill."

Rosa melted back, a millimeter at a time.

Ernesto tilted his chin. »What do you want?«

»Money,« the creep said. »And whatever else is valuable.« He gestured with the gun. »The nun's rosary. The grandfather's belt buckle. Rings, drugs . . . whatever you've got.«

Rosa glanced over her shoulder again. A few more meters to the toilets . . .

"Keep moving slowly," Luz said. "He's fixated on the woman's rosary. He seems to think the beads are some kind of gem."

Right, Rosa thought. *So why is she crossing with a coyote?*

Then she remembered the diamonds—Señora Mendoza's diamonds—attached to the collar of her dress. She resisted the urge to touch them.

She eased back another step.

»We'll start with you,« the creep said to the older man. »Empty your pockets, one at a time, then remove your belt. Quickly.«

The older man emptied one pocket. Setting a wad of pesos in front of the thief, he reached into the other. From this he withdrew a pocket knife, some coins, and a packet of Canel's. He unbuckled the belt.

Ernesto's hands settled on his own waistband.

Rosa held her breath. A few more steps, just a few more—

Something exploded, ripping the darkness with light and sound. The creep jerked and fired. Ernesto fell.

Rosa flung open the door to the portable toilet and darted inside. She shut the door, a millimeter a time. The creep's gun exploded again. She closed the door.

From the gully, the lonely woman shrieked, her voice too thin to sustain a scream. She erupted in prayer—loud, desperate prayer gilded with sobs and Latin.

»No problems!« the creep shouted. »I told you, *no problems!* Quit trying to come between me and God!«

Another gunshot split the night. The prayers dissolved into silence.

Rosa locked her jaw. Her eyes watered with fear and the sting of chemicals.

The creep's gun exploded three more times.

ELEVEN

HECTOR GLANCED OVER HIS SHOULDER AND TO HIS LEFT, looking for the fence. Darker than the night, it stretched ribbonlike, a kilometer or two away. It reflected nothing, not even the lights of Otay Mesa. He turned a little to look back the way he'd come. The end of the wall was no longer visible. He sighed and shuffled on.

There was no sign of Rosa and the others. Not a footstep, not even a blur of movement. A coyote and four *pollos*, moving across this barren landscape, with only a tiny bush here and there—wouldn't he have seen something? They must be further ahead than Alfredo thought. . . .

Straddling the border at the end of the fence, Alfredo had pointed. »Head that way. If you feel disoriented or confused, look back at the fence. Use it as a guide. You should catch up with them soon.«

Hector peered across the rolling plains. »I can't see them. They must be far ahead.«

»Not so far,« Alfredo said. He scuffed at a cigarette butt on the Mexican side of the border. »It didn't take us long to get here. If one of the *pollos* had enough time to smoke this, Ernesto must have started late.«

He clapped Hector's shoulder. »You'll find them. And if you don't, just keep walking. You'll either reach the safe house or a town.« He grinned. »Eventually . . .«

»Eventually,« Hector muttered. The desert tilted, deceptive in its gradual rise. His calves ached. He stumbled on a loose rock, swinging his arms forward, but caught himself before he fell. He slowed. Ahead and to the left, the desert rose to a sort of mesa. Hard to tell from here, but it looked as if a road perched on the rim of the mesa. Rosa and the others might be hiding there, at the base of the cliff. He picked up his pace.

Questions whined through his head like mosquitoes. Why had the spirits led him here? To be sure Rosa was all right? She had crossed and disappeared into California. That's what she'd wanted to do and she had done it. Surely God watched over her now.

So what was he doing? Why did he feel compelled to follow?

Hector kicked at pebbles. They clattered like dice. It was more than returning the ring, he decided. There was nothing left for him in México. The last two people he considered family, Rosa and his son, Leandro, were in California. It was time to leave Tijuana—and Gloria. To put even more distance between himself and Inez. A smile crept across his face. Perhaps once he gave Rosa the ring, he would go find Leandro. A letter from his son had arrived from someplace outside Sacramento. Auburn. »A town named for a woman's hair,« Leandro had written. »A friend of mine took me to a store and showed me a bottle of hair color. Can you imagine, Papá? Such a strange thing to name a town. You should see this place.«

»I would like to see that place,« Hector told the night. He peered into the dark again. A dirt road led from the little mesa, scarring the plain. Two portable toilets waited beside the road. Hector shook his head. Toilets, in the middle of nowhere! Leandro said the North Americans were crazy, but this—

Gunshots burst the quiet. Muffled by distance, they popped like firecrackers. Hector's gut twisted. Another round of firecracker gunbursts erupted.

He ran toward the fading sound.

ROSA CROUCHED AT THE CENTER OF THE PORTABLE TOI-let. The bubble gum sweetness of the cleansers and disinfectant twisted her gut. *This can't be good for the baby*, she thought, then had to stifle a giggle. A man waited outside with a gun, a murderer, and she was worried about disinfectant?

Footsteps ticked toward the portable toilets with the precision of automatic weapon fire. Rosa swayed to her feet.

She could slam the door in his face, stun him. She loosed the latch, then reached for the handle—

"Not yet," Luz said. "Rosa, you need to listen to me. Listen carefully."

Rosa trembled, hand still outstretched. Her mind divided itself between the approaching footsteps and Luz. She wet her lips, but dared not utter a word.

"Listen to *me*," Luz said. She moved so that she was no longer on the edge of Rosa's sight, but right in front of her. Her features, clothed in light, were indecipherable. Rosa shielded her eyes and turned away.

"Look at me," Luz said.

Rosa winced and turned back. She focused on Luz's eyes, two green spheres that glowed like sunlight on tender new shoots.

"I can save one of you," Luz said. "You or your baby. I cannot save both. I don't have the power. You must decide."

Rosa shrank from the spirit, an aching cold searing her to the core. "Luz . . ."

"Hush," Luz said. "Don't say a word. Show me. Trust your hands. But do it quickly."

Rosa tried to swallow, but her throat had cinched shut. Trust her hands?

She blinked and turned her head away. Her gaze settled on the toilet paper dispenser. *Trust your hands.* She snatched sheets of paper and began to fold.

"You or your baby," Luz said. "The decision is yours."

Rosa's fingers pulled and tucked the paper, bending it, flattening it. Her or the baby . . . a sob caught in her throat. What was the mother without the child? What was the child without the mother?

Trust your hands. . . .

The door slammed open. The murderer thrust the gun barrel in Rosa's face. »You bitch. Did you think you could hide from me?«

"You must decide," Luz said. "Now."

SOMEONE, A MAN, DARTED FROM THE SHADOW OF THE mesa, sprinting toward the portable toilets. Hector cleared his lungs and spat, then sucked at the air. To be running like this at his age—

He scuffled to a stop. The man had a gun.

The man stopped in front of the toilets. He lowered his head, listening, then crept to the first toilet. He stood, still as moonlight, gun aimed at the door.

Hector yearned forward, fear rooting his feet to the dusty earth. Was this monster after Rosa . . . or had he already killed her?

The man shifted his weight, stepping away from the portable toilet. He slunk toward the second, gun ready, hand outstretched to grasp the door handle. He moved with alarming silence and slowness, deliberate and unhurried. His fingers closed on the handle. He stood still for a full minute, then flung the door open.

His words carried across the plain. »You bitch. Did you think you could hide from me?«

Cursing under his breath, Hector ran toward him.

The man cocked the trigger. Fired.

Hector's stomach knotted around an imagined bullet. He doubled over, then forced himself upright and staggered on. He slowed, struck by the sudden silence. Hunching nearly to all fours, he stole closer, each footstep quieter than the last. Within ten meters of the portable toilets, he crouched behind a small, prickly shrub.

Not Rosa, he prayed. *Blessed Virgin, please. Not Rosa—*

The killer reached into the portable toilet and dragged a body from the narrow stall. Rosa crumpled to the dirt.

Setting the pistol by his foot, the killer knelt beside Rosa. Rolling her on her back, he lifted her dress and peeled back her underwear. He slid his fingers into her. With a snarl, he jerked them away. »Where is your money, bitch?« he said. He backhanded her across the face.

Her head flopped to the side, her sightless eyes staring at Hector.

Where were you, Tío? the eyes seemed to say. *I needed you.*

Hector pressed his fist into his stomach, trying to soothe the bile rising from his gut. Rosa's throat gaped, torn open by the bullet. A miracle her head was still attached.

The killer tore open her dress, exposing the mound of her belly and her bra. He grasped the bra, then stopped. A smile touched his lips. He released the bra and reached for the glint of silver nested between her breasts.

Hector gritted his teeth. The *milagro*. The silver girl. The killer's fingers closed around the charm.

Rosa's hand shot out and grabbed his wrist.

The killer screamed, jerking his arm, trying to break free. Hector slithered closer. Rosa turned to face her murderer, then lifted her head and shoulders. Blood poured from her ruined throat.

The killer shrieked again and lurched backward, his

fingers splayed and quivering. Rosa snapped her wrist, wrenching his. He howled with pain. Then Rosa picked up the pistol. She placed the barrel to the man's forehead and cocked the trigger. The stench of piss and fear choked the night.

The killer's lips moved, but only tight squeaks escaped him. Rosa's eyes narrowed. She pulled the trigger.

The bullet scattered the man's brain like dandelion seeds.

Hector crossed himself, shivering despite the sweat filming his skin.

Rosa flung the man's hand away, then set the pistol down. She tore the remnants of her dress away, keeping its collar knotted in her hand. Without hesitation, she removed the man's clothes and slipped them on. She stood. The pants hung unbuttoned from her hips. Letting the shirttails drape the sagging waistband, she slipped something into the shirt's breast pocket. Then she turned toward Hector. Her gaze met his.

Her eyes were cold and hard. A warning. *Don't come near me, old man.*

She buttoned the shirt over the *milagro*. Then she walked away, deeper into California, deeper into the night, until she vanished.

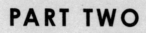

PART TWO

PART TWO

TWELVE

FOG FROSTED THE SUMMER MORNING. BOTH OPAQUE and clear, it softened the details of the neighboring houses, obscuring wooden siding and textured stucco with tufts of mist. Teddy inhaled, filling her lungs with the moist, chilled air. No one else stirred. It was too early for most people to go to work, too early for the children to play. Even her neighbor Rita, the earliest of the early risers, hadn't emerged yet to finish painting her house.

Teddy walked down the asphalt driveway past her car. Her fingers streaked the fine grit that had settled on the blue paint. That was one drawback to life in a semirural town like Watsonville—dust. From the strawberry fields, the lettuce fields, the zucchini fields. After sitting in the driveway for two weeks, the Civic resembled a donut sprinkled with powdered sugar.

Teddy stopped and rested her splinted arms on the trunk of the car. Extending from her knuckles to just below her elbows, the splints encased her arms in metal, foam, and Velcro. She winced. Her thumbs ached, from either the splints or the tube bandages beneath. She fumbled with one of the Velcro straps on the right bandage, then hesitated.

"Keep 'em on," the doctor had said. "We wanna get that inflammation under control. Tendinitis is a bear."

Teddy released the strap.

Tendinitis, the doctor had said. *Carpal tunnel. Probably both. Tendinitis could take months to cure. Carpal tunnel—well, with surgery . . .*

Surgery. Teddy bit her lower lip. She'd seen what that surgery could do. Her friend Jon, the art professor, had gone through it, wrists and elbows. The surgeon had been able to camouflage the scars along his wrists so that they blended in with the creases on his palms. But not the ones on his elbows. Those scars embossed his elbows, puckered like pale, badly stitched seams. He'd been allergic to the bandages. "Wonderful, huh?" he'd said, rotating his arms. "Gives the students the willies. Wouldn't be so bad if the operation had been a success. I can paint for maybe an hour before the fire starts jolting along my wrists and fingers. And sketching! Forget *that.*"

A shudder folded Teddy's chest. *No more hand-building, no more throwing pots, no more loading the kiln—*

She thrust her shoulders back and walked to the end of the asphalt driveway.

No banjo, no typing, no—

"Stop it," she said. She walked out into the street, following the faint crease in the middle of the road.

There were signs of life scattered about the neighborhood, but no life. The front of Rita's house faded from peach to green, from pale sandstone buff to celadon. Tarps and cans of paint waited on the cement porch. Two doors down, a tricycle stood beside the wooden posts of the mailboxes. Teddy imagined one of the neighbor children standing on the rusted seat, reaching into the cavernous metal boxes. A cat peeped from the hedge across the way, blinked at her, then disappeared. Teddy walked past the cat's hiding place toward the strawberry field at the end of the street.

The wind sieved the fog until only a cool damp clung

to the morning. Ripe strawberries scented the air. Teddy stopped at the shallow bluff overlooking the fields. Only seven o'clock and already row after row of small figures stooped over the emerald plants, the women in caps and white kerchiefs, desert style, the men in caps and cowboy hats. A dirt "road" bisected the field. Dust mixed with fog as a small blue tractor jolted and groaned along the brown swath. Two Portapotties swayed on the tractor's trailer, reeling like dropped dimes when the truck stopped near the workers.

A woman stood at the end of one green row, arms dangling at her side. She raised her right arm, then cradled it in her left hand. Her fingers probed her wrist only to settle at the heel of her palm. She massaged her wrist with her thumb, flinching from the shoulder when she hit a tender nerve. After a minute, she released her wrist. Wading between the rows of strawberries, she crouched beside a woman in a bright orange sweater. She reached to pick the scarlet fruit.

Teddy touched her own right wrist, then her left. Did the woman have carpal tunnel? Picking strawberries certainly looked repetitive enough. The pain must be intense. Why was the woman still—?

Because she has no choice. Teddy had savings and a good day job with benefits. This woman had pain and strawberries, maybe children. She probably had no other skills, no other way to feed herself and her family. She might not even be here legally, which meant—which meant—

"You should be glad all you've lost is a few weeks," Teddy said.

And your ability to do anything that matters to you.

Mist cooled Teddy's cheeks. She trudged back to her house to wait for the sun to wither the fog—the new highlight of her days.

•   •   •

THE RADIO PLAYED SOFTLY. TEDDY LEANED AGAINST the worktable beneath her studio window. Tatters of fog still pressed against the glass. "June in Watsonville," she said. "And July and August. One of the hazards of living on the coast."

The words spread to fill the room, gradual as haze.

"It's twelve-ten and this is *Out to Lunch*," the radio deejay said. "That's KPIG, one-oh-seven-oink-five. If you've got any suggestions, give us a call on the Swine Line—"

"No bluegrass," Teddy told the unseen deejay. "Nothing with a banjo. Please."

She squinted into the gray afternoon. Twelve-ten. It must be really hot over the hill in Gilroy to draw this much fog from the Monterey Bay. Teddy rested her chin in her hands. Lightning scorched the nerves from her shoulder to her fingertips. She lowered her arms, resting them on the worktable. Curls and pebbles of dried clay embedded themselves in the foam brace. Teddy ground a pebble to dust with her finger. Instantly she regretted it. Flinching, she waited for the pain to dim.

Massaging her wrist, she glanced at the tools scattered across the worktable: needle tool; three trimming tools; dried, mud-caked sponge; rolling pin; wire; meat tenderizer; knife. The wooden handles, coated with dried clay, still bore the imprint of her fingers and palm. Teddy prodded the sponge, releasing a puff of moldy dust. She sneezed and straightened without using her arms.

Emmy Lou Harris warbled on the radio. No banjo— thank God.

Teddy backed up until she felt the seat of the electric wheel. She sat, the wheel at her elbow, her arms dangling between her thighs. She'd managed to clean the wheel and the bats, though not very well. Thin swirls of dried clay lined the wheel head. A few lumps of porcelain stuck to the back of the trough surrounding the wheel. Her slip and water buckets sat on the small bench beside her. The water bucket was empty. The slip bucket still brimmed with watery clay sludge. Although a little thicker than she liked, the slip was still moist—and pliable. Teddy removed her splints and bandages.

She eased her hands into the bucket of slip. The mud oozed over her arms, coating her skin like cool, creamy silk. She closed her eyes, biting her lip to catch a moan. Just the feel of the clay sparked her imagination. An image swam into focus: a large vase, with leaves and honeysuckle curling away from the surface of the pot, rabbits and birds peeking from the foliage, carved from the leather-hard clay and enhanced with hand building. A mockingbird perched on the lip of the vase, shiny and iridescent.

But the vase itself hadn't been made and there was no way she could throw anything now. She might be able to hand-build a small piece, a pinch pot or a tile. She squeezed the liquid clay through her fingers, pretending to mold it into a ball, pretended to plunge her thumb into its center.

Her eyes winced open. Just the thought of pressing her thumb into a ball of clay hurt. Maybe she could mold something out of the slip—yeah, right. She could fingerpaint with it . . . maybe. She thought of Jon, unable to lift a paintbrush for any decent length of time—even after the operation. She scanned the shelves around her. There must be something she could do.

Bisque-fired pots, masks, and sculptures lined one wall, waiting for glaze. Teddy scraped the slip from her throbbing right arm. Some of the glazing required lifting—out of the question—but the finer work, with the oxides and the underglazes, she could do that. For a short time. But once she'd glazed them, then what? She couldn't load or fire the kiln herself, and since only she knew the kiln and how the slightest variation of temperature affected her glazes, it would be hard to trust anyone else to get it right. She scraped the clay from her left arm and went to the stainless steel sink.

Counting Crows wished Elizabeth good night over the radio. Definitely not a banjo song.

Teddy looked up. On the wall to her right, wrapped in plastic vegetable bags and shaded from the reach of the sun, waited ceramics in progress—cups without handles or ornaments, untrimmed pots, a clay banjo with a woman embracing its neck. All of them intended for her gallery show in August, none of them finished. If she could just work on them—but she couldn't trim or pull handles. These would have to wait. But for how long?

Maybe forever.

And the gallery show? She couldn't just call and say, "Hey, my arms are bothering me. How about six months from now?" Not to the Wren Gallery in San Francisco. Artists were booked more than a year in advance. She'd fallen into a slot because someone had canceled (died) four months ago, prompting the manager to offer it to her. An old friend from college, Suki loved Teddy's work. "This is a big break, Teddy," she'd said. "Your work will be seen by collectors from all over the world. People *beyond* Watsonville—*beyond* California . . ."

Teddy stared at her clay-encrusted arms. She had a few finished pieces. She could raid the display case at work—but those were all early pieces, not nearly as interesting or, well, *good* as her recent work. She glanced at the shelves of unfinished ceramics. If she could only finish them, there was nearly a show's worth—

Give it up, Teddy. With these hands?

She turned on the water and rinsed her arms. The slip melted away. Sadness filled Teddy. Was this all she'd ever be able to do in clay? Dip her arms in slip and wash them? She might as well tell her next-door neighbor not to bother anymore. Rita came over once a day to mist the unfired pieces so they wouldn't dry too much for Teddy to work on them. "My contribution to the arts," Rita liked to say.

Teddy turned off the water. "Well, Rita," she told the empty studio, "you'll have to find some other way to contribute. I can't keep wasting your time."

"Okay, piggies," the deejay said. "It took me ten minutes, but I finally found that Hot Rize album—"

Bluegrass. Teddy turned off the radio. She needed no other reminders of things she couldn't do.

SUNLIGHT SPILLED THROUGH THE LIVING-ROOM WINdow, flooding the window seat, splashing across the cherry-wood rocker, glinting off the glazes of the mugs on the racks above the TV. Teddy's banjo rested in its open case, the impression of the strings still visible in the case's silver velvet lining. Shoved against the base of the window seat, the instrument looked as if Teddy had just set it down. A music stand waited to one side of the window, a fiddle fake book clothespinned open to "Over the Waterfall." A page had drifted to the floor, unmoored from the book's spine. Teddy bent to pick it up, let her fingers dangle for a minute, then straightened without touching the paper. This way, she thought, it looked as if she was only taking a break. This way, she could pretend.

Funny that seeing the banjo comforted her, but hearing someone play tormented her with frustration and longing . . .

She sat in the rocker, scooting it to face the TV. She propped her right leg on the coffee table, nudging aside the acrylic cookbook holder. Letting her head fall back against the rocker's headrest, she stared at the mugs.

Fifteen mugs, each made a year apart. She had thrown the first, a lopsided blue blob with a pulled handle, at the end of her first ceramics class when she was fifteen. This year's mug hung on the second rack, a slender cylinder carved with cherry blossoms and foxes and painted in both vivid and soft colors. A few of the petals curled away from the body of the mug. She had planned to make a second one for the show in August—

She turned away. Her heartbeat pounded through her body, keeping time with the throbbing of her arms. She couldn't do any of the things she enjoyed, not art, music, swimming . . . she could read, but after a while the books, even the paperbacks, got too heavy to hold. The acrylic cookbook holder helped, but then it took forever to turn the page. She couldn't cook. Even if she'd been able to grip the handles of the pots and pans, their weight seared along her nerves. Canned foods were out. No way she could work the can opener. That left microwave dinners and take-out. Tasty as they were, she was getting tired of the burritos from the Harvest Moon Market down the street.

"You're falling into it," she said. "The self-pity trap. Come on, Teddy. Escape. Now. *Do* something."

But what? Daytime television—that included videos— depressed her. Another walk? She'd already tromped the bike path along Green Valley Road and hiked the trails around Pinto Lake. She'd even stopped at the oak tree and searched the branches for the Virgin. "Just a discoloration of the bark," Jon had said when she showed it to him. It didn't matter. In the right mood, with the right need, Teddy could see the Virgin, her head tilted to one side, haloed in people's belief. A profusion of flowers, real and plastic, adorned the wire fence protecting the tree. And on the benches facing the oak, people sat and prayed or simply sat. Sometimes they whispered to each other, usually in Spanish. No one whispered to Teddy, honey-haired, Anglo Teddy, but it didn't matter. Just being around people . . .

That's what she needed—people. But her friends and neighbors worked during the day. Well, except Rita. But watching her neighbor paint her house depressed Teddy even more. With each slap of the brush, Teddy's fingers tingled, anxious to wield the brush—to do something useful and satisfying and active.

She swung her leg down from the coffee table. She missed her day job. She missed greeting people as they entered the psychotherapy office, missed juggling the schedule when someone needed to change an appointment, missed offering tissues to those who left Paul's office in tears after a difficult session. She wouldn't mind typing Paul's psych evaluations and notes on his clients. She wouldn't mind *filing*.

Teddy smiled. "You are desperate, aren't you?" she said.

Where else could she go to be around people? Shops and malls, cafés . . . too expensive, too depressing. She hated shopping. Ride the bus . . . to where? Shops and cafés. And the library. But what a tease that was—all those books and no hands to hold them.

Thank God it was Friday. Maybe Kym or Lydia would like to take a walk on the beach tomorrow. Saturday night, she and Jon had tickets to see the Nuclear Whales at the Mello Center—all saxophones, not a banjo within hearing. Kym had suggested they go to a movie on Sunday. And then it was Monday and the beginning of another long, empty week, staring at her unfinished ceramics, watching Rita paint her house, pacing her living room. . . .

Teddy rocked herself to her feet. She crossed to the end table next to the TV and took the phone from its recharger, then hit speed dial three, wincing at the jab of pain. Waiting a few beats for the first ring, she pushed the button for speaker.

THIRTEEN

PAUL STEPPED OUT OF HIS OFFICE INTO THE WAITING room. Two sea-green sofas formed a cozy three-quarter circle along the edge of a blue and pink carpet. Cozy, but with room for warring couples to sit comfortably apart. Adolescents often declared their independence by slouching in the coral armchair that closed the circle. Those clients who had been coming awhile often put their feet up on the sand-colored coffee table, scooting the old issues of *Newsweek* and *Climbing Magazine* out of the way with their heels.

Sunlight reflected off the chalk-white walls, tinted by the papery flowers pressing against the windows. The flowers clashed a little with the ocean colors Teddy had chosen, but as his wife, Mary, pointed out, tropical fish came in the same brilliant reds and oranges. "Remember snorkeling in Hawaii?" she'd said. "The fish were bright like that. Electric blues, neon yellows, oranges, whites—"

"Yeah," Paul had said, stretching the word in his uncertainty. "I remember the coral and the underwater canyons. And the sea turtles."

"You only notice things that remind you of rocks." Wrapping herself around him, Mary had looked up at him with that seductive smile of hers. "What about me? How do I remind you of rocks? Is it my heart of stone?"

He'd pulled her close. "Naw. You're like a cliff. Whenever I see you, I just want to climb . . ."

A smile slid across Paul's face. He dismissed the memory and scanned the waiting room. His gaze flickered past the bookcase filled with Teddy's ceramics, pausing briefly on the Ken doll scaling a large, volcano-shaped vase. Mary had slipped Ken into the display. Where she'd found the doll-sized climbing gear, he had no idea.

He nodded at the client waiting on the sofa, Jeremy, normally a feet-on-the-coffee-table type. Not today, Paul noted. "Hello, Jeremy," he said. "Come on back."

Jeremy glanced at the temp, Raquel, sitting behind the built-in desk with its curved counter. His eyes narrowed. "Teddy's still gone?"

Don't read into it, Paul warned himself. "She's still healing. She'll be back as soon as she can."

Jeremy rose like smoke, still glaring at the hapless temp. "So long as you didn't get rid of her."

Okay, Paul amended. *Read into it.* "You're concerned about Teddy," he said, ushering Jeremy past the white counter. "So am I."

Jeremy stopped at the bookcase displaying Teddy's ceramics. He admired the delicately etched pots and the vibrantly glazed figures, his upper lip twitching into a passing sneer at the sight of the rock-climbing Ken. He turned to the temp. "Teddy's special," he said.

Raquel smiled, a reassuring smile. "You like her very much."

She's good, Paul thought.

"Teddy decorated this room," Jeremy said. He pointed to the display. "And she did these."

"I hope I get a chance to meet her before I leave," Raquel said.

The phone rang. She answered it. "Dr. Grant's office."

Paul touched Jeremy's elbow, urging him toward the

office. Jeremy ambled in, still scowling. Paul followed, trying to repress a grin. Most people bonded with the psychiatrist, not the receptionist.

He tugged at the door, but it wouldn't shut. He turned. Raquel grasped the knob, her face flushed from running across the room. "Teddy's on the line," she said. "She wanted to catch you before you started your session with Jeremy. Jeremy, Teddy said to tell you hi."

Paul excused himself and hurried back to the front desk. He picked up the phone. "Teddy? How are you? Any news?"

Her voice sounded flat, her tone colorless as quartz. "Paul? I know you don't have much time right now, but . . ."

"It's okay, Teddy." He switched ears. "What's up?"

Raquel rolled her chair to the far side of the desk. She placed her hands on the computer keyboard and began to type.

"Paul, I can't do this anymore," Teddy said. "Sitting around. I want to come back to work."

Paul hesitated.

"I *need* to," Teddy said.

Desperation added a little animation to her voice. Animation verging on hysteria. He imagined her heart-shaped face, thin lower lip caught between her teeth, hazel eyes searching his face. She reached to tuck her chin-length blond hair behind her ear with a splinted arm—

"How are your wrists?" he said.

A shudder rippled along the temp's shoulders.

Teddy sighed. "I can't do this anymore."

Paul stroked the phone cord. Boredom devastated Teddy. He'd always encouraged her to bring a book or her banjo to work, anything to keep her mind busy when she finished typing or filing. All this empty time must be killing her.

"Teddy, let me call you back," he said. "This evening. I'll talk to Mary. Between the three of us, we'll figure something out. But I'm not letting you come back if it's going to ruin your arms.''

Teddy's voice flattened again. ''Okay, boss. Thanks.''

Paul hung up and returned to his office. He assigned Teddy to his subconscious, demanding that it find a solution, then he focused on Jeremy. Jeremy became the entire world. For fifty minutes.

THE WOMAN SAT ON THE NEAREST COUCH, CHIN UP, shoulders back, looking both comfortable and regal in her simple black dress. Diamond earrings sparkled on her ears. A blue notebook rested on her lap under her folded hands. Paul smiled at her, then joined Raquel at the desk. ''I thought Penny was my last client,'' he whispered.

Raquel glanced at the woman, then back at the file she'd been organizing. ''She came in about half an hour ago and insisted on waiting for you. She gives me the willies.''

Paul tapped the edge of the desk with his fingers. ''I guess I better find out what she wants. Did you get her name?''

Raquel's jaw tightened. ''No.''

Paul nodded. He skirted the desk—

''Dr. Grant,'' Raquel said, her voice quiet with warning. ''She doesn't speak.''

Paul sat in the coral armchair and leaned toward the woman, his elbows resting on his knees. He opened his mouth to speak, then just looked at her. In her mid-twenties, her skin had the same rich gold-sienna tones as smoky topaz. Her eyes, a deep, earthen brown, gazed at him, drawing him in with their intensity. Something about the gentle oval of her face and the lift of her cheekbones reminded him of Mary. Why, Paul wasn't sure. It was the only similarity. That and the long, dark hair—although the woman had captured hers at the neck with a silver clip. Mary always let hers hang free.

The woman's pupils widened. She studied Paul with hungry concentration. He had the sudden feeling that he was falling into her gaze without anyone to belay him and catch his fall—that he was tumbling from a sheer rock face without harness or rope.

Paul scooted back, edging away from her. She blinked and his balance and stability returned. "I—I was told you've been waiting for me," he said.

The woman nodded. She wrote something in the blue notebook. Tearing off the page, she handed it to him.

"My name is Estelle," it said. "I want to work for you."

Paul nodded and tucked the note in his pocket. "I don't really need anyone right now. Can you . . . talk?"

Estelle touched her throat, then removed her hand.

Paul started. He'd been so intent on the woman's eyes, he'd been blind to the rosette of scar tissue blossoming at her throat. "I, uh . . ."

Estelle smiled.

"Dr. Grant?" Raquel said.

Paul turned. Raquel stood in front of the desk, purse in hand. "Would you like me to stay?" she said with a quick, pointed glance at the woman.

"No, no," Paul said. "Go ahead. I'll see you Monday."

He waited till the door shut, then faced Estelle again. "The only thing I ever need is a receptionist. You wouldn't be able to answer the phones. I'm curious—what did you think you could do for me?"

Estelle stood and crossed to the reception desk. Paul followed. Estelle glanced at the electric typewriter, the filing cabinets, the pen holder, the computer, then sat down at the typewriter. She switched it on. It hummed to life. She rolled a piece of paper into the platen and placed her hands on the keyboard. Within seconds the words "This is what I can do" appeared on the page.

Paul's subconscious tapped his conscious mind on the shoulder. He could almost hear it speak: *She can do everything Teddy can't do and Teddy can do everything she can't—namely answer the phones and talk to clients. Get Teddy one of those little headsets—*

Estelle's fingers tripped across the keyboard again. *"Yo hablo y escribo espanol tambien."*

"You know Spanish," Paul said. Not that he had any Spanish-speaking clients, but this *was* Santa Cruz. He drummed the edge of the desk. Could he afford to do this? He hated being without Teddy. After six years, she was like family. And if this woman realized it was only until Teddy recovered—

That's fine, a voice whispered through his mind. The hair on Paul's neck rose.

The click of the keyboard reclaimed his attention. "It would be unfair if I didn't tell you," Estelle typed, "that I'm only looking for temporary work."

Paul stared at the typewriter. It was perfect—too perfect. Raquel had already told him she planned to go on vacation next Wednesday. She could leave two days earlier and the temp agency wouldn't have to send a replacement.

He cleared his throat. "I need to think about this," he said. He crouched, pulling open one of the desk drawers. He flipped through Teddy's carefully prepared forms folders. Insurance forms, new client forms . . . where had she put that pad of application forms? He'd gone through dozens of receptionists before he'd hired her. Had she really thrown them away like she'd threatened to do? Release forms, waivers . . .

There. Behind the medical forms. Paul removed the pad and tore off the top sheet. "Here," he said, handing it to Estelle. "I'll need you to complete this—"

The phone rang. He answered it, turning away from Estelle. "Hello?"

"Hi," Mary said. "It's me."

"Hi, you," he said. "You sound a little down."

Mary took a deep breath, let it out. "It started. Just now."

Paul's shoulders sagged. He ran his fingers through his hair, then forced himself to smile. Infusing his voice with hope, he said, "Well. We'll just try harder next month."

"We tried hard last month," Mary said. "We did everything right. I think there's something wrong with me."

"Maybe there's something wrong with me," Paul said. "I'll get another semen analysis—"

He stiffened, embarrassed, then glanced over his shoulder. Estelle was gone. She'd left her application on the desk in front of the typewriter—folded into a seated cat. Something about the cat suggested that it had claimed this desk for its own. A note lay beside it. "See you Monday," it read.

FOURTEEN

AFTERNOON SUN FLOODED THE LIVING ROOM, SPILLING over the pine windowsill to pool on the blue carpet. It caressed the shoulders of the pale green sofa, sparkled on the cherry coffee table, warmed the seats of the two forest-green recliners. The entertainment center stood just out of the sun's reach, Paul's climbing shoes nestled at its base. Dried flowers, a gingham sachet frog, and other fadable things sprouted between CDs and videos or crouched, mushroomlike, beside the stereo and the television. Mary stood just inside this oasis of shadow, her shoulder touching the cherry frame of the entertainment center. She glanced at the ceramic near her elbow. A woman leaned from the body of a gourd-shaped vase, her arms flung over her head, face upturned to the sun or moon. "Which?" Mary had asked Teddy once.

Teddy had cocked her head in her birdlike way. "I'm not sure. I guess it depends on my mood. What do you think?"

Mary had studied the ceramic woman's parted lips and closed eyes. "I think she's drinking in the stars," she'd said.

But that interpretation relied on *her* mood. Today the woman flung herself into unrelenting darkness.

A cramp knifed Mary's uterus. She winced, cradling her bloated abdomen. Warmth might help. God knows the ibuprofen hadn't. Yet. She stepped into the sunlight.

It warmed her a little, but did nothing for the bloated heaviness weighting her abdomen. Walking to the window, Mary touched the pane. The lip of the quarry curled below her, bearded with blond, summer grass. It rose in a slight hill, a sort of pout, before dropping away. Mary pushed herself from the window. She was in no mood for the quarry's surliness. Not today.

She sank into the nearest recliner, shifting until the menstrual cramps ebbed a little. The heaviness remained. She leaned over and lifted the tumbler of Jamaican ginger beer from the coffee table. A paper coaster stuck to the bottom of the glass. She removed it, tossing it at the coffee table. It rolled to a stop between two frogs—one brass, the other quartz.

She pressed the damp tumbler to her left wrist. Its cold sweat calmed her. She took a sip of the forbidden liquid, closing her eyes as the spicy ginger burned down her throat. Forbidden, just like caffeine, just like alcohol, just like hot tubs—except for these five days each month when she knew she wasn't pregnant.

She'd tried all the folk remedies. Well, not all of them. She hadn't tried drinking Robitussin or injecting egg whites into her vagina before sex. But she had avoided things like ginger and licorice because someone told her they were emmenagogues. She stood on her head after sex, drank raspberry leaf tea at breakfast and after school, downed a glass of milk before going to bed.

Paul had modified his life, too. He'd given up coffee, his "liquid love." Mary smiled. That alone made her feel special, supported. They were full partners in the great fertility game. And coffee had only been the beginning: He avoided hot tubs, drank ginseng tea, no longer wore briefs. He dusted his cereal with wheat germ.

Raw oysters were his Robitussin and egg whites. "They're like swallowing snot," he'd said one night in the kitchen. "I'm just not desperate enough."

Mary had looked at the egg in her hand. She put it back in the fridge. "Me, neither," she'd said. There were just some things . . .

"Relax," her doctor kept telling her. "You're young, you're healthy—there's no need for invasive tests at this point. Just give it a little more time . . ."

Mary opened her eyes and set the ginger beer on the table. "A little more time," she said. "Three years, Doc. Isn't that long enough?"

Her voice settled in the still room. Wonderful. Now she was muttering to herself, the way Dad used to. A rueful smile touched her lips. As a teen, she'd been horrified whenever he talked to an empty room. What she wouldn't give to have him alive and babbling endlessly to his imaginary friend, Eileen—

The dull ache flared into another spasm. Mary doubled over with a moan. Taking a deep breath, she imagined it flowing from her lungs to her feet. She straightened a little. Maybe she should take another ibuprofen.

At least her period hadn't started yesterday, on the last day of school. That would have been much too much, being around children and knowing she wasn't pregnant. It would have been especially hard after the early recess. . . .

She'd gone out on the playground to talk to the principal, but hadn't been able to find her. "Lori," she called to the yard duty. "Have you seen Bridget?"

Lori shaded her eyes with her hand and scanned the yard—the metal play structures rising like dinosaur skeletons from the sand, the wooden planters and terra-cotta pots of the life lab garden, the huge, grassy field. "She went to break up a fight," Lori said, passing the hand over her forehead to smooth her short blond hair. "Over by the fence, I think, near the parking lot."

"Thanks, Lori," Mary said. She squinted across the

field—was that Bridget in the far corner, kneeling between two boys? Only one way to find out.

She avoided the handball court, stepping into the middle of a game of tag at the edge of the grass. Kids swarmed around her. One of her English as a Second Language students hid behind her, grasping the sides of her skirt as if they were handles. "Gabriela, what is this?" Mary said, placing an arm around the first grader's shoulders. "Am I the base?"

One of Gabriela's pink barrettes had come undone. The girl brushed a strand of dark hair from her cinnamon-brown eyes. What Mary wouldn't give to take her home. »No, teacher,« Gabriela said in Spanish. Then in English: "You are a tree."

Mary smiled. "A tree? *Un árbol?*"

Gabriela nodded. Another of Mary's ESL students, Jacinta, ran to join them. She cowered behind Gabriela. »Are we safe here?« she whispered.

Mary's smile grew heavy. Safe? She looked at Jacinta's broad, delicate face. »What are you playing?«

Leandro squeezed between Gabriela and Jacinta. He grinned at Mary, then leaned to look around her. He raced off toward the life lab garden. Another boy, José, swooped down on him with a yell and tackled him. Gabriela chewed the ends of her hair. »Now they will send him back,« she said.

A cold, hard knot formed in Mary's chest. »Send him back? What are you playing?«

»Migra,« Jacinta said. »We're trying to cross the border without getting caught.« She pointed to Luis, Hannah, and Mike. They crowded around Leandro and José. »They're the Migra.«

Mary held her breath. Rosie stood at the edge of her mind, blue dress rippling in the wind, dark eyes wide with studied ignorance and innocence. Standing in the dark on that hostile border, Rosie glowed as if touched by light. She looked down at the scuffed toes of her new sneakers, ignoring the border patrol's words. *"Niña?"* the younger officer said. "Honey, *comprendes? Ayuda* your mom, *niña.* Okay?" The officer's shoulder slid under Mamá's arm like a crutch. Mamá moaned, her face damp and twisted with pain—

»Señora Grant,« Gabriela said. »Are you all right?«

Mary looked down into the girl's face and saw Rosie in those brown eyes. Now a young woman, Rosie stumbled forward, exhausted and haggard, one hand trailing a wall to help her keep her balance. She looked like a younger version of Mamá, with the same rising cheekbones and delicately arched brows, the same oval face. But her lips, though full like Mamá's, curved in Dad's near smile. »I'm coming, Maria,« Rosie said. »Look for me . . .«

Gabriela grasped the sleeve of Mary's dress. »Señora Grant?«

Mary shook herself free of the vision. »I'm fine,« she said. »But I need to talk to Señora Monroe. You'll have to find another tree. . . .«

Mary burrowed deeper into the recliner. Clasping the *milagro* that hung from the chain around her neck, she tugged at the silver girl's feet. Like the other visions she'd had through the years, this one had been so strong, so *real.* Would it also come true? *Where are you now, little sister?* Mary wondered. *Where should I look for you?*

Tears skimmed her eyes. She clenched her jaw, tilting her chin to prevent the tears from falling. Dad, Mamá, Rosie . . . ghosts drawn by this new death, this unconceived, never-to-be-born child.

Mary released the charm, wishing it was as easy to release this crushing desire. Every month she forgot her promise to herself and Paul, and gave in to hope. She imagined the baby growing inside her, imagined it taking its first step, saying its first word. If it was a boy, it would look like Dad, all bright blue eyes and curly, pale hair. Or like Paul, with lean, creased cheeks and gray eyes under a thatch of feathery, tawny hair. He'd be tall, like Paul, not short like her. And if they had a girl . . . Mary forced herself to breathe through the knot in her throat. She always pictured a little girl with hair the color of bittersweet chocolate and eyes the color of polished coffee beans. She pictured Rosie, standing still and frightened and brave beside Mamá and the border patrol—

Mary stood. She leaned over the coffee table and picked up the quartz frog and the brass frog. She set them on their backs. Walking to the bookshelf, she overturned the glass frog, then went to the entertainment center. She wandered the room, turning every frog upside down. Like her heart.

PAUL STOOD BESIDE THE ENTERTAINMENT CENTER, SURveying the living room. A glass of golden liquid sat on the coffee table between two overturned frogs, one brass, the other quartz. Paul glanced at the entertainment center. The cloth frog lay on its back. A second brass frog nested upside down inside one of his climbing shoes. The glass frog on the bookshelf lay with its feet thrust into the air. So did the raku one that Teddy had made for Mary.

She's left no frog unturned, Paul thought, a grim smile touching his lips. A hard period this time, made worse by the fact that school ended yesterday. Without the distraction of lesson plans and staff meetings, Mary had time to mourn.

Paul stood still and listened. No sobbing—Mary rarely sobbed. She cried silently, her jaw set in grim determination, her eyes fierce. Paul picked up the cloth frog and set it on its feet. He couldn't face her grief just yet, not when his own was so raw. Frustration and loss had welled up inside him on the drive home, alternating between angry snarls and knots of tears clogging his throat. They had tried so hard for so long—three years. Sure, other people had tried longer—they or their friends made a point of telling him all about it. Including his climbing buddy, Abe Moss.

Moss had taken him to the Seabright Brewery one evening after a trip to the Pacific Edge climbing gym. Seated near a busing station and an open door, television flickering overhead, they waited for their oatmeal stouts to appear. Then Moss leaned across the table, his red beard skimming the foam. "You know, my sister and her husband had a helluva time having a kid," he said.

Paul's shoulders rose. He hunched over his beer. "Moss—"

"Took 'em ten years," Moss continued. "Well, eleven. They'd reach the end of a pitch and take a different route—drugs, hormones, insemination, you name it. They even did this thing where the doctor stuck a tube through her belly button."

Paul sipped his stout. "What finally worked?"

Moss straightened and leaned back. His wild brown curls haloed his square face. "Acupuncture. I think." He frowned. "Maybe it was the adoption. . . ."

Adoption. Paul squatted and retrieved the brass frog from his climbing shoe. He set it on the entertainment center next to Teddy's vase. He and Mary had gone around and around on the adoption issue. Maybe it was time to bring it up again.

Paul toured the room, setting frogs on their feet. *If only it was that easy with people*, he thought. But then he'd be out of a job.

In exchange for a world full of happy, adjusted people? He could live with that.

He took a deep breath and headed for the kitchen. The lemon-yellow walls and enamel-white counters cheered him. "A kitchen is a happy place," Mary had said while picking out the paint and tile. "It should *look* happy . . ."

It did, with its floral curtains framing snapshot views of the garden and the terrarium window box overflowing with herbs. The white counter formed an inviting L, dividing the cooking area from the breakfast nook at a conversational rib height. Tall oak stools lined the nook side of the counter, styled to match the oak breakfast table and chairs.

Mary sat at the table, staring out the window at the rosebush and the apple tree planted in the center of the yard. Her chin rested in her hand. A tendril of hair stuck to her cheek, pasted in place by dried tears. Paul went to her chair and knelt beside her. He leaned his head against her shoulder.

Mary stiffened and drew away. Paul looked up, but her gaze was still fixed on the roses and the apple tree. Or maybe it was fixed on something that wasn't there—

"When you do that," Mary said without turning, "when you put your head on my shoulder like that, I feel like you're asking me to take care of you."

"It's meant to be a sympathetic gesture," Paul said, rising. He sat in the chair next to hers.

She turned to face him. Her eyes, rimmed with tears, shone a deep sapphire blue. "It's never going to happen, Paul," she said. "We're never going to have a baby."

"You're sad and frustrated—"

"Don't use that reflective listening on me," Mary said, her voice dangerously steady. "Save it for your clients."

Paul pressed his lips together. "I'm sorry."

Mary picked up the glass salt shaker and studied it, turning it over in her hands. She set it down, then picked it up again. "Elissa at school—the one who teaches fourth—just found out she's pregnant."

Paul's gut twisted. "We can adopt—"

Mary looked at him. "And what guarantees will we have that we won't get a drug baby? I've worked with those children. They break my heart. More than that, they scare me. Sherry had one—the one that looked like a deer in the headlights. She was helping him at the computer that time and he started stabbing her with his pencil.''

"They're not all drug babies—''

"No.'' Mary's voice dropped to a shamed whisper. "They're not.''

Paul ran his finger along the edge of the table. "I'll get another semen analysis. The last one—''

"—was less than a year ago.'' Mary set the salt shaker next to the pepper mill. "I think something's wrong with *me*.''

Paul reached across the table and took her hands. "Hey, Dr. Aluri said your pap smears are healthy, your blood is healthy. You're menstruating—''

Mary's palms became damp and cold. "Maybe it's time for some of those tests.''

Paul squeezed her hands. "Dr. Aluri doesn't think they're necessary. Why do something invasive, possibly damaging, if you don't have to?''

Mary shrugged.

A shiver stole over Paul. "The next step is a hyster-osalpingogram, to see if her tubes are blocked,'' Dr. Aluri had told him. "If they are, the test can be worse than labor. And even when they're not—I don't know. I mean, I'm no fertility expert. But they shoot that dye up the tubes, and—well, nothing's supposed to go *up* the tubes. Everything's supposed to come *down* . . .''

Paul shifted in his seat. The thought of Mary being injured during testing scared him.

Mary withdrew her hands. "Maybe it's not a good idea. If the tests come back saying nothing's wrong, then what? What if the problem is that, subconsciously, I don't really want a child? What if my mind is against me? If it's telling my body not to conceive, because I'm scared or I secretly hate kids.''

The smile quirked across his face before Paul could quash it.

Mary glared at him, then smiled crookedly.

Paul winked. ''Right. You've just spent the last eight years teaching ESL in the elementary schools because you want to terrorize the little monsters.''

Mary raised her eyebrows. ''Some of the kids think so.''

Paul grabbed the legs of her chair and pulled her toward him. He dragged her into his lap. ''We're just going to have to keep trying,'' he said. He kissed her neck. ''You're only thirty. I figure we've got, oh, at least another thirteen years before we *really* have to start worrying.'' He kissed her nose. ''You know, that could be it. Dr. Aluri said it was possible we were trying too hard, stressing about it too much.''

Mary leaned back in the harness of his arms. ''Do you believe that?''

Paul thought a minute. ''Yes. I think I do. Maybe we should give up.''

Mary fingered the charm around her neck. ''It'll never work. We can *tell* ourselves we've given up, but we'll *know* we haven't.''

''Good point. Well, if we can't give up, we'll have to hope.''

Mary twisted away. He almost dropped her. She swiveled, staring out the window, her expression hard and closed. ''All hope has ever done is let me down,'' she said.

Paul laced his fingers behind her back, reinforcing his grip. He gazed at the side of her face, the defiant jut of her jaw, the cool distance in her eye. ''Not always,'' he said.

Mary looked at him. That crooked smile returned. ''When?''

''The day we met,'' he said.

They'd met at a party on Seabright Beach. Dressed in

a one-piece bathing suit, a Speedo, she looked ready for anything—unlike the other women, who had to constantly adjust and readjust their thong bottoms and string tops. Her arms and legs were toned, her skin was a warm pink under a frost of sunblock. A hint of shadow enhanced her sky-blue eyes. The silver girl dangled from a chain around her neck, her feet pointing to Mary's small, firm breasts. Paul listened to her laugh, eavesdropped on her conversations about film and education. When Moss challenged him to a volleyball game, Paul asked Mary to join him.

"Volleyball?" she said.

"You and me against Moss and Judy."

"I was hoping you'd ask," she said.

Paul hugged the ball to his hip. "To play volleyball?"

"No," she'd said, smiling. "You and me . . ."

With her legs, Mary pulled herself closer to him. The chair creaked under their shifting weight. She wound her arms around his neck and leaned into him. Paul nuzzled her neck, inhaling her freesia perfume. "So hope hasn't always let me down," she said. Sorrow underscored the forced playfulness in her voice. "But that's only once."

FIFTEEN

HECTOR STRAIGHTENED FROM A CROUCH. THE FOG HUNG in rags, a battered piñata of cold, morning air. The damp soaked through his jeans and blue shirt, chilling his skin. He breathed in through his mouth. The flavor of overripe strawberries and dirt drenched his tongue. It had taken him almost two weeks to reach Watsonville—he'd had to earn money in San Diego to pay for bus fare—and three more days to find his friend Rigoberto. In those three short days, strawberries and dirt had already begun to taste oppressive and flat.

He tamped the heel of his boot on the packed dirt between the strawberry field and the border of green corn. Rigoberto had told him that the corn protected the strawberries from road dust and exhaust. »Does it work?« Hector had asked.

Rigoberto had shrugged. »It must,« he'd said. »They do it every year.«

A car rumbled past on the other side of the corn. The tasseled stalks muffled the sound. It was early yet, too early for much traffic. Hector wondered how much sound would leak into the field when the rest of Watsonville woke. Trucks would rattle through the intersection, cars would whine and growl. Ambulance sirens would shriek, racing to the hospital on the corner. And here, in these fields, the only answer would be the soft grunts and shuffle of people moving, crablike, down the straight, green rows.

Rigoberto stood a few feet away, talking to some other men. A group of women in colorful sweaters and hats with kerchiefs stood on the far side of a blue tractor waiting to tow two portable toilets on an old trailer. Packs and cloth bags hung from the red metal rack attached to the trailer and leaning against the backs of the toilets.

Hector joined Rigoberto. »If this man does not hire me,« he said, »what will I do?«

»He has to hire you,« Rigoberto said. »I can't afford for you to stay with me for nothing. Even if you are an old friend of my father's. It's not the same in California.«

Hector nodded. That was certainly true. The people he'd met here, even the ones that had only arrived a year or two ago, they took you in, they took care of you, but their hands were not as open as they were at home. These people were losing México. Still, here was Rigoberto, sharing a trailer with five other men, insisting Hector stay with him . . .

Hector glanced at Rigoberto's pitted face. The drooping mustache hid a few of the pocked scars, but the man still resembled the moon. »Perhaps if we offer the boss a *mordida*,« Hector said.

»Ay! Don't do that,« Rigoberto said. »You only bribe people in this country if you are very rich. Otherwise they arrest you.« He tugged at the bill of his hat. »I wish you'd thought to buy *chueco* in Tijuana. The North American bosses are always asking for immigration papers. We'll tell the boss that yours got left at the trailer. Then we'll have someone make you a work permit and a social security card. Like mine.«

Hector nodded. He turned to a man in a John Deere cap. »You're sure there is work today? It's Sunday—«

»Would we be standing here?« the man said. »Use
your head instead of your balls.«

Hector shoved his hands in his pockets. Between the
leaves of the corn, a blur of metallic blue roared past.
Another car. There were lots of cars here—nearly everyone owned a car. Even the other farmworkers—they had
parked theirs at the edge of a field down the road. »In
North America,« Rigoberto had told him, »it is important to have a car. When I save enough money, *I* will
have a car.«

Hector scratched his jaw. By now, Maria owned a car.
Little Maria. He tried to imagine her as a woman. His
mind stretched and rounded the proud eleven-year-old
girl he'd left at the border. The face eluded him. The
body, well, his mind substituted Rosa's—

He touched his throat. Rosa's dead eyes gazed sight-
lessly in his memory. Her chest lay still, not with the
peace of sleep but with the shock of death. Dead. The
bastard had blown apart her throat.

Then she'd risen to take her revenge . . .

Hector crossed himself.

»It's the second one,« John Deere said. »Remember
Paco's? He found it behind the shed. Not a drop of blood
in it.«

One of the other men hissed. He tugged the bill of
his PG&E cap. »Kids,« he said. »Some crazy gang
thing.«

»Don't be stupid,« Rigoberto said. »Why would they
do that?«

»To get away with it,« PG&E said. »To see if they
can drain all the blood before someone catches them.«

Hector drew closer. »Drain all the blood?«

Rigoberto spat. »Come on! Gangs are more interested
in killing each other than killing goats.«

»*Chupacabra*,« Hector said.

»See?« John Deere said. »I'm not the only one. Just

wait till that thing discovers the farm up in Davenport—«

»Bonnie Doon,« a quiet man in a nameless red cap said.

»Bonnie Doon, Davenport,« John Deere said. »Somewhere up there. They'd better watch out or the *chupacabra*'s going to harvest the blood for them.«

Hector frowned. »Harvest the blood? Who's harvesting blood?«

Rigoberto waved his question away. »Someone's harvesting goat blood and giving it to humans.«

»They're using goats to grow antibodies,« the quiet man said.

»Yeah, well, when the *chupacabra* finds out, they won't have any kind of bodies left,« John Deere said.

»They'll have bodies,« Rigoberto said. »They just won't have blood.«

»What gang is going to go that far out of town just to prove themselves by killing goats?« PG&E said. »Look, the kids are proving they have balls. And they're proving they're above Mexican superstitions by scaring the shit out of old women like you—«

A flatbed truck loaded with shallow boxes bounced through an opening in the row of corn and onto the dirt track. The truck parked beside the portable toilets. »The boss,« John Deere said. He walked over to meet the driver.

The other men followed. Hector lagged behind, shaking his head. What was more fantastic—a *chupacabra* in California or someone raising goats for blood?

By the time Hector reached the truck, the other farmworkers had begun lifting boxes from the bed and heading out into the fields. Except Rigoberto and the quiet man. They stood beside a wishbone-legged man with tufts of gray hair peeking from under his black cap. Rigoberto spoke rapidly, gesturing with his hands.

The gray-haired man shook his head. »Rigoberto, I

don't have work for your friend,« he said, turning to Hector with a squint. His blue eyes opened wide. »My God, Rigoberto, did you really expect me to hire *him*? He must be at least fifty! You know I don't hire anyone over thirty-five.«

The quiet man stepped behind the boss.

»No, no,« Rigoberto assured him. »He isn't that old. He's had a difficult life—«

The boss snorted. He gazed at Hector. »Do you have any experience with strawberries? Any at all?«

»He has lots of experience!« Rigoberto lied. »He has done strawberries for years! Well, not *that* many years. Like I said, he's young still, he's just had a difficult life—«

The boss removed his cap and scratched the top of his bald head. Behind him, the quiet man raised a hand as if to bless him.

»I'm very sorry, but I don't have any work for you,« the boss said.

The quiet man laid his hand on the gray-haired man's shoulder.

A thoughtful look crossed the gray-haired man's face. He replaced his cap. »Then again,« he said, »what's an extra set of hands? I'll try you out for a few days, see what you can do. But you've got to get me those papers as soon as you can. I'm not having the Migra come down here causing a fuss.«

HECTOR WIPED THE SWEAT FROM HIS NECK, THEN reached for another strawberry.

»You need a hat,« the quiet man said.

Hector grunted.

»Your friend should have told you,« the quiet man persisted. »You get too hot without one.«

Hector nodded. They continued to work, plucking the red strawberries and arranging them in flats. The sun bled sweat from Hector's back. His lower back and knees ached from bending at the waist. Heat seemed to sear through his body—every joint, every pore. His mouth burned, it was so dry. He looked at the strawberry in his hand. Swollen with juice, it promised relief. He looked to the right and left without turning his head. Just one. What could it hurt?

»Don't eat it,« the quiet man said, adjusting the bill of his red cap. »Not without washing it. It's bad enough we work in the pesticides, but that we should eat them . . .«

»*Ni modo*,« Hector said. It can't be helped. But he placed the strawberry in the flat. »The pesticides, what will they do to us?«

»Maybe nothing,« the quiet man said, shuffling sideways to the next plant. »Maybe a lot. Some of them damage the nerves, even the brain. Others go for the lungs. The ones they use on strawberries, they're the worst. I don't even eat the strawberries washed.«

Hector dragged his flat to a new plant. »You know a lot. Antibodies, pesticides . . .«

The quiet man reached for another strawberry. »I read a lot. Spanish and English.«

»Spanish *and* English? Then why are you working here?«

»Here, in California, everybody reads.« The man grinned. »Enough people do, anyway. It's not special.«

»Yes, it is,« Hector said.

The man plucked another strawberry. They continued to work, shuffling down the rows of emerald plants, filling flat after flat with the dangerous red fruit. *If I could read English,* Hector thought, *I could find Maria and, hopefully, Rosa—*

A chill traced his spine, forcing his shoulders to curl. Did he really want to find Rosa? That look in her eyes as she stood over the dead man, buttoning his shirt over her blood-spattered breast . . . it still frightened him. For the first time since the fog lifted earlier that morning, he shivered.

Coward, he reprimanded himself. His cheeks warmed with guilt. How could he forsake her, his Rosita? How could he let the horror of one night persuade him to abandon her?

»Idiot,« he muttered.

The quiet man glanced at him, appraising him. They worked side by side in silence.

HECTOR AND THE QUIET MAN WALKED ALONG THE road, following the other farmworkers from the field. Dust had settled on the waiting cars, hiding the gleam of their paint. »You are a good man,« the quiet man said. »Why are you so hard on yourself?«

Hector looked at him, surprised. »I'm not—«

»Hector,« Rigoberto called. He sat on the hood of Alejandro's black Dodge Charger. »Alejandro and I are going out for a drink. You want to come?«

Hector sucked his lower lip. A drink would be nice, a cold beer . . .

But he had so little money. And he needed to find Maria and Rosa. »No,« he said. »There's something I have to do.«

Rigoberto hooted. »Don't be a woman, Hector. One drink.«

Hector shook his head. Rigoberto dismissed him with a brush of his hand. He tipped his chin toward the quiet man. »What about you, Eliseo? Come, have a drink.«

Eliseo lifted the bill of his red cap, then tugged the hat back in place. »Not tonight.«

»Not any night,« Alejandro said, opening the Charger's door. »Not Eliseo. Come, Rigoberto. Leave the children alone.«

The Charger rumbled to life, then jounced onto the road, dust billowing after it. Hector turned his back on the gritty cloud.

»This something you have to do,« Eliseo said. »Is this why you are so hard on yourself?«

Hector glanced at his companion. A slender man of medium height, Eliseo had the placid, gentle face of a saint. With his dark hair curling around the edges of his cap, he looked a little like a cherub, except that his face was broad and flat. And no cherub Hector had ever seen had had a mustache.

»I'm looking for friends, from home,« Hector said. »I have an address, but it's very old. I'm not sure how to find them.«

Eliseo nodded. »Do you speak English?«

»No.«

Eliseo raked his teeth along the fringe of his mustache. »Let me help you. Do you have the address with you?«

Hector pulled his billfold from his back pocket. A brown flake fell from the worn vinyl. He opened the billfold and removed the address Miguel had sent years ago. »These people will always know how to reach me,« Miguel had written. »In case someone needs to find me. Don't give it to Conchita or Rosa. It is better for them that they don't know anything that might lead to me. . . .«

Hector smoothed the wrinkled paper with his thumb. *These people.* Hector knew whose address he held. Or rather, whose address it used to be.

It was too much to hope that Miguel and Maria still lived there.

He handed the paper to Eliseo. Eliseo read it, then handed it back. »I know where that is,« he said. »It's not far from here. Come. I'll take you.«

Eliseo walked up to a crimson Camaro and unlocked the passenger door. A lacy, doily-like silhouette of the Virgin of Guadalupe had been glued to the rear window, her head bowed and her hands pressed together in prayer. Hector climbed into the car. It smelled of cinnamon and chocolate. Eliseo slipped into the driver's seat.

»It's been fourteen years,« Hector said. The press of the seat relieved some of the ache in his lower back. »They may not live there anymore.«

»And if they don't, I'll help you find them,« Eliseo said. He studied Hector's face, then frowned. »After we check out that address, we'll go to Thrifty's and get you a hat.«

THE GRINGO GLANCED FROM ELISEO TO HECTOR, AN EX-pectant look on his freckled face. »He says he only moved here four years ago,« Eliseo said. »He doesn't know who lived here before that.«

The gringo must have understood something of the translation—a word or two, Hector guessed—because he smiled. Eliseo said something in English. The man responded, then pushed the door several centimeters until it framed his face.

»He says he wishes he could help you,« Eliseo said. He touched Hector's shoulder and turned him away. »Come. Perhaps one of the neighbors—«

»Ask him if a woman came and asked him the same questions,« Hector said. »About twenty-five, with a dark complexion. She would have asked in English—good English. He might have thought she was from here.«

Eliseo nodded, then turned again to the gringo.

The stream of English bubbled past Hector. Jangling Conchita's ring in his pocket, he shuffled a step to the right and appraised the house. A sturdy little box, it boasted a balustraded porch and a small, neat yard of cropped grass. A drainpipe hung from the roof at an angle. Water and mud stained the stucco walls. Someone had patched one of the side windows with silver tape and a piece of cardboard. A good patch job, neat and serviceable. It would keep the rain out easily.

Hector nodded. A nice house, good-sized—at least two bedrooms—one that would comfortably shelter a family of ten or eleven. Miguel and Maria must have shared it with someone. Otherwise, how had they been able to afford it?

»No woman has come asking for your friends,« Eliseo said.

Hector glanced at the gringo. The gringo smiled again. Hector rolled his shoulder. »Thank him for me,« he said. »Tell him I'm sorry we bothered him and I appreciate his time.«

The gringo nodded after Eliseo's translation. »*De nada*,« he said, closing the door. His accent was terrible.

Eliseo steered Hector toward the house on the left. »Perhaps the neighbors—«

The door behind them reopened. The gringo shouted something.

Eliseo stopped, asked something in English, then thanked the man. He grasped Hector's shoulder, pointing him toward the house across the street. »He said the old man who lives there might know something. He's lived here forever.«

HECTOR AND ELISEO SCOOTED THEIR CHAIRS CLOSER TO the Formica table. Across from them, the old man, Mr. Lewis, shook his head, clasping and unclasping his hands before his onion-bulb belly. He leaned forward on the vinyl kitchen chair, not to get a better look at Hector but at a spot on the black and gray linoleum. »Tío Hector,« Mr. Lewis said, then mumbled something in English. He looked up, his gray eyes set in darkened folds. His face hung slack and pale. »She talks about you,« he said in halting Spanish. »When she is a little girl. I don't believe her.«

»Do you know where she is? And her father?«

The old man frowned. »Slower,« he said.

Hector repeated the questions.

The frown deepened. Mr. Lewis turned to Eliseo. Eliseo questioned him in English. Relieved, Mr. Lewis responded in kind.

»He does, but he wants to be sure you're who you say you are,« Eliseo said. »He says he wants to call her before he gives you her address.«

Hector grunted. A good man. Careful. Hector shifted. The vinyl cushion squeaked. »Ask him about Miguel, her father. Where is he?«

The old man's head drooped as Eliseo spoke. He touched his forehead with his fingers, pressing his nose to his palm. "Steven, Steven, Steven," he said. With a heavy sigh, he dropped his hand and began to speak.

Eliseo's jaw tightened. He began translating as the old man spoke. »He knows your friend as Steven. Twelve years ago, when Mary—he calls her Mary—when she was eighteen, her father was found dead in the Pajaro River. Shot he forgets how many times. Mary had nowhere to go. She was in her last year at the high school. She wanted to go to college, but couldn't afford to. Not if she wanted to eat. Mr. Lewis offered to take her in—if she promised to go to college. She lived here for four years.«

Mr. Lewis paused to watch Eliseo. When Eliseo stopped talking, the old man started up again. »She is a teacher now,« Eliseo translated. »She teaches English as a second language. To children. She is married to a doctor, a—« Eliseo frowned. »A minute, Mr. Lewis,« he said. He asked something in English.

The old man listened, then wrinkled his nose as if a great stench had filled the room. He growled something at Eliseo. Eliseo nodded. »She married a head doctor, a psychologist,« he said. »Mr. Lewis doesn't trust him.«

Mr. Lewis railed for a minute, then glowered at the linoleum.

A suppressed grin curled one corner of Eliseo's lips.

»He doesn't like psychologists. He thinks they're all ducks.«

Hector nodded. »Tell him I don't like them either.«

Mr. Lewis looked up again. »I know I like you,« he said.

SIXTEEN

MORNING FOG SWIRLED IN EDDIES OF VISIBLE AIR. Teddy hunched deeper into her cotton jacket and stepped onto the street. At nine or ten this morning, when the sun burned through, she'd be glad she'd worn a short sleeve blouse and cotton skirt. At nine or ten. Now she wished she had on her thick wool sweater, the plum one with the lavender and pale yellow leaves. And a pair of sweats.

"Hey, Teddy!" Rita called, waving her paintbrush. Perched on a ladder planted firmly in her flower bed, she looked delicate and small. The sparkle in her eyes offset her sixty-four years. She pushed her glasses higher along her nose. "What do you think? Looking pretty good, huh? I had to knock off for the weekend 'cause I had to take care of the grandkids."

Teddy stopped to admire Rita's handiwork. Not a trace of celadon marred the front of the house. Without the contrast, the sandstone-buff paint warmed to ripe apricot. "Looks great," Teddy said. "What color are you going to do the trim?"

Rita scratched her head with the handle of the paint-brush. A drip of paint matted her white curls. "Oh, I think green. A darker green. Sort of olive. Hey, where you going this early on a foggy Monday morning?"

"To work."

Rita frowned. "Oh, now, you aren't going to mess with those arms, are you? Teddy, you got to take care of yourself."

Teddy smiled. "I am. That's why I'm going to work. I'll talk to you later."

She walked toward the corner. Rolling one shoulder, she shifted the daypack. Weighted down with two cold packs, her lunch and her wallet, the pack pressed against her spine, a solid lump. She reached back and nudged it with the cuff of her right brace. The pressure sent a shock wave through her arm. Teddy flinched. "You need to lighten this thing," she told herself. "Leave one of the cold packs at work tonight. That'll help."

Sure, that'd help. And if she ate nothing but popcorn for lunch for the next few months, that'd help too.

She reached the corner and turned, then stopped.

A block away, on the bluff overlooking the strawberry fields, the wind parted the tall, sun-bleached grass to reveal a woman hunched in a wheelchair. Teddy shaded her eyes with her hand. Head thrust forward like a turtle, the woman wore a red cap, its attached kerchief flapping, a white blouse, and jeans. Her hands lay folded in her lap, and whether it was the wind quivering through the grass or the woman herself, her body seemed to tremble.

The woman turned, facing Teddy. Although unable to see the woman's eyes, Teddy felt their gaze locking on her. A gentle flutter filled Teddy's chest, a petal-soft sweetness that swirled and tumbled inside her like a warm breeze through wisteria. With the delicacy of a whisper, it murmured through her arms until, with a sudden fierceness, it rose to a scream at her elbows and wrists, a piercing, shrieking wail—

Teddy cried out. The pain stopped, leaving behind only the dull ache she'd grown accustomed to. She hugged herself, then realized she was kneeling in the middle of the intersection. She struggled to her feet, standing still for a minute before hurrying to the bus stop.

She glanced over her shoulder. The strawberry fields were still visible, but the woman in the wheelchair had disappeared, swallowed by the fog.

TEDDY STOOD ON THE SIDEWALK IN FRONT OF THE OF- fice. Bougainvillea crowded the restored bungalow, the oranges and reds vivid against the brown shingles. The glider stood in front of the picture window, its vintage Day-Glo throw pillow mashed under one arm. Teddy shook her head. She kept hoping some homeless person would take the monstrosity, but so far, no luck. Paul maintained that only a pillow that ugly would survive theft. Teddy—and Mary—argued that it deserved a worse fate. Teddy mounted the steps.

She stopped and peeked through the window. A black-haired, terra-cotta-skinned woman sat at the recep- tion desk, writing on a legal pad. The new secretary, Estelle, the one who'd made it possible for her to come back to work. Something about her seemed cool and distant. Her focused expression and the tilt of her head seemed removed, somehow dispassionate. She looked like the kind of person who watched and drew her own conclusions, taking into account only her own observa- tions. What was Paul thinking? The office needed some- one warm and reassuring, not a magistrate sitting in judgment. Teddy smiled crookedly. And what was *she* doing?

The door opened to a gentle push. Relief and home- coming washed over Teddy as she stepped into the wait- ing room. The cozy circle of sea-green sofas and coral armchair invited her in. The radio, barely audible, was still tuned to KPIG. Why, after only a month and a half, had she expected everything to be different? Why had she expected the stamp of someone else's personality— and whose? Not Paul's. He'd told her when she redecorated the waiting room that since she was the one who had to look at it all the time, she was the one to please. Not Mary's. Mary never interfered with the office. Well, except to "borrow" one of Teddy's ceramic figures, a nude, from the display shelves. Estelle had only started this morning—

Teddy turned to the desk. The woman sat watching her, dark eyes seeking Teddy's. Their gazes met. A weird feeling of recognition sparked in Teddy. Where had she seen this woman? *Had* she seen this woman? No, she couldn't have. She'd have remembered that blossom of scar tissue on the woman's throat. A rose, Paul had called it. It looked more like a dogwood flower.

Teddy coughed to clear her own throat. "Hi," she said. "You must be Estelle. I'm Teddy."

Estelle smiled and tipped her head. Her diamond earrings flashed. All traces of that coolness had disappeared, replaced by an air of earnest welcome. She stood, smoothing the folds of her simple black dress, then gestured for Teddy to come, join her. Irritation flared in Teddy—imagine being invited to her own desk. Then her annoyance dissipated. She was here, she was at work. And for the first time in all those long weeks, she had something to do.

The door to Paul's office opened. He stepped into the waiting room, all lean, long angles and easy grace. His arms strained the sleeves of his short sleeve cotton shirt, sinewy and strong. *Unlike mine*, Teddy thought.

Paul smiled, creases lining his cheeks. "Teddy?"

"Reporting for duty, Commander," Teddy said.

Paul laughed. "God, it's good to see you. Did you meet Estelle?"

"Just now," Teddy said. She walked behind the desk, slipping the daypack from her shoulders. She dropped it on her chair. "So where's this torture device you bought for me?"

"On the desk," Paul said.

Estelle held up a headset. Teddy took it with murmured thanks. The thing looked fragile.

Paul leaned over the desk, gray eyes earnest. "It was the lightest one I could find. Do you think you can get it on—without hurting your arms?"

"I think so," Teddy said. She fumbled with the headset for a few seconds, then set it on the desk. Ripping the Velcro tabs on her braces, she released her arms. They looked thin and frail without the padding. She put on the headset, adjusted it, then resplinted her arms. "There," she said. "No problem."

A dubious frown creased Estelle's brow.

The phone rang. Estelle pushed herself farther to one side. Paul stepped back. "It's all yours," he said.

Teddy took a deep breath. "Am I plugged in?"

Paul reached over the desk and tugged at a cord and box attached to the phone. "Uh . . . yes. All you have to do is push this button—"

Teddy pushed the button. A twinge crackled up her arm. She tensed until the pain passed. "Good morning, Dr. Grant's office," she said. "This is Teddy."

Silence.

Teddy readjusted the earphones and the microphone. "Hello? Paul, I don't think it's working—"

"Teddy?" a breathless voice said as Paul and Estelle moved toward her.

"Yes?" Teddy said, waving the others away. "Jeremy?"

Relief colored Jeremy's voice. "You're back. Will you be there tomorrow?"

"I sure will," Teddy said. "How are you?"

"Sick. Been in bed for three days. I was calling to cancel, but if you're back, I'll be there. See you tomorrow."

"Jeremy, wait," Teddy said. "Jeremy, if you're sick, you should stay home—"

A soft click.

''—and not give it to the rest of us,'' Teddy said. A grin spread across her face. ''It works.''

Paul smiled. ''Great. Oh, and I wasn't sure where to start, so I decided to leave Estelle's training up to you—''

The phone rang. Estelle reached across Teddy and hit the button. She made an apologetic face, then flexed her arm.

Teddy nodded thanks. ''Good morning, Dr. Grant's office,'' she said. ''This is Teddy.''

Paul waved and walked back to his office.

''Teddy!'' Mary said. ''Welcome back! How are your arms?''

Teddy grimaced. ''Awful. I feel like the armless wonder. How about you? What've you been up to?''

Mary's voice wavered for a second. ''Not much. Just trying to figure out which summer project to tackle first.''

That catch in Mary's voice—Teddy had heard that before, too many times. Mary's period must have started. Sympathy weighted Teddy. She knew better than to say anything. ''Any ideas?'' she prompted.

''I want to relandscape the yard,'' Mary began. ''Take out that pine tree before it falls down . . .''

Teddy glanced at Estelle, a tickle of guilt playing along her spine. She should be training her, giving her something to do besides just sitting there. But Estelle didn't seem to mind. She tore a piece of paper from the legal pad, folded it, tore it into a square.

''Sounds like a lot of work,'' Teddy said, eyeing Estelle. Estelle's hands folded and coaxed the paper into a crude bird. Teddy frowned. There was something familiar about the shape. She'd actually made one of those paper birds once. When?

The time Jon had insisted they experiment with origami. ''It'll help us realize our art in three dimensions,'' he'd said. Never mind that Teddy worked in ceramics. How three-dimensional could she get—

A *pajarita*. That's what the paper bird was called. A symbol of childhood in Spain and France. Teddy's gaze met Estelle's. Something in Estelle's eyes told her this *pajarita* wasn't for her.

It was for Mary.

SEVENTEEN

LATE MORNING SUN WASHED THE QUARRY WALLS WITH clear, liquid gold. Thin strands of red and pink highlighted the stone. *Like a woman's hair*, Mary thought, stepping back from the living-room window. Like Teddy's hair.

She paced behind the sofa, hugging herself to keep herself whole. She'd chatted blithely with Teddy about her summer projects, but all she really wanted to do was to curl up and hide. Hide from the world and its reflection of her expectations. Hide from Paul and his love for her and his desire for a family. Hide from her own treasonous body. "You're only thirty," everyone reminded her. Thirty. At this age her mother had had two daughters.

And at thirty-four, Mamá had watched one of those daughters disappear across the border.

Mary hunched her shoulders. Where was Mamá? And Rosie? The premonition, now four days old, still haunted her: *I'm coming, Maria. Look for me.*

Where, little sister? Where should I look?

Mary unfolded her arms, letting them dangle at her sides. The depression had hit harder this time, much harder. Usually she captured it by the third day of her period, caging the disappointment and anger into a tiny corner of her psyche. Until the blood flowed again.

She clasped the back of the sofa. To add to her mounting sense of loss, each period, each disappointment, conjured Mamá and Rosie. After all these years, her mother and sister had shed all reality and become ghosts. And like ghosts, they were drawn to death, even these monthly deaths.

She shouldn't have listened to her neighbor Nolan. She should have gone back to Mexico after Dad was murdered. But Nolan had urged caution. "Send a letter," he'd said. "You don't even know if your ma still lives there."

The letter had come back unopened two months later with "*No hay nadie con este nombre aquí*" scrawled in Mamá's handwriting. It lay on Nolan's kitchen table, waiting for her, when she'd gotten home from school. She circled the table, squeezing between a vinyl chair and the immaculate white counter, then slipped between another chair and a small black desk. Her thigh jostled the desk, shimmying the plastic stack trays that held bills and letters. She sank into the third chair and stared at the white envelope, stained yellow from passing through so many hands.

Nolan entered from the backyard. He sat in the chair nearest her. Mary continued to stare at the envelope. "I'm going down there to find her," she said.

"Mary, don't," Nolan said, pulling his chair closer to hers. "You got to think about why your ma did that. She must've had a good reason. Maybe she remarried and doesn't want the past to upset things. Maybe she just gave up on your dad. Just hurt too much to think about. Doesn't mean she doesn't love you. Just maybe it's easier for her to think of you and him as—" He winced. He'd put his foot in it, and he knew it. "I mean—"

"But she needs to know," Mary said. She looked up at him. "Rosie needs to know."

Nolan clucked his tongue and smoothed her hair with

his thick hand. "What do they need to know? That he won't be sending money anymore? Your ma just let us know she doesn't want anything to do with him. She's given up on him. Mary, listen to me. You got five more months of high school. You got good grades. You stay here, you can go to college like you always talked about."

Mary wiped her nose with the back of her hand. "Like I can afford it."

"You can afford it," Nolan said. "I'll take care of your room and board. You just get one of those scholarships and some kind of part-time job. We'll make it work. But Mary, you go to Mexico, you might not be able to get back into this country. You're illegal, Mary. You don't have papers. You could get stuck down there. And even illegal and all, you're not Mexican anymore. You're American. What're you gonna do down there?"

"But Mamá—"

"Your ma's made her decision," Nolan said. "Now you got to make yours . . ."

Mary released the sofa. Two damp handprints dimpled the green cushions. She picked up the quartz frog and set it on its back, then righted it and set it on its feet. She'd made her decision. Mamá had made hers. And now, if she could trust the vision, Rosie had made hers.

"I'll find you, little sister," Mary said. The words rang hollowly inside her. Dad had taken such comfort in talking to himself. It had never done much for her.

But then, she didn't have an imaginary friend named Eileen.

Mary chafed her arms with her hands. Funny that that was the one thing about Dad that still bothered her. Not his Irish past or his hand in the killings, not the vast reservoirs of secrecy he imposed on their lives or his refusal to speak Spanish. None of that prickled along her skin like his conversations with Eileen. Mary could still remember him stopping in midsentence while talking to

Mamá and answering some imagined question of Eileen's. Or his sitting alone in a room, confiding and laughing with an empty chair. In California, the conversations become more prayer-like. Dad's discussions with Eileen became wistful offhand remarks with no expectation of an answer. Lonely comments full of loss.

Over time, Mary developed a theory about Eileen. She had been a woman—a girl—that Dad had loved and been forced to leave behind in Ireland. Despite his love for Mamá, in moments of uncertainty or strain he turned to this Eileen, this memory of his purer self. The self without blood on its hands.

Mary squared her shoulders. She had too much time on *her* hands. She needed to immerse herself in one of her summer projects—work in the garden, rebuild Nolan's back steps, find someone to remove the dead pine tree. Maybe she should get a summer job. Too bad Paul had hired this Estelle. Working with Teddy would have been fun—

The phone rang. Mary went to the kitchen and slipped the cordless phone from its stand. Perching on the edge of the oak breakfast table, she gazed at the garden. The tomatoes looked a little wilted—

The phone rang again. She switched it on. "Hello?"

"Mary, Mary," Nolan said. Affection softened his gruff voice. "How's my girl?"

Mary smiled. "Good. How about you?"

"Slowing down, slowing down. How's the shrink?"

Mary rolled her eyes and tried not to laugh. "Paul's fine. You still saving next Thursday for me? We have a date to get some wood for those steps."

"Wouldn't miss it," Nolan said.

Mary slid from the table to her feet. Something in his voice . . . "Nolan, is something wrong? You sound a little . . . anxious."

"I had some visitors yesterday. Two fellas come by, Mexicans. Asking about you." Nolan paused. Mary imagined him pursing his lips into a tight, pink barnacle. "One of them," he said, "claims he's your Uncle Hector."

Mary sank into a chair. "Tío Hector? You're kidding, right? What would Tío Hector be doing here?"

"Picking strawberries, by the looks of his hands. And looking for you."

MARY SAT ON THE WHITE LOVESEAT BETWEEN THE APple tree and the rosebush, the cordless phone cradled in her hands. The sun baked down on her. The scent of hot, scorched cotton blended with the wine-citrus perfume of the last orange rose.

Looking up into the apple's twined branches, Mary thought of Paul. The day they moved into this house, he'd brought home two sticks, one thorny, one slender and leafless, and planted them four feet apart—in the center of the yard. "What are you doing?" Mary had said, circling the rose and the apple tree. "How am I supposed to landscape around this? They're right in the middle of everything!"

Paul smiled. "That's right," he said. He sat in the dirt between the two sticks and caught her hand. Pulling her down, he settled her into his lap, then sang her an old Malvina Reynolds' song, something about, if he loved her, he'd plant a rose and an apple tree. . . .

Mary touched the phone to her lips and smiled. Dad had always told her, "Mary, being Mexican *and* Irish, you need a man with a romantic streak as wide as a highway. Just be sure he's got more than a silver tongue." Dad would have been delighted. Too honest to be good at flattery, Paul excelled at the small, romantic gesture. And if the gesture turned out to be a little corny, well, that was Paul—and part of what she loved about him.

She'd left the rose and the apple tree where he planted them, letting the garden evolve around them. The tree and the bush now stood on an imaginary border between two worlds—herbs from Nolan's garden and vegetables on one side of the yard, flowers and ornamentals on the other. Sometimes she imagined herself as the rose and Paul as the apple tree. Sometimes she imagined herself as both, a blend of two cultures.

Today she imagined the plants straddling the border, afraid to cross. Tío Hector hadn't been afraid. And, if the vision was true, neither had Rosie. Unless—Mary lowered the phone and straightened. Unless the vision had been confused and it was Tío Hector she should be looking for.

Mary glanced at her watch. Four forty-six. The strawberry picking must be over for the day. Didn't those people start at some God-awful hour—five, six in the morning? Nolan promised to have Tío Hector call immediately. She glanced at her watch again.

Scuffing the ground with her sneakers, she stirred a small cloud of dust. This was Monday, Paul's late night. He'd be at the office till eight. She could meet Tío Hector here and the two of them could go to a café or something—

Guilt flashed through her. Why didn't she want Paul to meet her tío? Afraid he wouldn't understand? No, of course not. She just wanted Hector to herself at first, so she could find out why he was here, what news he had of Rosie and Mamá.

Be honest, Mary, she thought. Her skin started to prickle and itch. Having Hector to herself wasn't the real reason she hadn't told Paul. It was the panic that threatened to consume her whenever she tried to talk about her family. Dad had confided in Nolan, which made it possible for her to confide in Nolan; permission had been granted. She had told Paul a sketchy, stick-figure history of her past—including the story of the bombing and the men who had hunted Dad and murdered him—but only once, to the beat of her hammering heart. She and Dad had been so secretive and so careful for so long, it had been almost impossible to break silence. Whenever she tried, fear pounded in her ears, blocking all other sound. It menaced her: What if her stories reached the ears of those Irish thugs? What if those men or men like them came back to kill her—and Paul? What if her words inadvertently led the UDF to Mamá and Rosie?

Mary forced several deep breaths. Each came a little easier than the one before it. Chafing her right arm with her left hand, she smoothed away the last tingles. Calm touched her like a soprano touching a high note.

Wiping the sweat from the back of her neck, she took one last deep breath. There were other reasons she wasn't ready to tell Paul about Hector, she reassured herself. For one thing, she needed to sort out the wrongness of the premonition. She'd never had one that had been skewed before. Nor had she ever told Paul about them. Whenever she had a vision, she thought of telling him, but then said nothing. He'd think she was crazy. Or maybe that she was hearing voices. Like Dad.

The phone rang. She switched it on, then fumbled it to her ear. "Hello?"

"Hi, honey," Paul said. "It's me. Just thought I'd check up on my lady of leisure."

Mary forced the impatience from her voice. "Yeah? Well, I'm not the one who needs checking up on. How's the new woman working out? How are she and Teddy getting along?"

"Pretty good. They've divided the kingdom, which has been a little hard on Teddy. Estelle has claimed the computer, the typewriter, and the files, which leaves Teddy the phones and the clients." Paul dropped his voice. "It's a little weird, working with someone who can't talk."

Mary tugged at a rose leaf, rubbing it between thumb and forefinger. "How are the clients reacting to her?"

"Okay, I guess. Most of them are so glad to see

Teddy, they don't notice Estelle's silence."

"But you do."

Paul uttered a sheepish chuckle. "Can't help but. Sometimes, when I catch her watching me, I get the feeling that because she can't talk, she's a good listener. That somehow she hears or intuits things most people don't."

Mary released the leaf. Tío Hector would call back if he got a busy signal, wouldn't he? He wouldn't come all this way and give up. "That makes sense, doesn't it? If you can't talk . . ."

"Not necessarily," Paul said. "Even people who can't talk aren't always interested in what someone else has to say."

"True."

His chair scraped. "Listen, I've got a cancellation at six. I was wondering if I could coax you down here for a rushed, informal dinner at, say, Little Shanghai? Steamed buns, yu-shang eggplant, kung-pao scallops, whatever you want. I'll even call ahead."

Mary glanced at her watch. A minute after five. Tío Hector could call any time—

"I'm going to have to pass," she said. "I'm in the middle of something and I don't know if I can get it wrapped up by six. Rain check?"

"Rain check. I better go. Teddy's banging on the door. I love you."

Mary smiled. "I love you. See you when you get home."

"If you get everything wrapped up—"

"I know where to find you."

Mary switched off the phone and stood. Sweat drizzled between her breasts, bisecting her raspberry tank top. She went into the house and poured herself a glass of iced tea, then took the phone back outside.

•   •   •

MARY SET THE PHONE ON ITS BASE ON HER WAY through the kitchen. She looked at her watch. Six-ten. Maybe Tío Hector hadn't been able to stop by Nolan's. She fanned her tank top. A quick sponge bath, a fresh shirt, and she'd feel better. She passed through the living room to the tiled entry, then started climbing the stairs—

Voices mumbled outside the front door. Mary stood still, hand on the banister. The voices rose and fell to the tune of an argument. A word slipped through. *Aquí.*

Mary turned around and crept to the door.

»Knock again,« a man said in Spanish.

»She's not here,« a second man replied. »We'll come back tomorrow.«

Mary listened, straining to hear Tío Hector in either voice. One sounded so resolute, the other so weary. She placed her hand on the knob.

»Just once more,« the first man said. »You've come all the way from Tijuana to be intimidated by a house? Here, let's ring the bell—«

»What are you doing? Don't do that. What if it's not my Maria—?«

Mary opened the door. Two men in dusty jeans and caps stared at her, the older man ready to bolt. He removed his cap and squinted at her. One hand strayed to the collar of his blue shirt. He straightened the shirt, smoothed its front, fiddled with a button.

The other man—her age, maybe a little older— ducked his head and smiled. The ends of his mustache curved with his lips. ''Hello, señorita. We are looking for Mary Connelly?''

Mary looked past him to the older man. The high cheekbones, the wide set of his eyes . . . a bit of Mexico. Of Mamá.

Mary stepped onto the porch. »Tío Hector? Is it really you?«

»Yes,« he said. A tentative smile blossomed on his face. Creases spread like tears from the corners of his eyes. White streaked his black hair, lightened his mustache. *Has it been so long,* Mary thought, *or has it been so hard?*

She touched his elbow, then pulled him into a hug. His arms folded around her.

»I CAN GO,« ELISEO SAID FOR THE THIRD TIME.

Mary turned from the kitchen window. Tío Hector and his friend sat stiffly on the wooden chairs, each holding a glass of iced tea. Eliseo shifted, uncertainty oozing from him like sweat. »No, no,« Mary said. »Please. I just . . .«

She reached for her own glass of iced tea. The cold glass felt wrong. Hot tea, she needed a mug of hot tea. The warmth would soften the news, lessen its shock. Iced tea was such a crazy idea anyway. She needed something more welcoming for Tío Hector and his friend. She'd buy some horchata or some tamarindo. For next time . . .

»I wish I had waited to tell you,« Tío Hector said. His glass squeaked as he twisted it between his hands.

»I asked,« Mary said. »You would have had to tell me sooner or later.«

Tío Hector shrugged. He stared into his iced tea.

»They believe it was cancer?« Mary said.

Tío Hector looked up. »That's what they believe. It was quick. She didn't suffer long.«

Mary nodded. Mamá . . . dead. For two years. Numbness spread through her. Hot tea, that's what she needed. Something to keep her heart from freezing inside her. To keep her teeth from chattering so that she could ask the other questions.

She pushed herself to her feet and went to the stove. Lifting the copper kettle, she weighed it in her hand, then added a little water before setting it back on the burner. She turned on the flame.

Dead.

She's been dead for years, her mind whispered. *When she stopped writing to you. Move on, Mary . . .*

She took a deep breath, let it seep through her entire body. *Look for me.* She opened the drawer and pulled out a box of herbal tea. »And Rosie—Rosita. Where is she?«

»You haven't seen her?« Tío Hector said. »No, of course you haven't. She would have told you about your mamá.«

EIGHTEEN

ELISEO SLID INTO THE DRIVER'S SEAT OF THE CAMARO and inserted the key in the ignition. The car rumbled to life. »There's something you're not telling her about her sister,« he said, turning to Hector.

Hector looked out the passenger window at the grand, handsome houses that lined the street. Lawns spread like small parks in front of each, enhanced by flowers and an occasional tree. From here, he couldn't see into the back-yards, but from what he had seen of Maria's from her kitchen window, they were huge, large enough for a small orchard and garden. Maybe even room for a goat or a pig. A family of fourteen or fifteen could live com-fortably at Maria's and raise most of what they needed—

»What aren't you telling her?« Eliseo said.

Hector shook his head.

Eliseo sighed and pulled away from the curb. A green Accord passed them as they turned the corner. Hector swiveled, trying to catch a glimpse of the driver. »Do you suppose that was him?« he said. »The duck?«

»Perhaps. She invited you to wait and meet him.«

Hector grunted.

»She invited you to stay with her, too.« Eliseo glanced at him. »Her home is much nicer than Rigoberto's trailer.«

»If I decide to stay here, in California, I will need to make my own way,« Hector said.

»She is family—«

»She is North American.«

Eliseo said nothing. He guided the car onto Highway 1 and headed toward Watsonville. A silver BMW swerved to pass. The driver gestured rudely. »Go on, get a ticket,« Eliseo said. »Don't let me stop you.« He glanced again at Hector. »You don't want to stay with her because you are afraid you will tell her. About her sister.«

»Perhaps,« Hector said.

A hush filled Eliseo's voice. »Tell me about Rosa.«

»Rosa was a bright girl,« Hector said.

»Was?«

Hector's face grew warm. »Things change,« he said.

ELISEO STOPPED IN FRONT OF RIGOBERTO'S TRAILER. The Camaro vibrated in place. »I'll leave you here—«

A woman, Amalia, darted from between Rigoberto's trailer and Alejandro's. She stumbled to a stop, her shoulders slumping with disappointment. »It's not him,« she called over her shoulder. She glared at Eliseo and Hector, then walked back between the trailers, kicking at the wild tomatillos. A plump, leaf-enfolded globe fell from its stem.

Hector got out of the car. Eliseo switched off the engine, then hurried around the Camaro to join him. They followed Amalia to the pitted yard behind the circle of rusted trailers.

Hector skirted the lush plots of vegetables and chiles. A small child stood beside a tomato plant, clutching its leaves like a mother's hand and staring at the crowd gathered around Nelda's tiny house. Everyone was there—the men who lived in Rigoberto's trailer, the families from the other trailers, the neighbors from down the street. One of the women held Nelda, rocking and murmuring to her. The comfort seemed lost on the old woman—Nelda looked ready to take a swing at someone, if she could only figure out who. She glared from face to face, but everyone either met her gaze or gaped at something in front of her house.

Eliseo pushed past Hector. »What is it, *vieja*?« he said to Nelda. »What has happened?«

Nelda's scowl deepened. »The goat! Someone has killed my goat! But the bastard didn't want to eat her, poor little thing. No! The bastard left her body to rot in her little pen!«

Hector made his way to the pen, jostling people out of the way. The little goat slumped against the wall of Nelda's house, its head flopped to one side, its tongue hanging out. The little beast looked brittle.

»Now what am I going to do?« Nelda said. »There will be no milk for the grandchildren. No cheese. If I find the bastard who did this, I will fry his balls!«

Hector knelt beside the pen. Blood caked the goat's neck.

»What?« said Rigoberto's cousin Fermin. »Will you fry the balls of the *chupacabra*?«

Nelda spat. »This is California! There are no *chupacabras* here.«

Several of the men exchanged glances. Hector reached over the worn pickets of the enclosure and touched the goat. It was cold and much stiffer than it looked.

»This isn't the first goat to die like this,« Rigoberto said.

»Gangs,« said one man, one of the neighbors. »They are just trying to prove themselves. At least they aren't shooting each other. Or the children.«

»They might as well have,« Nelda said, shaking herself free of the comforting woman. »Without the milk and the cheese, the children will starve.«

»Ay, Nelda,« Rigoberto said, draping an arm around

the old woman's shoulders. »The children won't starve. We will all make sure of that.«

Nelda knocked his arm away. Muttering, she stamped into her house and slammed the door. The flimsy walls shook.

»We should butcher it,« Hector said, lifting the carcass out of the enclosure. »See if we can salvage anything.«

Rigoberto snatched the goat away. »I'll do it.«

Someone handed him a knife. Hector crossed himself and withdrew from the crowd. A girl with short, curled hair and a swollen belly stepped up to him and lay a hand on his elbow. She rested her other hand on her growing child. Hector looked down into her face, the face of a child, really, younger than Rosa. »It was not the *chupacabra*,« the girl said in a low voice.

Hector raised his eyebrows. »No?«

The girl shook her head. »I saw a woman approach the pen an hour before the goat was found dead. I tried to speak to her, find out what she wanted, but she ignored me.«

The girl leaned closer to Hector. »I think she did it,« she whispered.

NINETEEN

SUN GLAZED THE MORNING WITH CLEAR, YELLOW LIGHT. Not a scrap of fog clouded the day's vivid colors. Teddy tilted her face to the sun. It would be a little cooler this afternoon. She pulled her front door shut and tested the lock. A twinge sparked from wrist to elbow. Loosening the straps on the brace, she walked down the driveway past her car. One of the neighbor kids had written "Wash Me" in the dust on the Civic's back window. "I wish," Teddy said.

She stepped out into the street, then jumped back as two boys on bicycles shot past. A breeze followed them, riffling their black hair and wafting over Teddy in a warm gust. She leaned forward, looking both ways—in case the boys turned around and came back—then ventured into the street again.

"Hey, Teddy!" Rita called from her perch atop the ladder now planted between the side of the house and the garage. "You going to work again?"

"Yep," Teddy said. She stopped to admire her neighbor's work. From where she stood, the house was wholly apricot, except along the side across from the garage. There the apricot dribbled over the celadon like a second coat of thick glaze. "Looking good, Rita."

Rita set her brush on the paint tray. Wiping her hands on her jeans, she climbed down and met Teddy at the end of the driveway. Apricot highlighted one cheek and speckled her glasses. Teddy wondered how she could see. "It's coming along," Rita said. "I'm slow, but I'm good. I drafted Claudia, across the street, but she hasn't shown up yet."

Teddy nodded, surprised by a sudden wistfulness. She couldn't possibly miss watching Rita paint her house—could she? But somewhere inside she did—just as she missed hearing the three ice cream trucks creep past every day, the first playing "Pop Goes the Weasel," the second playing Scott Joplin's "Entertainer," and the third playing one jarring note, like a phonograph needle hitting a scratch in a record. And she missed the men pushing the refrigerated white carts, ringing their bells in time to their heavy footsteps. "What do they sell?" she'd asked Rita once.

"*Helados* and *paletas*," Rita had said. "Ice cream and fruit ices." She lowered her voice, glancing sideways at the ice cream vendor in question. "I worry about where the water for the ice comes from . . ."

Teddy chuckled to herself. She squinted at Rita's house. "Claudia will be here soon. She's probably giving her Chihuahua his daily dose of testosterone."

Rita nodded, her gray curls bobbing. "Yeah. That little scrotum with legs. Guess he makes her feel safe. Hey, d'you hear about the goat?"

"The goat?" Teddy asked.

Rita pointed to her house with the paintbrush. "Woman living across the gully, where those trailers are? Her goat was found dead, drained of blood. I'd bet you anything it was a *chupacabra*."

Teddy frowned. "*Chupabraca*?"

"*Chupacabra*." Rita nodded. "I wondered when one of those things'd get up here."

"What's a *chupa*—?"

A burst of ferocious, miniature barks shrilled toward them, punctuated by the click of claws on asphalt.

"Knock it off, Butch," an exasperated voice said. "You don't calm down, I'll have 'em cut off. Then where will you be?"

"There's Claudia," Rita said. She pushed her glasses higher along her nose. "Hey, Claudia! It's about time. You said you'd be here at quarter to eight. Hey, d'you hear about the goat?"

Teddy straightened. "Is it that late? I've got to run—"

She waved at Claudia and Rita, then hurried to catch the bus. As she neared the corner, she faltered. A woman sat in a chair at the end of the street, facing the strawberry fields.

Teddy slowed. It looked like the same woman—the same red cap with its attached kerchief, the same white blouse, the same jeans. But this chair was not a wheelchair. It looked like a kitchen chair, an old vinyl one from the early sixties, its frame made from metal tubing. The tufts of grass rippling around its legs made it hard to tell.

But the woman looked the same. Except—a little straighter, a little stronger. Her head still drooped, but she reminded Teddy less of a turtle and more of a heron, neck arched in watchful anticipation. Ready to strike—

Teddy took two shuffling steps, then turned down the cross street and hurried toward the bus stop. She looked away from the woman, but her gaze drifted back. The woman lifted her head, slowly, with the deliberate grace of a heron, and turned to face Teddy. Teddy's heart pounded. Any second the woman would raise her arms, two enormous blue-gray wings, and lift herself from the chair in two powerful flaps—

The woman's gaze sought Teddy's. Teddy ran.

TEDDY HUNCHED FORWARD SLIGHTLY, HER HANDS caught between her knees, and swiveled from side to side on her desk chair. Beside her, Estelle clicked along the computer keyboard, stopping every now and then to frown at the screen. Teddy swiveled in a complete circle and wished someone—anyone—would call. Even a solicitor. Or maybe someone would walk in. Those kids who sold framed pictures hadn't been in for weeks. They were about due.

On the radio, Richard Thompson apologized. "I misunderstood," he sang.

Teddy planted her feet, stopping the chair. She reached for the pint-sized yogurt container on the desk and cradled it in her hands. Its slight weight comforted her, gave her a small flicker of satisfaction. She eased it open, carefully, slowly, shoulders rising in anticipation of pain. None. Setting the lid on the counter, she stared into the container's murky, rust-colored contents.

Self-conscious, Teddy glanced at Estelle. Estelle was focused on the computer screen, her fingers racing along the keyboard. Teddy smiled, then brought the plastic cup to her nose and inhaled.

The slip's rich, moldy scent buoyed her. If she closed her eyes, she could almost believe she was in the studio. If she closed her eyes, she could forget the splints and bandages, her appointment with the specialist at lunch time, the pain pulsing from elbow to palm. She lowered the container and dipped her fingers in the liquid clay. The slip coated her fingertips. Such a thin layer; it began to dry to a gritty film, taking the moisture in her skin with it. Teddy recapped the yogurt container and set it by the phone. She waited till the slip dried completely, then chafed it off with a tissue.

She looked again at Estelle. Estelle leaned toward the screen, fingers racing. Teddy cocked her head and wondered who Estelle was—what her passion was, what she did when she wasn't at work. She wasn't one of those women who lived to shop. She wore the same short-sleeved black dress she'd worn yesterday, the clingy rayon sculpted to her full figure, its scooped neck showcasing the scar at her throat. Something about the dress suggested mourning. Or perhaps something about the way Estelle wore it—unadorned, plain, in stark contrast to her carefully applied makeup.

Estelle frowned and stopped typing. She pressed her glossed lips together, studying the screen. Jabbing the delete key, she wiped out two sentences, took a deep breath, then closed her eyes. She held her hands before her, fingers spread, lips moving. In silent prayer, Teddy thought, but as if praying to her hands. She opened her eyes and began typing.

"You've never used a computer before," Teddy said.

Estelle tensed, then turned to Teddy. Her eyes held . . . not fear, but foreboding. Caution.

Teddy scooted her chair closer. "Your typing is incredible. That's the hardest part. Knowing how to type."

Estelle's eyes narrowed.

Teddy shrugged. "The rest is just icing."

Estelle blinked.

"Icing," Teddy said. "On the cake. It's nice, but it's kind of . . . extra."

Estelle smiled. She saved the document and closed it, then opened a new file. Somehow she'd learned that much. In the new file, she wrote, "I like icing."

Teddy grinned. "Me, too."

"But let's practice on the plake instead of the cake," Estelle typed.

"Wait!" Teddy blocked the keyboard with a braced arm. "This is perfect. Instead of using the delete key and getting rid of everything, hold down the control button, the one with the apple on it. Move it to the 'k' in 'plake.' Now type a 't' over the 'k' . . ."

TEDDY SLOWED TO A STOP A HALF BLOCK FROM HER office. Jon stopped beside her. They'd said nothing since they left the doctor's office ten minutes ago. Once Teddy uttered the word "surgery," their silence had become as complete as Estelle's.

Teddy stared at the parking lot across the street, at the gingkos, liquid amber and pistache trees, planted in straight lines between the rows of parking spaces. The tree limbs created arbors of green leaves and sun. Across the lot, heat shimmered along the walls of Logos, the used-book store, and Frog Fitness. A woman in a business suit hurried out of Frog Fitness and crossed the lot, her left arm weighted by a heavy briefcase, her right by a workout bag. She stepped from the curb just as a man in a jester's cap rode by on a bicycle. With a haunting peacock's cry, the cyclist pulled on the handlebars, swerving around the entrepreneur. Another woman, arms overflowing with packages, slowed her pace while struggling to light a cigar. "Those'll kill you," the cyclist said before pedaling away.

The smoker bent her arm in an obscene salute.

"All God's creatures got arms," Teddy said.

"And so do you," Jon said.

The braces throbbed around Teddy's encased wrists. She looked up at Jon, startled anew by his latest haircut. His hair, which usually sprouted in kinky tendrils, had been cut close to the scalp, a soft lawn of tiny black and gray curls. She met his clear black eyes, his kabuki eyebrows arched even higher—a sign that he was concerned about her.

"Yeah, I've got 'em," she said, holding out her braced arms. "But they don't work."

Jon rubbed the side of his nose. The scar on his elbow shone white against his dark skin. "They will after the surgery."

Yours don't, Teddy thought. *Not very well.*

She started walking again. "But if the surgery doesn't work," she said. "What am I going to do? Everything I enjoy takes arms—my art, my music, cycling, swimming, cooking, reading—"

"You learn to modify the things you do," Jon said. Resignation colored his voice. "You learn to give things up."

Teddy hesitated. *Just say it, Teddy*, she chastised herself. *You and Jon didn't become close friends by pussyfooting around each other.* "I can't give them up," she said. "Those things are who I am. And I can't modify the most important ones. No one throws pots or does hand-building with their feet. Or plays banjo with their toes."

Jon smiled, stopping in front of the office. "Come *on*, Teddy," he said. "The banjo? Who'd *want* to play it?"

A grin quirked the corner of Teddy's mouth. "You *can* play jazz on a banjo. Bela Fleck does."

"Ah, Bela!" Jon nodded "How could I forget! But can he play classical?"

Teddy laid a braced hand on Jon's arm. "Thanks for going with me."

The fierce protectiveness in Jon's eyes betrayed his flip tone of voice. "I'm going to let you go alone, to hear the single most dreaded piece of news in your life? Think again."

Teddy hugged him, squeezing only with her upper arms. "Thanks."

"Call me when you get off work," he said. "We'll go to dinner."

"I'd love a home-cooked meal," Teddy hinted. "Something wonderful, like your famous shepherd's pie . . ."

Jon winked. "Flattery will get you everywhere. Call me."

Teddy hurried up the office steps. Pushing the door open, she went inside. Gina Ontello, Paul's three o'clock, leaned over the built-in desk, watching Estelle. "And that's me?" Gina said. "You really think?"

Estelle nodded. She held up a folded Post-It note and handed it to Gina.

Gina stared at the paper turtle on her palm. Sucking her lower lip, she contemplated the stubby paper legs and the little head just peeking from the creased shell. Slowly she nodded. "It's true. When people get too close . . ." She raised her head. "What do I want to be—what *will* I be? Show me that."

Estelle's lips parted slightly. She studied Gina, then reached for another Post-It.

Teddy drew closer. Estelle's fingers pulled and prodded the piece of paper, releasing the folds that stuck together with the weak glue. Within minutes she held up a tiny monkey.

Teddy winced. Gina—proper, reserved Gina—would hardly see herself as a monkey, present or future.

Gina plucked the monkey from Estelle's hand. And laughed. "Perfect!" she said, then started. "Oh, Teddy! Hi! Look what Estelle made for me!"

Teddy smiled. "They're wonderful—"

"Gina?" Paul said, venturing into the reception area.

Gina beamed at Paul. "Ready!" she said, walking past him into his office.

He raised his eyebrows, amused and surprised. He followed her. Stopping in the doorway, he turned to Teddy. "Teddy," he said. "How'd it go? With the specialist?"

Teddy nudged the plastic business card holder with her fingers. Estelle urged something into her hand. Teddy glanced at Paul, then away. "He wants—he says I need surgery."

A cough followed Paul's sharp intake of breath. "That cancellation at four . . . if you need to talk . . ."

Teddy forced a smile and looked up. "Thanks."

Paul backed into his office.

Teddy waited till the door shut, then walked around the desk and sat down. She opened her hand. A penguin nested on her palm, caught between the brace and her fingers. Its stubby, useless wings dangled at its sides. A hard knot formed in Teddy's chest. Eyes narrowed, she jerked to look at Estelle.

Estelle watched her, that same cool distance in her brown eyes, but also a wavering haze of concern. Estelle touched her fingers. A voice whispered through Teddy's mind: *It doesn't have to be this way*.

Teddy swallowed, shrinking from Estelle's touch. As Teddy's hand withdrew, Estelle collected the penguin. She unfolded it, smoothed the paper across the desk, then refolded it. When she finished, she set her new creation in Teddy's hand.

Warmth tingled through Teddy's arms. She took a deep breath, expecting to smell the sharp menthol of the salves her mother used to apply to her tired, childish muscles. The office smelled of the usual honeysuckle room freshener and dust.

Teddy looked at her hand. The penguin had been transformed into a spider: weaver, creator, artist.

TWENTY

PAUL FINISHED TAKING NOTES ON GINA, THEN STOOD, setting his pen next to the Gripmaster. Mary had given him the palm-sized device to strengthen and condition his hands. He used it as a paperweight—to Mary's dismay. "Use it right," she'd told him when she found out. "I don't want you potholing because you don't have enough hand strength."

He'd fought to keep a straight face. "Cratering."

Mary had glared at him, that crooked smile tipping to the right. "Craters, potholes. Whatever rock climbers do when they hit the ground. I don't want *you* doing it . . ."

Paul nudged the Gripmaster with a finger and smiled. Picking up his notes, he strode across the office, skirting the square of blue armchairs. He opened the door to the waiting room.

Teddy stood beside Estelle, pointing to something on the computer screen. Estelle frowned in concentration, pecked at the keyboard, then broke into a smile.

"It'll make things a lot easier," Teddy said.

Paul leaned against the door frame. Teddy and Estelle seemed to get along. He'd been worried about that, not just for Teddy's sake, but for the clients. He hoped that in his office, waiting room included, he'd created a safe place, a place where people could relax and rest on the ropes for a while. Two warring factions at the desk would undermine that. "Tension spreads like poison gas," Mary said once. "And it's easier to breathe in."

Paul pushed himself upright. "Teddy?"

She turned. Her eyes held all of her desperation. "Just a minute," she said. She pointed to the screen again. "Put the cursor here. Now, do a command V. Perfect."

Teddy's hand skimmed Estelle's shoulder in passing. "I need to talk to Paul for a few minutes. The answering machine can take any calls. If it's urgent, hit the intercom button and tap a pencil against the receiver or something."

Teddy's composure crumbled as soon as Paul shut the door to his office. Her desperation seemed to overflow, weeping over her face. Paul led her to the chairs. "Teddy—"

"Both arms, Paul," she said. She sank into the chair nearest the desk. "Both wrists and maybe both elbows. He thinks I might have cupital tunnel, too." Teddy pointed to her right arm. "It's like carpal tunnel except it's in the elbow."

Paul sat in the chair next to her, knee to knee. He took her fingers gently. "Will this fix everything?" he said.

"He says it will."

"You don't believe him."

Teddy shook her head.

"You're afraid," Paul said softly.

Teddy withdrew her hands. "Look at Jon. After all these same surgeries, he still has days when he can't paint a stroke."

"Worst case scenario?" Paul said.

Teddy gazed at the framed Kandinsky poster—"Blue Mountain, No. 84"—on the opposite wall. Teddy disliked Kandinsky—for the most part—but liked this one. "Why this one?" Paul had asked. "I think it's the colors," she'd said. "They're not as melted or smeared.

Everything is more recognizable—there are trees, horses and riders, a mountain . . .''

Paul wondered what else her mind found in the print today. Her life stampeding out of her control? Scars and shattered nerves?

"Worst case scenario," Teddy said, examining her nails. "I end up like Jon. Worse. A paintbrush isn't that heavy. Five to ten pounds of clay are. And a banjo . . .''

"Teddy, it sounds like—''

She made a face. "I know, I know. I'm feeling sorry for myself. People lose their arms and they go on. They figure out new ways to do things—like that woman, Joni something, who held the paintbrush in her mouth. And that Irish guy who wrote novels with his feet. But people can't play banjo with their mouths and they can't throw pots with their feet.''

Stung, Paul stared into his own cupped hands. Why did everyone assume that because he was a psychiatrist, he was going to tell them how to feel?

He uncupped his hands. *Teddy. Focus on Teddy.* "That's not what I was going to say. I just—you're facing the loss of your dreams. Possibly. I mean, maybe the doctor's right this time. But if he's not, then you'll have to cross the border into a very different world than the one you're used to. And that hurts. A lot.'' He shook his head. "I wouldn't just be hurt, I'd be angry. I'd be ready to tear the universe apart with my bare hands—''

Teddy looked at him, a slight curve to her lips.

"Well," he said, "all right. With my bare feet—''

She laughed. Guilty pleasure warmed Paul. *Right,* he chastised himself. *Make her laugh. Get her—and you—safely away from the pain. Idiot.*

"You can't get to mouth painting without going through grief," he said.

Teddy's smile faded into a thoughtful twilight. "I keep telling myself I haven't lost my arms till the bandages come off and the doctor says, 'We tried.' But it's hard. I can't *do* anything. Paul, everything I enjoy, every dream I have depends on my arms. My art, my music, even working here. You can't pay for both me and Estelle forever, even if we do make a whole receptionist.''

''There's your show—''

Teddy stared at him. ''Paul, I don't have enough pieces. I can't even finish the ones I've started.''

He took her hands again. ''Take the ones here at the office—''

The intercom hummed. The click of plastic on plastic filled the room.

Teddy pulled away. She stood, hunching her shoulder to dry her eyes. ''Phone. You better take it.''

Paul went to the desk and hit the speaker button. ''Estelle? Is the person still on the line?''

Teddy slipped out of the room.

Plastic tapped plastic twice. Paul frowned. Was that a yes? ''Go ahead and put the call through,'' he said, hoping he'd guessed right.

The phone clicked. ''Hello?'' he said.

''Hi, it's me,'' Mary said.

Paul picked up the phone and turned off the speaker. ''Hi, you. What's up?''

''I have to run an errand this afternoon. I won't be back till late.''

''How late?''

''Later than you.''

Paul shifted the phone to his other ear. ''I'll wait dinner—''

''Don't.''

''Where are you—?''

''I'm glad you warned me about Estelle,'' Mary said quickly. ''I was just about done with my message when the answering machine shut off and I heard someone tapping on the receiver. When do I get to meet her?''

A sudden click punctuated Mary's question.

''Mary?''

"Paul?" A frown colored her voice. "When did you get Call Waiting?"

"I didn't." Paul carried the phone to the door and peeked at the reception desk. Estelle squinted at the computer, then typed in a rapid flurry. Teddy, still shaken, stepped from the bathroom, a crumpled tissue caught between brace and fingers. "Probably static," he said. "So when do you think you'll be home—?"

"I'll see you tonight," she said. "Love you."

Paul had just enough time to say, "Love you, too," before Mary hung up.

Estelle glanced up from the screen and met his gaze. She averted her eyes.

Paul pressed the off button on the phone. Estelle's eavesdropping annoyed him, but it didn't worry him the way Mary's evasiveness did. She'd never been evasive with him before—not like this. Sure, she'd been fairly cagey that time she'd planned a surprise party for his thirtieth birthday, but that had been more playful. This was exclusive. *I don't want you in this part of my life,* her brusqueness implied. *You can't share this.*

Paul shut the door, then went to the desk and returned the phone to its base. He was probably projecting. Maybe she wanted to go to that support group for infertile women again and didn't want him to know. She'd done that once before. Teddy's weren't the only dreams threatening to shatter.

A deep loneliness seeped through Paul. Since that first volleyball game, he and Mary had always been a team. They shared everything—every dream, every excitement and disappointment, all the little stories they collected through the day, except for Paul's client confidences. They dabbled in each other's passions: He worked with her in the garden in the spring and summer, she went to the climbing gym once in a while and even went bouldering with him sometimes. He'd married a companion, a friend. And now, with this slow pulling away, being close to her was sometimes reachy.

How long had he felt that way? He tried to pinpoint it. The infertility meeting had been the first time she'd done anything without telling him about it. Although she *had* told him about it, two days later. "It made me feel weak," she'd explained. "Needing to depend on other people, especially people I don't even know. I felt like I was betraying *us* by needing someone else."

He'd pulled her close, stroking the top of her head with his chin. "Hey, those women know exactly what you're going through. You didn't betray us. Think about it—life's like climbing. Sometimes you need someone to belay you so you don't hurt yourself when you fall. When you do, you want people who know what they're doing."

"Ah," she'd said. "So I needed a roomful of Mosses. There's a thought . . ."

A good thought. Paul picked up the phone. He needed something physical, something to take him out of himself. He glanced at his watch. Twenty minutes before his last client, Oscar, arrived. He punched in Moss's work number.

"Law offices," Moss said.

Paul snorted. "What are *you* doing answering the phones?"

"Bad day. My receptionist broke her arm rollerblading on her lunch hour."

Arms again. What was it about arms? "She okay?" Paul asked.

"Yeah. But I need to scare up a temp for a few weeks. So, what's on your mind?"

Paul sat on his desk. "I need to climb. You want to meet me at the Edge at six?"

PAUL SAT IN ONE OF THE BLUE ARMCHAIRS, LISTENING. Oscar's footsteps thumped across the waiting room, followed by the creak and slam of the front door. Silence settled over everything like fine chalk. Paul pulled himself to his feet and walked into the empty waiting room.

Oscar's session had gone over by a good fifteen minutes; it was well after five. Paul basked in the splendid stillness. The magazines on the coffee table lay in neat, staggered rows, the rice paper shades had been drawn against the late afternoon sun. In the reception area, Teddy's and Estelle's chairs faced away from the desk so that their owners could slip into them easily. Teddy's sweater still draped her chair's shoulders. Nothing personal remained of Estelle.

Paul sat in Estelle's chair. He breathed in the quiet, trying to release Oscar. It had been an incredible session. Everything had gone along in the same rut he and Oscar had established. Oscar talked about his wife, his kids, the problems he had communicating with them, retracing familiar territory, as if going over the same pitches again and again would somehow help him redpoint the next session—as if psychoanalysis was an ascent to be scaled without falling. Then suddenly, at ten to five, Oscar took a different route. And, instead of exploring the old surfaces and handholds, he began exploring issues and ideas he had never brought up before. No way was Paul going to end the session just when it had truly begun. Especially since Oscar was his last client for the day— and since some of Oscar's newly revealed issues exposed his neglected feminine side.

Paul swiveled the chair and pulled at the filing cabinet drawer. Just a few notes on Oscar, then he'd meet Moss at the gym. Good thing he'd thrown his gear in the trunk this morning.

He plucked Oscar's file from the drawer. Flipping open the cover, he stopped. Estelle—it had to be Estelle—had clipped a paper butterfly to the inside cover. Glossy flowers, lace, and printed words spotted the folded butterfly's wings. Paul unfolded the paper, just enough to recognize a magazine ad for perfume, then quickly refolded it. He'd never figure out how to recreate the insect once he'd taken it apart.

He stared at the butterfly for several minutes, then set the file on his lap. He browsed through the rest of the files. Clients who had been in since Estelle started working here each had some sort of animal or figure paperclipped inside the front cover of their file. A monkey for Gina, an eagle for Jeremy, a possum for Hilde—each wonderfully appropriate, each revealing some personal, secret goal of the client's.

Paul drummed his fingers on the desk. Estelle's insight amazed him. What, he wondered, would she make for Mary?

What would she make for him?

PAUL WALKED DOWN THE STEPS OF THE PACIFIC EDGE. Housed in a former cannery, the climbing gym hunched near the railroad tracks. Its exterior resembled a box— a box with a wooden porch. Inside, three of the building's walls sloped into inclines and overhangs. Two "boulders" sat in the middle of the climbing area; a plastic owl perched on top of the larger one. Pinchers, slopers, and pockets pimpled every climbing surface, each handhold sporting a small colored flag. *Like party favors*, he'd thought on his first visit. And what a party!

At the bottom of the stairs, Paul stopped to look for Moss, who had preceded him out of the gym. Moss stood on the dusty lunarscape surrounding the tracks, his hair luminous in the evening light. The scent of salt, kelp, and diesel wafted from the yacht harbor less than a block away. Moss inhaled, his chest swelling. "Can you believe it?" he said, turning to Paul. "It's after eight and it's still light out."

Paul clapped his friend on the shoulder. "It's summer, Moss," he said. "Come on. Let's get a bite to eat."

They followed the tracks to Seabright, waited at the

corner for the light. "So, you talk to Mary?" Moss said.

"Left a message. She's not home yet."

Moss nodded. The light turned green. They crossed the street and headed for the brew pub. The aroma of malt and hops overpowered the breath of the sea. Moss made a beeline for the brewery's open door. He sank into the booth near the busing station. Paul sat across from him, the TV flickering as if desperate for his attention. He ignored it.

After they ordered, Moss leaned across the table, steepling his hands. "What's wrong?"

Paul played with his fork. "Nothing's wrong."

Moss tilted his head. "Oh? So why'd you bodge that pincher? And don't give me that reachy crap. A kid could've fired that. If I hadn't been there to belay you, you'd have cratered for sure."

Paul snorted. "If you hadn't been there to belay me, they wouldn't have let me climb."

Moss pretended to consider this. "Good point. So what's wrong? Is it the kid thing again?"

"I don't know." Paul stabbed his napkin with his fork. "Partly, I guess. I mean, all our lives, we're taught to believe that there are certain things we'll always be able to have if we want them—health, someone to marry, a baby. And when we don't get to have one of them . . ." The napkin shredded under the fork's tines.

Moss sat back. "Tell me about it. Do you see a Ms. Moss?"

"Maybe if you changed your name," Paul said.

The waitress set two oatmeal stouts between them. "Your salads will be ready in a minute."

"Great, thanks," Paul said. "Wait! Can I have another napkin?"

The waitress looked at the lacerated paper at his elbow. "Only if you promise not to hurt this one," she said as she walked away.

Moss took a sip of the stout. Foam dripped from his

mustache. "Why do you want kids? What will you be missing if it doesn't happen?"

Paul pressed his lips together. Why did he want children? "To—I don't know. To create new life. To give something back to the world instead of only taking. Children are the future. They're hope. And because I love Mary and I want to know there will always be a part of her in the world."

Moss made a gathering motion with his right hand, gesturing, *And . . . ?*

"And—I don't know," Paul said. "Selfish reasons. Having kids is kind of like being reborn. People seem to recapture their own childhood through their children. And to have someone to teach. You know, how to be a good person, how to make stuff, how to climb—"

"You can teach Mary," Moss said.

Paul gave him a dirty look.

"Hey, I'm serious. Teach her more about climbing." Moss took another sip of stout. "Have you guys talked about adoption? Like I said, worked for my sister."

"I thought you said acupuncture."

"Yeah, that, too."

Paul shredded the napkin further. "Mary doesn't want to adopt. She's afraid we'll get a drug baby."

Moss took another sip, then sucked the foam from his mustache. "What about one of those Chinese babies? Didn't you say Mary kind of wanted a girl?"

Paul set the fork down. "Mary's a little wary about that one, too. She's worried about the ethnic stuff."

With good reason, Paul thought. After her father brought her here, he'd forced her to sever all ties with Mexico, afraid the UDF would find them. "You're not to speak a word of Spanish," he'd told her, "except in Spanish class. And I don't want you hanging out with the Mexican kids."

After they'd been in Watsonville for a year, Mary learned how to get around his proscription. "Half the school is Mexican-American," she insisted. "It'll look weird if I don't have any Mexican friends." Her father relented, but raided her closet and cosmetic case periodically, tossing out anything he deemed "too Hispanic." Since the same fear of discovery prevented him from teaching her about her Irish heritage, she'd had nothing to fill the vacuum left by Mexico. . . .

"Ethnic stuff," Moss mused. "You could learn about China and teach the kid about her background."

"Hmm?" Paul said. "Oh. Yeah, we could do that." He lifted his arms from the table. The waitress rewarded him with a huge salad all but hidden under a slab of grilled fish. "But it's not the same as being raised in China."

The waitress set an inch-thick stack of napkins next to Paul. "Can I get you anything else?" she asked.

"Glass of water," Moss said. "Two."

She nodded and disappeared.

Moss hacked at his fish, reducing the filet to lumps. "Hey, there are a lot of Chinese-Americans out there who have never even been to China. Lot of Anglo-Americans who've never been to England."

Paul unfolded two napkins onto his lap. "That's what I said. I think it'd be harder to explain why she was rejected by an entire country because she was a girl."

Moss popped a bite of lettuce and Gorgonzola into his mouth. "I guess you'll have to keep trying. All that sex." He shook his head. "Life's tough."

Paul stabbed at a walnut. "It *is* tough. Because that's all it is now—sex. There's no lovemaking anymore. No tenderness or playing. Just, 'Gosh, honey, I might be fertile. We better do it.' " He lowered his fork, the walnut untasted. "I miss the love part. I miss Mary."

"Ah," Moss said, nodding. "*Now* we're getting to the crux."

Paul pried the walnut off of his fork. "Yeah. I guess so."

"So what's wrong?"

"Maybe nothing," Paul said. He speared a mandarin orange slice. "There's just this distance between us. At first I thought she was just depressed, you know, 'cause we've been trying so hard. But it's more than that. Lately she's been evasive and vague. She keeps trying to redirect my attention. She called to tell me she was going out tonight, but she refused to tell me where."

Moss munched on another mouthful of fish, Gorgonzola, and lettuce. "Sounds like she's hiding something."

Paul popped the orange in his mouth. "Yeah."

"Or someone," Moss said.

TWENTY-ONE

MARIA UNLOCKED THE CAMRY'S PASSENGER-SIDE doors, then went around to the driver's side. If the rusted trailers and staring farmworkers bothered her, she never showed it. Hector waved Rigoberto and the other men away. Rigoberto ignored him, his gaze traveling from Maria's bare legs and baggy shorts to her rounded breasts. When his gaze reached her chin, it dropped and traveled the length of her again. Hector hissed between his teeth. Rigoberto looked at him, reluctantly. Hector waved him away. Rigoberto leered at Maria one last time, then punched the shoulder of the man nearest him. The small group of men turned away.

Eliseo climbed into the back seat, reaching for the seat belt as he sat. Hector hesitated, running a hand over the plush upholstery. The fabric grazed his palm with the soft bristle of new carpet.

Maria swung herself into the front seat and reached for her seat belt. She leaned to the right to look at him. »Tío Hector?«

Hector jerked his hand away. He stroked the thigh of his pants, the denim coating his hand with dust. »I'm covered with half a field of dirt—«

Maria patted the passenger seat. »If it'll come off you, it'll come off the seat. I'm not worried, Tío.«

Hector brushed at his pants, then sank onto the seat.

The car smelled of sun-warmed raspberries. »This is very nice,« he said, stroking the dashboard.

Maria smiled. »Thank you. Now, where do we begin?«

Eliseo leaned forward between the front seats. »We talked to your friend, to Nolan. He said that no one has come looking for you—except us. When Hector described your sister, he said he would have remembered someone like that.«

Maria flinched, but only in her eyes. »Describe her to me,« she said.

Hector stroked his mustache. »She looks like your mamá.«

Maria's cheeks hollowed. »Describe her. For me. Please.«

Hector lowered his hand to his lap. »She has skin the color of rich caramel,« he said. »And eyes the color of chocolate. Large eyes. Sometimes, when she looks at you, she sees no one else. But other times her gaze drifts a little, dreams a little, as if she is listening to angels.«

Maria started. »Does she—does she talk to herself?«

Hector nodded. »Like your papá.«

»What else?« Maria asked.

»She has a mouth like an unfolding rose, soft and full. And cheekbones like wings. She had your mamá's roundness . . .« Hector inhaled the last word. *Especially since she became pregnant.*

Maria gazed out the front windshield, one hand gripping the steering wheel. Hector shifted in the seat, scuffing the heels of his shoes along the floor mat. He imagined Rosa as he last saw her, that gentle neck ruptured at the throat, those large eyes cool. And threatening.

Maria cleared her throat and started the car. »Where shall we begin?« she said. »Where did you go first when you arrived?«

»To Rigoberto,« Hector said. »I knew him from Nuñez.«

»Nuñez.« Maria bit the side of her lower lip. »And you, Eliseo. Did you know anyone when you came here?«

»A few people,« he said.

The car idled. Rigoberto peeked from behind the flour-sack curtains covering the trailer windows. Maria glanced at him. The curtain fell across the glass. Maria put the car in gear and did a U-turn in front of the trailers. »And Rosa knows me,« Maria said. »But she didn't try to find me. Yet. Tío, is there anyone else she knows in Watsonville or Santa Cruz?«

Hector thought a minute. »She knows Rigoberto, but she would never come to him.« Frowning, he lowered his head, then raised it again. »Señora Mendoza. She moved back here when her husband died. She and Rosa were friends.«

»I STILL CAN'T BELIEVE YOU FOUND ME,« SEÑORA MENDOZA said, leading them to a white wrought-iron table on her back deck. Hector lagged behind the others, peering sideways at the lush, meticulous garden. A thick lawn circled the wooden deck. Delicate, brightly colored flowers in oranges, purples, and pinks lined the dark wood fence and skirted the roots of three mottled white trees with leaves like pesos. Two large terra-cotta pots stood watch at the edge of the deck. Strawberries sprouted from little balconies in the sides of the pots, the tiny red berries veined with straw yellow.

Hector sighed. He would never get away from strawberries.

»It was fairly easy,« Maria said. »You were the only K. Mendoza in the phone book.«

Señora Mendoza laughed. »I guess that does make it easy. Can I get anyone anything to drink? I've got some fresh strawberry lemonade.«

»Thank you, señora, but water will be fine,« Eliseo said with a courteous dip of the head.

Señora Mendoza turned to Hector. Hector lowered his eyes. »Water, señora, please. If it's not too much trouble.«

»No trouble at all. Maria?«

»Lemonade sounds wonderful,« Maria replied, settling herself in one of the white chairs. Easily, gracefully, as if she were born to such luxury. As if she and the señora were equals.

Eliseo sat in the chair across from Maria. He pulled the cap from his head, ruffled his hair, started to put the cap back on, then lowered it to his lap. Hector hovered behind the chair between them. *Like a servant*, he thought. He scraped the chair away from the table and sat.

Señora Mendoza returned with a tray and four frosty glasses. She distributed them, setting the pink glasses in front of Maria and herself and the clear ones in front of Hector and Eliseo. She sat across from Hector. »I haven't seen Rosa since I left Nuñez,« she said. »Or heard from her. I wrote several times but she never wrote back.«

»To which address, señora?« Hector said.

The señora fixed him with a cool gaze. »To yours, Hector. And please, call me Kathy.«

Hector lowered his head. »We have not moved, señora. Perhaps they never arrived.«

Señora Mendoza sniffed. »Perhaps. And perhaps someone intercepted them.«

Hector frowned. Intercepted them? Then an image filled his mind: Inez, smirking as she burned the *bruja's* letters. It was more than possible. »Perhaps, señora,« he said.

A sullied satisfaction sparked in Señora Mendoza's eyes. She shrugged one shoulder and turned to Maria. »Anyway, I hoped that some day your sister would come looking for you and your father, and, well, look me up, too. How is your father?«

Maria stroked the glass of pink lemonade. »He's dead.«

Señora Mendoza stiffened, then nodded. She showed no surprise. »I'm sorry.«

»It was a long time ago,« Maria said.

Señora Mendoza smiled. »I remember teaching him how to 'talk like a Yank,' as he put it. After the two of you left, I taught Rosa. She spoke beautiful English. Anyone talking to her would never know it wasn't her first language. I worried a little when I left that she might lose it, with no one to practice with, but she assured me she had one friend she could talk to.«

Hector sat up. An English-speaking friend, in Nuñez?

»I asked her to come with me, so she could try to find you,« Señora Mendoza continued. »But your mamá was ill and Rosa wouldn't leave her. I told her that whenever she was ready to come, I'd make sure she had a job and a work visa. A green card if I could get her one. But I never heard from—What's that around your neck?«

Hector turned to Maria. She froze at the sudden attention, her hand raised to her breast. Caught between her fingers was a *milagro*, a silver girl. Hector started to cross himself, then curled his hand into a fist.

»Rosa had one just like it,« Señora Mendoza said. A tenderness crept into her voice. »She used to play with it when she was concentrating. Just as you are now.«

Maria bit her lip, looking much as she had the last time Hector saw her in México—young and vulnerable, but hopeful. She looked at Hector, a question in her eyes.

»She was wearing it the last time I saw her,« he said.

A faint smile gilded the corners of Maria's mouth. She sat quietly a moment, then asked the señora, »Have you seen anyone else from Nuñez here? Someone Rosa might know?«

Señora Mendoza laughed. »Not till today. There were so few people I really knew down there. Only Rosa. When my husband died—« She switched to English, gave that little half shrug again. »So you see,« she concluded.

Maria nodded. Eliseo drew back. Hector could well imagine what the señora had said: *I couldn't get out of there fast enough.* Not surprising. From the first morning she had arrived in Nuñez, the señora had been shunned for her independent, aggressive ways. A *mala mujer*, a bad woman, the townspeople said. She behaved more like a man than a woman. She even spoke to her husband as if she were his equal—ay, the shame she heaped upon him!

Hector played with the ring in his pocket. Nuñez was a lonely place for a *mala mujer*. And, for the señora, even lonelier after the señor died. Who could blame her for fleeing the town as if it were a prison?

SEÑORA MENDOZA WALKED THEM TO THE BACK GATE. It squealed a little when she pushed it open. »If I hear from her,« she said, »I'll call you. And if you hear from her, please, call me.«

»I will,« Maria promised. She took Señora Mendoza's hands in both of hers. »Thank you.«

»Glad to help,« the señora said. She drew the complaining gate closed.

Maria grabbed its handle. »Señora—Kathy. You said you were willing to find Rosa work. What . . . kind of job did you have in mind? Housekeeping or, well—«

»Restaurant work,« Eliseo said helpfully.

Señora Mendoza shook her head. »Oh, no, no. Some kind of clerical work. Like I said, her English was beautiful. And her typing skills—«

Maria's mouth dropped open. »Her typing skills?«

»I taught her to type,« Señora Mendoza said. »I only wish I'd been able to teach her how to use a computer. Oh, well. It wouldn't be hard for her to learn. She's quick.«

»Typing,« Maria murmured. Her hand went to the *milagro*. She pulled at its feet.

»I wanted her to have options,« Señora Mendoza said. »When she came here.«

Eliseo smiled. »You wanted to keep her out of the fields,« he said.

Señora Mendoza pinched her lips together, studying Eliseo. Soon she relaxed, convinced he hadn't meant it in a hostile or challenging way. »Yes,« she said. »I wanted to give her the best chance I could.«

MARIA SAT BEHIND THE WHEEL, STARING AT THE YELlow diamond-shaped sign on the corner of Señora Mendoza's street. »Typing,« she said. »That changes everything.«

Hector tried to imagine why. Rosa might type, but she had no papers. Even if she spoke beautiful English, the bosses would check to see if she was a citizen. Unless she stumbled into a clerical job with a sympathetic boss—how likely was that? Eliseo would know.

Hector twisted to look at Eliseo. »Is there much call for that? Undocumented typists?«

»There might be. I always go straight to the fields.« Eliseo shifted his jaw to the side, staring down at the floor mats in the back. He jerked upright. »Help organizations. Some of them take volunteers, some of them might know people who are willing to hire a woman without papers.«

Maria met Eliseo's gaze. »But it's not likely,« she said.

Eliseo deflated. »No. They would be under even greater scrutiny, I think, than a restaurant or a farm.«

Hector faced the windshield. Señora Mendoza's was

a rich neighborhood, with large, sprawling houses and more parklike yards. A small grove of the peso-leafed trees crowded the front left corner of the señora's yard. A shame. Such fertile land should be used to grow vegetables and fruits.

»Well,« Maria said, turning on the ignition. »I went to Barrios Unidos today, but no one there had heard of her—«

»Barrios Unidos?« Eliseo said. »In Santa Cruz?«

Maria pulled away from the curb. »Yes. They hadn't seen her.«

»But the address Hector gave her said you were in Watsonville,« Eliseo said. »Shouldn't we start there?«

Hector glanced at Maria. Her right hand left the steering wheel for a second, as if reaching for the *milagro*. It resettled on the wheel. »Who do we see in Watsonville?« she said.

A GRAY CAST SETTLED OVER THE LOW HILLS. EIGHT o'clock and the fog had come to reclaim the land. Hector gazed across the flat hilltop. Long, rectangular houses, duplexes, hunched in straight, barren rows. Like army barracks—or rows of strawberries. Hector made a face.

Narrow strips of lush, neatly trimmed grass separated the buildings. Hector frowned. Even with all this good land, not one vegetable garden had been planted. Nor did fruit trees dot the golden hillsides surrounding the migrant camp. Still, the homes looked comfortable, safe. Safer than Rigoberto's trailer.

Hector turned. His foot struck a bicycle tire.

»Careful,« Eliseo said.

The bicycle spanned the lawn and the cement walkway in front of the nearest duplex. A boy's small, worried face peeked from the window. Too afraid to come outside and claim the bicycle, he was also too anxious to let them roll it away without his knowledge. The boy shifted. The white curtains rippled, rocking a white vase with pink silk flowers. The boy steadied it with his hand.

Hector glanced at the parking lot. It, too, looked well-tended and clean. He recognized a few of the cars from the field. A couple strolled by, arm in arm. Mary came around the building to the right and stopped the couple. »Excuse me,« she said. »I'm looking for someone—«

»Rosa won't be here,« Eliseo said in a low voice. »You have to be legal to live here. No one would risk taking in a stranger.«

»But they might have met her,« Hector said.

»True.«

A man stepped out of the duplex across the lawn. Hector touched Eliseo's arm. »Come,« he said. »We can't let Maria do all the work.«

The man doubted he had met Rosa, unless—did she have a tooth outlined in silver, here? He tapped his front tooth. Hector shook his head. The man spread his hands in an apologetic gesture and went on his way.

Frowning, Hector turned again and stopped. Across the ravine, on the next hill, stood a collection of larger, bleaker, boxlike buildings. A wire fence surrounded them. »What is that?« Hector said.

»A correctional facility,« Eliseo said.

»A prison?«

»More or less.«

»In view of the children?« Hector shook his head. »What is wrong with North Americans?«

Eliseo smiled, a wry, cynical curve of the lips. »That's not the best of it. This camp is called Buena Vista. Would you call *that* a good view?«

THE SALTY AROMA OF ROASTED CHICKEN DRIFTED FROM the open rotisserie and filled the restaurant. Maria waited at the register to pay, pocketing the little wrapped mints. »Go ahead and find us a table,« she said. »It's on me.«

Hector made his way to a booth by the window and set his tray on the table. A bean slipped over the side of the paper plate. Hector lowered himself into the booth. His knees and back creaked.

Eliseo sank into the seat across from him. A pained expression lengthened his face. »She wouldn't take any money,« he said.

Hector ladled maroon salsa from a plastic cup with his fork. »She says she wants to treat us.«

»But—« Eliseo looked down at his tray. Beans, rice, tortillas, and three pieces of chicken were mounded on the paper plate. Eliseo shook his head. »I guess I'd feel better about it if we'd had some luck. Can you think of anything about Rosa, something she might be interested in or might need that would give us an idea where to look next?«

Hector glanced over his shoulder at the register. Maria leaned on the counter, her wallet open before her. »Rosa is pregnant,« he said.

Eliseo sat back, blinked, then leaned forward. »How far along?«

»Four, five months. I don't know.«

Eliseo lowered his voice. »Why haven't you told Maria?«

Hector mixed the rice and beans. »I don't know. I guess because the last time I saw Rosa—« He set the fork down. »She didn't look well. She may have miscarried.«

Eliseo pursed his lips. »That bad?«

»Like death,« Hector said.

Eliseo nodded. »I know where to go. Tomorrow. They're closed now. Tomorrow we'll go to Salud Para La Gente. Without Maria, if you prefer.«

Hector picked up his fork. »Without Maria.«

MARIA LEANED OUT THE CAMRY WINDOW. »CALL ME,« she said. »Tomorrow.«

»Tomorrow,« Hector said, backing away from the car. Rigoberto and a few other men gathered around him, anxious to get another look at Maria. Hector hissed at them, shooing them away with his hand. They took a step back, but continued to stare.

Nelda parted the men with rough, gnarled hands. The pregnant girl trailed after the old woman, clinging to a handful of Nelda's skirt. »You are a social worker?« Nelda said leaning into the open passenger window. »We need a goat. You get us one.«

»I'm a teacher,« Maria said. She held Nelda's gaze. Her attention invited the old woman to continue.

»The children need milk,« Nelda said. Grabbing the girl's wrist, she pulled her into Maria's sight. »She needs milk. So that her baby will grow strong.«

»Nelda, leave her alone,« Hector said, taking the old woman's arm.

Nelda shook him off. »The children need it to help them pay attention in class. If they are hungry, they cannot learn.«

Hector clasped the old woman's arm again. »Nelda—«

»It's all right,« Maria said. She smiled, a sad, regretful smile. »I don't know anything about goats. But here—« She reached into her purse and pulled out a twenty dollar bill. »Here's money for milk.«

»Thank you,« Nelda said, taking the money. She pushed herself away from the car. »May the Virgin bless you.«

The pregnant girl's eyes widened suddenly. She backed away from the car, skirting Nelda's broad hips. She cowered behind the old woman. Hector glanced from the girl to Maria. Maria's full attention rested on Nelda. She looked kind, not at all threatening. A little vulnerable, especially the way she tugged absently at the *milagro*.

»Tomorrow, Tío,« Maria said. »Call me.«

Maria waved, then drove away. Nelda watched dust trail after the Camry. »Her Spanish is good, very good for a *gavacha*,« the old woman said. She turned to look at the girl. »Isabela, what are you hiding from?«

The girl stepped away from the old woman, scuffing the gravel with her toe. She cradled her swollen belly and looked at the ground. With a huff of impatience, Nelda ambled off between the trailers.

Hector approached the girl. »Isabela,« he said.

She looked up at him, her eyes filling with dread.

»You're the one who saw the lady by the goat pen, aren't you?« he said.

Isabela nodded.

He softened his voice. »Why were you afraid of Maria, of the woman in the car?«

Isabela wet her lips. »The *milagro* around her neck,« she said. »The woman by the goat pen had one just like it.«

TWENTY-TWO

TEDDY STOOD AT THE DOOR TO HER POTTERY STUDIO, the origami spider nestled in her right hand. Fog clung to the morning like wool-gray gauze, not a hint of sun beneath the loose weave of mist. Teddy put her shoulder to the studio door and pushed. The door swung open. She went inside.

Setting the spider on her worktable, she stepped back to study it. Would it be difficult to duplicate Estelle's origami figures in clay? If she coated paper with slip and then folded it . . . she imagined Estelle's hands, sure and quick, creasing and opening the paper, squashing folds and tucking the tiniest corner out of sight. Teddy frowned. That would be impossible with slip-coated paper. But if she coated the folded origami *afterward*—

She nudged the spider with a finger. That might work. The paper would burn away in the bisque firing, leaving a thin-walled, fragile piece. Too fragile. No, the sides would have to be thicker, or the piece would never make it through the final firing. If she simply modeled the various shapes and planes of Estelle's figures on rolled sheets of clay, then reconstructed them . . . maybe. Definitely. The seams would look like creases. She could even add false creases to imitate the preliminary folds, like the ones that striped an origami crane's wings. The pieces could stand alone or be used to decorate sculp-

tures, vases, tiles—tiles, with one corner folding into a
leaping frog or the center rising into a bird with a long,
fanned tail. Why not? "If you can visualize it, you can
do it," as Jon liked to tell his students.

"I can visualize it," Teddy said. What an addition to
the show! Glazed in either an understated celadon or
even in the bright, rich origami-paper hues, the pieces
would provide a real contrast between her previous figures and carved works. Teddy placed her hands on the
table and leaned over the spider—

—and jerked back, arms lifted. Pain screamed from
elbows to fingertips, shredding her dreams. Pain unfolded her life, revealing not just creases but crooked
rips and worn holes.

She lowered her arms, careful not to let them touch
each other or her body, then turned and left the studio,
hurrying back to the house.

She glanced at the clock as she entered the living
room—twenty minutes before she had to catch the bus
for work. She went to the window seat, trembling with
frustration. Her right foot slid, nearly unbalancing her.
She caught herself and looked down. She was standing
on the fiddle fake book, her toe pointing to "Over the
Waterfall." Her breath hardened in her chest. Just what
she needed—another reminder of what she couldn't do.
With a kick, she shot the book across the room. The
mangled pages protested with rustles and creaks. Teddy
glared at the book, then her anger deflated. She stared
at the banjo, willing it to walk itself to the closet. It was
much too heavy for her to lift with these arms.

When the banjo refused to move, she picked up the
phone. Bracing herself against pain, she pressed speed
dial. Rita's cheery hello greeted her. "Rita?" she said.
"Can I ask you a big favor? Will you come over and
put my banjo in the closet?"

•   •   •

DAYPACK SLUNG OVER ONE SHOULDER, TEDDY marched toward the bus stop with her head down. She would not look at the strawberry fields. She refused. Not if that woman sat on the little bluff overlooking the emerald plants and crimson berries. Teddy scanned the ground for lucky pennies, but found only bits of glass and broken plastic toys. She started to peek, jerking her gaze away at the last minute. A rash of tingles spread across her neck, that feeling she got whenever someone was watching at her. "It's just the woman," Teddy muttered. Just that broken, sad woman, slumped in her vinyl and metal chair, buoyed by a timeless tangle of grasses and weeds.

The woman frightened her. Something about the weary hunch of her shoulders, the hopeless droop of her head—like a flower with a broken stem. Because the woman *was* broken. Whatever had happened to her had left her stranded on the edge, outside of life. Like Teddy.

Teddy locked her jaw. Projection, that's what Paul called this. Shifting her own disappointments and despair onto someone else. But even explaining all of that away, Teddy still feared the woman. Not the woman, not really, but the woman's gaze. Teddy gasped at the memory of that pain, that intense, blinding pain that had ripped through her arms as the woman's eyes met hers. She sucked at the air, unable to catch her breath. The sheer surprise of that pain had driven her to her knees, shocking her with its violence and its promise of obliteration.

But more horrible than that pain was the recognition in the woman's eyes: *We are sisters, we are the same. We can no longer move through our worlds with the grace we thought life owed us. . . .*

Teddy stopped. Another block and she'd be at the bus stop. Another three steps and houses would shield her from the woman's gaze. Teddy willed herself to take a step. Then she turned, slowly, as if fighting a stiff wind.

The woman sat on the bluff overlooking the strawberries, the grasses around the kitchen chair's metal legs trampled and ragged. She sat still, hands folded in her lap, shoulders high and proud. A defiant tilt lifted her chin. Nothing remained of the stooped resignation but the awkward splaying of her legs, angled as if she had little or no control over them.

Teddy swallowed, avoiding the woman's gaze. *This woman is getting better while I'm getting worse*—

Irrational fear plucked at Teddy's nerves—fear of the woman, fear of her growing health in the face of her own worsening condition. As if the woman drew strength—health—from Teddy. Why else would Teddy feel such agony when their eyes met?

Teddy pressed her lips together. The whole idea was ridiculous. Still, it gnawed at her. There was only one thing that would free her. She lifted her gaze to meet the woman's—

Pain crackled through Teddy's arms like a trapped electrical storm, tearing her nerves asunder, vibrating along her bones. Her muscles ached to contain the rage of that pain, but its heat threatened to dissolve them. She cried out. The daypack slipped from her shoulder, crashing to the ground. Teddy dropped to her knees. She swallowed the vomit rising in her throat.

ONLY THE CLICK OF THE KEYBOARD SOUNDED IN THE waiting room. The Pig had been silenced; the deejay had played one of Teddy's favorite songs, Mary McCaslin's banjo version of "Pinball Wizard." Teddy stabbed the power button, the pain a welcome distraction. "I used to play that," she explained when Estelle looked up, startled.

Used to, Teddy thought, *as in never again.*

She stared at the wall-hanging behind the sea-green sofas. Her gaze followed the threads of the weaving, over and under, as each color gathered itself into an image: mountains, reaching trees, clouds, a sudden star-burst of sun. Her mind composed and revised and re-worded a letter to Suki, the manager of the Wren Gallery: *Dear Suki, Due to circumstances beyond my control, I am forced to withdraw from my August show.* The words wove themselves into the wall-hanging, the handwriting sharp and staccato, reflecting the dissonance of her pain. *Dear Suki, It is with great regret—*

Estelle tapped her shoulder. Teddy started. The ringing phone breached her self-absorption. She lunged for the button. "Hello, Dr. Grant's office," she said in a rush. "This is Teddy."

After she hung up, she turned to Estelle. "I didn't even hear it. How many times did it ring?"

Estelle held up five fingers. Teddy grimaced. "Terrific. Keep this up and Paul will send me home."

Estelle returned her grimace. Pulling a scratch pad closer, she wrote, "What were you thinking about? Is something wrong?"

Teddy kicked the desk leg. "No more than usual. I just—I'm trying to face the fact I won't be able to do the show in August."

"Two months till August," Estelle wrote.

"Two months," Teddy said. She stared at the wall-hanging again. "I needed those two months to make new pieces. To make *enough* pieces. I can't. My arms aren't healing. They're getting worse."

The woman on the bluff watched from the depths of Teddy's mind. Teddy twitched. *Forget the woman,* she thought. *She's not stealing your strength. She's just curious. The pain is nothing more than coincidence.*

Her subconscious asked, *Do you really believe that?*

Estelle poked Teddy's leg. Teddy glanced down at the scratch pad. "What can I do?" it read.

Teddy cocked her head. "Can you throw pots?"

Estelle pretended to think about this, then shrugged. "How far?" she wrote.

Teddy laughed. Estelle grinned. "Seriously," she wrote. She underlined the words "What can I do?"

The laughter drained from Teddy. "There is something you can do for me," she said. "I need to send the gallery a letter of withdrawal. If I dictated it to you, would you type it up for me?"

Estelle's face betrayed nothing—no curiosity, no sadness, no annoyance. No eagerness. She simply studied Teddy, taking her in the same way the woman on the bluff had that morning—large dark eyes drinking from the depths of Teddy's being.

Teddy remembered to breathe, inhaling with a sharp hiss. Estelle blinked. Her resemblance to the woman on the bluff ended. Or did it? They could have been sisters—or was that just prejudice on Teddy's part? That old "they all look alike to me" excuse raising its ugly head. Dark eyes, dark hair, rich toffee skin—Teddy hadn't seen much more of the woman in the kitchen chair. Aside from the weary body, she had really only seen the woman's eyes. She hadn't noticed whether the woman had Estelle's wing-like cheekbones or her full lips or even her youth. In fact, Teddy's impressions of the woman had been of middle age, maybe even late middle age. Older.

Estelle touched Teddy's arm, then shoved the scratch pad closer to Teddy. "Ready when you are," it read.

TEDDY SWIVELED IN HER CHAIR. HER STOMACH RUMbled. She should have brought a snack. Jon was never late for movies or doctor's appointments, but anything else—like lunch . . .

She dragged her toes to stop the chair and found herself facing Estelle. Estelle leaned over to consult the cheat sheet she and Teddy had compiled, her finger tracing the blue ink. Flexing her hands, she placed them on the keyboard and moved a block of text. Her black dress whispered against the chair.

The same black dress. Teddy pressed her fingertips together, wondering at the feel of the fabric. Clean but slightly rumpled, the dress looked as if it had been washed by hand and allowed to drip dry. Was this Estelle's only dress—or her only work dress? Teddy shuddered. That air of mourning still clung to Estelle, like a note lingering long after the string is plucked. Estelle never "talked" about herself, although she seemed eager to find out about Teddy and Paul.

Teddy swiveled in a short arc. There must be some way to get a little insight into Estelle's personal life. Teddy hadn't been able to find Estelle's employment application. Damned if she knew what Paul did with it. In her employment folder, Teddy found an origami cat. Maybe he'd had Estelle fill out a card.

Teddy pushed the container of slip out of the way and reached for the card file. A twinge shot up her arm. After the jolt passed, she flipped through the cards until she realized she didn't know Estelle's last name.

"Estelle," she said. "Do we have a card on you yet?"

Estelle turned to her. Her pupils widened, then shrank to pinpricks. That distanced look sculpted her features again, this time tempered with caution.

A faint chill crept over Teddy. She forced herself to smile—warmly, she hoped. "You know, just your address and phone number," she said. "So Paul and I can get in touch with you if we need to."

Estelle tensed still further, then relaxed. She even smiled. Reaching for the legal pad, she wrote, "A phone? Be serious, Teddy."

Teddy shrugged. "Well, you know. You could have a housemate or something. Do you live with anyone?"

Estelle flinched, looking away. Loss played across her features. Her hand seemed too heavy to lift when she picked up the pen again. "I used to," she wrote.

Teddy held her breath, unsure how hard to press. Or

how far. "Did—did this person die? Is that why you wear black?"

Estelle's jaw hardened, her lips thinning to a fine line. Her eyes took on a vacant look, as if her spirit had evaporated.

Teddy ducked her head. "I'm sorry," she said. "It's none of my business—"

Paul leaned out of his office. "Teddy?"

Teddy removed the headset and hopped from the chair. She strode across the room, glad to have the interruption. Judging by the look on Estelle's face, not only had she gone too far, she'd gone *way* too far.

Paul's lunch hour client, Burton Powers, exited as she reached the door. A stocky man with a sweaty, ruddy face, he clasped Paul's right bicep. "It's all right, it's all right," he mumbled. "Don't know why I asked. Don't know what came over me."

"But it's no problem," Paul said. "Teddy can help you . . ." He frowned, puzzled. "What am I thinking? Teddy can't—"

Burton's face turned an even darker red. "It's all right, it's all right. Forget it."

He slipped past Teddy with a short nod, stooping beside the box of books he'd set by the reception desk when he arrived. Teddy had forgotten all about them. He hefted the box with a grunt, then plodded to the front door. It opened just as he got there. Jon backed onto the porch to let Burton pass.

Teddy turned to Paul. "What was that all about?"

Paul squeezed the bridge of his nose. "I'm not sure. Ten minutes before the end of the session, he broke off what he was saying and said he needed help carrying his box of books. A little voice told me to call you—I don't know. God, Teddy, there's no way you could lift that box. What was I thinking? I mean, *I* should have offered to help him."

"A little voice?" Teddy said. "That's not an expression I ever thought I'd hear from you."

Paul gestured helplessly with his hands. "I don't know how else to describe it. I heard this voice telling me to call you."

The absurdity of it tickled Teddy. "Physician, heal thyself," she said.

Paul blinked, then smiled. He gave her shoulder a gentle shove. "Go to lunch, Teddy."

"Right, boss," she said. She walked over to the reception desk, placed a hand on Jon's elbow. "Ready?"

Jon jerked to look at her. "Huh? Oh, hi. Hang on a sec. Estelle's making me something."

Estelle watched Jon from beneath her eyelashes. The scrap paper caught in the web of her hands grew smaller with each fold until she set it in front of Jon. A wounded bird leaned against his hand, its wing bent at an unnatural angle.

Teddy's chest constricted. She glanced at Jon.

He picked up the bird, turning it over and over in his hands. He nodded thoughtfully, catching his lower lip between his teeth. "Fair enough," he said. "Well, Teddy, you ready for lunch?"

Teddy knew how to read Jon. *Leave it alone*, his cool demeanor stated. *It never happened.* Teddy opted for flip. "I've *been* ready. Estelle, can I bring you back anything? Zoccoli's has great raviolis."

Jon turned the bird over once more, then set it on the desk. "Great sandwiches, too," he said.

Estelle shook her head. She made a shooing gesture with her hand.

Teddy backed away from the desk. "We're gone. Don't forget to mail that letter for me."

The phone rang. Teddy reached across the desk for her headset. Estelle brushed it out of reach, then pointed to the answering machine.

Teddy smiled crookedly. "Got it. See you in an hour."

Jon touched the small of her back and guided her to the door. Teddy followed him into the sunshine, forcing her shoulders to relax. They crossed Cedar Street, cutting across the parking lot behind Logos and Frog Fitness. Teddy stooped to pick up a penny glinting between the roots of a gingko. After wishing for her arms back, she checked the year—1987—then handed the penny to Jon. "Down payment on your thoughts," she said.

He pocketed the coin. "Just thinking about the bird."

Teddy wrinkled her nose. "It might not be you—"

Jon raised one eyebrow, his Jack Nicholson impression. It had taken him years to perfect. "Teddy," he said. "She makes something for everyone who comes in—a profile in paper. You said so yourself. Of course it was me." He shivered. "You should have seen the way she studied me. Suddenly I understood all those primitive people who thought photographers were stealing their souls."

They walked down the narrow foot ramp at the edge of the parking lot. Crossing the street, they headed through the ornate wrought-iron arch onto Pearl Alley, along the brick walkway running parallel to Pacific. Teddy floated her fingertips along the plaster planter—a ground-level balustrade—creating a courtyard around the entrance to the Pearl Alley Bistro. Geranium and bougainvillea leaves tickled her knuckles.

She peeked at Jon, trying to gauge his mood. "Come on," she said. "Who'd want your soul?"

He rewarded her with a grin. "You'd be surprised."

"Devil's been sniffing around again?"

"Left two messages on my answering machine." Jon shook his head. "It's amazing. I mean, I believed you, but to actually *watch* her make this little paper likeness . . . this *accurate* paper likeness."

They stepped out of the alley. The clothing on the

rack outside Shandry Dan billowed in the breeze, the bright colors and fabrics demanding to be touched. Teddy stopped to touch them. Across the way, a kid on a skateboard sailed down the exit ramp of the two-story parking garage and into the street. Teddy followed Jon down Walnut Avenue to Pacific. Gentrified forties storefronts stood shoulder to shoulder with retro art deco. Colorful awnings jutted like parasols to shade the sidewalk.

"Sometimes she makes two origamis," Teddy said. "One of the person as they are, one as they want to be."

"Is that how she explains it?"

"Well, no," Teddy said. She avoided a begging teenager with a boa constrictor draped around her neck. "No. We've never really talked about it. But I watch people's reactions. They recognize themselves in the first one and seem . . . encouraged by the second."

"Like she's seeing the future hidden inside them," Jon said.

"Or the future *they* want to believe in." Teddy looked up. "She only made one for you, didn't she?"

He nodded. "One. And nailed it."

Teddy winced. Was it worse to think the bird was Jon or would be Jon? "Hey, you're not a broken wing—"

"Teddy." Jon stopped beside the slatted wood-and-wire fence surrounding the vacant lot across from Blockbuster Music. "I try to wrestle with it, but I just . . . sometimes I wonder why I bother to get up in the morning. I lie in bed and feel sorry for myself. I can barely paint. I can't draw. On my good mornings, I'm a real Eeyore. 'Some people can paint and some can't. I'm not complaining, that's just the way it is.' "

They walked in silence. A lump formed in Teddy's throat. She already knew those kind of mornings, already dreaded waking to her useless and aching arms. Jon had been living with that same pain and resignation for three and a half years. Teddy hugged herself.

"She made you, what?" Jon asked. "A penguin and a crab?"

"A spider," Teddy said. And wondered whether the spider was the future or simply her own desperate, fleeting hopes.

JON SLOWED AS THEY APPROACHED THE OFFICE. "WHEN you were in college," he said, "did you ever get into that discussion about, if you had to give up one of your body parts, which would you give up?"

Teddy tapped her heel against the curb. "Oh, yeah. But I could never decide. But I always knew it would be hardest to lose my hands."

Jon nodded, squinting up at the sun.

"What about you?" Teddy said.

He sniffed. "My legs. That would be the hardest. Not being able to walk to the corner for a paper or go out dancing or go for a run on the fire trails at the University. So I guess in a way I'm blessed." He hugged her gently. "See you later. Think about that movie."

"Sure." Teddy shaded her eyes with her hand and looked up at him. "You don't want to come in, see if Estelle's made you another one?"

Jon's smile soured. He backed away. "No," he said. "I'm not ready to see my future."

Teddy nodded. She walked up the steps and went into the office.

TEDDY SLIPPED THE LITTLE DAYPACK OVER HER SHOULDER. "Thanks for locking up," she said to Estelle. "If there are any calls, just let the answering machine take them."

Estelle bowed her head with mock gravity, then made a shooing motion with her hand. Teddy saluted her.

Paul's door was flung open, and a client—Mr. Peterson, the new one—backed out. He spun and rocketed toward the door. "Evening, girls, evening. See you soon.

Got to run. I have to go to the goat ranch and pick up a friend.''

Estelle straightened.

Teddy grinned. "A goat?"

"Naw, naw," Mr. Peterson laughed. "I got a friend who works there."

A note nudged Teddy's fingers. She glanced down at Estelle's handwriting: "A goat ranch? In Santa Cruz?"

"A little north of here, somewhere on the coast," Teddy said. "They raise goats for—what is it? Human antibodies?"

"Plasma, transplants, whatever," Mr. Peterson said, yanking the front door open. "I can't keep it straight. It's too techie for me. See you next week."

The door stood open, resisting the wake of his passing. Teddy glanced at the latest note from Estelle. "No," she said. "They don't do transplants. The goats have human antibodies or human plasma in their blood, something like that—"

"Estelle?" Paul leaned out of his office. "Estelle, can you get me the file on Jessica Ingram? Teddy, aren't you gone yet?"

"Ten minutes ago," Teddy said. "See you tomorrow!"

She hurried outside, pulling the door shut behind her. The air smelled of the sea, a thick, brackish scent splendid with life. And cold. The fog seeped through the streets like a white stain spreading through the city. Chill bumps formed along Teddy's upper arms, above the braces. She shivered and went back inside to get her sweater.

Estelle's empty chair faced Paul's door. Teddy skirted it, snagging the collar of her sweater with one finger and lifting it from her own chair. Big mistake. Lightning traveled the length of her arm, splintering her nerves.

She sank into Estelle's chair, waiting for the pain to pass. She closed her eyes, forced herself to take a deep breath and relax. She opened her eyes. An origami creature crouched on the desk in front of her.

For once Teddy had a hard time figuring out what it was supposed to be. It looked sort of rodentlike, or maybe foxlike—except for the blunt nose. Teddy studied it. With its sturdy, bowed legs and powerful head, it reminded her of a badger. Interesting. Badgers were known for—what? Ferocity, cunning, and living underground—hiding. Who reminded Estelle of a badger?

"Jon, is that you?" Teddy said.

She leaned closer. Estelle had used a piece of copy paper for this one, apparently a rough draft of something. Lines of type striped the creature, creating odd markings. Notes from a client's file, maybe a letter—

Teddy snatched up the badger. "It can't be," she murmured.

But it was. Her crippled signature scarred the little beast's belly. Her letter of withdrawal. It hadn't gone anywhere—wouldn't go anywhere now. It would hide here among Estelle's other creations, burrowing into time until it was forgotten. And—an absurd thought crossed Teddy's mind—defending itself against any attempts to send it out into the world.

TWENTY-THREE

PAUL SAT IN THE BLUE ARMCHAIR ACROSS FROM THE Kandinsky, the phone pressed to his ear. The unanswered ringing echoed through him, hollow as footsteps in an empty room. His gaze traced Kandinsky's straining horses. The phone continued to ring. The horses lunged past the yellow and blue trees, desperate to break free.

The phone rang again. The answering machine should have picked up five rings ago—why had Mary turned it off? Where was she?

He hung up. Someone coughed, a soft, scratchy sound. He turned. Estelle stood beside his desk, cradling Jessica Ingram's file against the bodice of her black dress. Head tilted back, she watched him from under those dark lashes. She made no move to hand him the file. Instead she tipped her chin, a visual question. *What's wrong?*

He was reading way too much into the gesture. "Thanks, Estelle," he said. He stood and reached for the file. "Have a good evening. I'll see you tomorrow. Oh, wait. I still need a photocopy of your social security card—"

His eyes lost focus, so that Estelle blurred around the edges like a watercolor wash. His request evaporated from his mind, leaving only a groping sense of loss. What had he just said to her? He searched his memory:

He'd asked for Jessica Ingram's file; she'd brought it. . . .

Estelle still held the manila folder, not in any coquettish or surly way, but as if that wasn't the point. As if bringing it to him was of no importance and that wasn't the reason she was here. She queried him with a slight widening of the eyes that involved her eyebrows. Light flickered in her pupils. *You're upset about something,* she seemed to say. *What is it?*

The words formed in Paul's head, full and resonant, the voice uttering them rich with a timbre reminiscent of Mary's. *Stop projecting,* he ordered himself.

He cleared his throat. "Is there—do you need something?"

The light left Estelle's eyes. She pursed her lips, a slight frown creasing her brow. She set the file on his desk, then searched the broad, barren surface with her fingers, nudging the Gripmaster to one side. Her frown deepened. She looked up at him.

Paul joined her beside the desk. "Paper?" he guessed.

She nodded, then pantomimed writing. Paul rummaged through the top drawer, fishing out a pen and a colored notepad. Estelle accepted them, dashing off a quick note: "You seem distracted. Is anything wrong?"

Paul studied her crisp, light handwriting. He'd known this woman how long? Three, four days? For all she knew he was like this all the time. "No, nothing's wrong," he said, looking up. "I've just got a lot on my—"

Her eyes glimmered again, a gentle radiance flickering around her irises like the sun rising behind a weathered pinnacle. He leaned toward her, drawn by the same compulsion that drew him to climbing—the challenge of the unpredictable, the immovable. The lure of a silence not complete, but embracing. The wind might whistle through crags or chimneys, water might roar in a torrent down a sheer cliff, but the silence of the stone—

Paul pinched the bridge of his nose, closing his eyes.
He steadied himself, grasping the edge of the desk, and
opened his eyes. "It's nothing, really," he said, fighting
this crazy urge to tell her everything. "Just 'the little
disturbances of man,' to quote Grace Paley. Nothing that
won't sort itself out."

You don't believe that. The words rang in his head,
audible and full as if she'd said them out loud. He jerked
to look at her. She bent over the pad, writing another
note. Pushing the page across the desk to him, her fingers touched his. "Then talk to me. Maybe hearing
yourself think will help you sort it out," it read.

The touch electrified him, reeled him farther into her
silence. Paul clutched at his self-control. The woman
worked for him, for God's sake. He couldn't burden her
with all of this. Yet even as he clung to that, his hold
began to slip. He wanted to tell her. He *needed* to. But
whether it was his need or hers, he couldn't tell.

PAUL'S ELBOWS RESTED ON HIS KNEES. HE HUNCHED
forward in the blue armchair, the soft plush bristling
against his arms. Estelle sat on the nearest chair, her left
hand resting on his knee. Her face was as open as a
sheet of blank paper. *Ready to catch all my words*, Paul
thought, *and record them for all time.*

Estelle shifted. The movement blurred, the faint glow
around her body trailing light. Like a flickering candle
flame. Her fingers brushed his knee. She made that same
gathering motion with her right hand, the gesture Moss
used for "And?"

Paul took a deep breath, held it, then let it out. "And
I don't know," he said. "Mary and I have always talked
about everything. But lately she seems distracted. She
turns her back on me and gazes out the window, seeing
something—someone—that's not there. It doesn't feel
like a conscious decision . . . well, not usually. There are
times when I can see her retreat from me. Like when I

ask her how her day went or what she's been doing. I
don't know why she's excluding me. I mean, I try not
to judge her or solve her problems for her. And it's not
like I get impatient when she goes over old ground or
tells me a story she's told me before. Assuming this is
some old hurt she's mulling over. It's probably the baby
thing, but sometimes I can't help wondering if she's
been thinking about her family. She hasn't seen her sister or her mom since she was twelve, and her dad . . .
his death really shook her.''

Estelle jerked back. Her left hand fluttered at her
throat, then dropped to her lap.

A quiver passed through Paul, shaking him free. What
was he doing, rattling on about his personal life to a
person he barely knew? Telling her things he'd only
partially told Moss, voicing fears he hadn't voiced to
Mary? He fell back in the chair, lightheaded and embarrassed.

He rubbed the chill bumps from his arms, then turned
again to Estelle. A sense of loss engulfed her features,
drawing them taut. Her mouth became as pinched as the
rose of flesh at her throat, her gaze turned inward to
follow its own haunted paths. ''Estelle,'' he said, gently
touching her knee. ''What's wrong?''

She stared for a few seconds, still lost in that private
countryside, then blinked into focus. Her jaw tightened
as if she was willing herself to forget or accept whatever
had upset her, then dragged the pad into her lap. She
scribbled quickly.

Paul accepted the note. ''How did her father die?'' it
read. Paul smoothed the paper across his thigh. ''It was
a long time ago,'' he said.

Estelle tapped the paper, her finger jabbing his thigh.
Paul shook his head. ''I'm not sure,'' he said. ''We only
talked about it once. I'm not sure of the details—''

Estelle's hand closed over his knee. With a sickening
lurch, he fell into her silence once more. ''It happened

a while ago,'' he heard himself say. ''When Mary was eighteen . . .''

THE STORY UNFOLDED INSIDE HIM, REVEALING LINES and creases. Yet each crease was really only part of the same crease, connecting and veering away from itself. Paul marveled at the intricacies of the pattern, the mysterious beauty of it. The unseen hands that unfolded the story were sure and deft, not like his own when he'd pried open the butterfly. These hands knew how to rebuild him and the story afterwards. These hands wanted the tale's heart . . .

He saw Mary at eighteen, a slender, wistful girl with a serious face. Her hair, cut short and wispy, just skimmed her forehead, her blue eyes enormous without the tumble of hair to hide them. She came home from school to find Nolan sitting in the living room on the old Naugahyde recliner, the curtains drawn against the sunny afternoon. He twiddled an unlit cigarette between his fingers, twirling it like a baton. He stood when she walked in, tucking the cigarette into his pocket. His shoulders drooped, parroting the fleshy sag of his basset-hound face. ''Mary,'' he said. ''Oh, Mary. Come sit down.''

Mary touched the arm of the wooden rocker, guiding herself to its seat. The premonition she'd had that morning stalked through her, no longer fierce and hungry, but sated. Like a tiger after a successful hunt. ''Where— where's Dad?'' she said.

Nolan took a deep breath. His lips parted—then closed on nothing. Not a syllable, not a sound.

He struggled to drag the Naugahyde recliner closer to the rocker. Mary stood again and pulled her chair closer to his. Nolan waited till she resettled, then sank into the recliner. ''Mary, your dad's dead.''

Mary recoiled into the rocker, tensing her legs to hold it still. *They found him*, her mind whispered. *The UDF finally found him.* She wet her lips. "Where—what happened?"

"Three guys in a pickup saw two men, a redheaded fella and some other guy, running from the levee, near the Pajaro River," Nolan said, pulling the cigarette from his pocket again. He put it in his mouth, removed it. He spun it through his fingers. "Two of the guys in the pickup got out and went down by the river while the driver followed the two men. They found your dad facedown in the water. He was—he'd been shot. In the—"

"I don't want to know!" Mary blurted. The force of her words rocked her forward. She caught herself. "I didn't mean—I don't want to know. I don't want to remember him with a hole in his head or his chest or—or wherever."

Nolan hung his head. He raised it as if to add something, then lowered it again.

Mary stared at the ceiling. If only she'd been able to explain the premonition to Dad at breakfast. She'd tried, but he wouldn't listen . . .

He'd laughed. "Don't go to work? And what would I do all day? Stay home and watch soap operas?"

"And don't stay home." Just speaking the words gave them weight. A greater urgency crackled through Mary. "Go to a park or something. Or go hiking. You remember that trail, in Nisene Marks? The one that leads to that old cabin? Go there. If you do the whole thing and maybe go up to the campground, it'll take you all day. Just don't be around."

Dad looked at her, his eyes bright with wonder and fear. "Why are you telling me this?"

Mary squirmed. The vinyl kitchen chair creaked. "I don't know. Just a feeling."

"A feeling." Dad appraised her. "A feeling . . . or a warning? Is someone telling you things?"

"No," she said sullenly. "It's just a feeling, okay?"

He rose and knelt in front of her. "But where did it

come from?'' he said. ''Did you dream it? Or did you hear it—from a spirit, say, or . . . an angel?''

Mary glared at him. ''I'm not crazy. I don't hear voices or anything.''

Sadness and relief washed over Dad's features. ''No. No, of course not. Come on, now. Eat your breakfast. You'll be late for school.''

Mary's throat tightened. ''Dad, don't go—''

''Darlin', I can't call in sick because you have a bad feeling. Now eat up. Your eggs are getting cold.'' And he'd risen to go pack his lunch . . .

Mary brushed at her itchy cheek. Tears, and she hadn't felt them—on her skin or in her heart. Dead. The UDF finally got him. After all these years, why not just leave him alone? But no, they had to have their fucking revenge. She hugged herself. Why hadn't Dad listened to her? What could she have said to *make* him listen? What if, when he'd asked about spirits and angels, she'd told him Eileen had told her?

Mary smiled, a sour twist of the mouth. Right. Resurrect his own imaginary friend to convince him. She lowered her gaze and met Nolan's.

''You all right?'' he said.

''For now. It's not real yet. I mean, I believe you, but I can't feel it—'' She tensed. ''Do I have to, you know, identify him?''

Nolan shook his head. ''No. I already did that.''

Mary gaped at him. ''Wait—already? When did they find him?''

''Around noon.''

Mary lunged to her feet. ''And no one called me? No one came to the school to tell me my father had been shot?''

The cigarette disintegrated between Nolan's twitching fingers. ''I told them not to. I told them I'd tell you. I didn't want you to hear it at school.''

She stared at him. Her tension drained in hot, sticky

tears that burned the rims of her eyes. "Nolan, did he die quickly?" she asked.

Nolan nodded.

Mary took a deep breath, asked the one question she'd been avoiding. "What about the men who shot him? Did they catch them?"

"They tried to shoot the driver. The driver's friend had a gun. He killed them both."

Mary closed her eyes. That was one thing, at least, that she wouldn't have to worry about. That the Irishmen would come after her. . . .

PAUL JERKED AS IF WAKING. ESTELLE'S HAND WITH-drew from his knee, her fingers rising like doves. Paul frowned, trying to recapture his thoughts, trying to re-spool the story. He studied the beige carpet, searching for the lost threads.

"She knew who'd killed him," he said, his voice at a distance, as if he were standing outside his body. "Some men were after him—it's long and complicated. It was a revenge thing. Anyway, she knew. The mur-derers had staged the whole thing to look like a robbery. That's what the cops thought. She didn't set them straight. Sure, she could have demanded they track the killers down, but then it would just be a revenge thing again. Better to let it end. She was also afraid that if she caused trouble someone else would come after her. And maybe go after her mother and her little sister."

His voice trailed away. An incredible weariness set-tled over him. He rubbed his eyes, then looked up. Es-telle sat, hands twisted in her lap, her face turned to the door. A sheen of tears glazed her cheek lending her the same false fragility of Teddy's ceramics.

Paul cleared his throat. "Estelle?"

She turned to him, the sorrow in her eyes tempered by anger. *At me?* Paul wondered. Then her expression softened. She inhaled, deep and slow, reaching for the notepad. Without looking at it, she wrote a quick note. "Tell me about Mary," it said.

"About Mary," Paul said. He grasped the back of his neck, tugging at his hair. Everything he had poured out this afternoon was about Mary—what more could she possibly want to know?

TWENTY-FOUR

ELISEO LIFTED THE CAP FROM HIS HEAD AND RAN HIS fingers through his hair. He stopped walking at the edge of the parking lot, then turned to face Salud Para La Gente. »Nothing,« he said. »I guess we should call Maria.«

Hector looked up at the sky. Late afternoon, probably five or five-thirty. »Do you think we should check the hospitals first?«

Eliseo replaced his cap. »We could. Didn't Maria say she already checked them?«

Hector nodded. »Yes. But she didn't know to check the maternity wards.« He arched his back to the accompaniment of little cracks and pops. The boss was right. He was too old to work the strawberry fields. »What was that woman saying, about clinics?«

Eliseo took Hector's elbow and steered him toward Watsonville's Main Street. »There are too many of them. Let's call Maria.«

They turned onto the broad avenue. Eliseo scanned the storefronts. »Maybe we should have asked to use the phone at Salud Para La Gente,« he said. »Let's try this way.«

They turned left and walked toward the plaza. The signs and banners in the shop windows promised sales and bargains—in Spanish. Homesickness weighted Hector's stomach. He missed Gloria. A little. She would still be at work—

»What haven't you told her?« Eliseo said. »Besides Rosa's pregnancy.«

»Told Maria?« Hector said, stalling for time. Time to think, time to force Rosa's fierce, unholy eyes from his mind. »Nothing. There is nothing to tell.«

Eliseo's jaw shifted to one side as he studied Hector. Hector looked away. Two cannons stood facing each other along the front of the plaza. The nearest, a short, stubby cylinder, pointed across the lawn at a slender, more elegant gun. At the midpoint between the two, he would be caught in the crossfire. »Where did they get those cannons?« Hector asked.

»What aren't you telling *me*?« Eliseo said.

Hector's shoulders hunched involuntarily. He stroked his mustache. »It's nothing,« he said. »An old man's phantasms. A trick of the light.«

Or the dark.

Hector glanced at Eliseo. Eliseo still eyed him with suspicion. Tilting his head back, Eliseo said, »Did she lose half of her face?«

Hector recoiled. »No! What makes you say that?«

»You act as if it's something so terrible, no one must know. But, friend, think about this: If it is so terrible, wouldn't it be better for Maria to know and be prepared than to meet this horror unsuspecting?«

Hector's shoulders rose higher. It was true. How would Maria react if they found Rosa as he had last seen her, with her throat blown open and her eyes glittering with contempt? What if Rosa fell dead at Maria's feet, her spirit's goal reached, her need to get to Maria answered? It was too much to imagine, too horrible.

And what if he'd been wrong, back there in the desert? What if Rosa had not died, had only been wounded? It had been three weeks. In that time, Rosa might have healed. Or nearly healed. Perhaps that was why she hadn't gone to Maria or Señora Mendoza yet, because she wanted to wait until a scar formed over the rawness of the wound. If that was the case, it might be best to tell Maria that she'd been shot, so that Maria would anticipate the scar. But telling her that Rosa had died—no. He couldn't do that. Not after her body had walked away.

Hector weighed the ring in his pocket. It was heavy with Conchita's and Rosa's lives. »I watched Rosa get shot, in the throat,« he said. »And I saw her rise and kill the man who shot her.«

Eliseo's face remained impassive as stone. Whether this news shocked or offended him, Hector couldn't tell. They stopped at the corner across from the plaza. Children hung from the cannons, raced across the grass, swarmed over the pavilion. The faint scent of diesel hung in the air.

»A baby might not survive that,« Eliseo said at last. His voice held no judgment, only a quiet contemplation. »Let Rosa tell Maria about the baby. Let her tell Maria about the dead man, too. But the wound—I think you should prepare her for that.«

»All right. But how? Without telling her about the dead man?«

»We could tell her—«

A hand clapped Hector's shoulder. »Ah, you old bastard!« Rigoberto said. His voice floated on a current of beer. »What, you finally got tired of work, work, work? Come. I will show you where to play. And you, Eliseo?«

»I need a telephone,« Hector said. »To call Maria.«

Rigoberto raised his eyebrows. »Your niece? Find a girl for *you*, hombre. Ay, Hector, you're impossible!«

But he steered them across the street and through the plaza. Benches filled with men lined the dirt walkways. Several of them nodded to Rigoberto as he passed. »There is a phone at the library,« he said. »Although why I should lead you there just so you can talk to your niece . . .«

He sniffed and shook his head. »Ah, well. Afterwards, you will both come with me and have a drink. And not Peñafiel. A real drink.« He stopped suddenly, catching at Hector's arm. »Did you hear? The *chupacabra* found the goat ranch last night. The one where they raise goats for doctors, up north. Drained one of the goats, just like old Nelda's.«

Rigoberto started walking again. Eliseo fell in beside him. Hector stood still, a thousand bits of conversation and conjecture rushing to one eerie thought like iron filings to a magnet. *The milagro around her neck*, the girl had said. *The woman by the goat pen had one just like it.* The blood bubbling up from Rosa's throat. The sudden appearance of this *chupacabra* . . . announcing Rosa's arrival? The chill in Rosa's eyes, so unlike her— a ghost or a demon claiming her body from the brink of death?

»Hector,« Rigoberto called. »The sooner you make that call, the sooner we can have that beer.«

Hector blinked, then hurried to join them. »There won't be any beer. Not for me. After I call Maria, there's something I must do.«

Rigoberto jerked his hands in disgust. »Fine, fine. The phone is there,« he said, pointing. He spat at the sidewalk, then stalked away. »You try to help someone . . .«

Eliseo touched Hector's arm. »What do you have to do?«

»I have to go to the goat ranch,« Hector said. »Tonight and every night until I meet the *chupacabra*.«

»The *chupacabra*—?« Eliseo gaped at him. »You think . . . ?«

»I don't want to think,« Hector said. He pressed his lips together. »I don't want it to be true.«

TWENTY-FIVE

WAVES TUMBLED AND CHASED EACH OTHER TO SHORE, bursting into foam along the jetty and the beach. A couple followed the rim of the sea, the evening's last beachcombers, one woman dragging a mast of driftwood. A furrow deepened behind the two women. *Like a furrow of light trailing a shooting star*, Mary thought. She sniffed. A very slow shooting star.

Mary shifted on the sea wall. Sand milled her jeans. The first wisps of fog dampened her skin, shivered through her, melted into dried tears. She pulled at the collar of the flannel-lined windbreaker. Lucky for her that Paul insisted on leaving an old jacket in each of the cars. She stuffed her hands in the pockets, her right hand closing on a scrap of paper. She pulled it out. "I love you bunches," it read in Paul's handwriting. A love note, in case she wore the jacket. Mary smiled and looked out to sea.

The fog continued to sift over Capitola, blown in small puffs past the crescent of lights on the esplanade. She could still see the wharf, but dimmed as if in an old photograph. Breathing in through her mouth, she tasted salt and fish and cold. Judging by the fog-tangled dark, it had to be around nine, nine-thirty. Paul would be home, wondering where she was, what she was up to. There was a pay phone near the car. She'd call to let

him know she was on her way home. She swung her
legs over the sea wall and dropped to the sidewalk. A
man brushed past her, his breath another puff of fog,
this one warm with tequila.

Mary jangled the keys in her pocket. "Little sister,
where are you?" she whispered.

Here, somewhere, unless Tío Hector was wrong and
Rosa had gone searching for someone else. She had a
boyfriend in Fresno, Tío Hector said. *Had*, he'd stressed,
leaning heavily on the past tense as if to dismiss the
possibility Rosa could be there. But why not? Why assume she'd make her way to a sister and papá who had
never fulfilled their promise to send for her? Why come
all this way, with only an address copied from an old
envelope?

But if she did turn to friends—other than this boyfriend—why not turn to Señora Mendoza? *Kathy*, she
reminded herself. Kathy had offered to sponsor Rosa, to
help her find work—and acquire a green card. "When
did you get citizenship, Mary? When you married or
during the amnesty in '86?" Kathy had asked.

"During the amnesty," Mary said. "By the time Paul
and I got married, I had citizenship. All we had to do
was get a license."

Kathy chuckled. "Nice of Congress to make it so
easy." She sobered. "And when you filled out the papers, I bet you used the name you and your father took
here. It might be hard, possibly dangerous, to prove Rosa
is your sister. If the government found out you lied back
in '86, they might deport you. Me, I was born here. They
can't touch me . . ."

Mary stopped beside her car, peering across its roof
at the wave-battered jetty. Kathy spoke of Rosa with
such protective affection; Rosa must know she'd receive
a warm welcome there. And, from what Tío Hector said,
Kathy had been one of Rosa's only friends.

One of her only friends . . . why? Who had Rosa become? The way Kathy described Rosa's intelligence, her earnestness and determination, she sounded like an older version of the little sister Mary remembered. So why hadn't Rosa made more friends? Had she harbored a bitterness inside her, a festering disappointment and distrust, surely it would have colored the stories Kathy told about her. Surely it would have colored Tío Hector's.

No, the portrait they drew between them was of an affectionate, if quiet, person. What was that story Kathy told her? »One night Rosa came to my house around nine in the evening,« Kathy had said. »It was raining and her hair hung nearly to her waist, it was so heavy with water. She had two apples in her hands—shriveled, ugly things. Cold-storage apples, probably from someone's hoard.«

Tío Hector nodded. »From your Aunt Inez. Inez hid apples in the cellar.«

Kathy's face twitched into a suspecting smile. »Anyway, she handed them to me and said, 'Eat one today and one tomorrow. If I can, I'll bring you more.' I took them. They felt like cold, tiny elephants. I thanked her, then asked, 'Why did you bring them to me?' She said, 'You were coughing a lot today and I was afraid you were getting sick. A doctor won't come if you eat apples.' « Kathy laughed. »I'd been teaching her North American sayings. 'An apple a day keeps the doctor away,' that kind of nonsense! Imagine if I'd taught her, 'Don't lose your head,' or 'Sock-it-to-me,' or 'If your eye offends you, cast out your eye.'«

»The last one's biblical,« Eliseo pointed out.

" 'Sock-it-to-me?' " Mary said.

»She came home one day and told me something about stars,« Tío Hector said, shedding some of his meekness. »About wishing on stars and pesos. She said North Americans wished only on shiny things.«

Kathy grinned, shaking her head. »I remember, I remember! I told her North Americans wish on the first star and pick up lucky pennies, blow eyelashes off their knuckles . . . and make wishes on falling stars. She told me she didn't need star luck. 'I already have a star at my shoulder,' she said.«

Tío Hector's sparkling eyes dimmed. »She always acted as if there was something there . . .«

A car horn chirped. Mary shook the conversation from her mind and turned. A man leaned out of a boxy BMW. "Hey, lady," he shouted. "You coming or going?"

Mary opened the Camry door. "Going," she said.

THE FOG SHREDDED ABOVE SANTA CRUZ, DISPLAYING patches of midnight blue. Mary squinted, trying to catch a glimpse of the first star. To her right, a tiny spangle of light glittered. "Rosie, please find me," she whispered. "Come home to me."

The spangle of light moved slowly out of the patch of darkness. Mary screwed her mouth to one side. Great. She'd just made a wish on a plane. Was there a penalty for that?

Mary returned her attention to the road. Highway 1 swept into a tight fishhook, doubling back and under itself in a loop, sharing a lane briefly with Highway 17. Best to be all there for that one—even at this time of night, cross traffic could be tricky. Mary made the loop and headed toward Mission. To her left, another patch of fog peeled away. A star—or a plane—sparkled against the night.

Rosa had a star at her shoulder . . . Mary smiled. Her sister had a poetic streak, probably inherited from Dad. Certainly not from Mamá. Mamá was the practical one, the one who looked at a problem and solved it, while Dad dreamed his way around its edges. Mary swallowed, trying to loosen a catch in her throat. Although when Dad needed to act, he acted.

They made it, didn't they? She was in California,

waiting for a sister who looked like Mamá and talked like Dad—

The hair rose on Mary's neck. A sister who talked to herself, Tío Hector said. Who acted as if there was something at her shoulder. Like Dad.

PAUL HOVERED IN THE BATHROOM DOORWAY, A PER-plexed and uncertain look on his face. Worry always made his face longer, sort of pointed. Mary removed her earrings, trying to ignore his reflection in the mirror. "I just wish you'd left a note," he said.

Mary set the blue topaz studs beside the bottle of rubbing alcohol. "Yes, Mom."

The blue stones drew her gaze. So like the blue of Dad's eyes. So like her own. She got Dad's eyes—

"I worry when it's late and I don't know where you are," Paul said.

—Rosa got Eileen. Or had she simply made up her own imaginary friend?

Paul's voice intruded again. "I feel hurt when you shut me out."

Mary met his gaze in the mirror. "I" messages. He'd resorted to "I" messages: *I feel this, I'm angered by that.* Each phrase carefully constructed not to blame her, simply to let her know how he felt. Mary bit down on a smile, savoring the sudden warmth flowing through her. He tried so hard and he cared so much. But right now, all she really wanted was to be left alone to sort through the fragments of her sister, hoping that in piecing them together, she could find her. How did she phrase *that* as an "I" message?

"I'm sorry," she said, turning. "I didn't expect to be gone so long. The time just . . . slipped away. I didn't think."

Paul's nostrils flared. "Or you were thinking too hard."

Mary stiffened. She didn't need this. Not now. Not tonight.

Paul's shoulders sagged. "I'm sorry. I just—I feel like there's something going on, something you're trying to figure out, but I don't know what it is. We used to talk about everything, but lately it feels like we're keeping secrets from each other."

"I don't have—"

"The last few months, I felt like I've watched you striding into the distance. And now, in the last week, it's gotten worse. What is it, Mary? Is it the baby? We'll keep trying. Forget what the doctor says—we'll go to a specialist now. Three years is too long, even if we are young. Even if it does take some people five years."

Mary stared at him. Is that what he thought this was, her sudden preoccupation? Sadness spread through her. Of course it was. What else did he have to grab hold of? And it was true. She hadn't told him all of her thoughts about the baby, hadn't let him into all of her hurt and despair and anger. For whatever reason she'd held all that back, hoarded it, like Aunt Inez and her apples. For what? She couldn't make sauces and pastries with these corrosive feelings. She couldn't barter them for something more valuable or more wanted. She could only hold them and hope that they would shrink rather than swell.

"Mary?" Paul said.

She leaned against the sink, her hands clasping the lip of the Formica. *Give him the pain of being unable to conceive and keep Rosa and Tío Hector to yourself*, her mind pleaded. "I don't know, Paul. I have a lot of things to sort out. The baby's just one of them."

Paul touched her arms with his fingertips. "I can help you. Let me help you."

Mary let a smile escape. "You going to solve my problems?"

Paul smiled, encouraged by hers. "No. I'm going to listen."

Something in him seemed so touching and vulnerable. Mary looked away to collect her thoughts. *Give him the baby*, her mind insisted. But what if she hurt him with the weight of her own pain? *I'm not going to have a baby. Ever. It's pointless to even try. There's just that crushing death every month when the blood starts to flow. I hate my body. I feel like it's betrayed me. Like it's failed me. It's my fault we're not pregnant. It's my fault we can't have kids. And I'm not even sure—I am sure—I don't even want kids anymore. Yes, sure. Very sure. Why should we? Why disrupt what we have now? Why keep bashing our heads against a wall so our lives can be turned upside down? We're comfortable now. We can do what we want. Why should we share our lives with someone else?*

Because we want to, another part of her mind said. *Because a child is the future, is hope, is a way of giving to life and the love we have for each other.*

It all tumbled through her, a kaleidoscope of contradictions. Her students' faces blended and became part of her imagined child. How could she unleash this on Paul?

Why not tell him? He'd be able to weather it. His vulnerability made him strong, not weak. Strong enough to weather Hector and Rosa, too—

Her throat constricted, her skin prickling. She had talked to Hector and Kathy about Rosa and even about Dad—but they had been part of that life. And from what Hector said, no one had come looking for Mamá or Rosa since Dad died. No one but Hector had come looking for her—

Paul pulled her into his arms, her lowered head crushed against his chest. Mary wriggled, unkinking her neck. "There's so much—" she began.

Paper crinkled in the pocket under her ear. She frowned and pulled back. "What's in your pocket?"

Paul released her, reluctantly, and dipped his fingers into his pocket. "Estelle makes these," he said, removing a piece of folded paper. He handed it to Mary. "I found this one on the reception desk. I think it's a bird."

Mary examined the paper. It had been folded into a *pajarita,* a symbol of childhood. Its head and one wing had crumpled and started to unfold. Mary picked at the paper, unfolding it farther—

The vision snapped through her like a banner in a gale. She caught her breath, suspended in its crackle and wrench. Rosa's face peered out of the creased paper, sorrow embedded in her brown eyes. Then her face unfolded like the paper and became another face, a face Mary had never seen before. "Look for me," the unfolded Rosa said. Mary gasped.

The face vanished. Mary dropped the paper, backing into the bathroom sink. Try as she might, she couldn't remember a feature of the second face, only that it had been there. The only thing she could be sure of was that someone was coming, soon. But was it Rosa? Or was it someone else, someone with news of Rosa? Mary grasped the edge of the sink. Rosa, it had to be, but Rosa was in trouble. Mary must be ready for trouble—and for joy, too.

MARY HUGGED THE CUP WITH HER HANDS. THE HEAT warmed her fingers. She brought the cup to her nose and inhaled the spearmint tea. She smiled and took a sip. "You still growing your own spearmint?"

Nolan scooted himself away from the dinette table so that he could stretch his legs. "Of course. Still got me that whole garden of virtues on the side of the house— chamomile, rosemary, you name it. You about done?"

Mary swallowed, forcing the last of the tea past the lump in her throat. "Yeah, I'm ready. Let's go get some wood."

Nolan squinted at her. "You okay? You look like you been crying."

Mary stared into the mug. A residue of tea leaves

spackled the bottom. What fortune hid there, buried in the leaves? Her reaching across the rift separating her from Paul or her backing away, little by little, until even a shout couldn't touch him? Why hadn't she told him everything?

"Mary?" Nolan said.

Mary sighed and looked up. "Paul and I..." She propped her chin in her hand. How to explain this? "It wasn't exactly a fight. In fact, he probably thinks we cleared a lot of things up. And we did. We did. About the baby. About how I'm not sure I want to have one anymore. Maybe I'm just tired of trying. Maybe I'm trying too hard. Maybe I'm just growing out of whatever phase I was in where I thought I wanted one."

Nolan pursed his lips. "And Paul didn't take any of this too kindly?"

Mary flashed him a smile. "Sorry to disappoint you. Paul was great. But I wasn't. It's not just my doubts about having a baby that's come between us. It's that old fear thing again. I can't seem to find a way to tell him about my sister. Or Tío Hector."

Nolan grunted. "Now, it's not that I don't like Paul."

"You just think I could have done better."

"Not better. Different. Now, about that fear stuff. Mary, that's all over, those men trying to find you and your dad—"

"It's not all over. Not the fear—"

"Mary." Nolan shook his head. "You just got other fears. Maybe you're afraid Paul'll feel threatened by your uncle and your sister. Hey, it's not like you're asking either of them to move in—or are you?"

"Tío Hector turned me down flat." Mary slid in her seat and rested her neck on the back of her chair. "Rosa will have to live with us. Until I can get her a job and a place to live. Or whatever. No, I'm not afraid to move my sister in. But maybe I am afraid of sharing her, after all this time. I don't even know her anymore. She was

seven when I left. She was a sweet little thing, cheerful
and happy, the darling of Daddy's eye. Fiercely loyal to
me, even when I tried to shed her to get some time to
myself or with my friends. You know, a little sister.
Unformed, uncomplicated. But she's not a little girl anymore. She's a woman. She speaks English, she types,
she talks to herself."

Nolan grunted again. "So what you're saying is,
you'd like first crack at her."

Mary sat up. Across from her, Nolan swirled the dregs
of his tea. "Yeah, I guess I would," Mary said. She
frowned. "All these years, she's been *my* sister. I never
really told Paul about her, about the song Dad sang to
her or what she looked like. She was mine. *I* knew her.
Now, I don't know who she is. I can guess what she
looks like because Tío Hector says she looks just like
Mamá. But if Paul and I meet her at the same time,
maybe he'll understand her before I do."

Nolan fixed her with his no-nonsense look. "What?
'Cause he's a shrink?"

Mary pressed her lips together. "That has nothing to
do with him getting to know someone socially—"

"No?" Nolan snorted. "You don't think he uses all
that bullpuckey to size people up? You were lucky you
met him *before* he got all his fancy training."

Mary tried to repress a smile. "Why? Because I'm so
screwed up?"

Nolan crimsoned.

"Put your foot in it?" she teased.

"What I should've said, was that *he* was lucky he met
you before he started using his schooling to figure out
who he likes and doesn't like."

"He likes you," Mary said. *Although why, I don't
know, after all the silences and suspicious looks you've
given him over the years.*

Nolan waved that away. "Yeah, well. So what other
reasons you got? You afraid you won't like her and you

won't want to introduce them? Or that she's some beauty queen going to storm in here and snap him up?''

Mary blinked. Was there more to it than that lifelong habit of fear? Was she afraid she'd lose her husband to her sister?

Mary tried to shake this bull's-eye feeling. A year ago—several months ago—she'd felt completely secure in her marriage. She and Paul talked readily about everything, creating a closeness that sang through her. Their tangled lives swelled in her, a chorus of rich, intense passion that transformed her world. A child had seemed a natural way to celebrate this love. And easy—anyone could have a child.

Anyone but her. It wasn't Paul. His sperm count was high—so high, the doctor had warned her not to let Paul walk unattended past sperm banks or they'd snatch him. No, Paul was fine. But she wasn't. Not that he ever said or did anything to make her feel defective—but how could she avoid it? She wasn't a real woman. Real women could have babies if they wanted to. Only a broken, half-woman produced nothing but blood. Only a flawed woman. And what man would want to stay with such a woman?

Mary gritted her teeth. What a stupid thing to think! What was she, some throwback to the Middle Ages? Paul loved *her*, with or without a child. He'd told her so, in so many words and in so many ways. Stupid, the whole notion was stupid.

But then that tiny seed of insecurity she locked away deep in the back of her heart began to sprout. A broken woman, that's what she was. And why shouldn't Paul fall for her sister? Her sister might well have all of her good traits and new ones besides. Her sister was younger, possibly more attractive—especially if she looked like Mamá. And Rosa might even be able to have children. . . .

Nolan coughed. ''Don't mean to disturb you, but you

got that look on your face. Like you're wallowing in some mud puddle that's not yours. You want to talk some more?''

Mary hesitated. Wallowing, that was an accurate description. If she just kept that in mind—

"No," she said, standing. "Let's get some wood."

TWENTY-SIX

TEDDY STOOD IN THE SHADOW OF RITA'S APRICOT house, waiting for Rita to unlock the passenger door of the red Escort. Paint-splattered grass bordered the driveway.

"I figured, I have to go all the way to Santa Cruz to drop my grandkids off at the Boardwalk, I can take Teddy to work," Rita said, removing the key and ushering Teddy inside. Teddy climbed into the Escort, balancing her lunch on her knees. The car smelled new, although it was at least ten years old.

Rita climbed in. "And, if I work it right, I can even pick you up. What time do you get off? Six?"

"This is wonderful," Teddy said. "You don't have to go to all that trouble—"

Rita jammed the shift into reverse. "No trouble. It'll be better for the kids. Maybe they won't have a chance to spend all their money in the arcade."

At the end of the driveway, Rita lifted herself from her seat to peer into the street. Panic built in Teddy. They would be driving past the strawberry field and the bluff. The woman in the chair—

"I just remembered," Teddy blurted. "I need to pick something up at the Harvest Moon. Is that too much trouble?"

Rita shrugged. "Naw. What's a few minutes?" She

swung the Escort into the street. "So, you like the smell of my car?" she said. "Grandkids got me this little deodorant thing for Christmas. They said, 'Oh, Grandma, we can't get you a new car, but we can help you pretend—' "

Teddy let the words wash over her, rinsing away her panic. She couldn't face the woman in the chair today. Sure, walking or riding, she could force herself not to look—like people force themselves not to look when they pass an accident. And, had she been walking, she could have taken this same route past the market. She'd do that tomorrow.

TEDDY STOOD ON THE OFFICE PORCH, CLUTCHING THE bag from the Harvest Moon. The mango shifted to one side as she rolled the top of the bag tighter. She hadn't known what to get when she walked into the market, and then she'd seen the mangoes. Odd that such a tiny market carried produce at all—but mangoes? They also carried Mexican pastries, Slush Puppies, and tall votive candles decorated with the Virgin Mary. Not the usual corner-market fare.

"You're procrastinating, Teddy," she said. She opened the door.

Estelle, still wearing the black dress, sat at the desk studying the computer screen. Her mouth twisted to the side. Then she jabbed at the keyboard. Her mouth untwisted into a smile. She glanced at the door, her smile widening when her gaze settled on Teddy.

Teddy forced a smile. Her mind tried to undermine the effort. How could Estelle smile and seem happy to see her when she had lied to Teddy yesterday? And about something so important to Teddy. Why tell her the letter of withdrawal had been sent when it had been sculpted into something and left on the desk? Unless . . . the tightness in Teddy's chest relaxed a little. Unless that had only been a copy of the letter.

But it had Teddy's tortured signature in blue ink—

Still, a photocopy might have gone out. Teddy walked over to the desk. "I brought you something," she said and handed Estelle the bag. "I don't know if you like them."

Estelle peeked into the bag. Her lips parted and she looked up quickly. She nodded.

"Good," Teddy said. She sank into her chair. Estelle patted her knee, held up one finger in a just-a-minute gesture, then turned back to the computer.

After a moment's hesitation, Teddy turned on the radio. Van Morrison mumbled the blues. Safe.

She fiddled with the headset, watching Estelle. Should she bring up the letter? What if Estelle told her again that it had gone out? She scanned the desk, but there was no sign of the origami badger. It might be in a drawer. When Estelle went to lunch, she'd look for it. Unless Estelle took it home.

Teddy adjusted the headset. Right. Estelle had been especially proud of the badger and decided to hang it on her refrigerator. She looked again at Estelle.

The computer screen highlighted Estelle's face with a blue tinge. Her cheeks, normally hollowed to a fashionable leanness, rounded with a healthy glow. Her eyes sparkled. Teddy frowned, searching her memory for images of Estelle; had her eyes been so dull before that this sudden light made so much difference? Or had Teddy been so caught up in her own pain and self-pity she hadn't noticed how lively Estelle's eyes were?

The front door swung open and Paul walked in. "Hi, Teddy. Hi, Estelle. Sorry I'm late. Any emergencies?"

"Not since I've been here," Teddy said, turning to Estelle. "Anything?"

But Estelle looked past Teddy, her gaze fixed on Paul. That sparkle flared brighter still. A welcoming curve cupped her lips.

Teddy caught her breath and looked at Paul. To her

relief, he seemed oblivious of his effect on Estelle. Removing his jacket, he frowned at the floor. Dark circles underscored his eyes; his skin had that ashen, troubled-sleep hue. A fight with Mary? He'd been tense for days. A *long* fight with Mary. If Estelle made a play for him, how susceptible would he be?

The phone rang. By the time Teddy hung up, all that remained of Paul was the clapping of his office door and Estelle's gaze lingering on its broad wooden face.

"PICK UP, MARY, PICK UP," TEDDY MUTTERED, LISTENing to the ringing phone. She tapped her foot, looking from the front door to Paul's office door. Estelle wasn't due back from lunch for another forty minutes. Paul was with a client—for at least half an hour. The phone rang again. "Pick up, Mary," Teddy said.

How many rings did Mary and Paul have the answering machine on, anyway? It must have rung at least five times already—

"You have reached the home of Paul and Mary Grant," Mary's recorded voice said. "We can't come to the phone right now. If you leave your name, the time, date, and a brief message, we'll get back to you as soon as we can."

The message was repeated in Spanish. Teddy bit her lower lip. Now what? Any message she left might be picked up by Paul. Wouldn't that be great? *Hi, Mary. I just wanted to warn you that the new receptionist has the hots for your husband—*

The machine beeped. Words rushed out. "Mary, this is Teddy." She paused, forcing herself to slow down. "I was wondering if you'd like to have lunch with me tomorrow. I'll be at work till five and home around seven. Give me a call."

She pressed the button to hang up. Folding her arms over her chest, she stared at the phone. This really wasn't any of her business. Better to just stay out of it—

but Mary and Paul . . . she considered them friends. And it was hard to stand by while people and disappointments came between them. There was nothing Teddy could do about the infertility, but this thing with Estelle—she could defuse that. She hoped.

THE NOTE SLID INTO TEDDY'S FIELD OF VISION, NUDGING the base of the phone. "Are you all right?" it read.

Teddy's cheeks warmed. She turned to Estelle but couldn't meet her eyes. "I'm fine," she said.

Estelle considered her for a minute, then slid another note across the desk. "You're so quiet. Is something wrong?"

The breath swelled in Teddy's chest. She looked at Estelle, watched her carefully. "I was just thinking about my show," she said. "Wishing things were different. It's hard to let go of it, to know it's not going to happen. Suki probably got the letter today . . ."

Estelle nodded, her features creased with sympathy. *It's very hard to let go*, her expression seemed to say.

Teddy stared at her. Not a wince, not a hint of guilt or shame. Teddy cleared her throat. "You . . . did send the letter?" she said.

Estelle smiled. She patted Teddy's arm gently before reaching for the notepad. "It's all taken care of," she wrote.

Teddy tongued her front teeth. *Well, that's carefully worded*, she thought.

Paul's office door opened. Estelle sat a little straighter, smoothing her black dress across her thighs. Paul leaned into the reception room. "Estelle, can you get me Leticia Erlander's file?" he said.

Estelle nodded, rising from her chair.

"Thanks," Paul said and disappeared into his office.

Teddy pursed her lips. Paul was completely unaware of his effect on Estelle. "Estelle," she said.

Estelle looked up from the filing cabinet, a manila

folder in her hand. Teddy hesitated a moment, then said, "Estelle, he loves his wife. Very much."

Estelle stared at her for a minute, then smiled, a slow, crafted smile. Clutching the file to her chest, she leaned over the notepad and scribbled a quick note. "I'm counting on it," it read.

TWENTY-SEVEN

ESTELLE ENTERED THE OFFICE, STOPPING JUST INSIDE the door. She cradled the folder in her arms as if it were a baby. Paul looked up from the notes on his desk and froze, gripped by the fear of being alone with her. Unable to move—up, down, or sideways—he stared at her, the fear weighting his limbs like the slow burn of a hard climb. Something odd had happened yesterday afternoon, something creepy and unnatural. He never would have opened up like that to a near stranger otherwise.

Estelle hesitated, then walked to the desk. Paul broke through the fear and stood. He'd avoided being alone with her all day, finally giving in to the nagging doubt flitting through his mind: *You're making too much out of it. You needed to talk and she was willing to listen.* He'd relaxed and asked her for Leticia's file. Now another part of his mind whispered, *Yeah, she was willing to listen. Too willing.*

Watching her approach him now, he wished he'd gotten the file himself. He glanced at his desk and began rearranging his notes, to avoid her gaze. "Thank you, Estelle," he said, infusing his voice with false warmth. "Just set it on the desk."

But she held onto the file, the manila folder pale against her black dress. Paul looked up.

Concern furrowed her brow. *How are you?* she seemed to ask. *Have you talked to Mary?*

The questions reverberated in his mind like sound, so palpable and real, he answered before he caught himself. "We talked. She—things are fine."

Estelle nodded, unconvinced, and handed him the file. Paul took the folder and flipped through it, pretending to be absorbed. Her footsteps clicked across the room. With a muffled sigh, the door closed.

Paul's shoulders relaxed. He'd been unaware how hunched they were. The way he understood her unnerved him. And the way she drew information out of him. No, that wasn't fair. *He* was the one who had told her too much, been too open with her. It was like meeting a stranger on the bus and confiding his deepest hopes and fears only to find out the stranger was his new brother-in-law. Or like getting drunk at a party and telling an acquaintance his secret longings. His fault, not hers. He'd allowed himself to be drawn in by her attentive silence. Now he felt emotionally naked when alone with her.

Well, he didn't have to be alone with her. Next time he'd get the file himself.

He could fire her—but then what would he do about Teddy? *Let it go*, he told himself. He'd get over it. He just had to guard against any repeats of yesterday afternoon. He opened Leticia Erlander's file.

Clipped to the first page was a piece of paper folded into a pig. He ran his tongue along the inside of his cheek. What did people attribute to pigs? Intelligence, overeating . . . selfishness. A grin twitched across Paul's face. Well, if there was one thing Leticia needed to learn, it was selfishness. She'd swallowed that whole concept of love as sacrifice and her own selflessness and unmet needs as the ultimate expression of love. She'd become a self-appointed martyr who couldn't understand why the people she loved didn't love her back.

Paul stroked the paper pig. Selfishness, self-indulgence. Exactly what Leticia needed.

PAUL SET THE ERLANDER FILE ON THE RECEPTION DESK. Estelle picked it up and gestured with it toward the filing cabinet. "I'm done with it," Paul said.

"How about a late lunch?" Teddy said.

He swung to face her. "It's almost five—"

But Teddy gazed at the front door, the headset's microphone hovering in front of her mouth. "Okay," she said. "I can do that. Happy hour at the Palomar. I'll see if I can get the boss to spring me early." She turned to Paul and winked. "Why don't you come here? You can meet Estelle—"

Paul headed back to his office. Probably Jon or one of her other artist friends. He pushed open the door.

"Paul," Teddy called. "It's Mary."

"I'll take it in here," he said. His heart skipped a beat. Where was she in her cycle? He'd completely lost track. When had her period started? Seven days ago . . . too early to be ovulating. Still—

He picked up the phone. "Hi, beautiful."

"Hi. I just wanted to let you know I won't be here when you get home."

His gut knotted. "Won't be there?"

"I have an errand to run," she said, oblivious to the crack in his voice. "I should be home by seven, seven-thirty."

Paul pinched the bridge of his nose. An errand, not gone for good. He had to stop listening to Moss and his crazy ideas about Mary running off with someone. "Okay," he said. "Listen, do we need to do something soon?"

"Do something? What—? Oh. No. Not yet. I don't know. Maybe we should just skip it this month."

Paul sat on the corner of his desk. He held the phone in both hands, his last connection to Mary. "I don't—can we talk about this? Tonight? Let's go out for a late dinner—''

Mary clicked her tongue. "Listen, I've got to go. See you tonight."

"Love you," Paul said. The line was already dead. He held the phone for a minute, then returned it to its base.

Someone tapped at the office door. "Paul?" Teddy said.

"Come on in," he said, swaying to his feet.

Teddy opened the door and stepped inside. She shut the door. "My ride's here."

"So you're going home," Paul said, unsure how she wanted him to respond.

Teddy rubbed the side of her nose with her brace. "Um, Estelle's still here," she said in a low voice. She drew closer. "Paul, she's got—"

Paul held his breath. "Yes?"

"She's—" Teddy made a face. "Never mind. I'll see you tomorrow." She headed toward the door.

Paul darted after her. "Wait, Teddy. Never mind what? What has she got?"

Teddy cocked her head. She looked up at him, lips pressed thin. "You can take care of yourself. I don't know why I'm getting in the middle of it."

"Middle of what?" Paul said. "Teddy, what's going on?"

Two quick raps rattled the door. Teddy flinched. She reached for the knob. "I'll see you tomorrow."

"Teddy—"

Estelle stood just outside the opening door. Her wary look transformed into a smile. She gestured toward the waiting area.

"Hey! You ready?" a slender gray-haired woman called out. "The grandkids talked me into buying caramel apples, so I got you one, too."

Teddy glanced at Paul before turning to smile at her

neighbor. "Thanks, Rita," she said. She arched her eyebrows. "With nuts?"

Rita nodded. "Oh, you bet. Only the best. Hey, this is a nice place! Look, there's some of your pots and stuff! I like the Ken doll."

Teddy joined Rita. "A collaborative effort. See you tomorrow, Estelle. Take care, Paul."

Teddy and her neighbor swept out the front door, riding the current of Rita's rapid patter. A stillness settled over the reception area after the door thumped shut. Uneasiness prickled along Paul's spine. *Take care.* He glanced at Estelle. She bent over the desk, gathering her things, getting ready to go home. *She's got—*

What? Teddy couldn't possibly know about yesterday—

Estelle lifted her purse from her chair and slung it over her shoulder. She then picked up a small paper bag. *She's got . . .* Was she taking something she shouldn't, something that belonged to the office?

Paul feigned amiable curiosity. "What's in the bag?"

A childlike smile brightened Estelle's face. She reached into the bag and withdrew a mango. She pointed toward Teddy's side of the desk.

"From Teddy?" Paul said. "How thoughtful!"

A sudden thought struck him—what animal would Estelle make for Teddy? Certainly not a pig. Teddy might be generous, but she knew how to take care of her own needs.

Estelle drew his attention with a soft shuffle of her foot. She held out the mango, questioning him with her eyes again. *Would you like to share it with me?*

Paul shook his head. "No, no. That's your bit of gold." He hesitated. "Estelle, those animals you've been attaching to the files. Have you made one for Teddy?"

Estelle shrugged and nodded as if to say, *Sure. No big deal.*

Paul held his breath. "What did you make for Teddy?"

Placing the mango in the bag, Estelle went back to the desk. She set purse and bag beside the keyboard, then picked up a sheet of letterhead. She folded a corner to the opposite side, folded and tore away a narrow strip at the bottom. Unfolding the paper, she revealed a square. The paper began to change under her rapid fingers. Within minutes, she set a spider on the reception counter.

Paul marveled at the paper arachnid. Eight curved legs, a sturdy little body, tiny mandibles—all it lacked was thread. An astonished laugh escaped him. "That's incredible," he said. "But why a spider for Teddy?"

Estelle gave him an are-you-for-real look. She pointed to Teddy's ceramics. Paul nodded. Creativity. Artistry. "Yes, of course," he murmured.

He met Estelle's open gaze. Curiosity—and vanity— got the better of him. "What about me?" he asked.

Estelle smiled and reached for another piece of letterhead. She reduced this one to a square, too, before folding, unfolding, and bending the paper. She set a crude bird on the counter. It was just like the one he'd found on the counter two days ago. The one he showed to Mary last night.

Paul picked it up, turning it this way and that. But what did it mean? Birds often stood for freedom or flightiness. Or other things, depending on the bird. Eagles stood for pride and bravery, geese for pomposity and silliness, roosters for sexual prowess, parrots for talkativeness. He studied the paper bird. It looked suspiciously like a parrot. He didn't talk that much, did he?

Or was that the point? He *should* talk more. To Estelle. About personal things.

His head jerked up. Estelle eyed him with studied interest. She jotted something on a Post-It, then stuck it to the counter. "It's a *pajarita*," the note read.

"Not a parrot?" Paul said.

Estelle shook her head. Paul brushed the bird's head. *Pajarita*, little bird. What did that mean? That he was still a fledgling, learning to fly? Or that he needed to remember he still had a lot to learn? True enough. He smiled, wondering what Estelle would make for Mary.

Estelle brushed the skin below his lower lip with gentle fingers. A question flitted across his mind—*What's that smile about?*

"Mary," Paul said, then stepped back. "Just thinking about Mary."

That light flickered in Estelle's eyes again. She smiled. Collecting a paper and pen, she walked around the reception desk to join him. She cupped his elbow and guided him to the waiting area. That sense of falling rushed over him again. He dropped onto the nearest sofa, still flailing inside, snatching at any thought or inner strength that could prevent him from cratering.

Estelle withdrew her hand. He grasped hold of himself, but a heaviness spread through his arms and legs, anchoring him in the soft, plush cushions.

Estelle sat next to him, her knee touching his. She scribbled a quick note and set it on his thigh, sliding her fingers from the paper to the soft cotton of his Dockers. A blur of light trailed her movement. The falling sensation returned.

Paul glanced at the note. "Tell me about Mary," it read.

Paul wet his lips. "But I told you about her yesterday. I told you how we met, about her career, her family. What more do you want to know?"

Before he finished speaking, Estelle handed him another note. "What is she like with children?"

"She's great," Paul said. "Kids love her. Sometimes we run into some of her students at the mall or downtown and they always come over to talk to her. The younger ones hug her and hold her hand. She's very sweet to them."

Sweet—was that really the right word? Patient, loving, respectful . . . if those things could be called sweet, Mary was sweet to them. She gave each child her whole attention when they met, made the child the center of their shared universe until parents came to reclaim them.

Estelle squeezed Paul's knee. He looked up. She made that gathering motion with her other hand. *And?*

The fall accelerated. "Some friends of ours have a daughter," he heard himself tell her from somewhere far away. "She and Mary were very close—until they moved to the Sierras. . . ."

MARY CLEARED THE CHERRY COFFEE TABLE, SETTING the crystal frog and the brass frog on the blue carpet. With a grunt, Ashley tried to scoot one of the recliners out of the way. Her skinny, freckled arms trembled. The chair was too much for her five-year-old strength. She shoved the coffee table farther away instead.

Mary set a box of crayons and loose sheets of copier paper on the table, then sat beside Ashley. She smoothed a strawberry blond curl from the little girl's full-moon face. "It's not so far," Mary said.

Ashley nodded. She selected a purple crayon and drew a crooked house. "You do the sky," she said.

Mary picked out a blue crayon and scribbled above the house. "Do we need a bird in the sky?"

Ashley twisted her face, scrutinizing the drawing. "Two birds," she said. "And a sun and some stars. I'll make the stars."

Mary nodded. Beside her, the little head bent over the drawing. Green stars appeared above the house. Mary picked out a brown crayon for the birds.

Ashley's head popped up. "You can't do that! They can't be brown!"

"Ah. What color should they be?"

"Blue."

Mary suppressed a smile. "Just like the sky?"

Ashley frowned, the tip of her tongue peeking between her lips. "No. That other blue. The one that's kind of purply. That one." She handed Mary the blue-violet crayon, then picked out a yellow-orange crayon and drew a tiny, sad sun.

Mary left her bird unfinished, its wingless body suspended beside a green star. "The sun looks unhappy."

"She is," Ashley said. "She doesn't want to move. Not even if there is a lake and trees and things."

Mary set the crayon down. "You're very sad about leaving."

Ashley's frown deepened, her lower lip flaring into a pout. "I'm sadder that you're staying. Why can't you come with us?"

The breath caught in Mary's chest, squeezing like a vise. Why couldn't she? Why couldn't she and Paul just follow Ashley, Justine, and Erik to Truckee? "I'm sad, too," Mary said. "But you know what? You might be far away, but I'll always be with you. And you'll always be with me."

Ashley considered this. "She needs wings or she's going to fall," she said, pointing to the wingless bird with her crayon.

Mary drew wings on the bird, great arching wings to keep it aloft. She drew a second bird, close to the first. Ashley watched, scratching her eyebrow with the yellow-orange crayon. A flake of wax clung to the fine, blond hairs.

"That's better," Ashley said. She drew beaks on the birds. Selecting a black crayon, she drew smiles, little crescents on the sides of the yellow cones. "They're going to make the sun happy. She's sad because she wants them to visit her."

The vise in Mary's chest rose to her throat. "I'll visit you," she said. "And you can visit me."

Ashley looked up at her, then bent over the drawing.

With the black crayon she drew a smile over the sun's sad yellow mouth.

PAUL BLINKED, DISCONCERTED TO FIND HIMSELF IN THE waiting room rather than at home—and, curiously, startled not to be Mary. He'd felt the memory from the deepest part of himself, not as if it had happened and to someone else, but as if he were living it now. Love flowed through his veins, threatened to spill over at any minute in sad, red tears. To love so deeply, so unselfishly—to expect nothing in return. And to be rewarded with that sudden crayoned smile—

Estelle set a note on his thigh. "Did Mary ever visit?"

"Several times," Paul said. "But you know how it is with kids. They grow up, make friends, change. Unless you're there to see them through all their triumphs and tribulations, they kind of drift away. They're very *now*. But we've been up there or they've been down here, oh, once every two months or so in the last three years."

Estelle nodded, then wrote on her pad. She handed Paul the note. "Mary should have a child," it said.

Paul folded the note once. "Not all 'shoulds' come true," he said.

TWENTY-EIGHT

HECTOR HUNCHED DEEPER INTO THE THIN JACKET. THE sun had burned down all day, raising a rumpled, sweaty smell from his clothes and those of the other farmworkers as they bent over the strawberries. Now, in the coming dusk, a wind-borne chill seeped through everything, blown in from the coast. With few trees to block it, the breeze overlay the yellowed, grassy hills.

He followed Eliseo's lead and sheltered behind a curling, twisted oak. Beyond the tree, surrounded by a wooden corral, the barn had already turned gray in the fading light. Large and square, the building squatted on a plain of trampled earth and fragrant goat dung. A soft bleat escaped through the gate, slatted at the top so that the warm, woolen scent of goat drifted from the barn into the chilled yard. Hector wondered how many goats the wood and metal structure held. Here in California, it probably housed far fewer goats than the building could actually hold. North Americans never used all the space they had—in their houses, their offices, or their barns.

»Do you think we're too early?« Hector asked.

Hands balled in the pockets of a hooded sweatshirt, Eliseo shrugged. »Who knows? Didn't the *chupacabra* kill Nelda's goat in the evening? Before dark?«

Hector scuffed a foot across the dusty ground. »It did.«

He placed a hand on the oak's furrowed bark and leaned against the tree. The grooves bit into his palm, re-creating the wood's grain in his flesh. He swayed to his feet, tucking his hands into his jacket pockets.

It had taken a day and a half to find the farm. »Why would it be easy?« Eliseo had muttered after a trip to the library. All the librarian had been able to find was an article on the goats. »The company has had to face hostile neighbors, hearings on zoning, controversy on the ethics of the technology—why would they want anyone to know where they are?«

Eliseo crouched now beside the oak. »We can see from here,« he said. »Sit down. We may be here awhile. Better to rest a little.«

Hector sank to the ground. His lower back protested, the ache easing only when he sat. He scooted until his spine nestled against the tree. »I'm too old for these kinds of adventures,« he said.

Night deepened around them like a *gavacha*'s blush. Like Maria's blush. And, like Maria's eyes, the stars twinkled and glittered between the wisps of fog. He smiled to himself. Quite a woman, his niece. Ready to take charge and do what needed to be done. She'd always been like that, even as a young girl. There was that time when she was ten and the local bully stopped her and Rosa on the way home from the market. Hector had been sitting with his friends Carlos and Raul in the plaza. He saw it all.

The bully, a twelve-year-old boy named Enrique, towered over the two girls. Legs spread wide to block their way, he spat at Maria's feet. »What's in the bag, little gringa?« he said.

»Peppers, for my mamá,« Maria said.

Enrique sneered. »Such a large bag of peppers. Why would a woman cooking for gringos want peppers?«

He reached to snatch the bag away. Hector started to rise. Carlos patted his arm. »Wait,« he said. »The girl, she's brave. Let's see what she does.«

Maria passed the bag to Rosa. »Run,« she said.

Rosa darted around Enrique, then turned to watch from beyond the bully's reach. She held the bag of peppers close to her chest.

Enrique's eyes narrowed. He spat again at Maria's feet. »That was stupid, little *gavacha*,« he said, taking a step toward her.

Rosa crept closer, watching her sister. Maria ignored her, holding her ground as the bully swaggered closer. »You're the stupid one,« Maria said. »Picking on a little girl. And in the middle of the plaza.«

Enrique smirked. »By the time anyone comes to save you—«

Hector lunged to his feet, shaking off his friend's hand. But before he could reach Maria and the bully, Maria jabbed her fist into Enrique's crotch. Rosa darted forward then and smacked the bully across the back of the skull with the bag of peppers. Enrique dropped to the ground, writhing and gasping for breath, one hand clutching his crotch, the other clasping the back of his head. Maria spat at Enrique's feet. She took Rosa's hand and led her away. Rosa handed her the torn, crumpled bag. The neck of a Coke bottle protruded from one of the rips. »Maybe we should have told him about the Coca Cola,« Rosa said.

Maria shrugged. »He knows now,« she said.

Hector sighed. Yes, Maria sized up a situation and acted on it quickly. More so than Rosa. Rosa took time to think things through, as if consulting with someone. Had it been Maria that returned to México with Conchita, she'd have been across the border sooner. And, had she met the same monster Rosa did, she'd probably be dead.

Like Rosa? Hector scowled. That he didn't know.

She'd certainly looked alive, but her eyes were so strange and different—

»What do you plan to do if it is Rosa?« Eliseo said.

Hector shifted. »I don't know. Approach her, I guess. Tell her I want to take her to Maria.« He pressed his thighs together to warm his hands. »Do you think I should let her finish—if she attacks a goat?«

Eliseo grimaced. »I don't know. Maybe she needs it.«

»Needs it?«

»To stay alive.«

Hector chewed the ends of his mustache. »To replace the blood she lost in the desert . . . it's possible. I guess I haven't wanted to think about that.« He stared out into the quiet night, willing Rosa to appear. Nothing took shape in the darkness. »We'll let her finish,« he said.

Eliseo nodded. Silence wedged itself between them. Eliseo reached into his pocket and drew out something wrapped in white paper. He set it on the ground. Taking a knife from his pocket, he cut it in two. »Here,« he said, handing one half to Hector. »It's cold, but it's food.«

Hector squinted at the burrito. »Ay, Eliseo, you think of everything.«

HECTOR RESTED HIS CHIN ON HIS KNEES, SHAKING HIS head once to loosen sleep. He scanned the fog-shrouded darkness. »Do you think she'll approach from some other direction?« he asked.

Eliseo inhaled with a hiss. »She might. But the goats are here. She'll have to come here.«

Hector nodded. He sat up, stretching his arms and rolling the kinks from his neck. »What time is it?«

Eliseo glanced at his watch. »Eleven-thirty. Perhaps we should take turns sleeping. We won't be good for anything tomorrow—«

Hector silenced him with a hand on the arm. »There,«
he whispered.

A figure broke from the fog and drifted toward the
goat pen. The sway of its movement suggested a woman.
As it drew nearer, it became more real, more distinct:
definitely a woman, her long, dark hair curled by the
fog, her head held high by a curved and elegant neck.
She walked slowly, as if strolling across the plaza on
Sunday. At the edge of the wooden fence, she stopped.

»Is it?« Eliseo whispered, his voice barely a breath.

»I don't know,« Hector said.

Hiking her black dress above her knee, the woman
climbed into the corral. She walked across the trampled
ground, slowing as she approached the barn. She
stopped at the door, pressing her face between two slats.
Soft bleats greeted her. The woman clicked her tongue
at the goats. Holding up her hand, she rubbed her fingers
together as if calling a cat. Hector imagined the goats
swaying hoof to hoof, crowding each other, straining
against their pens to get at the woman.

She opened the door and entered the barn, disappearing from view. The goats fell silent.

»Can you tell?« Eliseo whispered.

Hector shook his head.

The woman stepped out into the corral, leading a
large, russet-colored goat. Shutting the barn door, she
knelt beside the goat, fumbling something from her dress
pocket. The goat opened its mouth to bleat. No sound
escaped its lips; instead it gummed the air like a dying
fish. The woman stroked its head, talking to it in a voice
so low Hector couldn't hear so much as a hiss. With a
chill he realized that, like the goat, not a sound flowed
from the woman's mouth.

Or was she speaking too softly? That had to be it. He
crept closer. A bit of gravel rattled under his foot. He
pressed low to the ground, trying to align himself with
a fence post.

The woman looked up. She peered into the night, a frown implied by the thrust of her chin. Turning toward Hector and Eliseo, she started to rise, still cradling the goat's head. Hector held his breath. Was it her? She looked like Rosa—but then, like that night in the desert, she also looked like a stranger. She *moved* like a stranger; her steps had less of a glide, her hips had moved sharply without that graceful roll from side to side, her arms had seemed heavy. Hector squinted, trying to see her face.

The woman listened to the fog. She turned her attention back to the goat, soothing it with caresses and unspoken words. The goat quivered. One hand still cupping the goat's chin, she raised the other. Something gleamed—a long, two-tined fork. The woman turned it in her hand so that the tines were aimed at the goat's neck. She plunged the fork into the animal's throat.

Eliseo grasped Hector's forearm. Hector leaned into his friend's grip.

The goat teetered on its feet but did not cry out. The woman withdrew the fork and pulled the reeling body into her arms, burying her face in its neck. The goat shuddered as she sucked at its throat.

Queasiness gurgled through Hector's stomach. The thought of the hot, sticky blood flowing down the woman's throat sickened him. It sickened Eliseo, too. Eliseo's grip tightened, threatening to cut off Hector's circulation.

Hector held his breath. Would that be so bad? Not to feel anything? This woman, this *bruja*, couldn't be Rosa. Not his Rosita. Please, God . . .

The goat wobbled on its feet, its head flopping away from the woman. She pulled back, wiping her mouth with the back of her hand. The goat crumpled to the ground.

The woman's shoulders slumped. Her head listed to one side, a desperate sadness radiating from her. She stroked the goat's body, as if to reassure its soul, then stood. Slipping the fork back into her pocket, she backed away. She crossed the corral and climbed over the fence.

Eliseo's breath seared Hector's ear. »Once she's farther away from the barn,« he whispered, »we'll stop her.«

Hector murmured. He raised himself into a runner's crouch. Eliseo's hand fell from his arm, exposing the sweaty skin to the fog. Hector shivered.

The woman stood for a minute, her face tilted to the sky. Without glancing at the barn, she walked back the way she had come.

Eliseo sprang after her. »Wait!« he called out.

The woman whirled toward them, her eyes wide with alarm. She ran.

Eliseo sprinted after her. »We won't hurt you! We just want to talk to you!«

Hector stumbled after them, his legs stiff and useless with cold. He paused to rub the cramps from his calves, then lumbered to catch up. Eliseo drew closer to the woman with each stride, his right hand reaching for her, grasping for a handful of her dress, her hair, her arm. Swerving right, then left, she eluded him until her toe caught in a gopher hole. She pitched forward, arms flailing like wings. Eliseo snatched at the waist of her dress and yanked her to her feet.

»We just . . . want to . . . talk to you,« he wheezed.

The woman hovered, suspended on her toes, ready to bolt at the first opportunity. Hector loped to a stop two meters away. The woman turned to him. His gaze fixed first on the rupture of scar tissue at her throat before traveling to her face. His mouth went dry. Those arched cheekbones, that rosebud mouth—and those desert-cold eyes, devoid of Rosa's warmth.

He cleared his throat, swallowing once. »Rosa,« he said. »Rosa, I've been searching everywhere for you.

I've found Maria. She wants to see you. Rosa, come with us. I'll take you to her.«

Rosa backed away, twisting once, trying to free herself from Eliseo's grip. She glared at Eliseo, her cheeks hollowing.

»It's all right,« Hector said. »This is Eliseo, a friend of mine. He's been helping me search for you.«

Eliseo nodded, smiling at her, trying to look welcoming. He succeeded only in looking frightened.

Hector held out his hand to her. »Come, let us take you to Maria.«

Carefully, cautiously, Eliseo took Rosa's hand. They both jerked as if connected by a live wire, Eliseo's hand wrenched from hers by an explosion of sparks. The sparks flared, tiny stars against the night, bathing both their faces in a white glow. They gazed at each other, eyes glittering with recognition and understanding. Eliseo held his hand up, palm facing her. She returned the gesture, and for a moment Hector thought they might touch again, creating another fountain of sparks. Then Rosa turned and fled. Eliseo lowered his hand. He watched her go.

Hector stared at him. Taking a deep breath, he darted after Rosa. Eliseo clasped his arm. »No, friend,« Eliseo said. »Let her go. When she is ready, she will find Maria. When she is ready, she will return to you.«

Hector pulled against Eliseo's restraint. He scanned the dry hills. Rosa had disappeared. Hector sagged into the emptiness of the gray night.

He turned on Eliseo, jaw trembling. »Why did you let her go?«

»There are things she needs to do,« Eliseo said. »Just as there are things I need to do. Come, let's go home.«

Hector shook himself free. »What do you need to do? What happened between the two of you? Don't lie to an old man. I saw the sparks.«

Eliseo sighed. »I shouldn't have touched her, but I didn't know. Come, it's late.«

He gestured for Hector to follow. Hector hesitated. Eliseo walked a few steps, stopped, turned to Hector. Hector kicked at the dried grass and plodded after him.

When they reached the goat pens, something caught Hector's gaze, a scrap of white. Eliseo passed it without a glance. Gaze fixed on Eliseo, Hector plucked the paper from the ground as if swiping at the dewy heads of the grass. An origami bird, a *pajarita*, made of stiff paper.

Eliseo glanced over his shoulder. Hector slid the *pajarita* in his jacket pocket, hoping Eliseo wouldn't notice. »Hector,« Eliseo said. »There is something you should know.«

Hector snorted. »There are many things I should know,« he said. »What are you willing to tell me?«

»There is very little of Rosa left,« Eliseo said. »In truth, I don't know that there is anything of Rosa left. That woman is—she is—«

Hector shook his head, bewildered and sickened. The truth of Eliseo's words rang through him. »What are you saying?« he said.

Eliseo hung his head, watching his feet rise and fall. »When Rosa talked to herself—did she listen as if someone was answering?«

The ringing in Hector's heart chimed louder. »She did. I overheard her a few times. Once I heard her refer to this other self as Luz.«

Eliseo nodded, then fell silent. Hector shuffled behind, uncertain whether to question Eliseo further. The answers loomed between them, large and frightening and unreal. That last would change as soon as they were spoken.

Hector shoved his hands into his jacket pockets. Paper crinkled under his right hand. Glancing at Eliseo, he drew the *pajarita* from his pocket. He kept his gaze fixed on the other man's back and unfolded the paper bird.

He glanced down. Printed across the top of the paper was a name and address. A business address, Hector guessed. Perhaps the address of the place this woman who was Rosa and not Rosa worked. Tomorrow he would go and see.

He balled the piece of paper and returned it to his pocket. He would go—without Eliseo and Eliseo's caution.

TWENTY-NINE

MARY SAT AT THE KITCHEN TABLE, STARING OUT INTO the garden. Browned petals fell from the last rose. Dust covered the white loveseat between the apple tree and the rose. A slight haze of neglect—or near-neglect—seemed to tinge everything. She really needed to weed a little, be sure everything was getting enough water. What would it hurt if she stayed home this morning and took care of her garden? What would it hurt if she stayed home and took care of *herself?* In the afternoon she could either meet Tío Hector or go back to Barrios Unidos. Or wait till evening and hit the salsa clubs and the bars again. Nothing Tío Hector or Kathy Mendoza had said evoked the image of Rosa the party girl, but perhaps, here in this strange, new place, Rosa had taken to the bars to meet people. Mary wrinkled her nose, remembering the loud music solidifying around her when she first walked into a bar—and the men peeling away that same shrouded layer with their lecherous gazes.

Mary hissed between her teeth. She turned over the stone frog in her hands, feeling its bubbled back, its webbed toes. Maybe this evening, when she met with Teddy for happy hour, she could enlist her aid. It might not be so unsettling if she had someone with her.

She set the frog between her thighs. But that was

hardly fair to Paul, for her to stay out late again. And with his receptionist. She should just enlist *his* aid, tell him the whole thing, although after keeping it to herself for the last week or so, how did she begin? *Oh, by the way, my uncle's in town and he says my sister may be in Santa Cruz. I know I should have told you . . .* Right. And when he asked, *Why didn't you?* somehow, *I don't know* didn't seem like an answer that he'd find very satisfying.

She lifted the frog from the seat and set it on the table. That feeling that Rosa would be here soon didn't help. When she'd climbed into bed beside Paul last night after returning from the bars, she'd snuggled close to him only to scuttle away quickly. A strange, sweet scent clung to him, a perfume almost, and that feeling returned: Rosa was coming, would be here soon.

Why such strong visions when she drew near Paul? Mary pushed the frog to the center of the table.

So far this morning, she'd managed to avoid him, slipping out of bed first, showering quickly and alone. She'd pulled on her jeans and padded down here. He hadn't surfaced yet, but he would soon. The stormy pounding of the shower had stopped several minutes ago—

The phone rang. Mary glanced at the clock. Ten to seven, too late for Tío Hector to call. He'd be in the fields by now. What had he insisted on doing alone yesterday? Had he found Rosa?

The phone rang again. Mary hopped from the chair and answered it. "Hello?"

"Mary, Mary. How's my girl?"

Her body relaxed. "Nolan! What are you doing up so early?"

"Couldn't sleep. I got something on my mind. I was wondering, maybe you could come for breakfast. You eaten yet?"

Paul walked into the kitchen, buttoning his shirt. He questioned her with a look.

Mary waved him away, then turned her back on him. "No, not yet—"

"Good!" Nolan said. "Then come on down and let an old man get something off his chest."

Mary glanced over her shoulder at Paul. "Twenty minutes soon enough?"

"What, you got wings on that little car of yours?" Nolan chuckled. "I'll have an omelet waiting for you, Princess."

Mary hung up. She avoided Paul's gaze. "I've got to go."

Paul's voice sounded tired—and hurt. "Now? Mary, I just—I haven't seen you. I don't even know when you came home, just that it was late. Or where you were."

"Want to give me the third degree?" Mary said, and instantly hated herself.

Before she could try to soften it, Paul said, "No. No, I don't. Or maybe I do. I wish it didn't matter to me where you were last night, but it does." His chair squeaked under his weight as he sat down. "You seem so . . . different lately. So . . . distant. I don't understand. If I've done something to upset you—or even if I haven't—I'd like to help. Listen, advise, distract, whatever you want."

Mary shook her head. She walked over to the table and touched the frog. "I just have a few things I need to sort out. On my own. I'm sorry."

Paul's fingers brushed her knuckles. "That's a hard one for me, leaving you alone, but I'll try. Mary, maybe we should see someone."

Mary flinched, meeting his gaze for the first time. Lined with tension and fear, his face looked years older. "Paul . . ." she began, then stopped.

He turned away. "I know, I know," he said. "Not one of my friends. Not someone in Santa Cruz. We can go over the hill."

He winced at the desperation in his own voice, a flush

of anger darkening his skin. "Maybe we should have gone long before this, talked out all the grief and frustration over the baby. But I thought we could do it, just us, sort through all the hurt and stuff—" He turned to face her again. "Who was that? On the phone?"

If Mary'd hated herself for the earlier comment, she hated herself even more for the lie that escaped her lips now. "One of the teachers from school. She wants to have breakfast."

Horror boiled in the pit of Mary's stomach. Oh, God, what had she done? What would it matter to Paul if she had breakfast with Nolan? But Nolan was tangled up in the search for Rosa and Rosa had been woven so completely into that frightened, protective silence—

A silence that might even protect Paul. *Go on, Mary*, she taunted herself. *Justify your cruelty.*

Disgust and fear quivered through her. She pushed past Paul, afraid to look at his face. "I've got to go," she said.

Paul caught her wrist. "Mary—"

She looked up at him. The lie reflected in his eyes. He knew, but he didn't know what she was hiding or what she was covering up. Neither did she, anymore. Her chest constricted around a hard, shattered ache. *God, please*, she prayed, *please. Protect me and promise me I haven't destroyed everything. I'll tell him everything tonight. Everything.*

Paul released her and shuffled back a step. "You better get going. I guess I won't see you till after your date with Teddy."

Mary clutched at him, pulled him into an embrace. His body, usually so yielding and so well molded to hers, hardened under her touch into a protective shell. She kissed him. "I love you," she said as she stepped back.

His shoulders drooped. He took a sip of air, started to

speak—then nodded. His voice strangled in his throat. "Go on," he said.

"THERE'S MY GIRL," NOLAN SAID, USHERING HER IN-side.

Mary kissed his cheek. "Hello, Nolan."

He ducked his head before looking up at her. He studied her face, a fearfulness etched into his own. Mary's heart contracted. What was this? Why did the two most important men in her life have to fear her?

Nolan led her to the kitchen. "I just finished your omelet. Jalapeños, avocados and potatoes. They been having a health scare about that Mexican cheese you like, so I put in Jack instead."

Mary inhaled. "Jack's fine. It smells wonderful."

"Good, good," Nolan said. He pulled out a chair for her. "You sit down and I'll serve you."

They exchanged small talk. Mary nearly grinned when Nolan started discussing the weather, but the seriousness with which he discussed it—no, the *need*—stopped her. Whatever he wanted to talk to her about took a lot of courage. She let him ramble.

After they'd both pushed their plates away, Nolan picked up a fork and began fiddling with it. "Now, Mary, what I got to tell you—it's hard, real hard for me," he said. "You might hate me . . ."

Mary waited for him to continue. He squirmed in his seat, setting the fork down, picking it up again, setting it down. Mary leaned across the table and touched his arm. "Nolan, go on," she said. "What could possibly make me hate you? You took me in after my father died, made sure I went to college, loved me. There's nothing you could tell me, Nolan, nothing, that would make me hate you."

Nolan swallowed, his face squinched with discomfort. "Mary, this is something I been meaning to tell you for a while, but just couldn't screw up the nerve to do it. I kept trying to think of the right time—the right time for *me*, I guess. A time when maybe it wouldn't matter so much to you and you could forgive me.''

His nervousness was contagious. Mary picked up her spoon and began to fidget.

''Yesterday, we started talking about the baby thing,'' Nolan said. ''And you said you just didn't think it was ever going to happen and you thought that was maybe fine 'cause maybe you don't really want kids anymore.''

Mary set the spoon down without a sound. She settled her hands in her lap. ''Yes. I may change my mind—''

A look of terror and misery filled Nolan's eyes. He swallowed again, forcing himself to continue. ''But you also said that maybe things were better this way. Kids would change things so much, keep you from doing stuff you want to do, maybe keep you from achieving goals and all.''

Mary nodded. ''Yes. Yes, I did.''

The fork spurted out of Nolan's hands and clattered to the floor. ''Well, that's what made me feel like I could tell you now. Mary, you can't have kids. Never.''

A bubble of disbelief rose in Mary's throat. ''What— don't know—it's not true—''

''It's true, Mary,'' Nolan said in a small voice. ''You haven't been to any specialists yet, but they'll tell you. I been dreading the day you'd decide to go to one.''

Mary shook her head. ''But, Nolan, the doctor says I'm healthy—''

''Healthy, but you haven't had a baby. He doesn't know. He figures your body's not ready and it's just going to take some time. He figures it'll happen without all them other doctors poking and prodding at you.''

Mary's hands knotted in her lap. ''He says a lot of the tests are invasive. He says they might do more harm than good. He's checked everything he can without forc- ing tubes and dyes and things and everything is normal. I have my period every month—''

"Well, I guess it didn't affect that," Nolan mumbled.

Mary stiffened. "What didn't affect that?"

"The stoneseed root. It does in mice, but . . ." His voice was barely audible now. "I put it in your tea. Every morning till you moved out. Stoneseed root. Grew it myself. I was so afraid, what with all the wildness and rampant sex and all, I was so afraid you'd go to college and some fool'd get you pregnant and all those dreams and goals you had, well, they'd just fly away. Just disappear."

A brittle stillness settled over Mary. "Tell me about stoneseed root," she said.

"Well, it . . . the Shoshone women used it."

Mary cleared her throat. "Why?"

"Sterility," Nolan whispered.

Mary shrank back in her chair. "No, that's—"

"For six months they'd drink this cold tea," Nolan said. His words accelerated, tumbling one after another. "I figured it might not be as strong in hot tea, so I just kept giving it to you. You had so many dreams and ambitions, I just didn't want to see them get lost in a mound of diapers. And the guys you brought around, well, they reminded me of me when I was their age— young and horny. Looking for an easy piece. And even though I trusted you, I didn't trust them. Suppose they weren't as honorable as me? Suppose they decided to force you? So I protected you the only way I knew how."

"Sterility," Mary said.

"Permanent," Nolan said, a twist of misery lodged in his voice. "I mean, you and your dad were Catholics, didn't believe in birth control. So I figured, if you didn't know, you weren't sinning and God would take it okay. He might hate me, but He'd be okay with you. And you'd be safe. You'd have a good life." He pressed his lips together. "Never occurred to me you'd want kids. . . ."

Numbness spread through Mary until she floated, lightheaded, to her feet. She stood beside the table, suspended in thought, all emotion dissipated like water in a hot oven. She grasped the edge of the table to steady herself. "I better go," she said.

Nolan gazed at her, his eyes pleading. "Mary, it was a terrible thing. A terrible thing. Please, Mary, forgive me. I know it's too much to ask, but maybe someday you can. Maybe someday you'll understand how much I loved you and wanted to protect you. And then you'll be able to forgive me for being such a stupid, stupid fool."

Mary blinked, but her emotions, her heart, failed to come back into focus. "I better go," she said, stumbling out of the kitchen. Everything seemed surreal, beyond assurance. Nolan's footfall trailed behind her, not too close, not claiming any of the warmth they'd always shared. Mary grasped the doorknob and pulled the door open. "I'll call you," she said, without turning.

SHE SAT IN THE CAR, STARING OUT AT THE LITTLE League diamond at Pinto Lake Park. The wire mesh of the backstop caged the dramas and comedies of children's baseball, keeping it from spilling onto the grass beyond the bases. Keeping the memories and hopes safe in that chainlink box, just as she had kept her own safe in the cage of her body. And now she knew that she'd been right. That cage was flawed. It couldn't hold that one dream, that dream of having children of her own. Mary tilted her head back against the headrest, letting her gaze wander to the horizon. Feeling—just a taste— seeped back. The hurt, the anger, the horror, thrilled through her hastened by sorrow.

She started the car and backed out of the parking space. When all feeling returned, it would crush her. When it did, she wanted to be some place safe. She wanted to be with Paul.

THIRTY

TEDDY REACHED THE CORNER BEFORE SHE REALIZED what she was doing. She'd been planning to go around the block and avoid the field altogether; now here she was facing it. Early morning sun shone on the strawberry plants, wept along the backs of the fieldworkers bending between the neat, straight rows.

Teddy averted her eyes and focused on the sun. A welcome stranger on summer mornings, its warmth burrowed to the core of her. She peeled off her light jacket as she hurried to turn the corner.

A tingle traced her spine, like a fingernail on a chalkboard. She strained not to look for the woman in the chair. The veins in her neck and along her temples ached, her jaw threatened to snap. She fixed her gaze on her goal: the bus stop at the end of the street, the one on Green Valley Road.

"She's not there," Teddy said to herself. "And even if she is, you don't need that kind of pain."

But pain seared through her anyway, burning through every nerve as she resisted turning toward the field. The tingle deepened to a taut vibration. With a muted groan, Teddy turned.

The woman sat in her chair overlooking the field. Teddy struggled to look away but could not. The woman's gaze locked on hers. Like a tether, it drew

Teddy to the woman, step by reluctant step.

Five feet from the woman, Teddy stopped. The woman stood, whole and straight, not the broken shell Teddy had first seen. Grabbing the brim of her cap, the woman pulled it from her head. Long hair tumbled past her shoulders, molasses-dark. She smiled, beckoning to Teddy with a callused hand. Teddy shook her head, but found herself walking to meet the woman.

Teddy wet her lips, still fighting the urge to move forward. *Let go*, a voice whispered through her mind. *Don't fight me. Let go.*

The woman coaxed with that same beckoning gesture. Teddy stared at the woman's fingertips, at the red and green stains smeared across her caramel skin. Then she looked up into the woman's face.

She searched the woman's features. Where in this face would she find Estelle? Not in the high, wide forehead nor in the square jaw. Not in the delicate, sculpted nose. She found Estelle beneath the thin, black brows, peering at her through those glittering brown eyes.

The eyes welcomed her, their gaze still pulling at her. Teddy stopped before the woman, startled to find they were the same height. They stared at each other, the woman studying Teddy with a delighted curiosity, Teddy scrutinizing her with fear.

The woman reached to touch Teddy's face. Her fingers hovered a hairsbreadth above Teddy's skin. Words flowed again through Teddy's mind: *Don't be afraid. I have something for you. A gift.*

Teddy swallowed through the tension in her throat. "What—what sort of gift?"

The woman withdrew her hands and displayed them to Teddy, palms up.

Teddy shook her head, confused. "I don't—what are you trying to tell me?"

Don't be afraid.

The woman reached for Teddy's right wrist. Gently,

she lifted the arm and removed the brace. She dropped the splint to the dusty grass. She then took Teddy's left arm and freed it.

The braces crossed like sabers in the grass at the woman's feet. Teddy shook her head. What was this woman thinking? That by getting rid of the braces, Teddy's problems would be solved? This just created a new one—how to get all that dust out of the absorbent cloth.

Teddy bent to pick up the braces. "Some gift," she muttered.

The woman stopped her before she touched the splints. Guiding Teddy with her fingertips, she urged her to stand straight and to again look her in the eye. She took Teddy's hands.

A shock jerked through Teddy's arms, the pain settling into steady bursts of sheer agony. She cried out, trying to twist her hands from the woman's. *Don't let go*, the voice whispered. *Sometimes there is pain before healing. Sometimes there is pain before joy. Don't let go.*

Teddy trembled. Her knees began to buckle, but the woman held her firm. Teddy leaned into her for support, shivering in the woman's grip. Pain lashed out in a white sheet, obliterating Teddy's vision. The world became nothing but all-consuming pain, flowing through her body like blood.

Then the pain turned sweet—too sweet, unbearably sweet. Teddy moaned. The fire in her nerves burned clean, turning agony to pleasure. Her body sang with the pureness of life. A laugh escaped her, breaking through the tears knotted in her throat. Still giggling, she rolled her head back and stared into the sky. The blue, embracing sky—

She jerked to look at the woman. The woman had released her, had taken a step back. Now she stood smiling at Teddy. Touching her fingers to her lips, she blew a kiss.

Teddy frowned, puzzled. Her body still hummed, alive with the sweetness of life. "What have you done?" she whispered.

The woman brushed her palms together, then held them up to Teddy. A quiver passed through Teddy. She raised her own hands, held them up to the woman. She closed her fingers to her palms, squeezing harder and harder, trying to find the barrier, trying to find the pain. She knotted her hands into tight, hard fists. The only pain was that of her fingernails scoring her palms.

Teddy murmured, unfurling her hands. The wrists, the forearms, the elbows—none of them twinged with a snap of nerves. She looked again at the woman. The woman still smiled, but within seconds her face seemed to shimmer, as if seen through a film of water. Her features wavered slightly and became Estelle's.

Teddy blinked. Estelle was gone.

The woman bowed her head and stepped back. Teddy tried to catch the woman's hands, but could not. "Thank you," Teddy said. "Thank you for giving me back my life."

The woman winked, then sat in the chair. She gazed out over the strawberry fields, her chin held high, her gaze encompassing the rows of emerald plants and the workers. She vanished.

Teddy flexed her fingers, turning her hands this way and that to admire them. She spread her fingers into wings, a dove's wings, or the legs of a spider—

A spider. Like the one Estelle made for her days ago. Teddy turned and ran home. She hoped she had enough gas to get to work. She hoped Estelle would still be at the desk, that she hadn't vanished like the woman in the chair.

THIRTY-ONE

RIGOBERTO YANKED HIS CAP ONTO HIS HEAD AND climbed out of the trailer. He swung to face Hector. »What am I supposed to tell the boss?« he said.

Hector looked up into the sky. Not a scrap of fog shrouded the morning light. Warm; he wouldn't need his jacket. »Tell him I'm sick.«

Rigoberto shook his head, disgusted. »And he'll think you spent the night drinking. You won't be welcomed back tomorrow. He could easily find a hundred like you.«

Alejandro's black Charger pulled up a few meters from the trailer. Clouds of exhaust struggled to conceal the world, to make up for the absent fog. Orelio, a young man with sleepy eyes and a flat, crooked nose, squeezed past Hector and out of the trailer. He mumbled something about »that last tequila« before plodding toward the waiting Charger.

Rigoberto glanced at the car, gesturing for Alejandro to wait. »And if you can't find another job tomorrow, Hector, what then? Rent is due in two weeks.«

Tomás and Guillermo pushed past Hector and out the door. They batted at each other, sparring until they reached the Charger. Hector shrugged. »I don't know what then, Rigoberto. *Ni modo.*«

»Can't be helped,« Rigoberto muttered. He slapped

the side of the trailer, turning to go. »I hope you know
what you're doing, Hector. This isn't Mexíco.«

Hector smiled grimly. No, it wasn't Mexíco.

HECTOR SIPPED THE WEAK COFFEE, WONDERING IF, NEXT
time, he should just eat the crystals and forget adding
the water. Maybe then it would taste more like coffee.
He spread the piece of paper in front of him, studying
the address. If he caught a bus to downtown Santa Cruz,
perhaps someone could tell him how to find the street.
He frowned at the tiny printing. There was a phone number. He could call this Paul Grant and ask him how to
get there—assuming the man spoke Spanish. But what
if Rosa worked there and she answered the phone? She
might run again.

No calling. He would get to Santa Cruz, then find
someone to direct him.

He glanced at the clock next to the sink. Ten past
seven. Too early to go to this Paul Grant's office. It
probably didn't open until eight or nine. Nine, then. It
might take an hour or more just to get to Santa Cruz—he
better take the seven-thirty bus to town.

Leaning back, he sipped the coffee. A calm settled
over him, a quiet pleasure. Outside the grimy trailer windows, the early sun brought color to the world, to the
small gardens, weathered trailers, and forgotten toys.
Hector smiled. He'd worked hard and early most of his
life. To have a morning like this—unhurried, silent—
was a rare luxury. He picked up the cup and rubbed it
against his jaw, letting its warmth pamper his skin.

Outside, someone moved between the trailers. Probably old Nelda. Hector set down the coffee mug. He
folded the paper and returned it to his pocket. Time to
meet the bus.

He picked up his cap. Pushing open the door with his
shoulder, he folded the bill of the cap before clapping

the hat onto his head. He looked up and stopped. Eliseo stood by the trailer steps.

Hector drew back. Rigoberto and the others hadn't been that long in the fields. Not long enough for Eliseo to notice Hector's absence. The crimson Camaro, engine purring, waited a few meters away. On the car's back window, the Virgin of Guadalupe's tilted, silhouetted head seemed attentive, curious.

»What are you doing here?« Hector said. »Did Rigoberto tell you I was sick?«

»I didn't go to the fields today,« Eliseo said. »I came straight here.«

Hector chewed the ends of his mustache. »Why?«

Eliseo bowed his head. »Because you need a ride. To Santa Cruz.«

Hector stepped down from the trailer, pulling the door shut behind him. »And how did you know that?«

Eliseo shrugged, spreading his hands. »I'm here to help you.«

Hector narrowed his eyes.

Eliseo smiled. »I was sent to help you.«

»Why?« Hector said. »Help me do what?«

»Help you find Rosa.« Touching Hector's elbow, Eliseo guided Hector toward the Camaro. »Where are we going?«

Hector glanced at him sideways. »To Santa Cruz,« he said.

Eliseo laughed. »Yes, but where in Santa Cruz? That I don't know.« He turned and met Hector's gaze. »God doesn't tell me everything.«

THE ADDRESS BELONGED TO A HOUSE WITH A SMALL porch and large windows. Bougainvillea crowded the porch and the side of the house. A wooden sofa stood next to the front door, a pillow covered in bright, festive cloth resting against one of the arms. Hector tried the door. It resisted him. He checked the name on the paper against the one on the door: Paul Grant, followed by a string of letters. Hector returned to the Camaro and got in on the passenger side. »It's Friday,« he said. »Perhaps they don't open on Fridays.«

»It's early yet,« Eliseo said. »Barely eight. Let's go get some coffee—«

»No.« Hector folded his arms across his chest. »I don't want to miss her.«

»All right,« Eliseo said, opening the door. »I'll get some coffee. You keep watch.«

Eliseo slammed the door, not out of anger, but because the door would not shut any other way. Hector winced, massaging his ear. He craned his neck so that he could watch Eliseo walk away in the rearview mirror. The man—could he call him that?—strolled across the parking lot, hands in his pockets. He disappeared between two buildings.

Hector slumped in the seat and stared at Paul Grant's door. »Take your time, Rosita,« he said. »I have enough to think about.«

More than enough. There was Rosa herself, out among the goats, sipping their blood. There was the flash of electricity when her hand touched Eliseo's. Now there was Eliseo himself.

Hector pulled Conchita's ring from his pocket. He turned it between his fingers, a small gold halo. And where was Eliseo's . . . ?

»God sent me to help you,« Eliseo had said once he'd coaxed Hector into the car. »To find Rosa.«

»If God sent you,« Hector had said, sarcastically, »does that make you an angel?«

Eliseo forced the car into drive. It leaped forward. »If you like. A guardian angel.«

Hector pursed his lips. »Mine or Rosa's?«

Eliseo smiled. »Does it matter?«

Hector turned to the passenger window. The fields streaked past, workers bending over strawberries, lettuce, and squash. The women's brightly colored sweaters blazed among the green plants, banners of yellow, red, orange, and blue. When the morning chill evaporated, the sweaters would disappear. The field would then be dotted with white.

»Why is God helping me find Rosa?« Hector said, turning. »Why doesn't He—why don't *you*—just take me to her?«

The tires squealed as the Camaro sped through a turn. »Because she is not in Heaven or Hell,« Eliseo said. »God cannot sense her on Earth. He thinks she is hidden.«

»How can that be?« Hector said. »How can a soul hide from God?«

Eliseo glanced at him, eyebrows arched. He said nothing.

They roared onto the highway, Eliseo easing the car up to speed. Hector marveled at the number of cars already on the road. What was it with these North Americans that they had to drive all the time?

»But we saw her,« Hector said. »Last night. You said there was very little of her left.«

»Very little. Only her body. But where her soul is—« Eliseo shook his head. »The body is animated for a reason. There is something that must be done. Perhaps when that task is finished, Rosa's soul will be released, but until then . . .«

Someone thumped on the driver's side window. Hector pocketed the ring and reached across the seat to open the door. Eliseo slipped in, two paper cups in his hands. The rich, oily scent of coffee filled the Camaro. Hector took one of the cups, lifting the plastic lid. Now *this* was coffee. He savored the aroma.

Eliseo set two packets of sugar on Hector's knee. »I didn't know if you take milk or sugar. I brought the sugar.«

»Black, always black,« Hector said. He touched his

lip to the cup, tentatively, then sipped. He smiled. Someday he would have coffee like this every morning.

»Good coffee,« Eliseo said, grinning at him. He dumped two sugars into his own. »They roast their own beans.«

Hector murmured. He took another sip. »Eliseo, who is in Rosa's body? Is it another angel? Is that why you couldn't touch her?«

Eliseo snorted. »I can touch her, but only for a second. You saw how the sparks flew.« He stirred his coffee with a wooden stick, took a sip. »It's not an angel. If it were an angel, God would know where Rosa is. It's something older.«

Hector stared at him. »Older than God?«

»Older than angels,« Eliseo said. »Well, older than angels on *Earth*. Look, someone is going in.«

Hector swung toward the office. A man hunted for the lock with a key. A pleasant-enough-looking man, almost handsome, but with angry, sad eyes. »That must be Paul Grant,« Hector said.

They watched in silence as Paul Grant finally opened the door. He went in, pulling the door shut after him. »Should we go in now?« Eliseo said.

Hector stared at Eliseo. The angel was asking *him*?

Eliseo met his gaze, clearly unsure. »Or should we wait till she shows up?«

Hector swirled his coffee. He had nothing to say to this Paul Grant. What if all the man saw were two farmworkers? What if he asked them to leave? If they waited for Rosa, they'd at least be able to talk to her before the man chased them out.

»Let's wait,« Hector said. He took another sip of coffee. It had lost all flavor.

THIRTY-TWO

PAUL REACHED FOR THE LIGHT SWITCH, THOUGHT BET-
ter of it. Let Estelle or Teddy turn it on when they arrived. The silence of a room without electric current
soothed him. He walked over to the couch and sank into
its embrace.

An affair. Mary was having an affair. She had to be.
Everything pointed that way—going out without explaining where she'd been, staying out late, avoiding
him both physically and verbally. Pretending he didn't
exist emotionally. And now lying. Paul let his head drop
against the back of the sofa. He stared at the ceiling.
How long had this been going on? Why hadn't he recognized it?

Someone rapped on the counter, a soft sound meant
to warn him without startling him. Paul let his head fall
forward. Estelle stood behind the coral armchair, hands
resting on its back.

"Hello, Estelle," he said, sitting up. "You're here
early."

She shrugged, walking around the chair. She sat. She
raised her eyebrows.

"Me, too," Paul agreed. "It was too hard to be at
home."

Estelle's eyes widened with alarm. She scooted closer,
reaching into her pocket for a pad of paper and a pen.

She scribbled a note, then handed it to him. "What happened?"

Paul stared at the note, at the letters tattooing the paper in dark blue ink. He'd told her so much already, why not tell her everything? Hell, what could it hurt? Hurt! He shook his head. *He* already hurt. Mary didn't know Estelle, would never know Estelle. It wouldn't hurt her. He sniffed. And if it did, so what?

He turned the paper over. "I think Mary's having an affair." He looked up and met Estelle's shocked gaze. "She . . . didn't say anything. I'm just putting two and two together. She got a call this morning and left. She lied about who it was."

Estelle studied his face, searching for something—reassurance? She dashed off another note and handed it to him. "But she didn't say she was having an affair. Could you be wrong?"

Paul bit his lower lip. Why was Mary's innocence so important to Estelle? "I could be wrong. But she's hiding something from me."

Estelle paced in front of the chair. Stopping abruptly, she turned to Paul and touched his knee. *Maybe it's her sister*, a voice whispered through his mind. *Maybe she's looking for her sister.*

Paul frowned. "Her sister? But she would have told me. I mean, why would she lie about—"

The door banged open. Teddy rushed in. "They're healed!" she said, holding up her braceless arms. "I drove here, I drove to work!"

Paul rose from the couch. "Teddy, shouldn't you have a doctor—"

"No! No doctors! Look!" Teddy raised her arms above her head in two victory fists. She laughed, rushing to Estelle. She grasped her by the shoulders. "You knew. That's why you didn't send the letter of withdrawal. But how did you know? Was that really you, out there by the field? Or some sister or cousin or whatever? How did you know?"

Estelle traced Teddy's arms, wrist to elbow. Teddy held up her arms, fingers spread, winglike. Estelle folded Teddy's fingers, gently, until they kissed her palm. Estelle bowed her head once, smiling at Teddy.

The smile vanished. A cold, harsh look crossed Estelle's face—pride mixed with cunning, wariness with fear. She backed toward Paul, hand dipping into her pocket, gaze fixed on the door.

Two men stood on the threshold, an older man with a graying mustache and sad, dark eyes, and a younger man whose eyes blazed. Both stared at Estelle. The older man glanced at the younger, seeking encouragement. The younger man touched his elbow and guided him into the office.

"Rosa," the older man said. *"Rosa, por favor. No tengas mieda."*

Estelle's shoulders rose. She drew closer to Paul, still fumbling in her pocket.

"Tío Hector," Mary said. She stepped into the office. "What are you doing here? *Por qué está aquí?"*

"Mary?" Paul said. He moved toward her—

Estelle stuck out her arm and stopped him. She held something in her hand, another origami, this one made of some fragile paper. She reached for her throat.

Mary stared at Estelle, her mouth opening slowly. Her eyes, rimmed with red, sparkled with tears. She blinked, sending one clear drop cascading down her cheek.

Paul pushed around Estelle's arm. "Mary, what's wrong? Are you all right?"

Mary swallowed. "Mamá?"

Estelle fished something from the bodice of her dress. A silver charm on a chain. Paul froze. A girl, just like the one Mary wore. Paul murmured low in his throat.

"Rosa?" Mary whispered.

The older man and the younger flanked Mary. Mary's

hand rose to her throat and drew out her own chain and her own silver girl. Estelle—Rosa—smiled.

Mary shook her head, dumbfounded. "You've been working here, all this time? This Estelle—"

Mary's eyes widened. "Star," she said, then laughed, a shrill of surprise. " 'She's young Rosie McCann from the banks of the Bann, she's the star of the County Down.' My God, why didn't I get that? Why didn't I see?"

A pleased smile freed Rosa's face. She nodded, a shyness touching her features. She held out the folded paper to Mary. It was a lily, an Easter lily, petals curled, nearly touching the trumpet-shaped body.

Mary crept toward her sister, each step slow and dreamlike. Rosa waited until Mary stood before her, then began to unfold the lily. She prodded open the lily's mouth with a finger—

And stopped.

Shock drained her face of all expression. She stared into the heart of the lily, her eyes bright with panic . . . and a growing relief. She looked up at Mary, shaking her head, then dipped two fingers into the lily and withdrew a second origami.

Paul wet his lips. A *pajarita*, like the one she'd made for him last night. Only this one was made of the same fragile paper as the lily. Mary puzzled at the paper bird, then looked up into Rosa's eyes. Some understanding seemed to pass between them.

"A child," Mary said.

Rosa nodded. She refolded the petals of the lily and slid it into her pocket. She touched the *pajarita* to Mary's abdomen, then unfolded it. Mary gasped once before cupping her stomach with her hand. The same way pregnant women cup their womb . . .

The creased paper floated from Rosa's hand. It lay on the floor between them, crisp and flat, not a crease or hint of a crease marring its smooth surface. A wondering smile touched Mary's lips.

Rosa drew the lily from her pocket. She glanced at Teddy with a twinge of regret, then shook her head as if to say, "It can't be undone." She then faced Paul. That voice filled his mind again. *Go to the phone*, it urged. *Be ready.*

Paul frowned. The phone—?

Now!

Paul scrambled behind the reception desk. Picking up the phone, he looked to Rosa for direction.

She nodded. Taking a deep breath, she began to unfold the lily. She hesitated at the last fold, her face rigid with fear. She pulled the last of the flower apart—

Blood gushed from her throat, the wound reopening in a torrent. She gurgled, gasping for breath, sinking to the floor. Hector rushed to her, gathering her in his arms. Numbed with shock, Paul dialed 911. Teddy snatched the phone from him and pushed him toward Mary— Mary, who stood trembling like an aspen, staring at her dying sister. Paul hurried to her and pulled her close.

The younger man knelt beside Hector and Rosa. He pulled Hector gently away, then pressed his fingers to Rosa's throat. Blood spurted around his fingers. His whispered prayers joined the canticle of Teddy's frantic instructions. The blood slowed to a thin stream, lining Rosa's neck like tears on a damp cheek.

"God bless you and keep you, Rosa," the younger man said. "He is glad to find you again."

THIRTY-THREE

ROSA WOKE WITH A START, GRIPPING THE BLANKETS. "Luz," she whispered, her throat raw and sore. She stared at the white walls, the woven wall-hanging, the lustrous pale wood furniture, the window overlooking a garden divided in two by an invisible border—one side vegetables and herbs, the other flowers and ornamentals. An apple tree and a rosebush stood watch at the border, their diligence not entirely successful. Bright and defiant, a cluster of golden poppies bloomed among the tomatoes.

Rosa frowned, trying to remember where she was. Mary's. She was at Mary's. "Luz?" she tried again. It came out in a croak.

Luz hovered at the edge of Rosa's vision. "Rest," Luz said. "I'm here."

Her voice calmed Rosa. "I thought you were gone," Rosa said. "I dreamed you were gone. Don't ever leave me, Luz. Please."

Luz turned as if to kiss her cheek. Rosa's skin warmed. "Until you send me away," she said.

Rosa relaxed into the embracing mattress. How wonderful it was—firm, but soft. She'd never slept on anything like it before. She traced the weave of the cotton blanket, following one blue thread, then another. North

America had been kind to Mary. Rosa smiled. Mary had been kind to Rosa.

She sat up, balling her pillow behind her, and gazed out the window. Mary, a wide-brimmed straw hat shadowing her face, wandered through the tomato plants. One hand rested on the swell of her belly, the other pointed to this plant or that. Her husband, Paul, walked beside her, stooping to examine the plants she pointed to. He plucked leaves, pulled weeds, fondled green fruit. Then he looked up at Mary, with that same love Papá had for Mamá—

Rosa turned away. She stroked her finger, feeling the roses entwined on Mamá's ring. "Tell me again, when is the baby due?" she said.

"Four months, a little less."

Rosa nodded. She released the ring and studied the wall-hanging. Threads of gold and purple pierced vibrant zigzags of blue and green. She could almost imagine hills in the rain—

"I was afraid to leave her with you," Luz said.

Rosa smiled, she hoped convincingly. "I know. She would have died with me. I was too weak." She reached for the glass of water on the nightstand. After a long sip, she turned—but, of course, so did Luz. "Why did you wait so long, to give Mary the baby? If you thought it was only the baby you carried?"

"I wanted to be sure Mary would love her. I wanted to be sure Mary was someone you would have liked and approved of."

"She's my sister," Rosa said.

"Yes, and she's been in this country a long time."

Rosa nodded. The core of Mary—her determination, her quick thinking, her devotion—all were still there, but overlaid with small, superficial changes. Cultural changes. Or were they superficial? Mary expected more now, expected to be treated with respect. Expected to be dealt with honestly and to receive what she saw as her due. She had a career, a luxurious home, a loving husband. Taking a job as a maid in a tourist hotel would never occur to her. Sleeping in a room with four or five other people would seem odd and uncomfortable to her. Being treated as less than equal would infuriate her. . . .

"Rosa," Luz said. Her fingers left trails of warmth along Rosa's cheek. "Rosa, are you all right?"

Rosa nodded, imagined Luz collecting the tears on her fingertips. "Just thinking about things that might have happened, but didn't. Is that regret, Luz?"

"What kinds of things?"

"What if Papá had sent for me and Mamá? Or what if we'd all made it that night? Would I be more like Mary now?"

"I think that's a form of regret," Luz said. "Even though there was nothing you could do about it—"

Someone rapped on the door. Rosa threw a questioning look at Luz. "Hector, I think," Luz said.

Rosa adjusted her pajama blouse. »Come in.«

The door opened a sliver, just enough for Hector to poke his head through. He smiled uncertainly, then entered the room. He hesitated before padding over to the bed. He handed her a plastic basket filled with strawberries. »How are you?« he asked.

»Stronger.« Rosa prodded the ripe red fruit with a finger. One of the berries wept juice. »These are beautiful. Did you pick them?«

Hector grinned. »No. Maria made me promise not to go back to the fields. I'm still taking care of her friend Nolan. Until Maria gets me a green card. Longer, if Nolan needs me.«

Rosa nodded. She'd heard about this Nolan. He'd taken Mary in after Papá died—Rosa flinched. After—after Papá was murdered. Now this Nolan was recovering from something. Not an illness exactly; Mary wouldn't say. It sounded to Rosa like a suicide attempt, but if Mary chose not to talk about it, who was she to press questions?

»You understand each other?« Rosa asked.

Hector raked his mustache with his teeth. »We are learning. His Spanish is simple but good. My English—« He made a flinging gesture with his hands.

Rosa laughed. She reached across the bed and patted his hand. »Mary will teach you—«

He jerked away as if she'd shocked him, then forced himself to reclaim some semblance of calm. He slid his hand under hers.

With great effort, Rosa thought. She withdrew her hand, pretending to scratch her face. Hector relaxed.

»Is—is she here?« he asked. »This . . . guide?«

Rosa nodded. »She's here. She's always here.«

"Tell him hi for me," Luz said sweetly. Rosa ignored her.

Hector grunted. »That's what Eliseo said. That she's always there. He said she kept your body alive until your soul could return safely.«

»She thought she was keeping the baby alive,« Rosa said.

"No kidding," Luz said. "That was quite a surprise you had for me."

Rosa bit back a response. Hector was spooked enough. »Tío, where is Eliseo?« she asked, touching the smooth skin at her throat. »I'd like to thank him.«

Tío Hector looked away. »Gone. He found you and healed you. Then the Lord called him home.«

Rosa nodded. *Why did God send an angel to find me?* she wanted to ask, but knew the answer would have to come from Luz, not Hector.

»Besides,« Hector said, his eyes smiling, »an angel shouldn't be picking strawberries.«

Rosa laughed and took her uncle's hand without thinking. It tensed in hers, then squeezed back. He slipped it free, shuffling backwards, reaching for the doorknob. »I must go,« he said. »I don't like to leave Nolan too long. He can get along all right without me— slowly, but all right—but he is so sad. He acts as if he carries some great sin that he cannot believe will be forgiven. I'll come back soon.«

Rosa scooted a little straighter, a little taller. »Tío, I want to thank you, too. For searching for me.«

»Ay,« he said, easing out of the room. »I had to find my Rosita. Could I leave her to butchers and fools?«

The door shut with a gentle thump. Rosa slumped against the headboard, the crown of her head touching wood. "Luz, will he ever be at ease with me again?"

"Patience," Luz said. "He saw your body rise from the dead and he saw your body drinking goat's blood. That he comes at all is amazing."

Rosa wrinkled her nose. "Did you have to drink goat's blood?"

"How else was I going to keep you alive?" Luz said.

"Lots of ways. Did it occur to you to try real food?"

Luz sniffed. "Your body and the baby needed blood and—I don't know, call me old-fashioned, but the thought of drinking human blood didn't appeal to me."

Rosa gagged. "That's disgusting."

"Besides, I didn't know you were there, too. I thought the only soul I held was the baby's."

Rosa selected a strawberry and dug out the pip with her fingernail. "You told me to trust my hands."

"*I* should have trusted your hands." Luz dimmed a little. "And I shouldn't have been so quick to give your magic away."

Sadness passed through Rosa. She had tried to fold something—anything—and could only make lopsided, spiritless cranes. Then she thought of Teddy and the beautiful vase Teddy had brought her three days ago. Cranes and flapping birds rose from the cylindrical walls of clay, ready to take flight. Between the birds, stars had been etched into the gritty, bisqued clay. Stars, for Estelle—for Rosie, the star of the County Down.

"I wanted you to choose the colors," Teddy had said. "Any colors you want."

Still weak and bewildered, Rosa had turned slightly toward Luz. "Tell her you want the colors of the sunrise," Luz said, "because this is a new beginning."

Teddy had smiled when Rosa repeated it, promising to glaze and fire the vase immediately. Twice since then she'd stopped by after work with her banjo to play for Rosa. The twangy strings took a little getting used to, but Rosa found she kind of liked the banjo . . .

Luz leaned closer. "I don't know how to undo it—"

"Don't," Rosa said. "Don't even try. Teddy needs it more than I do." She raised the strawberry to her lips and bit down. Sweet juice filled her mouth. "How much do you think Teddy knows, about Estelle? And about her healing?"

Luz sighed. "Not much. I think she's reconciled her own healing with the woman in the chair and forgotten any link between the woman and Estelle, now that she knows Estelle is Rosa, the long-lost sister."

Rosa arched her eyebrows. "*Was* there a link between the woman and Estelle?"

"Well . . . yes."

Rosa popped the rest of the strawberry into her mouth to hide a smile. A trickle of juice dribbled down her chin. She wiped it away with the back of her hand. "What are we going to do now, Luz?"

"Let's think about that when you're stronger," Luz said.

Rosa gazed out the window. Mary turned and looked up. She waved. Rosa waved back. Then each of them touched the silver charm at her own throat. Mary's other hand caressed the child growing inside her, the child she had prayed for and given up on. *Your child now, sister*, Rosa thought. *Keep her safe.*

Tugging at the silver girl's feet, Rosa turned to Luz. "What is there to think about, Luz?" she said. "We already know what to do."

"And what is that?" Luz asked.

Rosa smiled. "We will continue to take part in miracles."

VIRUS CLANS
A Story of Evolution

Michael Kanaly

The story of a research scientist on the verge of an extraordinary discovery: certain viruses are no longer acting in a random way. In fact, they seem to be intelligently planning where and how to multiply. And intertwined in this powerful drama is the story of the virus clans themselves, spanning millions of years as they evolve and make their own extraordinary discovery: to be the perfect hosts, human beings will have to be changed.

___0-441-00500-4/$12.00
An Ace Trade Paperback